The Longest Walk

by

Kirk Marty

Strategic Book Group

Strategic Book Group
P.O. Box 333
Durham CT 06422
www.StrategicBookClub.com

ISBN: 978-1-60911-661-3

In Memoriam

Russ Urban
Best friend and best Dodger fan

Special Thanks

To my wife for her love, patience and encouragement

Dedication

This book is dedicated to Vin Scully, Hall of Fame broadcaster, who for over sixty years has delighted, educated and entertained the child in all of us.

Foreword

In the fourth game of the 1926 World Series, Babe Ruth slugged an incredible three home runs. The Bambino reputedly launched those shots to keep his promise to an injured ten-year-old named Johnny Sylvester. Supposedly they lifted the boy's sinking spirits, and the hospitalized youngster enjoyed a swift recovery. The press ate it up, some suggesting that the Babe's heroics actually saved little Johnny's life. Many said Ruth didn't even know Johnny Sylvester existed until after that game. They were probably right.

Introduction

San Bernardino California is only ninety miles east of Los Angeles, which is home of the Dodgers. It might as well have been ninety light years away for the Stampede, a Dodger minor league ball club that called San Bernardino home in the year 2000. The jump from the minors to the Majors is not one many ballplayers can make.

After the rookie league, the minor leagues have three levels: Single-A, Double-A, and Triple-A. Class A is lowest in rank and ability. The Stampede was a Single-A team that bore little resemblance to their big league counterpart.

San Bernardino is located deep into the southern California desert. Summer is hot and dry, and this mid-sized, blue-collar city is, well, not quite as glamorous as LA. The Single-A "Dodgers" practiced and played their home games on a modest field on the outskirts of town. In a way, the players and residents toiled in unison, hoping their lots would improve. But it was only a hope, and for many only a distant dream.

If you were a member of the Stampede, the idea was to get out of San Bernardino as fast as you could. You also wanted to be going in the right direction—to a Double-A or Triple-A team. Going the other way pretty much took you out of professional baseball.

A-Ball is the edge, the cusp, the point of no return that leads to either higher levels or the search for a different life.

Chapter 1

Practice was over. Don Ogilvie headed for the place where he did his "special-occasion" drinking—a little neighborhood bar within crawling distance of his apartment. Most always he did his serious swilling at home. He didn't want to take the chance of running into someone who knew he shouldn't be hitting the bottle. For times like this, when Don was so downhearted he didn't care, only a shabby drinkers' bar would do.

He hadn't seen the inside of The Spigot in a long time. His last go-round was before the arrival of the Alvarez family, over a year ago. Oly Nevin, owner and bartender of this seedy San Bernardino tavern, was mildly surprised to see him walk in. It had been awhile. The place was never too crowded. It had a simple square-shaped bar with ramshackle stools all around. A beat-up pool table and a hastily hung dartboard completed the low-life, loser ambiance.

Oly had seen Don Ogilvie at The Spigot off and on over the last decade. He was familiar with his customers' drinking habits—at least at the bar. He knew Ogilvie was there for a bender. The big sixty-year-old, gray-haired, pink-faced bartender spoke as the crestfallen minor league hitting coach pulled up a stool. "Jeez, Don—where you been keeping yourself?"

Don did not feel like making small talk. "I've been around. How about a boilermaker? Scotch."

A heavy drinker himself, Oly Nevin knew when to leave his

customers alone. He set him up with a boilermaker, saying, "Let me know when you need another."

For Don Ogilvie, it was happening all over again—something he loved was being taken away from him by accident, bad luck. The first time it was his life, his baseball career that had been dangled so tantalizingly close; now it was little seven-year-old Roberto Alvarez, his best friend, his rescuer, his personal—if only temporary—redeemer, who was being torn from his heart. Incurable cancer is a cruel fate. The dark irony was not lost on him, and he grimaced as he drank. Life is not fair. This was a lesson he'd learned as a young athlete. He hadn't forgotten it, even though he was now over fifty years old. Why was he fated to endure it again—this time at the expense of an innocent kid?

And what about little Roberto's young parents, Antonio and Maria? What was all this doing to them? How could Antonio make it out of Single-A ball when his spirit was being crushed? How could Maria work if her sick child needed her? It was unbearable to think about. Ogilvie sat in the dim, dingy little saloon downing boilermakers. He and The Spigot were a perfect match—despair, with the faint stench of urine, mothballs, and booze.

He slipped out around 1 a.m. Way too gone to drive, he didn't even try. He left his car parked and walked to a nearby liquor store. He was so drunk the clerk didn't want to sell him the cheap bottle of whisky he put on the counter, but he changed his mind when he saw the disturbing look on Don's face.

The forlorn coach stumbled out to the street, only a block away from home. Guzzling freely from a brown bag, he rambled aimlessly and wailed, "Take me! Take me! I'm a worthless piece of shit! Leave Roberto alone!"

Don wasn't really talking to anyone, just railing against the injustice of it all. He repeated this mantra in various forms as he meandered back to his apartment. The fifth of Scotch was already a third gone. Staggering inside his monastic dwelling, he turned on the TV, imploded into his easy chair, took a last gulp and passed out.

A few hours later, a stranger awakened him in his apartment. "Hey,

Ogilvie—wake up!" the intruder demanded. Still drunk and in the early stages of an alcohol-induced sleep, he was slow to respond.

This time the voice was louder. "Wake up, Ogilvie!" Stuporous, the coach opened his eyes to see a short, bald, middle-aged man hovering over him. He was dressed like an umpire, black suit and shirt, but no cap.

Ogilvie was startled. "Jesus Christ! Who the hell are you?"

"Don't worry, I'm not here to harm you," promised the stranger as he turned off Don's TV.

Don paused and tried to collect himself. "Okay, who are you and what are you doing here? And how do you know my name?"

"I'm here because you asked me to be here," was the straightforward answer. The stubby man sauntered over to the breakfast bar and grabbed a stool. He put it directly in front of Ogilvie and sat down. "Don't you have any other chairs?" He surveyed the apartment and said, "You know, it wouldn't hurt to hang a picture or two in this place." He paused, then said, "I'll tell you who I am and how I know your name in a minute. I want to talk to you about Roberto."

That cleared Don's head enough for him to ask, "How do you know about Roberto?"

The stumpy little man sat back on the barstool with a toothy, Cheshire-cat grin. "I know all about Roberto. I know all about you too." His thin, raspy voice had a distinct New York accent.

Ogilvie was now awake. He was also a bit worried. The stranger didn't act threatening. Still, he noticed that although the man was dwarfish, he was powerfully built. You couldn't be too careful these days. Cautiously he said, "You're gonna have to tell me who you are or I'm going to ask you to leave. I don't want to call the police."

The man in black was fast to answer. "I assure you—you won't need to do that. My name is Drummond, Doctor Drummond. I'm here to give you a chance to save Roberto's life."

Ogilvie was confounded by the whole idea. *Why would a doctor come to my apartment at three in the morning?* he wondered. *Shouldn't he be at the Alvarez house? What do I have to do with this?* All he could do was repeat some of what he heard. "You're a doctor?" The reply wasn't what he thought it was going to be.

3

"Well, not exactly. I guess there's no easy way to say this. I'm Death—or the Personification of Death," said the baffling trespasser in a business-like way. "Yeah, I'm Death Personified. Death Incarnate. Death in the Flesh."

Now Don knew he was in trouble. Some nut from the local loony bin must have escaped and broken into his apartment. But how did he know about Roberto? He figured he could find out later. "I think you better leave," he said firmly.

Instead, Drummond began reciting facts as if he were reading from Ogilvie's dossier, with editorial comments thrown in: "Donald Alan Ogilvie. Born: April 7, 1948, Claremont, California. Mother: Margaret Rebecca Simpson. Father: Stephen Donald Ogilvie. Married June 6, 1946. Now retired and living in Bishop, California. You haven't talked to your parents in over a year. Sister: Mary Anne Ogilvie, born July 23, 1951. Married to Ronald Dean Hansen, June 20, 1978. You were best man. Two children: Robert and David. Whole family lives in Sunnyvale, California. You haven't spoken to your sister, brother-in-law, or nephews in over two years. Would you like me to go on?"

All the information was accurate. Don was puzzled. He came up with a new theory. He thought, *I'm dreaming. That's why this guy knows all this stuff. It's all in my own head!*

Drummond began speaking again. "No, you're not dreaming—and no, I'm not an escaped nut. I'm Death. Death Personified. Get used to it."

Don let out a nervous chuckle and said, "Did I say that out loud? Whoever you are, you can't be real. I've got to be dreaming."

Drummond didn't pursue it. "Fine. Think what you want. Just do me a favor and humor me. Listen to what I have to say. If I'm a mirage, then you have nothing to lose, do you?"

Ogilvie felt he had no choice. This guy wasn't leaving, and he was in no condition to make him. If he was dreaming, he was curious to see where the illusion might lead. "Okay, what do you have to say?" he asked, playing along.

Drummond swooped in like a used-car salesman smelling a quick sale. "I'm here to make you a proposition. You offered to exchange your life for Roberto's. You remember, out there in the street just a couple of hours ago. You were yelling, 'Take me! Take me!'" The squatty man mocked the drunk and distraught hitting coach. "Maybe we can work something out. Do you believe in second chances, Ogilvie?"

"No—never had one," was his cynical reply.

"Good, because you're not getting one now. But your best friend Roberto is," said Death Personified.

He continued. "Of course, you do get a chance to do something noble with your miserable life. You get a chance to die! You get a chance to trade your life for Roberto's! I know it's hardly an even trade, but you do have to win a contest first—or, a 'challenge,' as I like to call it."

Don was caught off-guard by the tangled direction of Drummond's plot. He warily asked, "What do you have in mind?"

The stocky little umpire's eyes lit up. "A baseball game. Actually, the best of seven games, like the World Series. You get to pick your own team. Anybody who's dead. If your team beats mine, you get to die instead of Roberto."

Again this was not an answer Don expected. He didn't anticipate a contest for Roberto's life. He asked Drummond, "I could trade places with Roberto?"

"Yeah, something like that. Anyway, the kid will be one-hundred percent fine, no strings attached. You just gotta beat my team first. Pick any dead Hall of Famers you want," said the dumpy man who resembled a human bowling ball.

"Why do they have to be dead?" Ogilvie questioned. He felt stupid as soon as the words left his mouth. Drummond stared at the floor and shook his head. Naturally, Death Personified would only have jurisdiction, so to speak, over dead ballplayers, not live ones.

Don then decided to ask, "So I could pick Ruth, Gehrig, and DiMaggio?" He found the whole idea bizarre, yet intriguing.

"Anyone you want, as long as they're dead as of today—July 17, 2000. Except for Ty Cobb. But anyone else. And by the way, you might find Ruth is more trouble than he's worth."

"Wait a minute, wait a minute," Ogilvie said, actually thinking out loud this time. "Let me get this straight. I get any dead Hall of Famers, except for Ty Cobb. Cobb's on your team, huh?"

Drummond nodded.

"If my team wins a best-of-seven series, then you let Roberto live?"

"Yes. But you're leaving out the most important part: I get to take you in exchange." Drummond tried to reassure Ogilvie by adding, "Don't worry. Your death will be quick and painless."

Don laughed. "You can have me, Buddy! I just want to make sure about Roberto."

"That's the deal," said Drummond.

Death's use of the word "deal" reminded Ogilvie not to be too trusting, particularly of a delusion or dream. He wanted more questions answered first. "If I do say yes, how do I know I'm not making a deal with the Devil or something?"

Drummond gave a crooked, Mona Lisa smile and said, "Believe me, we don't need to have the whole Devil-God conversation. First of all, you or any other human doesn't really know if such things exist. No one can prove it. People have 'beliefs'—only with me, Death, you don't have that problem. Everyone knows I exist. I prove my existence thousands of times every day. All I ask is that you make an agreement with something that you know is real. Death is as real as it gets, Pal. I'm not asking for anybody's soul—especially yours. I'm asking for your life in exchange for Roberto's. You just have to earn the privilege first."

Drummond added, "You know, if I were the Devil, I'd have to be giving you something for your soul, which in this case would be Roberto's life. Our deal is very different. If you win our Hall of Fame World Series, Roberto lives and you die. If you don't, everything stays the same, which means the kid dies. Nothing's guaranteed. That's the sport of it! The Devil, if such a thing existed, would have to guarantee Roberto's life in advance. Pretty boring. Everyone knows the outcome. My way's more exciting, don't you think?"

"Yeah, but something still gives me the feeling you could trick me," Don said.

"No tricks. You can call it off any time. Cross my heart and hope to die."

6

Seeing Don's blank reaction, Death Personified chided him. "Haven't you ever heard of gallows humor? Perhaps my delivery is too deadpan for you. Lighten up a little bit, Ogilvie! I'm giving you an opportunity not even the greatest Major League managers get. And, you get a shot at trading places with Roberto! I don't know what else I can do here. By the way, you'll notice that you're completely sober. I did that so I can have your real consent. By tomorrow morning, you're still gonna have a helluva hangover. I wouldn't want to deny you the fruits of your fermented cortex."

It was true. Don hadn't even noticed. He felt clear-headed. This convinced him more than ever that this dipsomaniac episode was an apparition or hallucination. He'd passed out before and could remember dreams where he'd acted perfectly sober. This time seemed so real though.

One of the earlier thoughts that had been in the back of Ogilvie's mind finally came pouring out. "So who else besides Cobb is on your team? Some superhuman ringers or something?"

"No—just Cobb and one other player you've never heard of. Believe me, they're both just as human as you are."

"But they're dead, right? I mean Cobb's been dead for decades."

"I said 'human,' not 'alive'".

"Well, aren't these guys gonna be a little too old to play? Most of them have been gone a long time."

"What do you think? I'm gonna give you a bunch of decayed skeletons? They're all coming from a time when they were alive and in the pros."

"Wait a minute, wait a minute," Don said again, trying to understand the setup, "how many do I get?"

"A twenty-four-man roster. Whoever you want, as long as they're dead," and then Ogilvie and Drummond said in unison, ". . . except for Ty Cobb."

Tyrus Raymond Cobb, nicknamed, "The Georgia Peach," born in Narrows, Georgia in 1886. Died 1961. Played Major League ball for twenty-four seasons. Set all kinds of records for hitting, fielding and base stealing. Cobb was considered the best all-around player of his day and probably of all time. Credited with setting the standard for the modern ballplayer, he was also the fiercest competitor and hardest player. Bar none. He was, by far, the meanest baseball player to have ever taken the field—and he was just as mean off the field. Many would say psychotic. When Ty Cobb played, he wasn't playing at all. He was dead serious. He played for keeps and didn't take hostages. He died old, wealthy, deranged, bitter, and alone.

Don Ogilvie thought if this was a dream, it was definitely an original. Then he said, "Well this sounds too easy. I get twenty-four dead Hall of Famers and you get Cobb and some other guy."

"Don't worry," said Drummond, "it's not going to be nearly as easy as you think."

"Well, who's the other guy? It's gotta be a pitcher, right?"

"Very good," said Drummond like a teacher praising a student.

"He's a pitcher all right. The best pitcher you never heard of— Clarence 'Hillbilly' Higgins. Died in 1947 at age twenty. Train ran over him near his home in rural Tennessee. Too bad. Major League baseball was just about to discover him. If the train hadn't been late that day . . . who knows." Drummond stopped himself from digressing further. "Anyhow, that's another story. You can't have him either."

Ogilvie's main concern at the moment had nothing to do with choosing Hillbilly Higgins for his team. More important questions were starting to pop up in his mind. "For the sake of argument, let's say you are who you say you are. Why give me this chance? You must get requests like this all the time."

"Not as many as you would think," answered Death Incarnate. "Not genuine requests, anyhow—and hardly any from people who aren't relatives. Those are the only ones I consider. Otherwise, every mother or father with a sick kid would be all over me. Besides, I don't do this very often—and only if it's not going to change history or the future. You don't need to worry about that. That's my job, and everything has checked out just fine. So whatta ya say?"

Things were still moving too fast for Don Ogilvie. He had more questions swirling around in his head. He started with one that wasn't too deep, "Look, all this seems a little crazy. What's with the umpire getup anyhow?"

Drummond was again eager to answer. "You were expecting a hooded black robe and scythe? The 'Grim Reaper' thing isn't in this year. You dressed me this way—you gave me this whole short-and-wide look. This is what your pickled brain came up with. I need you to take me seriously without scaring the shit out of you." Drummond looked himself over. "Apparently this is it."

Ogilvie was apologetic. "Sorry I couldn't come up with something better."

"That's okay," said Drummond. "It sure beats last time. I had to be a ten-year-old girl in a pink tutu. Really makes no difference to me. Death has no ego."

Ogilvie was prying. "Well, how do you do this whole 'personified' thing?"

Drummond appreciated the query, but replied, "No offense—it would be like explaining Einstein's Theory of Relativity to a chimp."

"No offense taken," said Ogilvie. "I like monkeys. Might make a good mascot for the right team."

Before Ogilvie could say anything more, Drummond started talking again. "Look, I'm very misunderstood. I'm not 'evil.' Every living thing eventually dies. Sometimes I bring relief when old people are suffering. Sometimes I take the very young like Roberto. There's nothing personal about it. It's business. It's my job."

Ogilvie said, "Yeah, but it's not fair when you take someone like Roberto."

"In a way, it's very fair," said a straight-faced Drummond. "The whole system is on 'automatic pilot.' Normally I don't get involved. You know, just 'let the bodies fall where they may.' That way no one gets special treatment. So if I were really going to be fair to everyone else, I shouldn't be doing this. That would be fair. That would also mean Roberto dies. So you can see what a unique opportunity this is for you— once in a lifetime."

Don Ogilvie decided right then that he couldn't afford to take the risk that he might be wrong. What Drummond was saying was starting to make sense. If this was a dream or only an escaped nut—what did it matter? Roberto would die anyhow. Even if there was just that one in a billion shot, why not take it? He so badly wanted to trade his life for Roberto's that he nearly gave his permission at that moment.

Death Personified stopped him by again speaking first. "Before you say anything, I have to warn you—if you're able to win our little World Series and you have to give your life, you may not feel the same about it then as you do now. I'm not just talking about the actual dying part. That'll only take a second. I'm talking about how, after going through this 'challenge,' you might be changed. You might value your own life a little more. It might make it tougher to go. And it only gets worse if you lose. Then Roberto dies anyhow, and you get to live out your life knowing you didn't save him. You'll have to watch him die. You may want to stop living yourself."

Don listened carefully to what Drummond said. He couldn't imagine anything that could possibly change his mind about giving his life for Roberto's—or at least trying. He knew what Drummond said about losing would probably be true. It would be harder to see Roberto die and then have to keep on living. He may not want to keep on living himself. Then again, that was pretty much the way he felt now. He looked directly at Drummond, sober and forewarned, and said, "I'll do it . . .."

Drummond hastily replied, "I don't think you really understood my warning. That's okay, because no one really does until the end. However, I do agree to your acceptance of my modest proposal."

"Wait a minute!" Ogilvie objected again. "You didn't let me finish. I'll do it . . . on one condition—that nobody finds out I'm trading my life for Roberto's. Especially the Alvarezes, and especially Roberto. They can't know." He wasn't so much trying to be heroic. He just knew little Roberto's parents would never go along with such an arrangement, no matter how magnanimous.

"I figured you'd feel that way. I can do that," said Drummond, "only it might be difficult because they're gonna be with you the whole time. I figure you want Antonio as your assistant, and Roberto's gotta be there so the players can see whose life they're playing for. And if Antonio and

Roberto are there, you can't leave out Maria. It wouldn't be right to break up the set."

Drummond was several steps ahead of Ogilvie. When he thought about it, he agreed with what Drummond was saying. He was fragile, a broken-down old alcoholic the Alvarez family had somehow managed to prop up and keep on going. There was no way he could do this without all of them being there. He thought he could make up a believable tale to feed them.

He told Drummond, "You're right. I'm going to need them there—and not just for the players, but for me. There's no way I can do this without them. They still don't have to know that I'm the sacrificial dead guy. You just tell them that they've been given an incredible break. I'll take the rest from there, okay?"

Drummond was smiling again, his toothy Cheshire cat grin, and said, "Okay, Pal, you won't hear anything from my end—but you better come up with a convincing story on yours, because these are not stupid people."

"Don't say anything or the deal's off, all right?"

"Fine with me," continued Death in the Flesh. "Then it's your problem. If they don't buy your story, it's your fault. Any other requirements you might have before we get this show on the road to the River Styx?"

Don felt sober, but his head was swimming. Drummond kept moving things along faster than he liked. "Wait a minute," he complained once more, "I still have a few questions, okay?"

Death Personified sat back in his throne-like roost, gave a sweeping gesture, and said, "Ask away."

"So where are we going to play these games?"

"Oh, don't worry about that," Drummond said confidently. "I've got a real nice ballpark called Drummond Field. We'll be playing in a place I call Limbotown. You won't find it on any map. You'll get to see all of it when you wake up tomorrow morning."

Ogilvie took this in and surmised, "Sounds like we won't be at Disneyland anymore, Mickey."

"Well, just think of Limbotown as a 'Never-Never Land' for dead people."

11

"I guess that makes you either Captain Hook or Tinkerbell," Don said, going along with the analogy.

"And you Peter Pan, which most ballplayers are anyway," said an acerbic Death Personified, now sorry for drawing the parallel in the first place. "Let's put it this way," he continued, becoming pensive for a moment, "Limbotown is a place I can bring both the living and the dead together without one world getting too mixed up with the other."

"Kind of sounds like *Field of Dreams*," mused Ogilvie.

"You're really starting to piss me off here, Pal," groused Drummond, plainly annoyed by the comparison. "We're here to play serious baseball, not just goof around playing exhibition games. And your life or Roberto's is at stake."

"How much time do we have to get ready?" asked an apprehensive Don Ogilvie.

"Plenty, by baseball standards. You'll have eight weeks with your team before the Series starts. That's two weeks more than your average spring training."

"Yeah, but what about picking my team?" Ogilvie wondered.

"When you wake up tomorrow, you'll be in the visiting team's clubhouse at Drummond Field, Limbotown. Waiting for you will be Antonio, Maria, and Roberto. You'll have until midnight, Limbotown Standard Time, to pick a team of twenty-four players. Anyone you want, as long as they're dead . . ."

Ogilvie joined the stout umpire by saying again, ". . . except for Ty Cobb."

Drummond finished by adding, "Your players will be there the next morning."

As Don began to think about it, he asked, "Where are the players going to stay?"

"Don't worry about that either," said Drummond. "You'll find that Limbotown has everything you need. There's a hotel, restaurant and, of course, a bar. We even have a movie theater. And don't worry about umpires, equipment or anything else. Drummond Field has it all; including video cameras and radar guns. I know what you're thinking and, yes, the umpires are honest. They're dead Hall of Famers too."

12

"I guess you've thought of everything," Don concluded.

"I think so," smiled Doctor Drummond, pleased with himself. He added, "You also need to know one more thing. You'll be the only one to remember any of this when it's over."

Ogilvie was stumped. "What do you mean?"

"Let me explain," offered Drummond. "Today's Monday, July 17th, 2000. You've got eight weeks to prepare for a seven-game series that might take another nine or ten days, if it goes all the way. The Alvarez family is going to be with you. I'm not going to have all of you just disappear for eight or so weeks and then suddenly reappear. But that's part of the beauty of Limbotown. You can spend a couple of months there, and when I deliver you back to San Bernardino it will still be today, July 17th, 2000. No one will even know you've been gone, except for you. Antonio, Maria, and Roberto won't remember a thing that happened in Limbotown, or that they were even there. I'll see to that."

Don was quick with a reminder: "Yeah, but if my team wins, Roberto goes back cured and I guess I get to go with you."

"That's right," said Death. "The Alvarezes still won't know what happened, only that Roberto will be miraculously cured, and you'll be discovered dead from a heart attack right there in your easy chair. First you have to win. If you don't, you get to go back with the Alvarezes to watch little Roberto die; and you'll still be the only one who remembers anything about Limbotown or the Series."

Drummond continued: "Like I said, you're going to have to come up with a good story for them when all of you wake up in Limbotown tomorrow morning. They won't remember anything when they get back, but they're going to have a lot of questions when they show up."

"I'll take care of it. You just don't tell them I'm trading my life for Roberto's," Don hammered home again.

"I'll live up to . . . well, I'll hold up my end of the bargain," said Death in the Flesh, trying not to make any more bad puns. "Remember, you can call the deal off any time you like, but then Roberto dies. Anything else you want to know?"

"Yeah, where are you going to be?" Ogilvie asked.

"I'll be there every day. I'll tell the Alvarezes everything, except

13

about you trading your life; and the same thing when the players show up. I can't promise anybody will believe a word I say, especially in the beginning. They'll all have to make up their own minds, just like you're trying to do now. Eight weeks or so in Limbotown should be convincing enough for everyone. The rest is up to you. Anything else?"

Don wasn't sure why he felt compelled to ask, "Do you have a first name?"

Death in the Flesh leaned forward on his barstool and said, "You already know it. I told you. It's 'Doctor.' You can call me 'Doc' if you like." Doctor Drummond then cautioned the suddenly familiar hitting instructor: "Let me give you some advice, Pal: Don't try to get too chummy with Death—there's no future in it."

As if ignoring a third base coach's "stop" sign, the unsteady and unsure minor league minion stared Death in the face and barreled through, declaring: "I'm ready as I'll ever be. Let's go!"

Drummond let out a resounding, "Good! Now close your eyes, Ogilvie—I'm putting you under. When you wake up, you'll be in Limbotown. We're gonna have a great series."

As he began to fall asleep, the dazed batting guru couldn't help thinking, *Death must be a baseball fan.* It seemed whimsical—but then, death can be that way.

Chapter 2

Blistering heat and a heavy layer of brown-orange smog had been hanging over the city for days. Bread was baking in open air. The local paper reported that a Hare Krishna had spontaneously combusted outside the airport. At dusk the polluted sky transformed into a beautiful but malignant aurora borealis. It was mid-July, 2000, in San Bernardino, California, the one-time home of the Stampede, a Dodger minor league ball club.

The Single-A team was in the last half of their season. There was no game that day, but the Stampede were working out despite the torrid weather—stretching, running, shagging fly balls, taking batting practice. Thwack! The sound of the ball coming off the bat hard. Thwack! Thwack! Then plunk. The sound of the ball not well hit.

The only relief from the swelter was in the air-conditioned clubhouse. The players were not allowed inside during practice. Only the coaches whose presence on the field was not needed were granted that privilege.

Two coaches and the manager of the San Bernardino Stampede sought refuge from the inferno. Manager William "Buck Nimble was trying to find the team's hitting instructor. The burly skipper was grilling his staff like helpless hamburgers on a fiery barbecue.

"Hey Ripper," Buck roared, "do you know where the fuck Ogilvie is? He was supposed to be here at ten, and it's almost eleven fucking o'clock!"

"Don't know, Buck," said first-base coach Frank "The Ripper" Holiday as he hurriedly looked for something to do in the next room.

Buck was bellowing now. "What about you, Squeaker?"

"Haven't seen him since yesterday," said Bobby "Squeaker" Johnson, the infield coach.

This time Buck wasn't really directing his bombast to anyone in particular. "Well he'd better fucking show up now! This is twice in the last week, and I'm getting damned fucking tired of it—and he better not fucking smell like booze!" Then, "Squeaker, go find Alvarez. He'll know where the fuck Ogilvie is."

"Damn, Buck, it's hot out there!" complained Squeaker.

The arteries in Buck Nimble's neck swelled, making his already ruddy face even redder. "It's gonna be a fuck-load of a lot hotter in here if you don't get Alvarez now! Or maybe you'd like to be out there for the rest of fucking practice."

"I'll go get him," was the infield coach's fast, resigned reply. Squeaker Johnson heaved melodramatically as he left the cool shelter of the clubhouse to look for the team's right fielder, Antonio Alvarez, who hadn't done anything yet to earn a nickname.

Buck Nimble was a hulk of a man. He had the physique of an aging wrestler, a sizable girth that he carried well. At six-foot-four and barrel-chested, he appeared and felt much younger than his sixty-five years. Only adding to his stature as a baseball elder statesman, his sandy-brown hair was mostly gray now. He had a deep, booming voice, born with a bullhorn where his mouth should've been. Buck always peppered his conversation with obscenities, especially any variation of the word "fuck." It was unconscious, and he really couldn't control it. To the uninitiated, it was as if both the wrath and voice of God had been visited upon them.

As lore had it, when Buck was bench coach for the Milwaukee Brewers, he capped off his introduction to the owner's genteel wife by blasting out, "It's a real fuckin' pleasure to meet you, Ma'am." After noticing the look of shock on the faces of the owner, his horrified spouse and anyone else within earshot, Buck realized his mistake and offered his apology, "Ah, Jesus Christ, Ma'am, I'm really fuckin' sorry about that."

As Buck's wife (called Mrs. Buck by everyone, including Buck himself) would later say about the whole incident, "My fucking husband doesn't fucking know how to talk to a lady." All those years with her profanity-obsessed mate had rubbed off on Mrs. Buck, and she suffered from the same affliction. The social graces were never the couple's strong point. Yet anyone who knew anything about professional baseball respected Buck Nimble as one of its best minds. He would've made a terrific Major League manager, except someone else always seemed to get the nod. A lesser man might've sunk into a cliché, but not Buck. He was too big for that, too pure. He was the original the stereotype was based on.

Now the big coach was ready to wind down his career. He knew he was getting too old to be a big league manager, so he decided to spend his last years before retirement in the minor leagues developing young players. Sure, life on the road with a Single-A team could be rough, but the obscenity-obsessed skipper was right where he wanted to be. All the others wanted to be somewhere else.

Buck had been a Major Leaguer. He'd had a mediocre career as a utility player who could play outfield, or first or third base. Never a regular starter, he was a solid if unspectacular competitor, mainly playing for the San Francisco Giants. Buck would recall his big league days to his new minor leaguers: "I wasn't too good a hitter, so I made up for it with my lack of speed." The strapping skipper also used this conundrum as sort of a "flash" intelligence test for his rookies. Those who laughed, passed. Those who looked puzzled were either truly brilliant or borderline idiots. Hardly any were brilliant.

Buck had always been blessed with a manager's mind. To occupy himself during his long spells riding the bench (and to keep his head in the game), he would think along with the coaches and ask questions about strategy, plays, substitutions, and the million other little details most fans and even most players didn't concern themselves with. This didn't go unnoticed. By the time he retired as a player, he had already been offered a couple of Major League coaching positions. He made it as high as bench coach. Yes, Buck wanted to be a big league manager, but he was also a realist. Who was going to hire an untested Major League skipper at age sixty-five?

Besides, to Buck, the big leagues were hardly recognizable anymore. Families used to own teams, not corporations. When he came to the Majors as a player in 1960, there was no free agency and salaries were paltry by today's standards. Ballplayers were money conscious even then, but love of the game still outweighed money. Athletes of that era were thought to be down to earth. Now money was everything. Players were "legal entities" with a coterie of lawyers, accountants, and agents in tow. Entourages and hangers-on were common. So were very expensive cars, mansions, boats (some big enough to be called ships), and other "toys." Too much money had made modern Major Leaguers as difficult and arrogant as Leona Helmsley at a tax audit. The idea of babysitting a bunch of immature, overpaid, Baby Hueys did not hold much appeal for Buck Nimble.

Even the minor leagues had its share of "bonus babies," talented athletes signed to contracts with large up-front payments. These prospects still had something to prove if they were going to make it to "The Show." If a minor league bonus baby wanted to drive his Porsche to practice, that didn't bother Buck. However, if that same player didn't put in enough effort at practice or especially during a game, the demanding but fair manager could make life as hard as artificial turf. Extra laps, longer drills—or even worse, a word to higher-ups that the player didn't have what it takes. Not all bonus babies made it to the Majors. Old Buck was happy with the power he had over his minor league wards. He felt like a lion tamer completely in charge of his wild beasts. Instead of a whip, gun, and chair, he had a bat, a ball, a barrel-chest, and that profane, thunderous resonance.

No one really knew how Buck got his nickname. Rumor was he gave it to himself. It supposedly happened toward the end of his playing career, when Buck knew he was going to be a coach. He figured it was bad enough to be a player without a nickname, worse still if you were a coach. He settled on Buck mainly because it seemed like half the players, coaches, and managers in baseball were "Bucks" or "Buckys." Buck didn't want a weird or strange nickname. This could easily happen if someone else thought of a name and it stuck—like "Squeaker."

Buck's infield coach, Squeaker Johnson, had suffered such a

christening. Squeaker, over fifty now, had also had an uninspired Major League career, although at least he'd made it that far. When he was barely twenty-one, Squeaker was invited (along with other minor league players) to spring training with the St. Louis Cardinals—a common practice that allowed Major League coaches and managers to see how their minor leaguers were coming along. It can be pretty intimidating for the Double-A and Triple-A players. Razzing and hazing by the big leaguers is all part of the experience. Some guys handle it better than others. Squeaker, known just as Bobby then, was an easy mark. When he'd first arrived at the Cardinals clubhouse, a new, young coach called Buck asked him his name. Bobby was overwhelmed to be in a Major League clubhouse with big league players all around. Nerves got the best of him and when he spit his name out his voice cracked wildly. After the laughter died down, Buck remarked, "We got a real squeaker on our hands, boys. Let's hope he can play better than he talks." Some thirty years later, Bobby Johnson was still known as "Squeaker."

Then there was The Ripper. You would think that Frank "The Ripper" Holiday's nickname had something to do with his being a decent hitter—as in, "He really ripped that ball!" In fact, The Ripper was not a solid hitter. His was also an undistinguished Major League career that indirectly led to his moniker.

The Ripper had a terrible temper as a player. When he struck out (which was all too often) or made an error, he would fly into a rage when he got back to the dugout. This did not please any of the several managers he'd played for. He was not a good-enough player to get away with this behavior. In an effort to curb his ire, Frank Holiday started keeping several sheets of paper in his back pocket. If he did something on the field he didn't like, when he got back to the dugout, instead of throwing a tantrum, he would start ripping up the paper. His nickname soon followed.

In baseball psychology, tearing up paper in anger would not be considered abnormal. In a game full of superstition and ritual, idiosyncrasies are not only tolerated, they are often encouraged, if it helps somehow. To this day, The Ripper still kept paper in his back pocket. Now, however, whenever a player made a bonehead mistake or the Ripper just got mad, a sheet would come out and the distinctive ripping sound would pierce the air. Everyone knew what it meant.

It was no coincidence that Bobby "Squeaker" Johnson and Frank "The Ripper" Holiday landed up on Buck Nimble's staff. Both had played under Buck when he was a big league coach with the Brewers. Neither was a kid anymore, which Buck figured could only help his youthful minor league charges. Buck liked Squeaker and the Ripper: not so much for their coaching skills, but for their reliability and unflagging loyalty to him. Like faithful Labrador retrievers, they were always there for the big skipper when something had to be done. Not so one Donald Alan Ogilvie, the Stampede's missing-in-action hitting coach.

Don Ogilvie did not have a nickname, and mercifully so. If Buck had decided to give him one, it would've been something like "Boozer" or "Boilermaker." Fortunately, the outwardly gruff manager liked Ogilvie enough not to purposely embarrass him.

Okay, so maybe he wasn't going to be the next Babe Ruth. Still, Donald Alan Ogilvie made it to the Major Leagues, only to have his lifelong dream squashed like a gnat on the windshield of reality—and all before he really had a chance to get started. He was about the same age as Squeaker and The Ripper, and unquestionably had more ability. He was a promising young outfielder when he first met Buck Nimble, who was managing Ogilvie's minor league team. Not only could Don Ogilvie hit the ball long and hard, he also had baseball smarts. You didn't have to tell him how to play the game—he knew. He reminded Buck of himself, except with more talent. The young player was always trying to learn the mental part of the game; when to bunt, when to steal, when to squeeze. He wasn't shy about asking Buck anything about a play or the game in general. He had a sharp head that always seemed to be tuned in to baseball. Buck only stayed with Ogilvie's minor league team for a season, and the two did not reunite until many years later. Buck Nimble never forgot about Don Ogilvie's baseball mind.

The aspiring Ogilvie was playing for the St. Louis Cardinals' Triple-A team when Buck managed there during the 1973 season. Both of them expected to be in The Show the following year—Buck as a coach and Ogilvie as a player. Buck made it back to the Majors as a coach and, in due time, as a bench coach, never to become a big league skipper. Ogilvie made it as far as spring training the next season. The Cards had an opening for a starting outfielder. He performed splendidly and won the position. Then came the unthinkable.

While running down a fly ball in a pre-season game, he caught a spike and blew out his right foot. At first everyone thought it was only a bad sprain. When the X-rays came back, it was diagnosed as a fully torn Achilles tendon. That's the thick cord-like muscle connecting the calf to the bottom of the heel. It's still a serious injury today, but it can usually be repaired and a career can continue. When Ogilvie suffered this fate in 1974, it was often career ending—especially when it didn't heal right. That's what happened to the would-be outfielder. Orthopedic medicine wasn't as advanced then. You were told to hang up your jockstrap and never look back.

Don Ogilvie was not the first athlete to have a promising future snapped clean by injury. For those who've had it happen, it is a reckoning like no other. Life can get very existential, very fast. Never is it fun bailing from a plane, only to set loose moths when you jerk the ripcord. Imagine striving for one goal, one desire, one mission in life—to become a professional athlete. It's a lottery with lousy odds, but given hard labor and a break, those with skill and drive can make it. Don Ogilvie made it, only to be denied. He was Roy Hobbs—a life destroyed faster than a silver bullet.

One measure of character is how adversity is faced. The violin player who will never play again still has choices—everything from jumping into a volcano to rising from its ashes like a crispy sacrificial virgin. But first, the poor bastards must play out the hand Chance dealt them from the bottom of the deck. At least Don Ogilvie could still walk and talk. He was not left an invalid or an incompetent. He had normal use of his body and mind. He would just never "play the violin again."

Let's face it, many other accidents can be far more devastating. Sometimes you sit in a wheelchair for the rest of your life. Take Roy Campanella, the Dodger Hall of Famer whose brilliant career was guillotined by an automobile accident, rendering the once vital catcher a quadriplegic. Or perhaps worse, you have brain damage and you're pretty much lobotomized like old R. P. McMurphy in *One Flew over the Cuckoo's Nest*. Of course, you can be unluckier still and wind up like Lou Gehrig. Having a terminal disease named after you is no consolation.

For those who survive, there are many inspirational stories of people overcoming their heart-tugging tragedies to lead quote-unquote happy, fulfilling lives. First, however, they were tempered in the crucible of their own misfortune. Having had their anguish melted away, leaving only acceptance, they made their peace. All of these people have at least one thing in common: they got past their catastrophes, stopped feeling sorry for themselves, and then found something to do. It doesn't always work out that way.

Don Ogilvie never got over it and never stopped feeling sorry for Don Ogilvie. He would not admit this, especially to himself. Maybe he was better off never having played in the big leagues. Often, a taste of honey is worse than none at all. He didn't see it that way, of course.

And although Ogilvie was careful to stay away from other drugs as he climbed the mountain to the Majors, beer and liquor were as much a part of American baseball as bankruptcy, taking the Fifth, or cheating the stockholders is a part of America today. It was no big deal to get plastered after a game. Hell, it was even encouraged back then. Besides, he wasn't a drunk, just a guy having a few with the boys. But that all burst apart, along with his foot.

His life headed into a tailspin. It was slow at first, like a roller-coaster car being towed to the top of that first big drop. He let his bitterness destroy what he'd already built. After all, Donald Alan Ogilvie had a college degree. A baseball scholarship made that possible. While at school he met his wife, Katie, a wonderful, loving, understanding woman who stood by him after his injury and attempted in vain to help him.

Finally, his escalating drinking ruined everything. He tried teaching for a while at a high school where he could also be the baseball coach. Being around baseball only made him miss it more. Missing it more made him drink more. Drinking more only made him withdraw further and further into a dark, all-consuming vortex of warped logic and cryptic dreams. Luckily, he and Katie had decided to delay starting a family until after he made it to The Show. He was in no condition now to be any kind of father.

Don Ogilvie was remarkably able at galling not only whoever happened to be his employer at the time, but also his friends and family. After losing more than a few jobs and all of his self-respect to alcohol, he managed to lose his wife. Katie didn't run off with anybody or anything dramatic like that. When she felt that she had done all she could do and it still wasn't helping, staying became too painful. She could no longer bear witness to her husband's self-destruction. It was like watching Prometheus having his live innards ripped out and eaten by ravenous birds every evening. Hard to stomach.

Don Ogilvie was determined to bottom-out faster than a Russian submarine. His unavoidable divorce did it. His drinking became worse yet, and for over a year he was homeless. Surviving in public shelters, he panhandled for liquor. He was so deep into the jungle, he didn't even know he was in the jungle anymore.

By the time he woke up one day and somewhat came to his senses, over ten years had gone by. It was 1986. Don Ogilvie was almost thirty-eight. Somehow, something had swum up from inside his whisky-soaked soul and made him go on. It was really nothing more than a survival instinct, like a wildebeest running helter-skelter from the deadly bead of a hungry lion. Ogilvie's body augured that too much more of this would be fatal, even at his fairly young age. On the one hand, he truly was trying to drink himself to death. On the other, he didn't have the guts to consciously commit suicide. It was this dilemma that kept him alive in a half-hearted, tortured sort of way.

He decided to re-enter the human race by swearing off baseball. It was baseball that caused his bad luck, or so he believed. For a while it worked. He joined A.A. and stayed sober. He toiled his way up from stock clerk to assistant manager at a local grocery store and found an apartment to rent. But there was still something missing. Ogilvie was a man with a broken dream, and he didn't have a new one. So it tore at him and ate him up inside like invisible termites. The twisted nightmares returned. Every so often he fell off the wagon. These episodes were sporadic and never lasted too long. He was able to hold onto his job.

That Don Ogilvie ended up as an assistant manager of a supermarket in San Bernardino was predictable. He'd grown up in southern California and attended high school in Claremont, a small city about sixty miles west. He went to Cal State Fullerton on a baseball scholarship. After his divorce, when Ogilvie just drifted and drank, it was mainly in southern California. When he regained consciousness and became serious about finding a job, he still wanted to live in the area. It also had to be a place that wasn't expensive and was just big enough to get lost in. San Bernardino was made to order.

A half-person like Don Ogilvie oozes sadness. It isn't noticeable at first, but becomes so to people who are around for a time, like fellow workers or regular customers. Ogilvie gave them the feeling that they were looking at one of those cheesy paintings of a lost soul, a wayward apparition with oversized, vacuous eyes. He was almost too courteous and friendly at work. This was only a thin veil that could not fully shelter his crushed spirit, and only made his attempts to seem content pathetic to those who could see otherwise. He had no friends. He preferred to be a loner. And beyond his TV set, he had no personal life.

Ogilvie hadn't been kind to himself during his years of heavy boozing and it showed. By the time he sobered up, his face had already developed that craggy appearance—more inroads than a Los Angeles street map. His body was mushy, and he sported a hefty beer paunch. He hadn't kept up any regular exercise since he left organized baseball, not even when he was a high school coach. He was out of shape. He was pear-shaped.

At six-feet-two, Don's playing weight was 195. He now weighed 255 pounds—not bad, considering all of his self-inflicted wounds. His brown hair had started to recede and turn gray. His countenance was plain, even common. It was an able façade to the unaware, masking problems far deeper than the lines on his face.

For Don Ogilvie, while a day seemed to drag on forever, the years flew by. It was now 1997, and he was fifty. He'd been working in the same grocery store for over ten years and probably would've worked there forever. Then Buck Nimble walked in one day.

Ogilvie knew the Dodgers had a Single-A ball club in San Bernardino. He never gave it a second thought. By the time he'd started working at the supermarket, he was already old enough for his big league career (if he'd had one) to have ended. Baseball had not been a part of his life for a long time.

It was a real shock for Don Ogilvie when Buck Nimble ambled in that fateful afternoon. Don instantly recognized his old coach. His heart pounding harder than John Henry's sledgehammer, he gushed sweat like water over Niagara Falls. Teeming perspiration was his normal, telltale reaction to stress or crisis; and Buck was the most vivid reminder of Ogilvie's star-crossed past since he left professional baseball.

The strapping coach had just landed the job as skipper of the San Bernardino Stampede. He'd never been to San Bernardino before, let alone lived there, and he was trying to cash an out-of-state check. Only a store manager or assistant could approve it. The checker directed the robust Buck to Don's booth, since Don was the only manager there that day. He was hopeful his old minor league mentor wouldn't recognize him. No way in hell was he going to recognize Buck.

Don walked to the manager's cubicle at the other end of the store and hoped the big man wouldn't remember him. He was fairly sure he wasn't going to be "made" anyhow. It had been over twenty years since he'd seen Buck, and Don had been hard on himself. Old Buck, on the other hand, looked great—in shape, tan, eyes clear.

Don mopped his brow with a thin, crusty handkerchief. Beads of water immediately reappeared and slid off his forehead. There wasn't much he could do to dam the monsoon coming from his armpits, which had already soaked through the worn cloth of his white, short-sleeve shirt. Ogilvie turned his back as Buck Nimble approached him.

With his trademark atomic-bomb voice, the newly employed manager started in: "Hey, Pal—I'd really fuh . . . I'd really appreciate it if you could approve this check for me." The profanity-loving Buck was becoming a little more careful about using obscenities in unknown situations.

Ogilvie took a deep breath, turned around, did not look at Buck Nimble, and took his check. "Do you have two forms of ID?"

25

"Yeah, sure," Buck said. When he was done pulling stuff out of his wallet, he handed the IDs to Don and got a clear look at him. You could almost hear the bells and whistles going off in his head. "Say . . ." Buck began slowly. Ogilvie cringed because of what he knew was coming next. ". . . didn't you play minor league ball?" The grocery store clerk briefly thought about lying. It was too late. Buck was reading his nameplate under the unforgiving fluorescent glare of supermarket surrealism. "Yeah, you're Don Ogilvie. I remember you. I'm Buck Nimble. Remember me?"

It was hard for anyone to forget Buck, particularly Don Ogilvie. "Sure, Buck," Don said, trying to act like he'd just recognized him. "I just never expected to see you here."

"Well, hell," said the animated coach, "I'm gonna be here in San Bernardino at least through the season. I'm managing the Dodger's Single-A team." Don was about to say something just to be polite, but Buck was on a roll. "You know, I really remember you now. You were a helluva hitter and a damn smart ballplayer. Didn't you make it to the Majors?"

Just hearing that question out loud made Don Ogilvie's stomach flip like a pancake. He answered anyhow. "I tore my Achilles tendon at the Cards' spring training camp. I had surgery, but it never healed right. That was pretty much it for me."

"Damn fucking shame." The big manager actually seemed sympathetic. "You know, they can usually fix that one now."

"Yeah, I've heard. Too bad I wasn't born about fifteen years later, huh?"

"Well, no use crying over spilled beer, right?"

Ogilvie thought to himself: *That's all I did for over ten years after my foot let me down.* Now he was crying not just for his lost big league career, but also for a lost decade.

The flustered employee stared at Buck, wondering what to say. He was blanking. Not to worry—the gears and wheels were going around in old Buck's head again, and he took the lead. "You know, you were the guy who used to ask me all those questions about plays and strategies. I'll bet you coach some local team around here."

"Jeez, I haven't done that in a quite awhile. Really been out of the game for a long time," Ogilvie said, his voice trailing off to a whisper.

"Well baseball is just like sex. Even at my age, you never forget . . . you're just not as good at it," said Buck, chuckling at his own quip. Don was not sure where the sturdy manager was going with this. Buck then made a sudden and unexpected invitation. "Why don't you come down to one of our games and sit in the dugout with me? I'll bet you forgot how much fun it is."

Ogilvie thought this a strange request. If Buck had only wanted him to see a game, he would've just given him a ticket. Don knew he had something else in mind when he asked him to sit in the dugout, but what? Maybe he just felt sorry for him.

Buck kept on talking while he reached into his pocket. "Look, here's a clubhouse pass. We got a home game here on Friday night. Think you can make it to that one?"

"I'll have to check my work schedule . . ."

"Well, we got home games on Saturday and Sunday, too. I know you can make it to one of 'em. Now promise me you'll come!"

Buck Nimble was a hard man to refuse. Don wasn't planning on making it to any games. He nodded anyhow.

"Good!" trumpeted Buck. "I'll expect to see you."

As soon as the newly hired manager of the San Bernardino Stampede turned to leave, Don grabbed the open roll of paper towels affixed to his booth and began to stuff wads of it in his armpits, and when he finished his shift that night, he headed for the closest liquor store. He wouldn't buy alcohol at his market because some of the employees were familiar with his problems. In fact, Ogilvie was not working Friday, Saturday or Sunday. He didn't need to check his schedule. He needed to drink himself into the next millennium through the weekend. He needed to forget all about Buck Nimble and his invitation.

It didn't work. He got good and toasted on Thursday night, and stayed that way all day Friday. Saturday morning he had a terrific hangover. He was going to douse it with more booze when he realized that if he didn't make it to one of those games, Buck would come looking for him. It was just the kind of thing the blustery skipper would do. He decided to go to Sunday's game. He was sick most of Saturday, but felt decent enough Sunday morning. The game started at 1 p.m.

Ogilvie knew right where the ballpark was, even though he'd never been there before. The weather was nice. Puffy white clouds broke up the baby-blue sky like giant floating cotton balls. It was late spring, and the oppressive heat of summer had yet to arrive—except in Don Ogilvie's hands and face, which were both more flushed than a ballpark toilet. He was schvitzing like a Rabbi at a Nazi Party reunion. He wished he could control this involuntary deluge, but it was almost like trying to stop the sun from rising. Instead, he bought a San Bernardino Stampede cap from a vendor as he approached the turnstile. The hat helped soak up the betrayal of his nerves. He gave his clubhouse pass to the ticket taker and was told to check in with a man with a clipboard standing off to the left. The man with the clipboard did not look up. He heard Ogilvie approaching and simply said, "Name."

"Don Ogilvie," he said clearing his throat. He knew his name wasn't going to be on any list.

"Don Ogilvie," the man with the clipboard repeated and then raised his head. "You're in the dugout with Buck. You've been on the list since Friday. Buck was asking about you." Before Don could say anything, the man added, "It's the third door down on the right. That'll get you into the clubhouse. From there, just follow the signs to the dugout."

Being at a ballpark after such a long absence was a chimerical adventure for Don Ogilvie. His dread was replaced by a lightheaded feeling mingled with a sickeningly sweet anxiety radiating from the pit of his stomach. His legs felt as rubbery and worn as old tires. For Don Ogilvie, making his way to the Stampede bench was a cross between a Fellini movie and an out-of-body experience. He wasn't sure it was really happening, and he was equally unsure what Buck had in mind. Gingerly traversing the tunnel from the locker room, he stepped into the far end of the dugout. He felt self-conscious and out of place. He was damp and sticky all over.

Buck spotted him a few seconds later. "Hey, Ogilvie!" Buck let fly. "Come over here. You're gonna sit by me." As he passed the players, they nodded at him. Plainly, Buck's welcome to Don was not lost on them. It was a sign of respect for Buck. When Ogilvie made it over to the other end of the dugout, Buck greeted him with a handshake and a slap on his moist back. "Hopin' you were gonna make it Friday or Saturday," said Buck while first inspecting and then wiping his wet hand across his uniformed chest.

"I had to work," Don said, lying.

"Well you're here now and that's all that counts," reassured Buck.

"What am I doing here?" Don asked, thinking out loud.

"I just want you to enjoy the game!" Then it came out. "And I thought maybe you could help me figure out what's wrong with my hitters."

Don felt relieved to know why Buck wanted him there, but also anxious because he wanted his "professional" help. Sweat streamed from under his cap and down his short sideburns to the line of his jaw. "Jeez, Buck," Don said haltingly, "I've been out of baseball so long, I'm not sure what end of the bat they use anymore."

Buck chortled, "Bullfuck! You got a good baseball head and you were a helluva hitter. I know you can help me."

Don replied, "I'll try."

After the National Anthem, the San Bernardino Stampede took the field. The visiting team made three outs without scoring a run, and then it was the Stampede's turn at bat. As the leadoff hitter for the Single-A "Dodgers" entered the batter's box, Buck leaned over to Don. "Tell me what you think of this guy's swing." Ball one. No swing. Second pitch. The right-handed batter swung and missed.

Don could see what was wrong. "His swing's okay, Buck. He's just shifting his weight and hips too soon; not keeping his hands back. If he hits the ball, it'll be a weak grounder to the left side." Third pitch, swing—contact, and a weak grounder to the left side for an easy out. Buck turned and smiled at Don. Buck was pleased. Not so much with Don Ogilvie, but with himself for trusting his instincts about his former protégé.

Next hitter, the San Bernardino Stampede's light-hitting shortstop. He dug into the batter's box and went through a preset ritual of tugging at his cap, looping the bat a couple of times, and then waggling it back and forth while waiting for the pitch. This one was going to be simple. Don didn't even have to watch him swing. He commented to Buck, "This guy thinks he's a helicopter. With all that bat movement, he won't be able to catch up to the fastball. Strike out swinging or an out to the right side." Pop-up to the first baseman.

Third hitter—the traditional spot for the team's best hitter. After watching him fan by taking three graceful swings at the first three pitches, none of which were strikes, Don said to Buck, "He's got a nice swing. I wouldn't mess with it. But he's swinging at bad pitches. He's taking more hacks than Lizzie Borden. Needs to be more patient. Wait for a strike. If he does that, he'll walk a lot more and raise his average thirty points."

And so it went. When a player returned to the dugout after making an out, Buck would motion to him, introduce him to Ogilvie and say, "Hey Don, tell him what you told me."

Ogilvie tried to be as low-key as possible. After all, he was just some old guy in the dugout sitting next to Buck. He didn't want the players to be resentful, and they weren't—at least while Buck was sitting there. Buck liked how Don got along with the players. It was as though he was one of them, an equal, not a superior or an underling.

By the end of the game, Don Ogilvie felt right at home. Thankfully, his cataclysmic perspiration ebbed like the Nile returning to its banks after the rainy season. His coaching resulted in a few hits and thank-yous from grateful players. Some asked about Don's baseball background. When they did, Buck would step in with his two bits, "This guy played for me in Triple-A before most of you fuckers were even born. He was gonna be a great fuckin' Major Leaguer, only a bad wheel took care of that."

One of the players asked about his injury. When Don told him it was an Achilles tendon, the player remarked, "I thought they can usually fix that one."

"Yeah, they can now, but not back in medieval times. Besides, it never healed right," Don said without hesitation or fear. It was strange. After a queasy start, being back at the ballpark turned out to be good for Don Ogilvie. The biggest surprise was that he didn't mind the question about his foot. When he thought about it later, the reason struck him. Time. In 1974, when he first knew his baseball career was over, the emotional wounds were still gaping. When he tried coaching high school baseball, it was when he'd figured he would have been in the middle of his Major League career. This was always in the back of his mind. Now he was old enough that if he'd had a big league career, it would've been long over. He might've been some kind of coach now, anyhow. Instead of wanting to hit the bottle, he wanted to hit the ball. He felt rejuvenated, full of energy. He couldn't wait for Buck to ask what he knew Buck was going to ask him. Yes, he'd be glad to be the new hitting instructor for the Single-A San Bernardino Stampede.

He gave notice at work and signed a contract with the ball club. For a couple of weeks, he worked both his old and new job. He'd worked at the same store for ten years. He didn't want to leave them in the lurch or blow-up any bridges, as he'd done with his life so many times in the past. If things didn't work out, he wanted a place he could go back to. He also needed work in the off-season. Minor league coaches only made about half as much as a box-boy.

The rest of that first season went just fine for Don Ogilvie. He fell in love with baseball all over again—this time as a coach.

But the first half of the next season was rocky. Ogilvie thought he had everything straightened out. He couldn't understand why he still battled bouts of depression and cravings for alcohol. One followed the other. It was the old, repetitive cycle. It turned out that his return to baseball became a real dilemma. He loved being back in the game, but he began to hate that it reminded him of the playing days he'd never had. Living his life through the team was about as satisfying as watching a stripper while blindfolded.

Just as he did when he worked at the supermarket, he occasionally gave in to his demons. Rather than miss a game or a practice, he would still show up, only wound a little too tight for Buck's taste. The big skipper was reserved at first. However, after about the third incident in as many months, Ogilvie endured the full ranting and raving, riot-act lecture from old Buck behind closed doors. The door helped muffle the burly manager's booming voice, but everyone knew what was going on. Don was a skilled and likable coach. The players and other coaches always pulled for him. Still, it was only a matter of time before Buck would have to let him go.

Happily for Don Ogilvie, something happened at the beginning of the 1999 season that truly helped him. It was the arrival of Antonio Alvarez, right fielder, wife Maria, and six-year-old son, Roberto.

Chapter 3

Antonio and Maria Alvarez had been high school sweethearts in Whittier, California, and married soon after graduating. Both were practicing Catholics, although not fanatics. Their common faith and love solidified their youthful marriage. Little Roberto soon followed. He became the center of their life.

Antonio, an excellent student and a fair athlete, had been accepted at UCLA on an academic scholarship. He made the baseball team as a walk-on. It was not an easy existence. The Alvarezes had little money and a baby—generally a poor combination. Nevertheless, they made it work. Antonio went to classes and played ball, and Maria held as many jobs as she could. They both somehow succeeded in being wonderful parents to little Roberto—and Roberto, with his unconditional love for them, completed the able trio. What a beautiful family they made. By the time Antonio graduated and eventually signed with the San Bernardino "Dodgers," he and Maria were mature beyond their years (at any rate, well past the stunted maturity of Don Ogilvie, now fifty-plus).

Antonio Alvarez felt fortunate to be signed to a minor league contract with the San Bernardino Stampede—first, because he had already spent the better part of two seasons with other Single-A clubs, neither in California, and second, to chase his dream not too far from home. Of course, he understood the life of a ballplayer was inescapably the life of a vagabond. The opposing team's field might be anywhere.

Antonio always wanted to be a Major League player. At least he made it to Class-A ball. He was not a bonus baby, and not blessed with a world of talent. That he'd made it this far was proof of his hunger to be in the Bigs and his willingness to work hard—very hard. Yet if he didn't advance from A-ball soon, his chances of making it further would be less than winning the lottery.

Players in Antonio Alvarez's position could always cheer themselves with miracle stories. Mike Piazza was a favorite of the 1990s. The former Dodger, then Met, catcher was drafted in the sixty-second round. They'd almost run out of rounds. He may well have been selected only because former Dodger manager Tommy Lasorda happened to be friends with Mike's dad. The would-be receiver put in lots of grinding work and became a star on both coasts.

Unfortunately, for every Mike Piazza there were 10,000 who didn't make it. At some juncture, every unheralded minor league player thinks he's going to be the next Mike Piazza. Nearly all of them are wrong.

Antonio Alvarez knew he would have to strive harder still if he was going to make it to The Show. By minor league standards, he was only average: average height and build, average speed, average throwing-arm, average fielding, and barely average hitting. His only real physical asset was his unusual strength. Always the strongman on any of his teams since high school, he often bested and embarrassed athletes twice his size, but only when it came to feats of power. Regrettably, strength alone does not transform into baseball brilliance. What Antonio Alvarez lacked in ability, however, he made up for with his big heart. No one had more desire to play hard and win than Antonio Alvarez. Had he been endowed with the same gifts as Don Ogilvie, his future as a big leaguer would have been secure.

Maria was patient with her husband's ambition to play Major League ball. She believed he would move up the minor league ladder. If he didn't, it wouldn't be the end of the world for her, but it would seem that way to Antonio. If that happened, Maria and little Roberto would be there to piece back together the jigsaw puzzle of Antonio's burst balloon. Like Don Ogilvie, Antonio Alvarez had made sure he got his college degree. If things didn't pan out in baseball, he'd have his education to fall back on. The Alvarez family all prayed that day would only come after Antonio's big league days were over.

Desire, heart, and—sadly for Antonio Alvarez—even great strength do not a Major League career make. Paradoxically, a few of his teammates who were superior athletes but lacking his discipline and hunger, stood no better chance of making it to The Show than Antonio. He knew he would have to improve to get further. He needed help.

Don Ogilvie needed help too. His bouts of melancholy and binging were starting to become more frequent. Were it not for the Alvarez family, Ogilvie would've slipped further, and eventually been fired by Buck. Their arrival at least delayed the inevitable.

When Antonio Alvarez arrived in San Bernardino in 1999, he immediately sought out Don Ogilvie. Not that he'd ever met him—he only knew he was the batting coach. Antonio reasoned—correctly—that the most important skill to master was hitting. Hitting was more noticeable than fielding. Big league teams prized it over almost anything else. Babe Ruth, baseball's most heralded slugger, started out as one of its most successful left-handed pitchers. He won almost a hundred games in less than five seasons! Hardly anyone remembers that Ruth pitched, and fantastically well at that. Everyone remembers the home runs. Antonio Alvarez was on the right track. If only he could harness his power when smacking a baseball.

Requests for help with hitting were expected, and Don Ogilvie was eager to oblige. It was also his job. With Antonio Alvarez, it became something more. In baseball parlance, the two hit it off, right off the bat. But it was the Alvarezes' six-year-old son, Roberto, who changed the doleful hitting instructor's life forever. His parents brought their lively boy to practices and Antonio's extra batting sessions with Ogilvie. The two became fast friends.

The first time they met, little Roberto asked Don, "Hey Mister, do you think you can teach my dad to hit better?"

Ogilvie answered, "Sure, Roberto. But don't call me 'Mister,' okay? My friends call me 'Don.'"

"Am I really your friend?" asked the hopeful youngster. No grown-up had ever offered to be his pal. He treated Ogilvie's offhand comment like a coveted invitation to join one of those secret clubs kids make up.

Crouching to be eye-to-eye with Roberto, the Stampede's batting coach sensed how seriously the six-year-old was taking the matter of friendship. He didn't want to hurt his feelings by being too casual in his reply. "I believe we can be best friends," Ogilvie earnestly told the wide-eyed boy.

Struck by his sincerity, Roberto reached into his pocket and pulled out an assortment of boyhood treasures: a yo-yo, some stamps, a few coins, and his prized cat's-eye marble, a boulder at that. He presented the blue-green orb to Don to seal their new bond.

The grateful coach reciprocated by giving little Roberto his full-sized outfielder's glove. It was his favorite. He gave it to him with the advice, "This glove may be big for you now, but you'll be able to use it sooner than you think."

Roberto was dumbstruck by the enormity of Don's offering. He and Don had just met. His open-mouthed, mute expression of thanks was more genuine appreciation than Don Ogilvie had seen in a decade.

Don treated little Roberto like they were peers—and in a way they were. It wasn't that the youngster was precocious so much as Ogilvie was childlike. They were enthralled to be each other's best friend.

It was no coincidence that Antonio named his son after the legendary Pittsburgh Pirate right fielder, Roberto Clemente. The mercurial star was tragically brought to ground when he died in an airplane crash in 1972 while delivering supplies to earthquake victims in Nicaragua. Only thirty-eight at the time, he was still playing for the Bucs. A black Puerto Rican, Clemente is revered by all Latin players, the first Hispanic to make it into the Hall of Fame. It was no coincidence either that Antonio Alvarez played right field.

Antonio was a student of the game. Like Don Ogilvie, he loved baseball. And like Don, Antonio also knew some baseball history. Of course he knew about modern-era greats like Mantle, Musial, Aaron, and Clemente, but he'd also read about old-time greats like Ruth, Cobb, Mathewson, and Wagner. Together Don and Antonio would tell a rapt Roberto about these heroic players of the past, the legends of baseball, the ghosts of the game.

36

Who knew what type of ballplayer little Roberto might turn into one day. Neither Antonio nor Don cared about that in 1999. Roberto was just a wonderful kid, full of light and life, charming as a leprechaun. He was also smart, as sharp as a diamond ring on a pimp's pinky.

Antonio, Maria, and little Roberto came to think of Don Ogilvie as family. He was invited to dinners at the Alvarezes' apartment. He brought presents for Roberto, mostly baseball stuff—balls, caps, trading cards, things generally pilfered from the Stampede clubhouse. They often wound up in the street playing catch and teaching Roberto how to hit. The fun always began with Roberto asking his father and Don, "Who was the best player there ever was?"

Either Don or Antonio, or both, would answer, "Babe Ruth."

This would always be followed by little Roberto's next question: "Did he bat left or right?"

"Left!" they would all chant, including Roberto.

Then would come little right-handed Roberto's proclamation, "I'm gonna bat left!" They would play until it was too dark to see the ball.

Don Ogilvie, never having had a real family of his own, figured this would be as close as he would get. He savored the feeling. He knew he should've had a couple of grown-up kids by now and maybe even some grandchildren on the way. It's funny how an injured foot can change the entire course of a life.

When the Alvarez family arrived in San Bernardino, there was little sign of Don Ogilvie's drinking. At first, he was reluctant to share his mottled past with them. He wasn't sure they would understand. Antonio and Maria were religious and moral people. They had to be to have such a strong marriage at such a young age. Slowly, Don began to fill in the blanks of his life. He admitted that he still suffered fits of gloom, usually followed by falling off the wagon.

Much to Don's surprise, the Alvarezes were forgiving. As it turned out, Maria's father had been an alcoholic. He was gone now, his drinking having contributed mightily to his early checkout.

The year of the Alvarez family's arrival was Ogilvie's best in many seasons. The special friendship between Don and little Roberto was like a balm on the festering sore that was the minor league coach's

37

life. There was no depression and no drinking the remainder of the year.

Little Roberto also became the team favorite. He was the Stampede's official batboy for home games, and their unofficial mascot. Most of the coaches and players went out of their way to keep an eye on him. Don advised him, "Don't be afraid of these guys, Roberto. They're just big kids and you're a little one. That's the only difference. All right, so they get to use swear words and you don't. Other than that, just treat 'em like you would a kid your own age."

After becoming best friends with Don Ogilvie (who little Roberto charitably regarded as an adult), he learned not to be cowed by blowhard grownups—especially profane ballplayers. The fearless Roberto, who would soon be seven, could banter with the best of them. He kept the team loose and in high spirits. He may have been small, but his quick sense of humor was more than a match for his much older "teammates," and they loved him for it.

A choice example was little Roberto's first encounter with the Stampede's behemoth first baseman, Billy "Big Ass" Washington. The surly infielder acquired his nickname because of his huge thighs and buttocks, which looked as if they were about nine sizes too big for the rest of his body. This also accounted for his brute strength. After practice one day, Roberto was standing in the doorway between the clubhouse and the dugout, unwittingly blocking Billy's path.

As the immense first baseman approached the little batboy from behind, he rudely commanded, "Get the fuck out of my way, Kid. You're just a two-ounce shrimp and I'm a 600-pound shark."

"Hmm," mused an unflappable Roberto. "You must've lost some weight." Big Ass, much to the delight and derision of the other players, had been duly humbled by a forty-eight inch, fifty-five pound, six-and-a-half-year-old.

Nonetheless, Maria Alvarez was worried about exposing her young son to the foul language so common among baseball people. Buck Nimble, of course, was in a category all by himself. His fascination with and constant use of the F-word was second to none. Roberto was old enough to know what swear words were, just not what most of them meant. Maria and Antonio never used them. But they also knew profanity was ingrained in the sport, and there was nothing they could do about it. Maria just didn't want Roberto coming home with questions like, "Why does Buck call me a 'little fucker'?" Or the big one: "And what's a 'little fucker' anyhow? You know I'm not that little anymore!"

Antonio and Maria did a good job of explaining to their curious offspring that simply because most of the players and coaches cursed like they had Tourette's Syndrome, it wasn't okay for him to do it. Grasping this, he was able to honor his parents' request—he didn't want to do anything to jeopardize his privilege of going to practices and being batboy. Occasionally, if he wasn't sure, he'd ask his mom or dad, "Was that a bad word?" Other times he was simply rhetorical: "That was a really bad word, huh!"

For Don Ogilvie and the Alvarezes, the balance of the 1999 season was as easy as shagging lazy fly balls. And while Antonio's hitting improved, it still wasn't enough to get him out of A ball. The Stampede coaches (mainly Don Ogilvie) hadn't figured out how to make Antonio's Schwarzennegger-like biceps hit home runs, although the potential seemed to be there. In what turned out to be the highlight of his third Single-A season, Antonio silenced a bigheaded Billy "Big Ass" Washington in an arm-wrestling contest. They didn't even have to the hold the third match in the best-of-three competition. Buck decided a guy this strong was worth another look.

The 2000 season was decidedly different. Don Ogilvie knew this would be a make-it-or-break-it year for Antonio Alvarez. No matter how it turned out, it was not going to be a fun season for coach Ogilvie. If Antonio progressed enough, he would be sent to a Double-A team. If he didn't, he'd probably be released. Either way meant the loss of the Alvarez family for Don Ogilvie. It was never discussed. Still, Don and Antonio had a silent understanding about this unhappy fact.

Buck was tempted to let Antonio go after the end of the 1999 season. He didn't. He was keenly aware of the positive sway the Alvarez family and little Roberto had over his cloudy-eyed batting instructor. It made him a better coach and a better person. Plus, Antonio was stroking the ball a little more often.

Nevertheless, both Buck and Don knew Antonio was not going to be a Major Leaguer. They never talked about it. They didn't have to. It was a given. But it was a touchy subject for Don and Antonio. Don knew if he told Antonio his real opinion, Antonio would be devastated. On the other hand, if he just strung Antonio along, it would only be giving him false hope. Don wanted Antonio to think about being a coach, because he would be a natural. He had a light touch that players liked, and he was just as knowledgeable and savvy about baseball as either Buck or Don. Ogilvie figured if he ever brought up this idea to Antonio, it would be the same as telling him he was not going to be a big league player, only in a back-handed sort of way, which would be even worse. Don felt hypocritical about it. How could he ask Antonio to abandon his hope of going to the Majors while the vaporization of that little dream had been the undoing of Don Ogilvie?

This quandary and the likelihood that the Alvarez family would be somewhere else the next season were enough to push Ogilvie over the outfield bleachers. First came the sorrow and the self-pity, then the intense boozing. Yet he very rarely missed a practice and never a game. Regrettably, though, he would show up under the influence. He was able enough, even glassy-eyed and unsteady, but Buck was getting less tolerant though—and as much as Antonio Alvarez had come to care for the down-and-out hitting instructor, he wouldn't cover for him.

Don Ogilvie's studio apartment was a model of simplicity and order. It looked like a monk's retreat. It also looked like he just moved in, but in fact, he'd been there for over ten years. No pictures hung on the walls. Some clothing and other personal effects were stored in boxes tidily arranged in a corner. The kitchen didn't get used much because the batting coach preferred cheap take-out chow. Still, the apartment was not cluttered with old pizza boxes or other evidence of fast food. Having been homeless had made an impact on Don Ogilvie. His place wasn't much, so he paid tribute to it by keeping it neat and clean, albeit Spartan. He wasn't a sloppy drunk, just a miserable one.

The apartment itself was a long rectangle, like a boxcar on a freight train. The front door opened immediately into a living area that consisted of his easy chair, a side table, and a television. Beyond that was the kitchen, which also had a small breakfast bar with two stools. After that was the bathroom and sleeping area. Studio apartments don't have a separate bedroom.

When he drank, he hardly ever made it as far as the bed. He customarily passed out in his easy chair in front of a droning TV.

That night Don Ogilvie had been drinking. He awoke at 10:30 the following morning when the phone rang. Knowing it was Buck, he didn't answer. It was already hot, and he'd already sweated through the clothes he'd been wearing since the day before. The TV was still on. He was late for practice again. He took a quick shower, put on some fresh practice garb, and tried to shake the cobwebs from his fuzzy brain. Then came the moment of reckoning, as it always did the morning after. Was he going to keep on drinking?

The decision was made one way or the other while pouring that first cup of coffee. There sat the remainder of the previous night's excess, about half a bottle of cheap Scotch. On this morning, there was no hesitation. Don Ogilvie poured half a cup of coffee and filled the other half with the leftover booze. He slurped it down in three large gulps, nearly choking on the last one. After recovering, he poured the rest of the whisky into a plastic flask he could use to nip on the rest of the day. He threw a stick of gum in his mouth. Ogilvie then got into his twenty-year-old car and made the short drive to the ballpark. It was a few minutes past eleven. He was over an hour late.

Antonio Alvarez was chasing fly balls under the unrelenting summer sun when Squeaker Johnson motioned him in. Buck wanted to see him. This could be unsettling for a minor league ballplayer. A trip to the manager's office was often followed by the cleaning out of one's locker. Occasionally it meant moving up to Double- or Triple-A. Most of the time it was not good news. Antonio knew this visit with Buck was not going to be about him. He too was worried that Don Ogilvie was missing again. They both knew why he wasn't there. Buck was frustrated and angry.

As Antonio entered the clubhouse, the big skipper was standing there, his face as red as a baboon's butt, yelling, "Alvarez, where the fuck is Ogilvie!?"

A feeble, "I don't know, Buck," was the best Antonio could muster. He was telling the truth.

"Was he with you guys last night?" Buck said, toning it down a notch or two.

"No, not last night."

"Have you seen him this morning?"

"No, sorry Buck."

"You're not covering for him are you?" Even the mammoth manager thought this was a stupid question, only he couldn't stop himself in time from asking it. Buck Nimble knew Antonio Alvarez well enough to know he didn't lie—not even for Don Ogilvie.

"No, Skip, you know I don't do that."

"Yeah, Kid. Sorry I asked. I'm really fucking pissed off here, and you just happen to be Ogilvie's best friend." After a short pause, he added, "Except for Roberto, of course." Such was the well-known status of little Roberto's friendship with the unpredictable hitting coach.

Before Antonio could say anything more, Buck sidetracked himself by asking, "Say, where are the wife and kid this morning?"

Everyone had gotten so used to Maria and Roberto coming to practices and games that it was noticeable when they weren't there. Sometimes Maria had to work. When she did, Antonio would bring Roberto. Buck saw little Roberto as much a part of the team as Antonio, Don Ogilvie, or even himself. Aside from his duties as batboy for home games, the unofficial mascot had established himself as the team's bona-fide good-luck charm. The Stampede were on their way to winning their second straight Pacific Coast League championship since the arrival of the Alvarez family; and it wasn't Antonio's hitting that was making the difference. Buck and the players liked having the guileless, disarming, big-hearted little Roberto around. They practiced better and played better. He was the catalyst in their chemistry. Like adding soda to water, he made the team pop.

So when Buck asked Antonio where the wife and kid were, it was more than idle conversation. He cared.

42

Antonio's reply wasn't idle chit-chat either. "Maria had to take Roberto to the doctor again. His appetite hasn't been that good for the last month; his energy level is down too. He has a cough he can't seem to get rid of. They gave him some tests and prescribed some medicine, but that didn't seem to do the trick. They're running some more tests and stuff. I'm sure it's nothing serious."

Buck's reply was sincere, for Buck, "Yeah, he does seem to have a cold or somethin'. Well, we need that little fucker around here—just to keep Ogilvie in line, if nothin' else."

As if on cue, Buck and Antonio could see Ogilvie's heap pull into the parking lot. Buck's response was scarcely contained. "Well fuck, here he comes. Alvarez you go out there and tell Mister 'I'm late again' that the boss wants to see him."

Antonio left the clubhouse to intercept him. Ogilvie was already halfway to the field, hoping that Buck hadn't seen him, so he could pretend he'd been there all along.

Watching the pathetic Ogilvie shuffle into the clubhouse inspired Buck to ratchet up his spleen for a good chewing-out. He greeted Don as he came through the door. "Ogilvie, get your fucking, worthless ass into my office."

Squeaker, who had just come back into the clubhouse, hurriedly left again upon hearing Buck's "invitation" to Ogilvie. The Ripper sat at his desk outside Buck's office trying to read a magazine. As Ogilvie entered the office and Buck slammed the door, the Ripper could still hear just about every word of the ticked-off manager's tirade. He put his fingers in his ears. It was like trying to block out a heavy metal band by tearing a piece of the Ripper's paper. Then, taking an "If you can't beat 'em, join 'em" approach, the Ripper tried counting the number of times Buck used the F-word. After less than a minute, he wasn't able to count fast enough. It became so unpleasant that he finally went into the equipment room, where the tirade was more muted.

With Buck's harangue over, Don left the clubhouse to help with batting practice. He too noticed the absence of little Roberto and Maria. He asked Antonio about it and got the same story Buck did. He knew that Roberto had been suffering from a lingering cold.

Don Ogilvie was not the type of person who had premonitions, so he didn't know how to decipher the strange knot that swelled up in his gut when Antonio said that Roberto was at the doctor's again. It felt like an overdose of Vic's Vapor-Rub on his inflated belly. He was afraid something was wrong. He didn't share this feeling with Antonio, and chalked it up to the stifling heat, his hangover, and his continued nipping. With that thought in mind, he furtively looked around to make sure no one was watching, then took a hefty swig from his flask. The cheap Scotch burned as it went down. It took the mysterious feeling with it. He searched for a fresh piece of gum.

In less than thirty minutes, Squeaker came out of the clubhouse, again to summon Antonio to see Buck. Don and Antonio faced each other wondering. If Buck was going to release Antonio, he would've done it on the earlier visit. Now that Don was at practice, Buck didn't need Antonio to find him. Something else was going on. The peculiar sensation sprang up in Don Ogilvie's gut once again. This time he nearly said to Antonio, "It's Roberto." But he didn't. After Antonio left for the clubhouse, Don took another good-sized nip. This time the uneasy feeling didn't go away.

Antonio was not in the clubhouse very long. When he left, he headed straight for the parking lot. Don saw him and chased him down. Antonio was nervous as he spoke. "Buck says the doctor's office called and I have to meet Maria and Roberto there now."

Don was both upset and demanding. "What's this really about, Antonio?"

"I don't know, Don. I guess I'm going to find out."

"Look, if you don't make it back today, call me later to let me know what's happening. Okay?"

"Okay."

After Antonio got into his car and drove away, Ogilvie secreted another fortifying choke from his flask and returned to practice. The weird feeling remained in his stomach the rest of the day.

Over three hours later, Antonio, Maria, and Roberto pulled into the parking lot between the clubhouse and the field. Little Roberto bounced out of the car with cap on, ball and glove in hand. He looked healthy enough. He raced toward the field to greet Don, who scooped him up and held him in his arms. Antonio and Maria followed, their gait slowed by the burden of bad news. Don did his best not to seem worried, even though the odd turmoil in his belly tried to give him away. He simply asked Roberto, "Hey partner, what'd the doctor say?"

He hesitated. "I guess I got a disease. Leukemia. I've heard of it. It's a kind of cancer. I could even die from it."

Don felt like he'd taken a hard sucker punch to the mid-section, as if the air had been knocked out of him by a mad Mike Tyson. His knees buckled and he struggled to hold his best friend.

While he was trying to recover from the jolt, Roberto continued: "The doctor says I have to take some medicine that's going to make me feel sick. You know, it's funny, I don't feel sick now, but to make me well, they're gonna give me medicine that makes me feel sick. I don't think I understand that part too well."

By this time Antonio and Maria were only a few feet away. Maria's eyes were teary, Antonio's face like chalk.

Maria took Roberto from a stunned Don Ogilvie's arms and said, "Come on honey, Daddy needs to talk to Don for a minute."

Roberto protested. "How come I can't stay with Dad and Don?"

"Come on, Roberto," said Maria trying not to cry, "it'll only be for a minute . . . and I'll play catch with you."

Roberto offered a reluctant "Okay."

Don and Antonio began to walk toward the clubhouse. Antonio didn't look at Don. Still in shock, he just stared straight ahead. "He's got leukemia. Kind of a rare form. There's no cure."

The gnawing sensation that had been confined to Ogilvie's abdomen suddenly spread everywhere. He was numbed, dumbfounded, destroyed. "There's gotta be some kind of mistake," pleaded the desperate coach.

"No. They've tested him a bunch of times and the results have been confirmed by three separate doctors."

Ogilvie grabbed Antonio's arm and stopped walking. The two men faced each other. The devastated hitting instructor was going to pieces like a shattered plate-glass window. His eyes flooded and his vocal chords tightened. He couldn't get out the unspoken question.

45

Antonio sensed what he was trying to ask, so he answered. "Maybe six months. Probably less."

Don hopelessly tried to gather himself. He asked Antonio, "How much does Roberto know?"

Antonio fought to keep his feelings under control. He paused, took a deep breath, then spoke in staccato bursts. "He knows he's very sick. He knows he could die. The doctors don't want him to know much more than that. They don't want to discourage him too much. They think he'll have a better attitude about treatment if he doesn't know everything."

"Well maybe they're right," said a dazed Don Ogilvie.

"Maybe so," answered Antonio, "but at some point we're going to have to tell him there's no chance. He's a very bright kid, and I think he already suspects the worst." Antonio continued: "It would be a good idea if you came over for dinner tonight. Help us feel more . . . normal. Help take Roberto's mind off of today."

Don knew he was not ready for this. He needed to sort things out in his own screwed-up mind before he could put up any kind of front for the Alvarez family, and especially Roberto. And, of course, dealing with disaster was never Don Ogilvie's strong suit. He knew he was going to have to get stinking drunk first. Maybe then he'd be ready to cope with this calamity.

Antonio could tell from the look in his batting coach's eyes that he wouldn't be coming to dinner that night. He knew what Don Ogilvie would be doing. He was hurt and disappointed, but at the same time he wanted to join him in drowning their sorrows. Antonio, the father of a terminally ill child, was not afforded this luxury.

Ogilvie's excuse was lame but honest. "Not tonight. I don't think I can handle it tonight. Tomorrow night for sure."

Antonio decided not to press him, saying only, "Okay, but tomorrow for sure."

Antonio then left to talk to Buck. He was going to need some days off to be with Roberto and Maria and a lot of doctors. Buck was more than accommodating.

Chapter 4

Don Ogilvie couldn't tell how long he'd been asleep when he awoke to the sound of Antonio Alvarez's voice. He wasn't sure where the voice was coming from. It echoed from down a long passage or hallway.

"Don. Don Ogilvie. Where are you Don?" Antonio called out.

It was a good question. Don Ogilvie had already opened his eyes. He had no idea where he was. He was suffering a painful hangover from the previous night's binge. His head throbbed like a giant toothache. His throat was as dry and barren as an old woman's womb. Taking a hurried look around, he rubbed some sleep from his eyes. He was still sitting in his old easy chair. Problem was, he and the easy chair were no longer in his apartment in San Bernardino. They all appeared to be sitting in a manager's office in a clubhouse. It was not the manager's office for the Single-A Stampede. It was way too nice.

He cleared his throat and responded, "I'm over here, Antonio." The bewildered coach still hadn't the foggiest idea where "here" was. Then it all came rushing back to him like a shot of cheap tequila. The bad news about Roberto. The big bender. The stocky umpire who claimed he was Death Personified and called himself Doctor Drummond. And, oh yes—the little arrangement he made with the good Doctor. *It can't be real*, he thought. *Or can it?*

Don sat in his easy chair, trying to sort out all that had happened in the last twenty-four hours. His hung over head was not immediately up to the task. It didn't matter. Antonio, Maria, and Roberto wandered into the office, sparing him from further taxing his alcohol-soaked brain.

As he came in, Antonio exclaimed, "We found you!"

Right behind were Maria and little Roberto. Before he could get up, Maria hugged him and Roberto leapt into his lap. Don grunted when Roberto plopped down on him. They hugged and kissed.

Next came the inevitable and anxious questions from Antonio: "Where are we, Don, and how did we get here?"

Ogilvie wished his head would stop pounding as he replied, "I think I know where we are—I just have no idea how we got here."

"Well there's a sign out there that says 'Drummond Field, Limbotown.' Isn't there a Limbotown in southern Ohio somewhere with a Double-A team?"

"Maybe," said Don, "but I guarantee you this is not Ohio. How did you guys get here?"

Antonio deferred to Maria. She didn't have much of a clue either. "It was the strangest thing," she began. "We cried ourselves to sleep last night in our apartment. When we woke up this morning, we were all in a hotel room. We dressed in our own clothes that were in the closet and went downstairs. The place looked deserted. We found a woman named Maggie at the registration desk that told us we could find you here. We tried asking her some questions but she wouldn't answer any of them. She said you could explain everything."

The thought of "explaining everything" nearly caused Don's head to explode like an overripe carbuncle. How could he explain the deal he made with Drummond? He wasn't sure he understood it himself. He couldn't tell the Alvarezes that it included trading his life for Roberto's. They would never stand for it, benevolent and generous as the gesture might be. He'd also made it a point with Drummond not to disclose that part of the agreement. Drummond's warning that Ogilvie had best come up with a good story for the Alvarezes was now making itself all too clear. While Don groped for some words, he was given a temporary reprieve by no less than Death Personified himself, Doctor ("That *is* my first name") Drummond.

Death strolled through the front door of what was now Don Ogilvie's

48

office—that is, "Manager" Don Ogilvie's office. He was again wearing his all-black umpire outfit. He looked like a medicine ball with legs.

"Hi, Don," Drummond said to Ogilvie, as if they were long-time buddies—an apparent reversal of his admonition from the night before.

"Jeez, I'm glad you showed up," said Don. "I was just going to tell everybody why we're here, but I'm not sure I know where 'here' is. Why don't you introduce yourself to the Alvarezes? That should get things going."

Drummond peered at Ogilvie, realizing he would never be able to explain anything to anyone without being taken as daft or looped. The stubby umpire took over by saying, "Don't worry. I'll fill everybody in."

The Alvarezes witnessed this brief exchange between Ogilvie and Drummond with a bit of misgiving but mainly curiosity. Much like Don the night before, they weren't prepared for what Drummond was about to tell them. He addressed the Alvarez family informally, even nonchalantly. "You might've guessed who I am by now," Drummond began. The vacant stares returned by the Alvarezes prompted him to add, ". . . or not."

He continued: "This will be hard to believe when I first say it, but I assure you I am who I say I am, and you will know it before you leave Limbotown in about eight or nine weeks. I am Death—at least in human form. I like to think of myself as Death Personified. Death Incarnate. Death in the Flesh. I call myself 'Doctor Drummond.' You can just call me 'Doc' if you like, although I've noticed a lot of people don't like being on a first-name basis with Death. Your friend Ogilvie might be the exception. He asked me my first name last night."

Antonio and little Roberto were looking agape at Don. Maria focused her attention on Drummond, trying to size him up. Drummond could sense the inevitable disbelief as he started to speak again, "No, I'm not insane, a kook, or even an eccentric billionaire. This isn't a dream or a hallucination either. And no, Mrs. Alvarez, this is not some cruel joke."

Antonio and Maria considered Drummond in silent amazement. As he had with Ogilvie the night before, he was answering their questions before they spoke. Mind-reading helped Drummond convince people that if he was not Death, he was definitely something other than human.

Death Personified went on: "I know this is a tough break for Roberto. That's why I brought all of you here. You're going to get the chance to save little Roberto's life. No guarantees, mind you—just a chance."

Even though this was the first time Roberto had heard that his death was a certainty and not just a possibility, he consoled his parents. "Don't worry, Mom and Dad. I'm not going to die. Don's going to save me!"

Antonio and Maria remained speechless. Drummond and Ogilvie were both momentarily taken aback by little Roberto's uncanny intuition.

The Alvarezes were too startled to ask any questions, so Drummond played both parts. "How can we save this child's life, you ask? That's easy." Death in the Flesh turned squarely to Antonio and kept talking. "You and John Barleycorn over there," he said while vaguely pointing to Ogilvie, "are going to manage a baseball team. You're going to play a best-of-seven series against my team. If your team wins, Roberto is cured and lives. If you lose, Roberto will stay the same and die."

Don sat in his easy chair, slowly nodding his head up and down. This was the second time he had heard this. He was almost beginning to believe it. He could tell Drummond was being careful not to reveal that Ogilvie's life would be traded for young Roberto's if they won. He swapped a confirming eye with Death Incarnate.

Ogilvie looked at a confused and astonished Antonio, Maria, and Roberto and said, "Yeah, we get to pick any players we want as long as they're dead"—Ogilvie and Drummond again chorused in unison—"except for Ty Cobb."

Ogilvie asked Drummond, "What's the name of your pitcher?" Don turned to Antonio and said, "We don't get him either."

"Don't worry about my pitcher," Death Incarnate advised. "You already have too many choices."

Finally, Maria recovered enough to ask, "How can this all be possible?"

"Well, Mrs. Alvarez," said a polite Drummond, "you and your family have been given an opportunity that's one in a million. I already told Ogilvie I won't or can't do this very often. My system is always on what I like to call "automatic pilot." You know, when your number's up, it's up. No outside interference. But occasionally I can make an exception. It's my choice. If I feel the situation is right, I can create a chance—or 'Challenge,' as I like to call it. And, of course, I can't do anything to change history or the future."

"This must be an answer to our prayers," concluded Maria.

"Sorry to disappoint you, Maria; if I can use your first name. I'm not God. I'm not an angel or a messiah. I'm not Satan either. I know you have strong religious beliefs, but this is not an answer to a prayer. On the other hand, you might call it a response to an inquiry made by our friend, Mr. Ogilvie. He brought this matter to my attention. And remember— you have to win a seven-game series against my team. Trust me, it won't be easy."

"Is that why Don is here?" asked Antonio.

"Yes," said Drummond, thus assuring Ogilvie that his secret was safe. "Your friend Don pleaded your case for you, you might say. That's one reason he's here. I just had to come up with a fitting challenge to save Roberto's life. The 'World Series' thing was the logical choice. Ogilvie's here to manage, because he's already a coach. That's another reason he's here. No offense, Antonio," he said to little Roberto's young father, "but your players might not respect a twenty-five-year-old manager." Drummond wigwagged at Ogilvie, saying, "Of course, they might have a problem with Johnnie Walker here too."

As if on cue, Ogilvie let out a sort of burping sound, lifted Roberto off his lap, waved his arm at Drummond and mumbled, "I'm going to be sick. Where's the bathroom?"

Drummond rolled his eyes at the Alvarezes while replying, "Out the door to your right."

Ogilvie hurriedly left the room. There was an awkward silence. Maria spoke at last, asking the black-clad umpire, "Is that the only reason Don is here, to manage? Is there anything else you haven't told us?"

Death Personified quickly saw that at least Mrs. Alvarez questioned whether Don Ogilvie's involvement was deeper than advertised. He discreetly glanced at Roberto to see if his child's insight had alerted him to anything more. Evidently, it hadn't.

Drummond still responded frugally, "You already have more

information than you need. Yes, he's here to manage, and you're all here to help. You know you wouldn't want it any other way." That much was true. The Alvarez family could only agree.

Death's explanation of Ogilvie's role seemed to satisfy their questions for now. By this time, Ogilvie was timidly making his way back to his office.

Death in the Flesh spoke to him. "I was just telling Antonio and Maria that the reason you're here is to manage—and the reason they're here is to help you. And, of course, your players are going to want to know who and what they're playing for. And that's pretty much it. Right, Ogilvie?"

The pale-faced coach looked meekly at Drummond. He knew that while he was puking his guts out in the bathroom, the good "Doctor" had bailed him out by creating a semi-plausible reason for his being there. That was supposed to be his job. But at least the secret of his chance to trade his life for Roberto's was safe—for now, anyway. Death Personified, for whatever reason, had helped Ogilvie. And, for whatever reason, it wouldn't be the last time.

Worry filled Maria's face as she asked Drummond, "But what about my son? He'll need medicine and doctors, and . . ."

The Ultimate Umpire held up his hand to stop her. "No need to worry about any of that. Nothing will happen to Roberto while he's in Limbotown. You have my word on it. He'll feel just fine the whole time he's here. Everything in Limbotown is at your disposal. Take a look around. I think you'll see I've thought of everything. If I haven't, just let me know, and I'll take care of it. And, oh yeah—everything is on the house. Free. Food, accommodations, entertainment, everything. You're my guests while you're here."

Ogilvie tried again to probe Drummond about his team. "The real mystery is how your team of two players is going to beat our team of Hall of Famers. I don't care if it's Ty Cobb and Jesus out there—they're not going to beat a whole team full of Hall of Famers! Anyhow, I'm sure Jesus wouldn't have anything to do with old Ty." Don looked at Antonio, and both chuckled. Like most ballplayers, they were very familiar with Cobb's reputation. Pretty much anyone who'd come in contact with or knew Ty Cobb was sure that if there were a Hell, Cobb would be there. He would probably be mayor.

"Well, let me give you something to think about," Doctor Drummond said to everyone. "My team only has two players, but we're gonna cover every position."

"How can that be?" asked a skeptical Ogilvie.

"You'll find out soon enough. I told you it was going to be hard. You don't even have half an idea yet. You've got until midnight, Limbotown Standard Time, to pick a team. On that shelf behind your desk are some reference books that'll tell you about all the dead Hall of Fame players. Choose twenty-four. I'll be back at midnight to pick up the list. Tomorrow morning your team will arrive. I'll be there to tell them why they're here. From then on it's your show. I've got some things to do now. Feel free to take a look around."

Death Personified waltzed out, leaving the small, dazed group in Ogilvie's office.

Roberto, who had barely said a word while Drummond was in the room, tugged at his mother's dress and whispered, "Hey Mom—I know that guy Drummond."

Maria gently told her son, "Honey, that can't be. We just met him this second, except for Don."

Roberto insisted. "I *know* him. I just didn't recognize him at first. I saw him in a dream I had the other night before we went to the hospital and found out I was sick. He didn't look the same, but it was him."

Don, Antonio, and Maria stared quietly at one another. If anyone needed anymore proof of Drummond's identity, this was more than enough.

Don broke the short silence by asking, "Hey, what's outside?"

"Mostly a baseball stadium," said little Roberto. He was remarkably unaffected by Drummond's presence, even though he understood who he was. He was still just a kid—and this was, so far, a great adventure for him.

Antonio added, "There's also the hotel we were in last night, and what looks to be a movie theater across the street. That's about it. After that, the whole place seems to be surrounded by a big fogbank."

Ogilvie read the clock in his office. It was nine o'clock. He asked Antonio, "Was it daytime out there?" Antonio nodded. "Good," said Don. "Then we've got all day and until midnight to pick a team. I think Drummond is right. Let's take a look around first."

The Alvarezes hadn't yet viewed the inside of Drummond Field. They'd found Don by entering the visitor's clubhouse through a door on the outside of the stadium. And Don Ogilvie, of course, had been "deposited" in his office without seeing anything.

Don, Antonio, Maria, and Roberto left the clubhouse through the door marked "To Visitor's Bench." At the end of a short tunnel they arrived at the dugout. It opened up onto the most magnificent outdoor baseball stadium any of them had ever seen. It was a glorious day, with blue skies stretching to the foggy horizon that surrounded all of Limbotown. There wasn't a cloud to be seen. None of them noticed that there was no sun.

Admittedly, the Alvarezes hadn't seen a lot of Major League ballparks. Don had seen many more. They all had experienced Dodger Stadium, which is still one of the most beautiful ballparks around. Drummond Field was not only pastoral, it had a very special feel—the kind of sensation ballplayers would get standing in the outfield in Yankee Stadium, knowing they were playing on the same hallowed ground as Ruth and Gehrig and DiMaggio.

Despite this air of tradition and history, Drummond Field appeared to be newly built. At the same time, it felt like an old ballpark. Some stadiums, like Camden Yard in Baltimore, tried to capture this mix of old and new. Drummond Field managed to bring together the best of the combination—an artful collage of the old ball parks with modern conveniences, including an electronic scoreboard and a colossal video-screen. Happily there were no swimming pools, waterfalls, giant Coke bottles, or sushi bars in sight.

The playing field was real grass, expertly manicured like the greens at a country club golf course. Its color—brilliant emerald. In the sunlight (or whatever accounted for the daylight in Limbotown), it shone like a jewel. The dirt infield and encircling warning track was mixed with crushed brick. Its blood red hue and the lush green grass complemented each other perfectly.

The spectator stands formed a semi-circle around home plate, extending to the outfields on either side. There were no bleachers. Not a bad chair in the house. The seats themselves were color-coded by section, blue, gold, and light green. The outfield walls and other façades were trimmed with smart-looking brickwork.

The stadium and playing field were symmetrical. The distance from home plate to the foul poles (according to the numbers on the wall) was 350 feet; the power alleys in left-center and right-center, 390 feet, and to straightaway center field 415 feet: A little sign on the backstop behind home plate stated that Drummond Field played at sea-level conditions: No cheap home runs here. Still, a ball hit inside the park had a lot of room to roam. The outfield was an open range.

Don estimated the stands could hold no more than thirty-five, maybe forty thousand people. He wondered if there would be fans. If so, where would they come from? Maybe their World Series would be played with only the players watching. Don Ogilvie suspected that Drummond would provide an audience. The Ultimate Umpire would've picked a different park, without stands, if he intended to play without onlookers. Ogilvie had not figured out Drummond, but knew he did everything for a reason.

The Alvarezes and Don Ogilvie walked quietly from the dugout toward home plate. They were in awe of grand Drummond Field and its enchanted surroundings. Little Roberto was scarcely able to utter a muffled "Wow".

Don felt a twinge in his stomach. It hit him. He would be managing the best ballplayers who ever lived (and died) in perhaps the best ballpark ever built. For the moment, he brushed aside his uneasiness and remarked, "Whatever they have outside this park can't possibly be better than this." He was right. The rest of Limbotown, which wasn't sizeable, was very stylish, although less inspiring by comparison.

They agreed to split up, explore what there was of Limbotown, and meet back at the stadium in two hours. Don and Antonio would then pick their team and have their list ready for Drummond's return at midnight.

They all exited the field through a tunnel in the stands between home plate and first base. A small, paved two-lane street with sidewalks on either side appeared in front of them. The Alvarezes went left and Ogilvie went right.

Chapter 5

Don trod toward the hotel where the Alvarez family had found themselves when they awoke. He went past it to find the "end" of Limbotown, if there was one. Across the street from the hotel was another building with a marquee and sign that said "Limbotown Theater." About fifty yards farther down the road was the all-encircling fogbank Antonio had told him about. Don marched down the avenue until it disappeared into the haze. A few feet before the imposing fogbank stood a small signpost facing away from him. He stepped to the other side and read the words: "Now entering Limbotown. Population: It depends." Ogilvie smirked, recognizing Drummond's peculiar sense of humor.

He wanted to see if there was anything on the other side of the misty barrier. He was afraid at first, not knowing if he would fall off a cliff or something. He took a deep breath and stepped inside. Engulfed by cloud, he took two more steps forward and found himself in the exact same spot he'd been just before entering, except now he was facing the opposite direction. Seeing the sign "Now Entering Limbotown" directly in front of him, he thought he must have somehow gotten turned around, so he tried it again. The same thing happened. The novelty of this phenomenon had him trying it several more times. It didn't matter where he entered the foggy wall that bordered all of Limbotown—he was placed right back at the point of entry, only facing exactly 180 degrees in the other direction. Whatever and wherever Limbotown was, it was not located in the middle of a cornfield in Iowa. A normal person could not get beyond its vapor-fence border. The fogbank must've been a good fifty feet high. After pacing about half of it, Don estimated the size of Limbotown at about two miles square.

He decided to check out the hotel. Striding back on the town's only street, he passed the movie theater. The marquee was empty, as was the ticket booth. The exterior was embellished with an elaborate art deco façade and other minutiae. It was a swank building but it did not summon the magic of Drummond Field. Ogilvie wondered what entertainment Drummond would provide there. He didn't try to get in.

The hotel was directly across the boulevard from the theater. It was several stories high, also finished in art deco style. The main entrance was ornately festooned. The massive front doors were open. Over the huge portal was a large brass plaque that proclaimed "Hotel Limbotown."

Ogilvie walked into a well-appointed, high-ceilinged lobby with white marble floors and a large circular fountain in the middle. Light poured into the great room from a huge domed skylight above. To the left was a substantial, maroon-colored mahogany registration desk. There were large potted plants all around. The walls had fancy wallpaper and were decked out with paintings, photos, and other collectibles depicting old ballparks, players, and anything else to do with baseball. Not a soul was to be found.

Ogilvie called out, "Anyone home?"

He was startled by a female voice saying, "I'm in the dining room." He thought that this must be the woman, Maggie, who told the Alvarezes they could find him at Drummond Field.

The dining room was to the right of the lobby. Its open entrance was marked with a dignified sign. Don viewed the spacious room and walked in. Along the far wall stretched a stately mahogany bar coupled with tall leather-backed chairs. Dark wood booths and paneling outlined the other walls. Dining tables were neatly arranged everywhere else. Baseball memorabilia was plentiful here as well.

Don couldn't see anyone. Then, like a jack in the box, a woman popped up from behind the bar. She stood across from Don and said, "Hi, I'm Maggie Briggs. I was just putting a few things away. You must be Don Ogilvie." She extended her hand to shake his. He moved closer and clumsily put his hand out to meet hers. Don Ogilvie was never the same after that moment.

Before him stood the most extraordinary woman he'd ever seen. Her wavy hair was the same color as the deep red mahogany bar. It fell past her shoulders. Her eyes reflected the striking emerald green of Drummond Field's well-manicured grass. Her lips were full and naturally red. When she engaged Don's eyes, his knees almost gave way. Her dark eyebrows arched, dimples formed at the corners of her mouth, and her verdant eyes sparkled as she smiled at him. Her skin was not as fair as a true redhead's, but then neither was her hair the same red. Still, her olive complexion complemented her angelic face. Ogilvie thought she was perfection. To him, she was an ageless beauty, although she must have been over forty.

Like that, he fell in love. The "Thunderbolt." Love at first sight. He tripped hard and fast. Nevertheless, he was confused. This had never happened to him before. He didn't think love at first sight was possible. Then again, he didn't think that Drummond or Limbotown was possible either. The balky coach hadn't had a true romance since his divorce, and nothing close to approaching love. His occasional encounters were more like bodily necessities. They never went anywhere. He wasn't relationship material.

He questioned his new emotions. He didn't even know this woman. Yet the fire was there: clear, strong, and undeniable. Feeling light-headed, butterflies danced in his beer belly. Luckily, his habit of shedding water like Hoover Dam had not been triggered. "Love" had thankfully managed to clog his pores, for now.

As Don continued to grip Maggie's hand, he tested his ability to speak. "Hi, I'm Don Ogilvie." He knew he was holding on too long for a handshake, but there was something wondrous in her touch, and he couldn't bring himself to let go.

Maggie cheerfully replied, "Yes, I know." She tried to make him relax by adding, "Please call me Maggie. I guess I'm what you'd call the manager of the Hotel Limbotown." She was able to escape the embrace of Don's hand, which he then brought to his forehead in a sign of embarrassment. Fortunately, it wasn't wringing wet. *Better to be a dry moron than a wet one*, he rationalized.

Don Ogilvie partially regained his composure. He tried to ask a fitting question: "Is this where my players are going to be staying?"

"Yes," Maggie said, "and they'll be eating here in the dining room. Would you like something to eat? Everything's on the house, compliments of your host, Doctor Drummond."

Don hadn't thought about food until just then. He was hungry. "Sure, how about some bacon and eggs?"

"We've got a great chef here. You could have eggs benedict, or anything else you like."

"Bacon and eggs will be just fine. Thank you, Maggie," he said, trying to come out of his love trance.

She eased toward a double door at the end of the dining room that Don correctly guessed led to the kitchen. She was wearing a black, mid-calf skirt and a plain white blouse. She had an athletic figure that her outfit did not disguise. As she went she said, "I'll be back in a minute, Don."

Hearing Maggie say his name made him feel woozy. He had it bad. He was so wrapped up in his own euphoria it didn't even matter what Maggie might think of him. He took a seat at the bar.

In what seemed like only a minute to Don—but must have been five—she came through the double doors carrying his bacon and eggs, as well as toast and orange juice. She placed the well-prepared breakfast in front of him with a simple, "Here you go. Would you like some coffee with that?" That's when he made his first mistake. It didn't take long.

Without thinking Ogilvie said, "What I'd really like is a cup of coffee with about two shots of Scotch in it."

The light instantly disappeared from Maggie's eyes. The radiant smile vanished. Don Ogilvie felt like a man overboard. She turned around to pour a cup of coffee from behind the bar, and without looking at him asked flatly, "Is Dewar's okay?"

Again, without thinking, he said, "Yes, it's better than I'm used to." He tried to bite his lip. It was too late. Maggie served the spiked coffee with a clang. His reaction was swift and automatic. He took a first sip to make sure it wasn't too hot. Then he downed the rest in two gulps and followed that with a noisy exhale that sounded like a horny sea lion in search of a one-night stand. He knew having his morning drink was doing nothing to ingratiate him to the splendid manager of the Hotel Limbotown. That his alcoholism was stronger than his newly aroused passion was a disturbing revelation to Don Ogilvie that love alone did not conquer addiction. Considering his horrendous hangover and recent purge, he knew he would only feel better if he drank something first. Such were his alcoholic ways. He finally started to eat.

Foolishly presuming he could damage himself no further, he asked Maggie a stupid question outright. "Why does my drinking bother you?"

Maggie glowered at him flabbergasted. "You've been given a one-in-a-million chance. Don't you think you should try to make the most of it?"

"So you know why I'm here," he said, viewing Maggie a little differently now.

"Of course I do." She took a deep breath and continued. "Look, I 'work' for Drummond, so to speak. Everyone here does, in one way or another. Other than you and the Alvarez family, everyone else you'll meet here—including me—is dead."

Ogilvie's head was spinning again, and this time it wasn't the Scotch. "What do you mean, 'dead'?" he asked.

"At one time, some of us here were like you," the beautiful woman explained. "Some of us had the same chance you're getting now. We had to face a challenge, and then try to overcome it. The man you know as Doctor Drummond appeared as someone else for each of us, but it was him every time."

Ogilvie, struggling to comprehend some of what Maggie said, asked, "So Drummond is who he says he is; and you're dead?"

"Oh yes, I'm dead," Maggie solemnly submitted, "and Drummond is who he says he is. He'll keep his promises too. The very few of us who were lucky enough to win our challenge were allowed to exchange our lives for someone we had chosen. Like you and Roberto."

She noticed the concern on his face. "Don't worry, no one will tell the Alvarezes. None of us wanted anyone to know either—least of all the person we were trading lives with, or their families or friends. Anyway, it's a requirement Drummond has. You have to want to keep that part secret to be considered in the first place." Ogilvie was not thinking about his secret for the moment. He just wasn't exactly comforted by the fact that his new-found love was, well, dead.

Maggie continued: "And if you succeed, you not only get to save a life, you'll get to see other challenges, like I'm doing with you."

He was buoyed by the news that he might be able to join Maggie if he won his Series. This seemed to be a wonderful bonus on top of saving Roberto's life—which, of course, would mean Ogilvie would then be dead.

He asked, "If I win my Series, then not only does Roberto get to live, but I get to see the next man or woman like me? And, you'll be there too?"

Maggie responded, "That's right. But first you have to win, and that's going to be very difficult."

Ogilvie appeared nonplused at this opinion. "Not with the team I'm going to have," he answered confidently.

Maggie, frustrated, said, "You've got a great opportunity here, but you don't know how hard it's going to be. These things are never easy. Hardly anyone is able to do it. It takes someone in a lot better shape than you. Drummond doesn't usually even give someone like you this kind of chance."

Ogilvie wasn't sure if he should be offended. "What do you mean 'someone like me'?"

Maggie sighed. "How can I put this delicately? Your life is a mess!" Ogilvie was distraught that Maggie Briggs was evidently privy to all of his troubles.

She continued. "I know all about you. I guess it's one of the perks we get for winning Drummond's challenge. Your life has not been a model of achievement, now has it? You gave up on yourself after you got injured. You sure didn't meet *that* challenge very well. Your solution was to try to drink yourself to death. That won't cut it here."

Maggie was raising her voice. She threw her words at Ogilvie like tiny, sharp darts, deflating his ego faster than a blown tire. "The best thing you've done in the last twenty-five years is offer your life for Roberto's. And you didn't even know that it was possible when you did. Drummond doesn't usually give this chance to people who have so little to lose, like you." For good measure she needled him further. "And, you're old! You've already lived a good part of your life. You're lucky Drummond happens to be a big baseball fan, or you wouldn't even be here."

Ogilvie winced. He'd eaten about half of his breakfast, but Maggie's words made him lose his appetite. He put his fork down, beheld the woman he'd just fallen in love with, and said sadly, "I guess you don't think much of me."

"Well, I don't right now," was the predictable reply. "Don't get me wrong," Maggie clarified, "I'm always pulling for the challengers like you. I used to be one too. I just hate to see you throw this away, like you've done with most of your life. Like I said, this won't be easy. Drummond will see to that. For one thing, no one here can refuse you a drink if you want it. On average, maybe one out of ten thousand challengers make it. Your odds are probably more like one in a million— at least for the time being. You're going to need to have your head on straight, especially when your players get here."

Ogilvie tried to put up a good front by saying, "Well, the players don't get here until tomorrow, and tomorrow's a new day."

"You still have to pick your team before midnight," Maggie reminded him.

"Yeah, well I've pretty much done that already."

Maggie started in again. "How much do you really know about these guys? Have you ever met any of them, let alone know them?"

It annoyed Ogilvie, being interrogated about the one thing he understood best—baseball. It didn't matter that it came from Maggie. He defended himself saying, "Look, they're here to play baseball. I know all the guys I'm picking can do that better than anybody."

Maggie was shaking her head from side to side. "You're oversimplifying things. These are human beings you're dealing with, not robots. They've got personalities and problems all their own. You'll see what I mean in a few days, especially if you don't stop drinking. Plus, you owe it to Roberto and his parents to give it your best effort."

Don knew Maggie's intentions were sincere. Still, he was weary of being picked apart. He tried to change the subject by asking, "Where's everyone else? I mean the other people like you?"

Maggie knew what he was doing. She felt she'd let him have enough for one day, so she answered his question. "They'll all be here tomorrow. A few are like me—successful challengers. Drummond likes to call us 'The Chosen Ones' because he chose us, like he chose you and we chose who we wanted to trade our lives with, and did—but not until after we passed our test. There aren't many of us. The rest of the help here and the fans for the games are going to be regular dead people. Except they don't think they're dead. They'll be like your players: plucked by Drummond from a moment in time when they were still alive. Drummond likes to call them 'The Lucky Stiffs.' They get to have a little adventure and excitement, like watching or playing some great baseball games. I guess that qualifies them as lucky."

Ogilvie asked, "At the end of my time here in Limbotown, I'll either be a Chosen One or a Lucky Stiff. Right?"

Maggie corrected him. "Not quite. You'll either be a Chosen One or just dead." She added, "Well, Drummond does pick a lot of failed Chosen Ones to be his Lucky Stiffs when the occasion arises, like now. He's sentimental that way. But no matter how you become a Lucky Stiff, you're still dead and don't know it. The Chosen Ones know they're dead."

Ogilvie wasn't exactly sure how this worked. "Don't the Chosen Ones tell the Lucky Stiffs?"

"They usually don't believe it, even when they're told. They know they'll be dead someday. Since they're taken from a past moment in their lives, they think they're still alive. In a way, they are—at least for a little while. They're dead again after they leave Limbotown. And they don't remember anything anyhow."

"I'm still not sure I understand," Ogilvie said.

"Take someone like Lou Gehrig," Maggie said, giving an example. "My guess is he'll be on your team." Ogilvie nodded in agreement as she continued. "He died in 1941. Drummond might take him from 1927 during his playing days. He won't know he's dead now because he's coming from 1927, when he was still alive."

"I think I get it."

Maggie finished by explaining again, "The same thing will be true for the rest of your players and the other Lucky Stiffs. They're all taken from an instant in time when they were living, even though they're dead now. In Limbotown you can do that. As you'll see, it's a very different kind of place." Don Ogilvie already knew Limbotown was a different kind of place. Where else could a live man fall in love with a dead woman and not be arrested?

Taking a gamble, Don asked Maggie a question of a very personal nature. "So what did you have to do to become a Chosen One?"

When he heard the answer, he regretted having asked it. Maggie riveted her eyes to his. "I don't think you've earned the privilege to know that yet."

There wasn't anything Don Ogilvie could say.

Once again the fuzzy-headed coach was saved by the Alvarezes. Maria, Antonio, and Roberto ambled into the Hotel Limbotown dining room and joined Don and Maggie.

Antonio remarked to Don, "Well, we're back. Strange place. Especially that fog bank. I guess no one gets out of here without a special pass or something." Antonio noticed Ogilvie's half-eaten breakfast and said, "Looks like you already met Maggie."

Maria quickly sensed Don's feelings for Maggie Briggs. The room was thick with his love. Antonio, however, was oblivious to it. Little Roberto, whose child's intuition was unfettered, recognized it too. Don knew they knew. It made him feel transparent and self-conscious. What he didn't know was that Maria and Roberto also detected some feelings from Maggie for him. He would've paid big money for information like that.

Little Roberto traded smiles with Maggie. He turned to Don and said, "She's really pretty, huh, Don?"

That was an observation no one could dispute. Ogilvie rejoined in a way he felt would not completely give himself away. "Yes, Maggie and your mom are the two prettiest women I know."

Maggie and Maria blushed. Neither of them was immune to flattery. Don was glad to learn this about Maggie. He knew it was going to take more than adulation to gain her trust and respect. Her love seemed to be out of reach for now.

Ogilvie hadn't finished his breakfast and it was already time for lunch. Antonio said, "Gee, I'm really hungry. I'm sure Maria and Roberto are too. We haven't had anything to eat yet today." He asked Maggie, "Any chance we could get some sandwiches or something?"

Maggie replied, "Of course. You can have anything you want. Everything's on the house, as I'm sure Doctor Drummond told you. He wants us to make your stay here as comfortable as possible."

Don thought this was a good time for him to leave. "I better be getting back to the clubhouse and start putting a team together."

Antonio said, "I'll be there right after I eat."

Little Roberto spoke. "I want to go too. But I'm kind of tired." Maria and Antonio wore troubled expressions, believing their son's illness was affecting him.

Maggie comforted the nervous mother and father. "Don't worry. Roberto's going to be just fine while he's in Limbotown. Nothing bad can happen to him here. He won't be sick. He won't need a doctor either. The trip here can be a little fatiguing, especially for children. He'll feel better after a nap."

"That's good news," said Maria. "That's what that Doctor Drummond said to us earlier. I'm not sure I believe him. With all that's been happening, it's hard to remember everything."

"Don't worry about Drummond," Maggie said. "He keeps his word."

Maria announced to the small gathering, "Roberto and I are going to stay here and sleep for a while. We'll see you at the clubhouse later."

"Fine," Don said. "I'm leaving now. I'll see Antonio after lunch." He focused on the attractive manager of the Hotel Limbotown. "It was very nice to meet you, Maggie." His goodbye was, thankfully, more poised than his hello.

Maggie was cordial, nothing more. "It was interesting meeting you, Don. Good luck picking your team." He left through the lobby.

Little Roberto and his mother looked at Maggie, then at each other. They formed an unspoken pact. They liked Maggie. They liked that Don liked Maggie. They both wanted Maggie to like Don. They both were going to do their best to help Maggie like Don.

Ogilvie reentered the clubhouse and made his way to his office. The shelf above his desk held the reference books Drummond had suggested he use to pick his team. He looked at but did not reach for them. He paused to contemplate his sudden infatuation for Maggie and what she'd said to him. He knew he wouldn't stand a chance with her unless he changed, and that he wasn't sure he'd be able to do to her satisfaction. Still, she was the kind of woman who made him feel alive. She ignited some primal spark in him, as if his heart was a dormant furnace roaring to life after many years of neglect.

He sat down behind his desk. He searched the drawers for some paper and a pen. The desk was well stocked—a little too well stocked, he decided when he looked in the lower right-hand drawer. There he found a fifth of Scotch. Drummond had thought of everything.

Earlier, Death had helped Ogilvie explain to the Alvarezes why he was here. Now, he was tempting him, putting an obstacle in front of him. It was the same with Maggie. Was Death Personified trying to help him, or was she an obstacle too? Maybe she was both. It would be a pattern repeated by Drummond many times during Ogilvie's stay in Limbotown.

Contemplating, he gazed at the bottle in front of him. He'd already had a drink at the hotel. He didn't think another would do any harm. Taking two good-sized swigs, he capped the bottle and put it back where he found it.

Then, without using the books, Ogilvie started jotting down some names. It was quite a mix of players from the old days, a few more recent names, and a healthy dose of some great players from the old Negro Leagues, before Jackie Robinson broke baseball's color line. An imposing list it was. Ogilvie grinned at his tentative roster. A team like this would be practically unbeatable, certainly against Death Personified's two-man squad. Or so he thought. He still didn't understand Drummond's or Maggie's earlier warning that "this isn't going to be easy."

The Alvarez family finished their lunch in the hotel dining room. Antonio helped Maria take Roberto upstairs. Their room was on the second floor, accessible by either stairs or the main elevator in the lobby. That morning they had walked down the stairs to the lobby. This time they took the elevator up. The elevator cab was distinctively decorated, like the rest of the hotel. It had one of those old-fashioned elevator devices that required someone to operate it. Neither Maria nor Antonio was old enough to remember such a contraption. Conveniently, the elevator also had a panel of buttons. They made it to the second floor without incident.

Maria and Antonio helped make little Roberto comfortable in the small room adjoining theirs. Maria told him he should try to take a nap. He was tired and didn't need much coaxing. Maria advised the youngster that when he woke up, if she wasn't in the room next door she'd be downstairs talking to Maggie. He was instructed to take the stairs, not the elevator. Maria soothed him by saying, "I'll probably be back before you wake up."

Roberto answered sleepily, "Don't worry, Mom—I'll find you."

Maria and Antonio walked back downstairs together. Antonio asked, "What do you want to talk to Maggie about?"

Maria thought out loud. "Lots of things. I think she knows what's really happening here. I have many questions for her. I'm just not sure how open she's going to be." She added, "If you didn't notice, Don really likes her. My feelings tell me she has a good heart. I think she needs to know more about Don. If she got to know him the way we do . . ."

Antonio cautioned her. "I'd be careful about playing matchmaker in this place. He may never see her again after we leave. Don's going to have enough on his mind with the players and the games, and everything else."

Maria was both disappointed and direct with her husband. "I guess men aren't very romantic. Don't you think the love of a good woman could help Don? It sure didn't hurt you."

Wisely, Antonio was not about to argue that point.

Maria told Antonio that she and Roberto would deliver dinner to the clubhouse around 7 p.m. Antonio left for the stadium, while Maria went back to the dining room to see Maggie.

She found Maggie Briggs washing glasses behind the bar. She offered to help. Maggie countered, "That's a very kind thought. Please remember you're the guest here. Anyway, you didn't come down here to help me tend bar. Why don't you pull up a seat?"

Maria sat down on one of the stools and spontaneously remarked, "What a strange place this is."

The beautiful Maggie's response was not encouraging. "Yes, it sure is. It's a weird mixture of real and unreal, live and dead, all rolled into one."

Maria wanted to hear more about Limbotown, but for the moment she wanted to learn more about Maggie. She didn't want to seem too personal. Not sure how to phrase her next question, she tested the waters by asking, "What's a nice woman like you doing in a place like this?"

Maggie laughed. She knew this was Maria's way of trying to break the ice, loosen her up so she'd be talkative, tell her what was really going on. She didn't mind. It was only natural for Maria to be nosy about her, Limbotown—and, of course, Death Personified. She tried to say as much as she could without giving away anything.

"I guess you could call me an employee. My employer, as you know, is the man you call 'Doctor Drummond.'" Maggie seized Maria's attention. She lowered her voice. "He is who he says he is. And, yes—he can spare Roberto's life."

"I think I believe you," said Maria. "Soon I hope to trust you. I guess we have Don to thank for this chance. I just hope he'll be okay."

"That's why he's here. He asked for it, so he has to help pull it off. He needs to straighten himself out first," Maggie firmly stated. She felt guilty misleading Maria about the real truth of Ogilvie's entanglement with Drummond. She couldn't tell her that Don's agreement also meant he would trade his life for Roberto's. Then there was the small matter of first winning a seven-game series.

Maria tried to help Don. "Sometimes, when he disappoints you most, he'll bounce right back and do something wonderful. He can surprise you." Even Maria was hard-pressed to think of an example, though.

She wasn't making much progress for the fuzzy-eyed hitting coach, so Maria returned to her original question. "What's with Limbotown?"

Maggie was more talkative on this subject. "It's anything Drummond wants it to be. It could be the Grand Canyon or an entire planet—or even bigger than that. And all the people you'll see here were real people. Like your players. Most of us just weren't as famous."

"How long have you been working for Drummond?" asked a curious Maria.

"Too long," was the hazy yet genial reply. "Maria, I know you have a lot of questions, so let me tell you all I can tell you. I'm a bit different than most of the others you'll meet here. I'm sort of a permanent employee of Drummond's. There are a few others. Everybody else you'll meet here is like Drummond told you—dead, although most don't believe it. And they won't remember a thing once they leave here. Drummond likes to call them 'Lucky Stiffs.' I, on the other hand . . . well, I know I'm dead and I get to remember what goes on here. I really can't tell you more than that. I've told you more than enough."

"This is all pretty incredible," Maria said, dismayed. She was confounded that Maggie, like the players, was real but also dead. Except Maggie knew she was dead. It made Maria feel odd. She didn't directly say this to Maggie. Instead she lamented, "I'm still overwhelmed. Maybe I'll get used to it in a few days."

"Don't worry," the lively redhead advised. "When the players get here tomorrow, you won't have time to think about it."

Having established a rapport of sorts with the mysterious Maggie Briggs, Maria didn't force things. Maggie had at least been candid about Drummond and Limbotown, although more evasive about herself and Don's presence. Maria thanked Maggie for talking to her, and left to check on Roberto. She learned that getting the friendly but equivocal hotel manager to open up on some subjects was going to take time. It was far from certain that she would open up at all.

Antonio found Don Ogilvie at his desk, pondering his list of players. "Hey, Skipper, how's it going?" he eagerly asked.

Don didn't react at first. It hadn't completely sunk in that he was now a manager—the manager of perhaps the strongest, most talented team of baseball players ever assembled . . . on paper anyway. Sportswriters, managers, and other baseball professionals are often called upon to offer up their own lists of all-time, all-star teams—teams that couldn't exist because everybody played at different times. Some players were dead, and most of the living ones would be too old. Therefore, an actual game could never be played. Oh sure—it was fun to talk about and speculate. To Don Ogilvie, his list was no more real than that.

He would soon be reminded there was a big difference between a piece of paper and a human being. A good baseball manager is not only a student of the game, he is also a student of human nature. Ogilvie knew this. His failure to take it into account would be a big mistake. Maggie had tried to warn him earlier.

Don finally peeked up from his list and replied easily, "We're going to have an exceptional team, Antonio. I think we should still check the reference books to make sure we didn't forget anybody. I've already got too many names as it is. The hard part's going to be getting it down to twenty-four."

This was true. There would be many great names on the final list, and many, many more that deserved to be there. Twenty-four proved a difficult number.

With that, Don and Antonio set out to revise the list, pare it, check the books, and make final selections. They picked a team of stupendously talented individuals, the best at their positions. However, baseball is a team sport. Don and Antonio discussed it in a way. They tossed about the idea of importing a whole baseball team, like the legendary 1927 Yankees. They knew that Ruth and Gehrig would make their list, why not just take the entire crew? They all knew each other and played well together. It might've made managing much easier. It was an idea they should've given more thought.

Neither Don nor Antonio could resist the temptation of putting together their own dream team. People had seen the '27 Yankees and all the other great teams of the past play. But nobody had ever seen Babe Ruth bat in the same lineup with Joe DiMaggio and Mickey Mantle; or Josh Gibson, the great Negro Leaguer catch for Christy Mathewson. The opportunity to put together a team like this was too tempting, too overpowering. They were being baseball romantics, idealists, innocents.

Don and Antonio knew a lot of the guys they'd picked had never played together. They believed the eight weeks they had to get ready was more than enough time for a group of professionals of this caliber. In nearly every way, they would be proven wrong.

When Maria and Roberto arrived with dinner, they were still dutifully working on the list. Mother and son didn't stay long, knowing the manager and his assistant only had a few more hours to make their final choices.

At exactly midnight, according to the clock in the clubhouse, Drummond reappeared at Ogilvie's office. Don and Antonio exchanged hellos with the stocky, umpire-clad personification of Death and handed him their list.

He read it for a moment, then broke into his signature Cheshire-cat grin. He was more than amused. "Boy, you guys are making this easy on me. You've got some terrific talent here, but you're never going to be able to get them to play together. You'll see what I mean after everybody gets here tomorrow morning."

Ogilvie tried not to look worried. "Well, we think eight weeks is plenty of time."

Drummond was laughing now. "Eight years wouldn't be long enough. First of all, you've got the biggest fuck-up in the world on your team—Babe Ruth. I told you about him. He's two tons of trouble. Second, you've got a lot of the old Negro League players teamed with white players from when the Major Leagues were still segregated. You're just asking for it there. I could go on, but those are two big ones right off." Then with a wry smile he added, "If you were going to insist on having Ruth, you should've just taken the rest of the '27 Yankees."

Drummond could surely overhear words as well as read thoughts. Don and Antonio spied one another as if they had just signed on as Captain and First Mate of the *Titanic*. They'd hoped for more like the *Love Boat*.

Death Incarnate consulted the clubhouse clock and said, "Well, it's past midnight. Too late to change now." He folded up the piece of paper with Don and Antonio's team on it and slipped it in his back pocket. As he began to walk out of the manager's office and vanish into the darkness of the clubhouse, he reminded them, "Your players will be here in the clubhouse at nine sharp tomorrow morning. I'll be here too."

After Drummond left, they agreed there was nothing they could do now to change the list. Perhaps Death in the Flesh was only trying to psyche them out. They decided they should try to get some sleep. Don declined to go to the hotel, telling Antonio he would sleep in his easy chair in the office. That way he would be there when the players arrived. What Ogilvie was actually thinking about was the remainder of the fifth of Scotch in his desk.

As soon as Antonio left, he reached into the drawer and pulled out the bottle. It was not only there, it had been refilled! Yeah, that Drummond really had thought of everything. He took a long pull, then another. Ogilvie then read his copy of the team roster:

- Outfielders: mostly Yankees.
- Joe DiMaggio—the Yankee Clipper, Joltin' Joe, who owned centerfield.
- Mickey Mantle—The Mick, a switch-hitting homerun superstar.
- Of course, George Herman Ruth—the Babe, the Bambino, the Sultan of Swat.
- Roberto Clemente—little Roberto's namesake, the gazelle-like Pittsburgh Pirate right fielder and power-hitter.
- James "Cool Papa" Bell—a legendary Negro League outfielder with the speed of a jaguar.
- Oscar Charleston: a renowned Negro League center fielder who could also play first base.
- The diminutive and speedy Jimmy Crutchfield, also of the old Negro Leagues.
- Infielders:
- At first base—not just another Yankee, but the quintessential first baseman of all time: Lou Gehrig, The Iron Horse.
- Buck Leonard: who was considered the Negro League equivalent of Gehrig.
- Honus Wagner—the Flying Dutchman, considered by many as the greatest shortstop of all time.

- John Henry Lloyd—a black player from the days before the old Negro Leagues were even formed, and also considered by many as the greatest shortstop of all time.
- Jackie Robinson—the Dodgers' historic and gifted infielder, first to break Major League baseball's color line.
- Rogers Hornsby—the best hitting, right-handed second baseman ever.
- Jimmy Foxx—Double X, a powerful hitter and versatile infielder who could play several positions.
- Harold "Pie" Traynor—the unrivaled Pirate third baseman.
- Judy Johnson—the Negro League's best third baseman.
- Catchers:
- Josh Gibson—sometimes called 'the black Babe Ruth' because of his amazing home run power.
- Roy Campanella—the star receiver of the old Negro Leagues and then the Brooklyn Dodgers.
- Pitchers:
- Satchel Paige—the outspoken and flamboyant Negro League star who pitched into his early sixties.
- Don Drysdale—Big D, the tough Dodger right-hander.
- Walter Johnson—nicknamed "The Big Train" for his blazing fastball.
- Cy Young—the first major league pitcher to hurl a no-hitter, with baseball's most prestigious pitching award named after him.
- Christy Mathewson—the gentlemanly, Bucknell-educated strikeout artist.
- Carl Hubbell—the incomparable, left-handed screwball pitcher from the old New York Giants.
- Dizzy Dean—the white, personality-soaked Arkansas-born Cardinal right-hander, who greatly admired Satchel Paige.

As the weight of Drummond's warnings settled in, Ogilvie tried not to panic. They had great players. Why wouldn't these guys want to play together? It would be a once-in-a-lifetime experience—it would be fun. Naturally, it would be Ogilvie's job to make them into a team. How hard could that be? He was about to find out.

Ironically, Ogilvie's Hall of Fame squad had many players with stories far more tragic than his own. Josh Gibson, Lou Gehrig, and Roberto Clemente all died before their playing days were through. Roy Campanella, rendered an invalid in an automobile accident, was an all-star the season before. Although retired from baseball, Christy Mathewson died prematurely at age forty-five from the poison gas he was exposed to in WWI. Dizzy Dean, at age twenty-eight, suffered a freak, career-shortening injury. Ogilvie knew he did not have the patent on bad luck. However, it would be a painful and humbling lesson for him to learn how others had dealt with it.

He took another long pull on the never-empty bottle, put it back in its drawer, walked to his easy chair, and sank into it. He was thinking about Maggie, about Chosen Ones, Lucky Stiffs, and dead Hall of Famers. He wondered what other surprises Drummond and Limbotown had in store. The would-be manager fell into a restless, uneasy sleep.

Chapter 6

O gilvie was startled awake by Drummond's yelling. He wasn't yelling at Ogilvie though. Death's grating exhortation was coming from the dugout tunnel and getting louder. "Ruth, get your fat, drunken ass into that clubhouse! And the rest of youse guys too!"

The foggy-brained manager shook his head and tried to focus on the clock on his office wall. Nine o'clock straight up. He'd overslept again. Standing up from his easy chair, he took a short inventory of himself. His clothes were rumpled, hadn't been changed in three days, and he was beginning to waft rotten. Although not as bad as the day before, he was hung-over. Rubbing some sleep from his eyes, he also tried to brush away a few wrinkles and walked into the clubhouse. He knew what was coming. Nonetheless, he could barely believe what he was seeing.

Slowly, steadily, the clubhouse started to fill with his players. They were dressed in old-fashioned street clothes from various eras, and they carried beat-up duffels and luggage. They looked like a bygone group of Damon Runyan characters. They also looked disoriented. Ogilvie, on the other hand, was stunned. Here were the real Joe DiMaggio, Christy Mathewson, Lou Gehrig, Satchel Paige, and all of his other picks come to life. He couldn't believe it. He couldn't stop himself from smiling, chuckling. The budding manager was giddy at the sight of his dead Hall of Famers.

Nearly all the players had entered the clubhouse when Babe Ruth, hefting a suitcase and duffel bag, tripped and literally fell face-first into the room. He rolled from his stomach to his back and lay spread-eagle on the clubhouse floor, moaning weakly. He didn't look good. He must've been at least forty. The Babe was even more unkempt than Ogilvie: shirttail dangling beneath a soiled jacket, sporty cap askew. His size was elephantine. If he had wandered into a police station alone, they would've arrested him for illegal assembly. The eyes in his round, bulldog face were glazed over and bloodshot. As the big man gasped for air through his dry lips and raspy windpipe, Ogilvie instantly recognized the symptoms. Babe Ruth had a humongous hangover.

Directly behind Ruth was Death Incarnate—Doctor Drummond, dressed in his familiar umpire get-up. The roly-poly embodiment of Death gazed down at the huge, wretched homerun king sprawled on the floor, then at Ogilvie, and said, "You have to be careful what you ask for—you just might get it." This was not what Ogilvie had expected.

It was not clear if Ruth was reacting to what Drummond said to Ogilvie when he cried out, "I've been attacked by a fucking midget umpire!"

Ogilvie and the others burst into laughter. Drummond could only smirk while slowly swaying his head side to side. The Babe then let out a fart that erupted like Mt. St. Helen's, destroying all in its path. The odor was downright sulfuric. As those standing closest to Ruth choked, their chortling turned into pleas for mercy while they tweaked their faces into pained expressions and waved their hands around in a futile effort to disperse the noxious fumes.

The Bambino said to himself, "That feels better." Still on the clubhouse floor, the hulking giant rested his head on his duffel, took a deep, noisy breath, and closed his eyes.

Antonio, Maria, and Roberto had followed Drummond and Ruth's inauspicious entrance into the clubhouse. Hardly anyone noticed them. They walked over to Don, softly said good morning, and stood by him, seeming every bit as muddled as the Hall of Famers. Although he was not able to match all the faces with names, Ogilvie quietly tried to identify the players for the Alvarezes.

Drummond got up on one of the benches to be seen and heard better.

He wasn't very tall. What his body lacked in height, his gravelly voice made up in volume. He began speaking. "I know you're all wondering how you got here, why you're here, and where 'here' is. I'm going to try to explain. Please be patient, because it's going to take a few minutes. First of all, let me introduce myself. My name is Doctor Drummond. I'll be your host for the next eight weeks or so."

A collective cry rose up from the crowd of players when Drummond said "eight weeks," most complaining about games they had tomorrow let alone all the games they'd miss in two months.

Drummond tried to stem the uprising by saying, "I know this sounds impossible, but none of you will miss any games or any other plans you've got. When you leave here, it will still be today for all of you. I can't really explain it beyond that right now. You're just going to have to trust me on this. You don't have a choice anyhow." The hubbub momentarily died down.

He went on. "You're in a place I call Limbotown. We have everything here you'll need: great food and drink, a fine hotel, and even a movie theater. Everything's free. As you can see, we also have a wonderful baseball stadium. You're all going to get a chance to play in it too." The players were not happy with what they'd heard so far. Those who were not protesting reacted with blank expressions or flustered looks.

Drummond paused before going on. "I've brought all of you here under rather unusual circumstances. You see, where I come from the date today is July 17th . . . 2000." There were scoffs from the small audience.

Undeterred, Death in the Flesh pressed on. "That's right—the year 2000. But I'm not from the future. Actually, you guys are from the past, and from different times in the past. For instance, Ruth is from 1935, Christy Mathewson from 1905, and Don Drysdale from 1965. Some of you guys know or have heard about each other. Others not. The two things that all of you have in common is that, by the year 2000, you're all in the Hall of Fame. And you're all dead."

Upon hearing this, Ruth tried to sit up or turn over, his enormous gut and pounding hangover making it difficult to do either. He managed to raise his head and declare, "I know I'm not dead yet because I feel like

I'm dyin' right now!" Most of the players chuckled. However, it was a nervous laughter.

Ruth again struggled unsuccessfully to sit up. Drummond sarcastically implored the players, "Would you guys help Moby Dick get in the boat before someone tries to put a harpoon in him?" A few more chortles.

Lou Gehrig and Joe DiMaggio each grabbed one of the big man's arms, hoisting him high enough to plant him on a clubhouse bench. It was fitting that the greatest New York Yankee of them all was assisted by two other Yankee greats.

As Drummond was about to continue, Christy Mathewson, the Hall of Fame pitcher who came from 1905, asked, "What's the Hall of Fame?"

"Fair enough question," said a patient Death Incarnate. "A lot of you guys are from a time before the Hall of Fame was founded. The Hall is just what it sounds like. All the greatest players from the history of the game are nominated, then elected by a group of professional sports writers. It's very hard to get in and considered the highest honor. It wasn't started until 1936, so that's why a lot of you guys don't know about it yet."

Drummond motioned toward Ruth saying, "Babe, the Blue Ox here, is one of the charter members. Also Ty Cobb, Honus Wagner, Walter Johnson and, oh, Christy Mathewson." A large, stately grin graced the New York Giant's handsome, clean-cut face.

Then, like a bell going off in his head, Satchel Paige, the great Negro League (and later Major League) pitcher stood up and asked, "Does that mean us Negro League players are in the same Hall of Fame?" The clubhouse was momentarily muted—strangely enough, not because of Paige's question, even though it was provocative, but because of Paige's outfit.

Fashion-wise, Satchel Paige was a man ahead of his time. Dressed in a full-length, reddish fur coat, probably fox, his head was decked out with an outlandish deep purple chapeau that was finished off with a feather boa hat band the same color as his fox overcoat. Most of his fingers sparkled with gaudy, bejeweled rings. Paige was Superfly in cleats, Liberace with a fastball. Had it been the late 1960s or early '70s, Satchel would've had a nickname like "Huggy-bear" or "Big Daddy." Paige didn't know he was dressed like a latter-day pimp, and might even have inspired such a "uniform." His apparel drew peculiar expressions from white and black players alike.

Drummond, unfazed by Paige's costume or the players' double-takes, proceeded to answer. "Believe it or not, Mr. Paige, you're all in the same Hall of Fame. In fact, the Major Leagues started hiring players from the Negro Leagues in 1947, and the old color line was broken forever. Ask Jackie Robinson," Death said, gesturing toward the Dodger legend. "He was the first black player in Major League history to do it, and there have been many more since."

Paige eyed Robinson, who nodded. The young, fur-clad Satchel triumphantly announced, "Damn—I knew we'd do it!" Paige was not only ahead of his time when it came to clothing, but also civil rights. He was an early and outspoken critic of baseball's color barrier, although at the time he was but a voice from left field. Paige's enthusiasm was not shared by many of the white players milling about the Drummond Field clubhouse. With the exception of the other black players and the few modern-era whites, Drummond's words dropped like thuds. Not just the part about color-blind baseball, but the whole idea of playing ball in Limbotown as well.

The players were starting to form cliques. Understandably, those who knew each other grouped together, mainly along racial lines. The exceptions were Don Drysdale and Roberto Clemente. They both entered Major League baseball well after Jackie Robinson had broken the color barrier. They knew each other. Clemente, little Roberto's namesake, was both black and Latin. Drysdale, the big, white right-hander, played against Clemente, and also played with former Negro Leaguers Robinson and Roy Campanella on the Brooklyn and then Los Angeles Dodgers.

As Drysdale and Clemente stood together in the clubhouse as the only visible sign of baseball's integration, they felt an ominous sense of déjà vu. Would the battle need to be fought again?

While Drummond spoke, a murmur arose from the gathering. It was not a good omen. The seeds of division and discontent were being sown. Ogilvie felt it. He knew now he would have to deal with it. He just had no idea how. Once again, he was blanking, caught up by the certain fear that Drummond would soon be turning the players over to his care. Ogilvie had no idea how to keep himself from running out of the room and vomiting like the day before, let alone how to solve a thorny racial problem. Death Personified's prediction of trouble was already coming true.

Rogers Hornsby, the thickly muscled, good-looking Cardinal second baseman who had mourned the death of baseball's color barrier when it finally came about, bluntly asked, "How much are we getting paid to play with the darkies?"

This racist remark in fact gave Ogilvie hope. Maybe even a self-admitted bigot like Hornsby would make an exception if the money was right. But Drummond hadn't mentioned that the players were to be paid, and Ogilvie hadn't negotiated for it either.

Death in the Flesh was equally blunt in his reply to Hornsby, flatly stating, "Nothing." Seeing and hearing the grimaces and grunts throughout the room, he rapidly reminded the players, "Don't forget, everything here is free. All the food and booze you can eat and drink. And wait till you see the first-class hotel we're putting you in. Great room service. It's free, and everyone gets their own deluxe room!" This slowed the rebellion once more.

Drummond's offer of deluxe accommodations may not have sounded like much when compared to today's world of astronomical athlete salaries. Still, most of Ogilvie's players came from a time in baseball when decent accommodations and good food were anything but guaranteed. Even the well-heeled teams were often forced into substandard hotels. It wasn't so much that the owners tended to be tightwads (although many were notorious cheapskates)—it was more the unflattering image from which old-time ballplayers had suffered.

Organized baseball was never an elitist pastime. In the beginning, this was an understatement. It was not polo, with its corps of wealthy, aristocratic participants and spectators. Baseball was a grassroots game that anyone could afford to play, and many did. Its appeal obscured all social and economic lines. Any given turn-of-the-century Major League game drew millionaires to dirt farmers, scoundrels to politicians—the latter two groups virtually interchangeable.

Like most other professional sports, baseball originally attracted poor immigrant athletes. It offered an alternative to working in the coal mines, the farm, or the general store. Many of the early players were bumpkins and rubes. They were rough and tumble, not averse to drinking, gambling, swearing, and just being plain old rude, crude, and crass. Otherwise, they were an exemplary bunch. There were exceptions, naturally, like the polished, educated Mathewson.

For the most part, the country that embraced baseball as its own invention and national diversion shunned its players as social outcasts—or at least misfits. Sure it might be okay to take your daughter to the ballpark, but heaven forbid that she would want to marry the first baseman. It would be years, decades, before the players' general reputation improved to the point of public acceptability. Some would argue it hasn't happened yet.

Given their pariah status, the better hotels were hesitant to sully their hallways, rooms, and lobbies with turn-of-the-century ball players. They didn't want to scare off the carriage trade. When the early players did get the rare, fine accommodations, they truly relished it, put mustard on it, and savored it like a Coney Island hot dog.

As might be expected, the Negro League players had had it much worse than their white counterparts. Forget about bad hotels. The old Negro League teams were often not allowed to room in even the seediest flophouses. The old Jim Crow attitudes were applied equally in the North as well as the South. The Negro Leaguers usually slept in their overcrowded buses—or, like Blanche DuBois, depended on the kindness of strangers.

The players did not readily cast aside Drummond's offer of grand accommodations. Death Personified was again trying to help Ogilvie. Ogilvie, in contrast, viewed Drummond's offer of free, unlimited food, liquor, and private rooms as an invitation for a nonstop party. Ordinarily, he would've joined them. Now, he was worried about how he was going to control his players in this freewheeling atmosphere. The duties of managing were beginning to weigh in.

He took for granted that no one could leave Limbotown. That would help—or so he thought. For Don Ogilvie, ignorance would not be bliss in this mysterious place. What he didn't know was going to hurt him. He didn't know nearly enough about Limbotown—or Drummond—to make any of his assumptions. Among the many things Ogilvie did not know: there was a way to leave Limbotown—at least temporarily. Naturally, the players would discover it before he did.

Having recaptured the players' attention with the promise of first-rate lodgings, Drummond decided to start getting everything out in the open. "There's another reason you're not getting paid," he explained. "You're all here to do a good deed—to save a life, if you can."

Drummond gestured for Ogilvie and the Alvarezes to come forward. "This is Don Ogilvie, and this is the Alvarez family: Antonio, Maria, and their seven-year-old son, Roberto. I've brought them here for a very special reason. You see, Roberto has leukemia, a type of cancer. In his case, it's fatal. He doesn't look sick, and he won't be sick as long as he's in Limbotown. But he's going to die within a few months of the time he leaves here. Maybe less."

The news of little Roberto's impending death was too fresh in Antonio and Maria's minds. Hearing it again from Drummond gave way to their tears. Roberto tried to comfort his parents. Some of the players looked on sympathetically. Others were not moved.

The Ultimate Umpire carried on with his speech. "You guys can save this kid's life. All you have to do is play a seven-game series against my team. Of course, you have to win."

Then finally it came. The irascible and racist Hornsby asking Drummond, "Well, who the hell are you, anyway, that you think we can save this little brown kid's life by playing baseball?"

Drummond flashed his toothy grin and acerbically replied, "I was wondering when one of youse geniuses was going to ask me that." Drummond began to pace back and forth on the bench he was standing on. He became histrionic. He was all but shouting. "I'm the guy that brought all of youse here! I'm the guy that made this entire place. I'm the guy that made it possible for everyone to come from a different time. I'm also the guy that's responsible for little Roberto's dying. You see, I'm Death! Death Personified. Death Incarnate. Death in the Flesh."

There was stunned silence for a second. Ruth, suddenly coming to life, wise-cracked, "Ah, you're not Death. You just look like Death warmed-over."

The players couldn't help guffawing, breaking the tension of Drummond's always shocking pronouncement. When the noise died down Death Personified tried to top Ruth's jibe. He failed miserably saying, "That's rich, Ruth. Especially coming from someone in your condition!"

The players barely snickered at Death's retort. They were plainly backing the Babe, no matter his condition. The unfazed Doctor Drummond went on. "Youse guys can laugh all you want, but you're all dead and you're all under my control. You only think you're alive because I let you think it!" Feeling he was coming on too strong, Drummond backed up a little. "Look, you're here as my guests. It's an honor to be selected to come to this place. It's a gift to have your life back, at least for a little while, and to play the one thing you all love— baseball. You'll see we don't ask for much here. One of the things we do request is that you play ball. You don't have to believe anything I say. Make up our own minds. I just want you to listen. You've got eight weeks to get ready. Since everybody comes from a different date, we'll be using the calendar from where I came from. So no matter what day it was where you came from, it is now Monday, July 17th. Forget about a year. You'll get used to it. There are clocks and calendars all over Limbotown. Other than that, all youse guys have to worry about is playin' ball. Don Ogilvie here is going to be your skipper."

The would-be manager made a tentative nod toward the players. Except for a few dubious glances, he was ignored. Drummond was wrapping up. "I'm going to turn this meeting over to him now. When Ogilvie's done with youse, you can all take your luggage over to the hotel and check in. Leave your gear. Your stuff will be put into lockers here." Drummond climbed down off the bench and started walking out of the clubhouse.

"Hey wait a minute!" demanded Satchel Paige. "Who's on your team?"

Drummond turned around and casually answered, "Just Ty Cobb and a pitcher." Paige cocked his head and squinted, trying to comprehend.

"It's all yours, Ogilvie," said Death Personified, grinning his clenched-teeth smile again as he left the room. The clubhouse was abuzz with bewildered players.

Don Ogilvie was not exactly exuding confidence as he cleared his throat in an attempt to also clear his head. His armpits let loose like Victoria Falls. He wondered what Buck Nimble would do in a situation like this. Hell, he wished he were Buck. Or better yet, he wished Buck was here and he could be Buck's assistant. Buck would know what to do. Don Ogilvie didn't have a clue.

Spurred on by supportive nudges from the Alvarezes, Ogilvie stepped atop the same bench as Drummond had stood on and began speaking. "I know you all must be a little surprised to be here. I know I am." The noise began to lessen as Ogilvie plodded on. "You see, the Alvarezes here are kind of my adopted family. Roberto is my best friend." Even Ogilvie thought he sounded more like an elementary school "Show and Tell" than a baseball manager. The few players who seemed to be listening were skeptical.

He tried to explain more. "I'm the hitting coach for the San Bernardino Stampede. We're a minor league team for the Dodgers. Antonio is an outfielder there. That's how I met his family, and we all became good friends. You see, I'm kind of the one who asked for a chance to save Roberto's life. Believe me, I didn't think it was possible. Especially this way. So anyhow, Drummond shows up and makes this proposition that if I can manage a team of Hall of Famers and beat his team in a seven-game series, then he'll let Roberto live. I sure didn't believe it at first either . . . but here we are!"

The players were barely listening. Ogilvie anxiously cleared his throat again. "Anyway, Antonio and I picked you guys to be on our team. We hope you can help save Roberto's life." He paused, not sure what to say next. He was still shedding water like a flying fish. It was hard to miss.

Taking advantage of the awkward break, the irritated, caustic Rogers Hornsby asked Ogilvie, "We know the other nutcase thinks he's Death, but who the hell are you? The Johnstown Flood?" Most of the players laughed at Ogilvie's expense.

Misunderstanding the real intent of the question, he answered, "For those of you that didn't hear, my name is Don Ogilvie."

Exasperated, Hornsby shook his head. "We know you got a name. What have you done in baseball? Are you in the Hall of Fame, like the rest of us, or just some nobody?"

The difficulty of the task ahead was again made painfully clear to Don Ogilvie. He at once saw that he would have no respect from or credibility with his players. If Buck were here, he could tell them about Don's promising major league career cut down before it started, what a great hitter he was, and a damn good coach too. He knew he would look egotistical (and with no apparent reason) saying it himself. Nevertheless, he had to say something.

"Uh, well, I had just got an outfield spot with the Cardinals and I tore up my Achilles tendon. That was it for my playing days. So I went into coaching after that." Ogilvie conveniently left out the gritty details of what happened in the lost years between his "playing days" and becoming a coach.

Hornsby said to the loosely formed assembly, "Just like I thought: A nobody."

Little Roberto could stand it no longer. His friend was under attack. He got up on the bench with Don, staunchly defending him to Hornsby and the rest. "He's not a nobody. He's my best friend. He's the best hitting coach there is. And before he got hurt, he was going to be the best hitter on the Cardinals. Now he's going to be a great manager." Roberto postured as if he was ready to fight anyone who disagreed.

The players, Hornsby included, were impressed by little Roberto's moxie. So was Don. Buck Nimble couldn't have done a better job himself. But despite Roberto's praise, the players were not similarly taken with Ogilvie.

Hornsby remarked directly to the "nobody-manager," "Well, you got the kid convinced, but not us." Ogilvie was going to have a lot of convincing to do.

Realizing he wasn't going to top Roberto's pep talk, Ogilvie figured it would be a good time to wind things up and let the players get acclimated to Limbotown. Besides, he was running out of things to say.

"This is a travel day," the nobody-manager said. "I want you guys to see what there is of Limbotown and then check into the hotel. Like Drummond said, leave your equipment here. Our first practice is tomorrow morning. Be here by ten to dress. See you then."

The clubhouse gathering began to break up. The first thing on the players' minds was how to break out. Even though they found Drummond Field as beautiful and wondrous as Don Ogilvie had, the players were determined to get home, Limbotown notwithstanding. Invariably, they encountered the same phenomenon with the fogbank as had Ogilvie and the Alvarezes. At first they were amused by it. But amusement shortly turned to disappointment and dismay.

After a couple of hours of scouring Limbotown and failing to escape, the players, tired, hungry and perplexed, made their way to the Hotel Limbotown. The common belief was that neither Drummond nor Ogilvie could be trusted. Limbotown was some elaborate trick. Still they could not explain how they all came from different dates and times. The players were coming to the unhappy conclusion that Limbotown was not your usual stop in anyone's league.

Ogilvie and the Alvarez family sat in the now-empty clubhouse. They were at once ecstatic and stupefied by what had just happened. Their dead Hall of Famers miraculously showed up all right, they just weren't going to be cooperative. Both Maggie's and Drummond's warnings that "this isn't going to be easy" dogged Don Ogilvie like his habitual hangover. He had foolishly overlooked human nature. These guys had ego, pride, vastly different personalities, superstitions, staggering athletic ability, and the unforgiving prejudices of their times. He knew the players would not have to like each other in order to play well. They would, nevertheless, need respect for one another—not to mention, respect for their manager. Insurrection would otherwise take hold. He had to devise a way to build, perhaps even manufacture this respect. The thought gave him a headache. He wanted a drink.

Fighting off the urge, Don instead thanked his little friend for his big show of support, saying, "Buck would've been proud of that one, Roberto. I know I sure am."

They were surrounded by bags and duffels of old-fashioned, possibly antique baseball equipment. Don and Antonio looked wearily at one another. Who was going to put all this stuff away? They needed a clubhouse manager.

Auspiciously, one emerged from the dugout tunnel. He was an old, small, gray-haired man, wiry in build, wearing a New York Yankee cap and carrying a clipboard. He approached them and introduced himself. "The name's Charlie McManus," he said. They all exchanged names and handshakes.

Turning to Ogilvie, Charlie McManus stated, "Doc Drummond's asked me to be your clubhouse manager." Seeing Ogilvie's astonishment, he added, "If that's all right with you."

"Of course. Of course, Charlie," said Don Ogilvie. "I just didn't know you were coming. Is it all right to call you 'Charlie'?"

"You betcha, Mr. Ogilvie. That's what everyone calls me. Mr. McManus is my father's name!" It was hard for Ogilvie and the Alvarezes to picture Charlie McManus's father. Charlie himself looked like he was about ninety. He couldn't have been that old, but his deeply furrowed and rugged face made him look like a well-worn leather bag.

"Well, Charlie, have you ever managed a clubhouse before?" asked Ogilvie.

This brought forward a hearty snort from Charlie McManus, followed by a lifetime smoker's cough that sounded something like a garbage disposal with a spoon in it. When he recovered, he said, "I've been the stadium suprvisor for the New York Yankees for the past thirty-seven years! I've seen 'em all come and go, from Ruth to Mantle."

Ogilvie vaguely remembered hearing of Charlie McManus. He was now embarrassed for asking about his credentials. "Sorry, Charlie," said an apologetic Ogilvie, "I know who you are now."

Charlie McManus seemed satisfied. He then got to the job at hand, saying, "Doc Drummond tells me you're going to manage a team of All-Stars against his team. I hear we're trying to save this little boy's life!" Then he lowered his voice: "I also hear you've got some of the old Negro League players playing with some of the old major leaguers. I'll see what I can do to arrange the lockers to keep the peace."

"That's fine, Charlie," said an appreciative Ogilvie, adding, "but remember, every player here gets equal treatment."

"Oh, believe me, I like ballplayers of any color," said a sincere Charlie McManus. "Of course, the Yankee clubhouse is integrated now. You just got to get the players to respect each other. It's not easy mixing up a clubhouse for the first time."

Ogilvie replied, "Yeah, everyone here seems to know that but me."

"Do you have any of my old Yankees on your team, Mr. Ogilvie?" asked a hopeful Charlie McManus.

"Only Babe Ruth, Lou Gehrig, Joe DiMaggio, and Mickey Mantle. And please call me Don."

"It sounds like the start of a great team. I'm sorry though, Mr. Ogilvie, it just wouldn't be right me calling you by your first name, you being the manager and all," said the revered old Yankee clubhouse skipper who'd been on a first-name basis with all the Yankee greats.

"If you don't mind," he continued, "I'll get started with assigning lockers and putting this gear away. I've got a couple of young assistants who'll be here in a little while to help, if that's okay."

"No, no, not at all. That's great," said a relieved Don Ogilvie, who was having visions of the bantam and decrepit Charlie McManus expiring from multiple hernias while stowing the players' heavy duffels.

Ogilvie turned to the Alvarezes. "I think you guys should get back to the hotel and make sure everybody's getting checked in okay. I'll be by in a little while to eat and get a room." Antonio, Maria, and Roberto said their goodbyes and obediently left for the hotel.

Curiosity got the best of Don Ogilvie, and he asked his new clubhouse manager, "Hey Charlie, are you a Chosen One or a Lucky Stiff?"

Charlie McManus looked at Ogilvie like he knew what he was asking. Then a void filled his face and he answered, "Huh?"

Ogilvie mumbled, "Never mind." He mentally noted, *Lucky Stiff.*

He left Charlie and his clipboard alone in the clubhouse to brood over locker assignments while he retreated to his office. The lower right-hand desk drawer opened virtually self-propelled. The always-full bottle of Scotch was there to do his bidding. He took two big gulps and began planning for his first practice tomorrow morning.

It was check-in time at the Hotel Limbotown. Actually, anytime someone showed up to check in, it was check-in time at the Hotel Limbotown. The players, in ragged groups, having exhausted every possible avenue of escape, began walking resignedly to the hotel entrance. Where else were they going to go? They didn't want to sleep in the clubhouse. That left either the movie theater or the hotel. The movie theater had lots of seats, but the hotel had rooms with beds and bathrooms, and a dining room and a bar. The players didn't want it to appear as if they were doing anything either Drummond or Ogilvie had told them to do, but in this case it seemed like there was no choice if they wanted a place to stay. It was well after lunchtime. Most of them hadn't even had breakfast before being "transported" to Limbotown. They were hungry and tired. They'd been dragging their luggage around all day. Everyone needed a shower. A musty cloud of cheap cologne and perspiration enveloped them.

Splendidly attired doormen now graced the main entrance to the Hotel Limbotown. As the players approached, the doormen summoned bellhops to relieve the weary travelers of their bags, and opened the elaborate front doors. They were mollified by what they saw. The marble floors gleamed like glass, the indoor water fountain bubbled soothingly, and the walls abounded with baseball memorabilia, the players recognizing themselves in some of the photographs. The bustling staff was courteous and eager. They addressed their guests as "Mister," followed by their correct last names. Few of the players were used to such hospitality. Taking in the opulence of their surroundings, they became revived and cheerful. They slapped each other on the back and offered to buy each other drinks. The helpful staff reminded them that they couldn't really "buy" drinks because everything was free. This only led to more joking and backslapping. Everything was fine until the contingent of Negro League players, led by the sartorial Satchel Paige, came into the lobby.

Most of the white players had already entered the hotel and were at the registration desk getting rooms. When Paige and his teammates came in, the lively hotel was overtaken by a wary silence. It was one of those situations where anything could've happened, except that it would no doubt be ugly. The Alvarezes, who were monitoring the check-ins for Don Ogilvie, were overmatched. Antonio and Maria, Hispanic, younger than most of the players, and unknown to them, were not in a position to do anything.

Aware of this turning point, the fearless and gorgeous manager of the Hotel Limbotown, Maggie Briggs, briskly walked from behind the registration desk to the middle of the lobby, and in a pleasantly firm voice said, "Welcome, everyone, to the Hotel Limbotown. We hope your stay here is a pleasant one. If there is anything I can do to assist you, please let me know. I'm the hotel's general manager, Maggie Briggs. Please feel free to call me Maggie if you'd like. We're very friendly and informal here."

By this time the striking Maggie had everyone's eye. Over forty or not, she could still command the attention of a room full of men. Among those more deeply affected by Maggie's taking center stage was George Herman Ruth. He of the gargantuan hangover was instantly revived by this vision of loveliness. Ruth was struck by the same Thunderbolt as Ogilvie. Whereas Ogilvie had never been stricken by the Thunderbolt before; the Babe had been its willing target many, many times. All of Ruth's appetites were, well, Ruthian—including and notably women, marriage and fidelity notwithstanding. He remarked to Lou Gehrig, who was sitting next to him, "Gosh, Lou, she's the most be-u-ti-ful dame I ever seen!"

Gehrig, almost talking to himself, said, "I wish I had a nickel for every time I heard you say that, Jidge." "Jidge" was how most other players and Ruth's friends mispronounced his first name. Ruth had picked up the sobriquet in Boston, where he'd begun his professional career. It was a thickly accented New England bastardization of "George" that would've made the Pepperidge Farm man proud.

Ruth sat on the edge of his lobby chair, watching and listening intently as his new love interest, Maggie Briggs, continued to speak. "As I'm sure you've all seen by now, this is the only hotel in town. We have a policy here of treating all of our guests with courtesy and kindness. That also means that the guests will be expected to treat each other the same way. There are no exceptions to this rule. We're going to check in everybody on Don Ogilvie's team. You will all get your own room and private bath. As you know, everything here is free, including food and drink. All of you will eat in the dining room. We also have an adjoining lounge. And, of course there's room service too. There are no restrictions here for any guest. Now do I have everyone's promise that we're all going to treat each other nicely?"

Before anyone could say otherwise, Ruth, pale and unsteady, rose to his feet and spoke to the comely manager. "Ma'am, I'm sure I speak for all of my other 'colleges' when I say that we will respect the wishes of the be-u-ti-ful and gracious management of this fine hotel and act like gentlemen at all times. Furthermore, anyone who don't will have to answer to me personally." Ruth then tipped his cap to a mildly surprised Maggie Briggs.

She smiled and blushed at this public display of favoritism. It helped her cause, however, and she acknowledged him. "Why, thank you for your generous offer, Mr. Ruth. Your pledge is gratefully accepted." Ruth resumed his seat with a contented smile on his face.

It was clear to everyone in the room that the Big Guy was sweet on the be-u-ti-ful Maggie and there was no sense in upsetting the love-struck Bambino. Even in the Babe's weakened state, a player would've stood a better chance against a charging rhino during mating season.

Registration continued without incident. All the players were checked in, and some began filtering down to the dining room to eat. By now the elevator was manned and operated by the impeccably outfitted, five-foot, four-inch Burton P. Stansberry, III. No matter the time of day or night, he always seemed to be in the elevator. Some would later speculate that he also lived there. He was short and trim, and slim of build. His boyish good looks, easy smile, and smooth features belied his true age of thirty-five or so. Always cheerful and friendly, he normally greeted his customers by saying, "Great day to be alive, isn't it!" Likeable as he was, some of the ballplayers got on his case about being short. It was the kind of petty and cruel locker-room banter common in junior high school. It didn't take long for Burton P. Stansberry, III, to become "Burt the Squirt" to Babe Ruth, Rogers Hornsby, and a few of the others. The elfin Burt, however, was a Chosen One with a quick reply. He gave Ruth and the others as good as he got. He often returned Ruth's slurs with nicknames like Sasquatch, Bigfoot, Orson Welles, the Missing Link, Doctor Moreau's favorite pet, and the Hindenburg. When Ruth and the others didn't "get" some of the cracks, he told them, "The Babe is just a man ahead of his own time." He could really show Ruth and his goons something if and when he wanted too. He'd give them a chance to come around first. If they didn't, he'd give them a lesson they wouldn't soon forget.

Although Maggie would tell him about it shortly, it was best that Don Ogilvie had not witnessed the lobby repartee between her and "Jidge"—not because of the Babe's newfound affection for Maggie (he would find out about that soon enough), but because it would have given him false hope about the racial problem. Only hearing about Ruth's promise to act "like gentlemen" might spur his Pollyanna belief that it would carry over to the ballfield. This would not be the case.

Instead, Ogilvie showed up a couple of hours and a few drinks later. The Hotel Limbotown was still humming with activity from the arrival of its new guests. The nobody-manager tentatively made his way to the registration desk to get a room. He hadn't changed clothes or showered in three days. Flies were beginning to nest. He prayed Maggie would not be there. She was.

Her greeting wasn't exactly flattering. "We've got some fresh clothes for you up in your room. Do you mind if I have what you're wearing burned?"

"As long as I'm not in them," Ogilvie laughingly replied. As tired, dirty, and boozy as he was, just seeing Maggie lifted his spirits.

She knew she was seeing him at his worst. She had no mercy and confronted him. "You almost missed a small riot in the lobby this afternoon. Some of your white players didn't want to let your black players stay here."

A concerned Ogilvie asked, "What happened?"

"Well, since the team manager wasn't here, and the poor Alvarezes couldn't do anything, I was the only one left to plead for calm. Luckily, Mr. Ruth came to the aid of a lady in distress. He was really quite gallant. He promised me that all the players would behave themselves or they would have to answer to him personally."

"Babe Ruth said that?" Ogilvie asked optimistically. He was naïvely hoping that any racial discord was working itself out on its own.

He also made note of Maggie's sharp jab about his untimely absence in the face of crisis. Too tired to fight or argue with anyone now, especially her, he let go her parting shot and only asked for an 8 a.m. wake-up call. He found his room and showered, allowing the warm waters of Limbotown to soothe and cleanse him. Lying down on the bed, he drifted into a deep sleep.

Chapter 7

If he dreamed that night, Don Ogilvie could not remember. His sleep was buried and still. The nine o'clock wake-up call brought him back from a comatose slumber. Feeling refreshed and energized, he was looking forward to the first day of practice.

He grabbed a quick breakfast in the hotel dining room. He wanted to say good morning to Maggie, but she was nowhere to be found. Some of the players were also having breakfast. None of them acknowledged Ogilvie, but he wasn't worried. They didn't really know him yet. The first day of practice was meant for everyone to get acquainted and to fix a routine. He figured things would naturally fall into place, given a little time. He figured wrong once again.

As he walked to Drummond Field, knowing he was going to have to deal with the race issue somehow, Ogilvie was again bolstered by Ruth's pledge of civility. Even if the promise was made only to Maggie and only covered the hotel, Ogilvie reasoned it would have to help things at the ballpark too.

When he arrived at the stadium it wasn't yet 9:45 a.m. The cluttered clubhouse was hardly recognizable from the day before. The new clubhouse manager (and old Yankee Stadium honcho) Charlie McManus had assigned lockers and neatly stowed away uniforms, equipment, and other gear. Ogilvie was pleased. He was also amused at some of the old-time stuff he saw. Fielders' gloves not much bigger than your hand, the fingers not even tied to each other, like on modern gloves. How could you catch a ball in something like that? He saw bats that looked more like thick, wooden dowels. They weren't tapered like today's bats. They were just as thick at the handle as they were at the barrel. Sure these old bats wouldn't break or crack as easily as the thin-handled, bulging-barreled bats used by players now, but he still wondered how you could hit a ball out of the infield with one of those things.

The chain-smoking little clubhouse manager, Charlie McManus, came out of the equipment room holding a cup of coffee in his hand. "Good morning!" he said energetically. "Got a cup of Joe for ya."

"Thanks," said a grateful Ogilvie, taking the mug from Charlie's hand. "And thanks for the great job on the clubhouse. Everything looks . . . great!"

"Well that's what I'm here for," replied a sunny Charlie McManus, glad to have a boss who didn't take him for granted. "Of course, I've been here since 7 a.m. That's when Mr. DiMaggio likes to start his off-day workouts."

"DiMaggio's already here?" responded an encouraged Ogilvie.

"Yeah, he's doing some stretching and running on the field," the rough voiced Charlie said.

Don Ogilvie thought, *Wow, DiMaggio's been here since seven! That's a good sign.*

Just before ten, Antonio Alvarez, dressed in his San Bernardino Stampede uniform, found Don Ogilvie in his clubhouse office. Ogilvie was getting into a practice uniform given to him by Charlie McManus. "This is the big day," said an excited Antonio. "What do you have planned?"

"A light workout today," said Ogilvie. "I don't want to push it. These guys need to get to know each other, and us too."

"Sounds good to me," agreed Antonio.

Don asked, "Where's Maria and Roberto?"

"They're still at the hotel. They'll be here in about an hour."

"Good. I want them here too—especially Roberto. The players need to know who they're playing for."

At exactly ten o'clock, three other players came into the clubhouse: Roberto Clemente, Don Drysdale, and a very young-looking Mickey

Mantle. Charlie McManus intercepted them and showed them where their lockers were. Ogilvie, watching the goings-on from his office, instructed Antonio to tell the trio to dress for a light practice and sit tight until the other players showed up. Antonio was intimidated. Here was not only the Hall of Fame player he named his son after, but also two other baseball legends.

Recognizing that "I'm so nervous I'm going to vomit" look in Antonio's eyes, Don cajoled him. "C'mon—these guys won't bite. Besides, you're much closer to their age than I am."

Shored-up, yet still uncertain, Antonio made his way over to the small gathering. Drysdale and Clemente seemed to be only a few years older than Antonio. Mickey Mantle, on the other hand, looked maybe seventeen. Antonio took a deep breath, extended his hand first to Roberto Clemente, and said, "Hi, I'm Antonio Alvarez. This is a real honor meeting you. My wife and I named our son after you."

Roberto Clemente smiled, shook Antonio's hand, and said in his Puerto Rican accent, "Nice meet you. Your leetle boy mus' be very courageous. Dat some spitch he give yesterday. Too bad on his leukemia."

"Yes, we're very proud of him," said a still-shaky Antonio Alvarez. Antonio then turned to Drysdale and Mantle, shook hands, and exchanged introductions. He was relieved to see that the very young Mickey Mantle was apparently as discombobulated as he was.

When Antonio asked the players to dress for a light workout, Don Drysdale, the big Dodger pitcher, remarked, "It's definitely going to be light. I think we're the only ones who are going to show."

"What do you mean?" questioned a worried Antonio.

"Well," Drysdale began, "Ruth and most of the white players are back at the hotel dining room having a party. They don't look like they're about to come down here. And all the black players are sitting at a couple of tables with their suitcases, like they're goin' somewhere. I think you better tell your skipper."

"Yeah, I think I better," said a dejected Antonio.

Antonio relayed Drysdale's words to Ogilvie. He came out of his office and introduced himself to the players. He found it a bit strange to be talking to Roberto Clemente, Don Drysdale, and a disturbingly youthful Mickey Mantle. Ogilvie had watched them play when he was a youngster. In Limbotown, the players hadn't aged but Don Ogilvie had. Forty years ago, he was just another adolescent rooting for his baseball idols. Now he was a fifty-something nobody-manager, considerably older than his players. With Ruth, Gehrig, Mathewson, and the other old timers, it didn't matter as much. Ogilvie wasn't old enough to have seen them play. They had long since retired or died. For Ogilvie to now be in charge of his childhood heroes was surreal. He had to stop himself from having another one of his out-of-body experiences. After the "hellos" were swapped, Don Ogilvie asked Don Drysdale, "Why do you think no one else is going to make it?"

Drysdale told him about the party taking place with Ruth and his band of merry men, and also about the sullen and isolated black players. After hearing it for himself, Ogilvie finally abandoned his simplistic hope for spontaneous racial harmony. The question was, what was he, nobody-manager Don Ogilvie, going to do about it? He didn't have any good ideas. In fact, he didn't have any ideas, good or bad. He didn't want to appear helpless, even if he was. It was now past 10:30, and no one else had shown.

Ogilvie told the three players, "Get your stuff on. Antonio will take you out to the field. Do whatever you usually do to warm-up. I'm going to the hotel, and I'm coming back with the rest of the team." He sounded like a manager in charge. Now if he could only be as in charge as he sounded.

Ogilvie wasn't sure what to expect when he got to the hotel. He stood at the entrance of the dining room in his practice uniform and just observed. It was much as described, except things had gotten even more raucous. At two tables near the bar were Babe Ruth and most of the other white players. The Babe was holding court in between giant gulps of what was in front of him—which seemed like the entire breakfast menu. Ogilvie saw large platters of eggs, pancakes, French toast, waffles, sausages, bacon, hash brown potatoes, what looked to be a half-eaten ham, a stack of toast, two or three gallons of orange juice, and several large schooners of beer. All in all it was a fairly typical Babe Ruth meal. Diamond Jim Brady would've approved.

98

At the other end of the dining room sat the black players. In between the two groups of players sat other people. Ogilvie wondered who these others were and where they came from.

Maggie was behind the bar. Each time the Babe went for a swig of beer, every thirty seconds or so, he would hoist his heady schooner in the direction of Maggie and the bar, as if toasting them. He wouldn't drink from the heavy glass goblet until he caught Maggie's eye and winked at her. Even without having witnessed the previous day's banter between the two, it was obvious to Don Ogilvie that he and the Bambino were both enamored of the same woman. This revelation did not do much to clear his head.

Maggie noticed Don at the dining room entrance and apologetically rolled her eyes at him. Ruth noticed Maggie noticing Ogilvie. Ogilvie walked over to the bar and took a seat. Discreetly gesturing toward Ruth and his crew, he asked Maggie, "How long has this been going on?"

"Close to an hour," was her matter-of-fact response.

"Where'd the other people come from?" Ogilvie was asking her about the assortment of apparently new "guests" at the Hotel Limbotown now flittering about. She told him that they were the hotel, theater, and stadium staff and their families. There were tailors and barbers, maids and maintenance men, chefs and servers, laundrymen and dry cleaners, and so forth. Then there were the movie theater people—projectionists and ushers. After that, there was the entire crew it took to run Drummond Field: groundskeepers and locker room attendants, and the stadium's own set of ushers and concessionaires for the Series. Also, those who would operate the electronic scoreboard and colossal video screen, and on and on . . . In total, they were some 700 strong, baseball fans all. There was no other place to put them up in Limbotown. The "employees" worked in shifts. When they were off, they were treated like the other patrons. Most were Lucky Stiffs, with a couple of Chosen Ones, like Maggie, mixed in. Anyhow, Drummond wanted it this way. The Hotel wouldn't seem real without guests, other than the players. This gave the appearance of a "live" hotel with normal guests, Maggie explained. *Maybe in the Twilight Zone*, thought Ogilvie. Like the players, these Lucky Stiffs had also been given a Limbotown orientation of sorts to—

initially, at least—calm their fears and curiosities. Having been told about the same as the players, they were about as unbelieving. It was Maggie Briggs who gave them their footing, their stability, in this tiny, ethereal Eden.

Ogilvie sat sideways on his barstool to survey the entire scene again. He came full circle and refocused on Ruth. Ruth returned his stare, unsettling the nobody-manager. The Babe paused from his mass consumption for a moment and quietly conferred with the other players at his table. He again looked up at Ogilvie and, while motioning him over, said, "Hey, Ovaltine! C'mon over here a minute."

The Bambino was notoriously bad with names, sometimes forgetting the names of his own teammates and coaches. He often resorted to calling people "kid" (pronounced "keed" in 1920s' New York slang). It was hard to get someone's name wrong this way. That Ruth even attempted Ogilvie's name was a complement—only Ogilvie didn't know it at the time.

The nobody-manager cringed, squinted at Maggie and said, "Wish me luck. I have a feeling I'm going to need it." He cautiously walked over to the table.

No one could conjure up a better baseball hero than Babe Ruth. A Deadhead on acid at a Phish concert didn't have better hallucinations than this. If Babe Ruth hadn't been real, they would've had to invent him. But then, how do you invent genius? How do you imagine the most enduring sports icon of the last century? How do you dream about perfection, and then make it come to life? Every once in a while, nature screws up and it happens.

Babe Ruth wasn't exactly handsome. He was perhaps the only human being to have a face that looked more like a bulldog than Winston Churchill. Everybody loved him for it though. And it never seemed to hinder his luck with women. At just under six-foot-two, barrel-chested, and with stovepipe legs, Ruth was imposing—Paul Bunyan with a bat. Instead of boots, a plaid shirt and a big axe, Ruth had cleats, a Yankee jersey, and a big "axe" of his own. At one time it was a fifty-six ounce bludgeon that would've taken a Paul Bunyan to chop down in the first place.

Even though he was the best-known celebrity-athlete of the Roaring Twenties, he was wholly unaffected. He knew only how to be himself, which was more than enough for most people. Describing Babe Ruth's personality and appetites as unconstrained would be like calling the Grand Canyon a ditch. Ruth did everything bigger (and generally better) than anyone else. He hit more home runs, ate more food, drank more beer, bedded more women, stayed out later, smoked more cigars, laughed louder, drove more expensive cars (that he usually wrecked), made more money, spent more money, got in more trouble, had more fun, and was the most beloved sports figure in America. He was well beyond a superstar. He was a living legend, a masterpiece, Santa Claus in a Yankee uniform, part of Americana. He could do no wrong. Even when he did, his adoring public quickly forgave him. He was bigger than life, and he knew it. He was as big and as brassy as they came. Despite all this, people identified with Babe Ruth. He was one of them—a regular guy. All too approachable and friendly, the Bambino had a real soft spot for children. He was also child-like, childish, petulant, selfish, irresponsible, immature, and totally and completely irrepressible. But as wild and raw as he was, the Babe's feet were ordinarily planted firmly on the ground—though he did get knocked off of them frequently enough, both in and out of baseball games.

He loved the limelight. He loved being the center of attention, and he usually was. Fame and adulation were not burdens for Babe Ruth—they were his fuel. If Ruth hadn't been a sports hero, he might've ended up as the strongman for a carnival, or President of the United States. It was no surprise that he was on a first-name basis with whoever was in the White House, assuming he could remember it. When the Babe met President Harding one summer, he greeted him in typical Ruth fashion by forgetting Harding's name and simply quipping, "Hot as hell, ain't it, Prez?" In 1930, when a reporter asked Ruth if he thought it was wrong that his salary was more than President Hoover's, he supposedly shot back, "Well I had a better year than he did." Whether the quote is accurate or not, the Babe in fact did have a much better year than Hoover. He hit forty-nine homers, again leading the league. Hoover was voted out of office the next election, still wondering why everyone was so upset about the Depression. Even when a president shared the spotlight with Ruth, it wasn't big enough for the both of them. Politicians were forced to give way to the more favored Bambino.

Virtually all baseball players liked George Herman Ruth, too. They couldn't help it. It was almost impossible to dislike him. A garrulous, good-natured practical joker, he was the best ball player anyone had ever seen, and just a big kid at heart. He was a perfect match for Major League baseball—which is, after all, a child's game that happens to be played by adults. Who better to be champion of the sport than Baby Huey with a magic bat?

By the time Ruth made it to professional baseball at age eighteen, he was fresh out of Saint Mary's Industrial School for Boys, in Baltimore, Maryland. He landed up there as a youthful offender when he couldn't stay out of trouble, and his parents were too busy to keep bailing him out. He was not a criminal, however, and his offenses were far from heinous—stealing change from his father's bar, for instance, and treating the local kids to ice cream. (The Bambino, of course, making sure to get his fair share.)

He was not an orphan, as was often reported and corroborated by Ruth himself. The fib was not malicious. The Babe intended to offer his story as inspiration to the real-life orphans out there. His love of children was as boundless as centerfield at Yankee Stadium.

At Saint Mary's, he fell under the influence of Father Matthias. He was probably the only person who could command the young Ruth's respect. At a towering six-six, Father Matthias, dressed in his black robes, must have commanded just about anybody's respect. Ruth, although still prone to find trouble, flourished under the good Father's guidance. When Father Matthias introduced him to baseball, George Herman Ruth found his purpose in life, his calling.

As good as he became under Father Matthias's tutelage, Big George was still not sure he was worthy of professional ball until the day he was signed by Jack Dunn, the owner of the then-minor league Baltimore Orioles. Father Matthias released Ruth into Dunn's care as an eighteen-year-old baby-man. Despite his years at the Industrial School, he was largely uneducated, unworldly, and uncouth.

That year at spring training, the veteran ballplayers were warned not to harass the big rookie. Ruth was a favorite of club-owner Dunn. Prospects in this category were referred to by the other players as Dunn's "babes." Considering Ruth's enormous size compared to the average baseball player of the time, nicknaming him "Babe" was the equivalent of calling him "Tiny." In the Babe's case, the handle not only seemed to fit, it stuck. By the next season, he was playing for the Major League Boston Red Sox.

With Ruth's emancipation from Saint Mary's and his employment as a professional ballplayer, it was like setting free a wild animal. He was ready to conquer the world. He was ready to revel in life's bounty, drain every ounce of pleasure out of it.

To Babe Ruth, every day was a great day to be alive. This contributed to his aversion to sleep. There was too much to do, experience, and enjoy in any given twenty-four hours. Sleep was a waste of time. There would be plenty of time for that when he was dead. When asked what it was like to room with Ruth on the road, a teammate once remarked, "I've never roomed with the Babe, only his suitcase."

The name "Babe" may've had a better ring to it, but it may as well have been "Bacchus." He was a hedonist of mythical proportions. Ruth made debauchery his personal art form. Married most of his baseball career, Ruth considered it only a technicality and not an obstacle to his pursuit of the fairer sex. Branding him a Lounge Lizard would be too kind. Barroom Brontosaurus was more like it.

And like most everything else about the Babe, his timing was perfect too—and not only the way he could judge a pitch and hit it out of the park. His arrival as a New York Yankee was just in time to save the entire sport of professional baseball. It's true. What else could be more fitting for the Sultan of Swat, the King of Baseball, than David coming to slay Goliath?

And the evil two-headed Goliath that Ruth of York was charged with slaying? Gambling, of course—and boredom. Or perhaps more accurately, fan complacency. Curing the boredom problem was easy for the Babe. His part in eliminating gambling was indirect, but no less important.

The boredom problem? Until 1919, baseball had largely survived as a game of finesse rather than power. The Major Leagues were lousy with so-called "Punch and Judy" hitters. Batters poked at the ball, hoping to hit it over the head of an infielder or between them for a base hit. Most home runs were not hit over the fence. The fence could be a quarter mile away. Baseball stadiums at the turn of the century were vast affairs. Many parks had large outfields with fences several hundred feet away from home plate. Some didn't really have fences—at least, not all the way around. A batter might have to hit the ball 500 feet to clear an outfield wall, if there was one. Most home runs were hit between outfielders who could then run after the ball until they faded into the horizon. The batter simply ran around the bases and scored before the ball could be retrieved and thrown back in. Because the hitter was customarily running as fast as he could, the now-familiar home run trot wasn't seen much then. Later, when new stadiums were built or old ones remodeled, they brought in the fences.

The other reason for lack of home runs in the old days was the ball. In fact, the period up to 1920 was known as the "dead ball era." The ball itself was made up of loosely coiled yarn held together by stitched cowhide. The stitching formed a horseshoe-shaped seam still used today. This early ball was not nearly as hard as the ball used after 1919. Hitting a pulpy ball for distance was like trying to run in quicksand.

Once the batter hit the dead ball, it would dent or ding it, all to the pitcher's advantage. A lopsided ball can make more crazy dips and curves than an old mountain road. Prior to 1920, umpires were instructed to keep the same ball in play as long as possible. This meant the ball would be scuffed and dirtied to the point of blackness. Players would intentionally darken the ball with tobacco spit, mud, or whatever. This was all tolerated until 1920.

Punch and Judy hitters, combined with a beanbag of a ball, made for a lot of low-scoring games. The post World War One American fan, looking forward to the prosperous and fast-paced decade ahead, found this defensive style of play, well, dull. Monotonous. Boring.

Two things changed all that in the Roaring Twenties. The first was the introduction of what was then called the "jack rabbit" ball. (Today, the ball is simply referred to as "juiced.") Unlike the dead ball, the jack rabbit ball was tightly wound and had a cork or rubber core. When hit solidly, it made a cracking sound, not the thud of the old ball. Being harder made it travel farther. Umpires were now told to replace the orb whenever it was scuffed, nicked, or sullied. The new, milky, round ball was easier to hit, and hit for distance. To the old dead-ball era players, it was like hitting a grapefruit-sized, white neon super-ball with blinking red lights. In the 1920s, batting averages rose as fast as the stock market.

The second thing to change baseball forever in 1920 was Babe Ruth. He roared right along with the Roaring Twenties, conceivably louder than anyone else. When Ruth started out in Major League ball in 1915 with the Boston Red Sox, he was a terrific left-handed pitcher. There was only one thing he could do better than pitch—and that was hit. By the 1919 season, Ruth was doing very little pitching and a lot of hitting for the Sox. He was one of the few players who could hit the old dead ball out of the park more than a few times a year. In fact, in 1919 he hit twenty-nine of them, a record he would proceed to break many times.

By 1919, the Red Sox knew Ruth was the premier hitter of the game and a fan favorite. Spectators found it more exhilarating to watch Babe Ruth strike out than to watch a series of bloop singles. Naturally, when Ruth connected for one of his trademark high-arcing home runs, the crowd went wild. Ruth was anything but a Punch and Judy hitter. He always swung from the heels. It was a big swing. It was dramatic. The fans loved it.

By this time, Ruth had taken over the title of baseball's best player from the aging miscreant, Ty Cobb. The Georgia Peach, who played most of his career during the dead-ball era, believed that both Ruth and the home run were overrated. He needled the Babe for his record number of strikeouts while maintaining that the long-ball would ruin the chess-like strategy of the game. Cobb made sure, like he did with everybody else, that the otherwise genial Bambino would grow to detest him. Ruth brushed off any comparisons with the cretin Cobb by stating, "Hell, I could hit .400 every season too if I only tried to hit them itty-bitty singles."

He was also one of the first players to use a modern-style bat—thin at the handle, with a large barrel. When he hit the ball with that bulbous club, it frequently flew out of the stadium, much to the delight of the crowd. The fans demanded more. Ruth gave it to them.

In what is still considered the worst trade of all time, Ruth was shipped to the New York Yankees, then a struggling team looking for respectability. Ruth would start the 1920 season as a New York outfielder. The die was cast for the Yankee Dynasty that followed.

What made the trade possible were the financial straits of the Red Sox owner, Harry Frazee. Old Harry's main business was that of a Broadway producer. Unlike Ruth, Frazee hadn't produced a big hit in years. He desperately needed money to subsidize his latest Broadway venture. The owners of the Yankees, Col. Jacob Ruppert and Jacob Barrow, were only too happy to accommodate Harry with cash and loans. In return, the Yankees got Ruth. The rest is legend. Ruth went on to set records in almost every offensive category, and led the Yankees to ten pennants in thirteen seasons. Baseball was no longer a dull, defensive game.

The name "Harry Frazee" remains about as popular today in Boston as the name Sherman is in Atlanta. The Boston loyalists claim the trade jinxed their franchise. There is empirical evidence to support this theory as well. Prior to the infamous trade, the Boston club was considered one of the elite teams in the league, having won several World Series, their last in 1918—the year before Ruth was sent to New York. Since the trade, Boston could not claim even one World Series until 2004. Eighty-six years was a long time, if you're a Boston Red Sox fan. The phenomenon has since been labeled "The curse of the Bambino."

Then there was the gambling problem. The other way Ruth saved baseball was to help reestablish the game's honor after the 1919 World Series fiasco. No sooner had the American public finally started to embrace the game as its national pastime than a scandal broke loose that shook baseball to its cleats: The 1919 "Black" Sox.

The 1919 Chicago White Sox were owned by Charles Comiskey, who also owned the stadium where the Sox played—Comiskey Park. Despite all his wealth, or perhaps because of it, Old Charley was a well-known cheap bastard, like many of his fellow ball club owners of the time. Only Comiskey was even more so. Before the 1919 World Series, many of the White Sox players had asked for raises on the strength of their great season. All were flatly turned down. Some even came away with salary decreases!

A pivotal group of players rebelled. In exchange for promised money from gamblers, which most of the players never saw, the Series was to be thrown by the heavily favored Sox. Word of this collusion came to light before the Series. Few took it seriously. However, when the mighty White Sox lost to a relatively weak Cincinnati club, a formal investigation was launched. The Sox' star hitter, Shoeless Joe Jackson, was implicated, along with several other players. Some of the players, Shoeless Joe included, were permanently banned from the game. A few of them were even tried in criminal court. No one was convicted. The infamous gamblers behind the scandal, Arnold Rothstein and his henchmen, were never brought to justice.

The ignoble disgrace severely tarnished and impeded baseball's budding stature as the national game. The figure of the scruffy-faced paperboy confronting Shoeless Joe Jackson with his immortal words, "Say it ain't so, Joe," left an indelible blemish on the sport and in the public's mind. After staining their own image and all of Major League baseball, the 1919 White Sox were appropriately dubbed the "Black Sox."

In order to restore the integrity of the game, the baseball owners turned to Judge Kenesaw "Mountain" Landis and elected him baseball commissioner. To say that Landis had an undistinguished career as a lawyer and a jurist would be generous. Gomez Addams was Clarence Darrow by comparison. Nonetheless, he was a world-renowned hard-ass, and that's what baseball needed—or so the owners thought. They gave Landis sweeping powers previously unheard of. He was appointed for life. Unfortunately, he was far too stubborn to die at a reasonable age.

The gruff Landis swiftly moved to solidify his authority and placed lifetime bans on the players he considered guilty or involved in the Black Sox debacle. He established rules designed to prevent future scandals. Although he was effective, Landis turned out to be a megalomaniac tyrant who ruled baseball as his private fiefdom for over two decades—kind of an American-style Rasputin. He also resolutely supported baseball's unwritten rule against hiring black players, although he publicly denied it. Ruth, Cobb, and Hornsby, among many others, would also have their run-ins with Landis.

Ruth's role in repairing the faith in the game was more oblique than Landis's, but just as vital. At the start of the 1920s, fans still had the bad taste of the Black Sox fiasco in their mouths. Ruth was like a heavy dose of Listerine. In his first season with the Yankees, he belted fifty-four home runs, which surpassed all of the old records by miles (including his own of twenty-nine a year earlier). He recaptured the imagination of the justifiably disgruntled and alienated fans. Ruth's accomplishments shortened America's memory and gave baseball a fresh start. The game needed a new hero, someone to make them forget the Black Sox. The Babe had a way of making people forget a lot of things.

George Herman Ruth created a new dimension in baseball. His fellow professionals recognized it. Some described him as a "Force of Nature," others, as the "Missing Link." Whatever the comments, they were testimony to his uniqueness and his tremendous ability. An adolescent off the field, on it he was just the opposite—a man among boys. They didn't break the mold after Babe Ruth was born. There was no mold to begin with.

His presence transcended charisma. He had a magical quality, like the purity of a child's belief in Santa Claus or a boy's love for his dog. He was the essence and heart of baseball, its elemental core, its strength.

Don Ogilvie would have to find a way to tap into that wellspring of absolute energy. The Babe, of course, was only a human force of nature at best. Ogilvie and the Alvarez family were battling, perhaps, the supreme force of nature: Death. Not even Babe Ruth in his prime could match that kind of power.

Indeed, death found its way to the Bambino's doorstep all too early. He died in 1948 at the age of fifty-three from throat cancer. Some say it was more from a broken heart when he realized he would never achieve his greatest ambition—managing a major league team. It was hard for any owner to reconcile the Babe's wild lifestyle with the discipline required for managing. As they often said of him: "How can he manage a team when he can't even manage himself?"

Still, Babe Ruth was a magical player in a magical game. For some reason, baseball has always had a streak of magic in it. Nothing gives itself more to real drama than baseball. Yeah, there are thousands of uneventful contests every year. Then there are games that become something more. The crowd, the stakes, and the heroics of the players can make it extraordinary. A few of these games have a chance to be mystical, mythical, so elevated that there is no longer a game but a study in life. Ascribing a supernatural, cosmic quality to baseball may seem grandiose or maybe absurd. But not when it comes to Babe Ruth. Consider two examples:

One is Ruth's controversial "called shot" home run hit against Chicago Cub pitcher Charlie Root in the third game of the 1932 World Series. It's still talked about and disputed today. Did he point toward the centerfield fence and then promptly smack the pill out of the park? The motion was plainly made and the home run just as surely hit, yet was it a called shot? Probably not, but no matter. Such stuff became the fodder of the Babe Ruth legend even while he played.

An earlier fable was Ruth's alleged promise to hit a World Series home run for a hospitalized kid by the name of Johnny Sylvester. In the fourth game of the 1926 World Series, Ruth hit three home runs, supposedly for little Johnny. The roused ten year-old soon rebounded, his injuries wondrously overcome. The press ate it up, some implying that the Bambino's drives actually saved little Johnny's life. Many say Ruth never even knew Johnny Sylvester existed until after that game— and they're probably right. Still, there can be no doubt that little Johnny's belief that the Babe hit those homers for him raised his sinking spirits and inspired his recovery. Such is the might of a child's faith and the Bambino's wizardry.

Whatever the truth, the myth and parable surrounding the Babe during his playing days and continuing long after his death are without precedent. There are many such stories about Babe Ruth. No player in the history of the game has garnered such folklore. With Ruth, the line between reality and fiction was always blurred. This would seem to make him a natural for the ethereal realm of Limbotown.

Don Ogilvie and Roberto Alvarez would need genuine magic from Babe Ruth if they were to stand a chance against Death Personified, Doctor Drummond. They could only hope that little Roberto would be Ruth's real Johnny Sylvester. This time, the Babe's daring could save a child's life instead of just giving a sick kid hope. Babe Ruth did not need to give Roberto hope. If hope were the cure for his leukemia, Roberto would soon be healthy on his own. Nevertheless, Don Ogilvie knew that a Babe Ruth home run in Limbotown at the right moment could do so much more for little Roberto than it did for little Johnny Sylvester. It could save Roberto's life.

The pressure this might put on a mortal ballplayer would perhaps be too great a load. Not for the Babe. He welcomed pressure; he craved it like a cold beer on a hot day. He wanted to be at the plate when the game was on the line. He loved the challenge. And more often than not, he delivered. Sure he missed opportunities now and then, proving he was, after all, human (despite rumors to the contrary). But then the exalted status of Babe Ruth was not conceived by these rare exceptions. It was founded on his uncanny knack for getting more big hits in more big games than anyone could ever remember. If you ask a youngster, even today, who was the most famous baseball player of all time, you always get the same answer: Babe Ruth.

Don Ogilvie and little Roberto Alvarez desperately wished that Babe Ruth would also be their answer. He was Casey at the Bat who didn't strike out. He brought joy to Mudville, New York City, and all of America. Would Limbotown be next?

Chapter 8

Don Ogilvie approached Babe Ruth's table with equal parts awe and apprehension. He wondered if he should say anything about the Babe calling him "Ovaltine." "It's a pleasure to meet you, Babe," said a star-struck Ogilvie adding, ". . . and, by the way, I'm not named after a cup of hot chocolate. The name's Ogilvie. Please call me Don." They shook hands.

Maggie pretended to be busy behind the bar. She pretended not to be interested in what was going on or what was being said. In truth, she was hanging on every word or nod of a head. She was very curious to see how Don Ogilvie was going to fare.

"Yeah, sorry about the name. I'm not good with 'em," said an honest Ruth to Ogilvie. "Have a seat," the Babe said in between bites and swallows of the spread that lay before him. Ogilvie took the empty chair next to him.

Ruth and the rest of the players in his group were in white shirt sleeves, some with odd-looking, quaint ties, mostly hand-painted stuff, like 'nose art' on a WWII bomber. No coats or jackets. Seeing Ruth up close confirmed the nobody-manager's worst fears. The Babe was old, out of shape, and horribly dissolute. Except for the bulldog face, Ogilvie could've been looking into a mirror. Ruth offered him some food and drink. Ogilvie politely declined. He asked Ruth straight out, "How old are you, Babe?"

Ruth, unperturbed, replied, "I don't know. I don't keep track of them things. All I know is, it's 1935 where I come from and I'm missing a game today." At least Ogilvie was able to determine that the Babe was still playing, although to what effect remained to be seen.

Ogilvie got right to the point. "I hear you guys don't want to come to practice. Is that true?"

Ruth scanned the table, which included most of the remaining white players, and said, "We got a number of problems here. But first of all, let me say we're sorry about that kid. Too bad about that illness. You know I like kids too. A lot. What is he, anyway, Puerto Rican or somethin'? Anyhow, we can't play with the nig . . . I mean the darkies over there—even if we wanted to. Commissioner Landis would have our asses. Probably suspend us, or even throw us out of the game for good. I don't know. Ain't that right, Hornsby?" said Ruth, asking for support from the smug Cardinal second baseman.

Hornsby faced Ogilvie and repeated, "That's right."

The Babe went on. "And of course, we're not getting paid. Yeah, this hotel and saloon are nice, but we gotta have money. We're pros. We get paid for this kinda stuff."

It was clear to Don Ogilvie that the Landis threat was a convenient excuse. The real heart of the problem was race, plain and simple. Money might have had something to do with it too, but not nearly as much.

Ogilvie was stymied by his limited knowledge of baseball history. He knew that exhibition games between professional black and white teams took place all the time during Ruth's era. Strangely enough, these games had been allowed by "Emperor" Landis until about 1943. Nonetheless, Old Landis felt this was a way to continue to keep the leagues separate. If the blacks had their own league, why would they need to play in the whites' league? "Separate but equal" was the widely held belief of the day. Separate but unequal was the reality. Although Ogilvie couldn't recall any integrated teams of the time, he couldn't understand what would make it such a big deal. But it was a big deal.

What made it even harder for Ogilvie to understand was that Ruth himself had often been the victim of racial taunts. This was well known. Even though the Bambino's lineage was mainly German, there was no getting around it—he did have black features. His complexion was

112

ruddy and brown, his lips fuller than most, and his nose could only be described as flat and pug. He was often called "nigger-lips," or just "nigger" by some of his less-refined opponents. And Ruth, unlike Hornsby, was not known as an unbending segregationist. Ogilvie believed all this might make him a little more open to the idea of playing with the Negro League players. Evidently not.

There was little question in the nobody-manager's mind that the square-jawed Hornsby was behind the whole rebellion. The other players were going along with him. Hornsby selected Ruth as their spokesman to deflect attention away from himself. Ruth probably did believe Hornsby's yarn that Commissioner Landis would suspend him.

Ironically, as Ogilvie would later learn, Hornsby hated Landis and would've done just about anything to piss him off—except play with black ballplayers. That was the one thing that Hornsby and Landis agreed on. Otherwise, the handsome Hornsby was well-known as a heavy gambler, rumored even to have bet on his own games. Landis, having been hired to abolish gambling in baseball, had had his share of confrontations with Rogers Hornsby. Generally, Hornsby came out on the short end of the bat. Despite this, none of Hornsby's indiscretions kept him out of the Hall of Fame. His wagering reputedly made Pete Rose look like a church-going bingo novice.

Ogilvie hoped the on-field combination of Ruth and Hornsby would be like "thunder and lightning." Perhaps that would come to pass. He could see that off the field he would be dealing with a different type of storm. The rookie manager's negotiation with Ruth and Hornsby was more like trying to bargain with the Town Drunk and the Village Idiot.

Trying to play it straight, Ogilvie set out to assure the Babe and the rest of his party about the Commissioner Landis nonsense. "Don't worry, Babe—we're well out of Landis's jurisdiction here. The only guy you got to worry about is the Final Commissioner—Death . . . Doctor Drummond."

Ruth was skeptical. He quipped, "If that little bastard is Death, I'm Santa Claus."

Not Ruth or even Ogilvie saw the parallels between the Babe and Old Saint Nick. But there were others in the Hotel Limbotown who did.

Both were American originals. Just as baseball evolved from English cricket and other stickball games, Santa Claus sprang from the European version. Americans added the red suit, the flying reindeer, the name "Santa Claus" and claimed Saint Nick as their own. Americans have always claimed baseball and Ruth as their own. Both Ruth and Santa wore "uniforms." Both loved children and loved making them happy. Both were big and jolly. Both remain as fabled figures, confusing the line between fact and fantasy. And both have been credited with performing minor miracles. Both are held sacred and beloved by their followers, and they still receive fan mail. What makes that even more astounding is that most people are reasonably sure that Babe Ruth, unlike Elvis for instance, is dead. Santa Claus is pretty much immune to things like death. Santa should be receiving fan mail.

Admittedly, Santa Claus was not known as a womanizing carouser like Ruth. Then again, we don't know much about Santa's personal life. He could retreat to the North Pole in the off-season without people beating a path to his door. Not that they didn't want to. The North Pole was a tough place to get to, and Santa would already be busy getting ready for the next Christmas.

Ruth, on the other hand, enjoyed basking in the adulation of his admirers, and particularly children, any time or any place. The press never played up the skirt-chasing, heavy-drinking angle, of course. They considered a player's private life, well, private—a novel concept by today's standards. It was always Ruth's charitable, Santa Claus-like generosity and his unrivaled affection for kids that made it into the news. His other extra-curricular activities were benevolently overlooked.

Ogilvie was still trying to deal with the race issue, and the ridiculous notion that "Attila the Hun" Landis would suspend the white players if they played with the black players.

Ogilvie appealed to Ruth and the others. "I guarantee all of you, Landis won't suspend you, fine you—or even find out about this."

Ruth was doubtful. "How do you know that?"

Ogilvie shot back, "I know, because where I come from it's the year 2000. I know the history of baseball, and I know that no such thing ever happened." Actually, he remembered only a little baseball history.

114

But the new manager sensed he might be on to something, so he continued his thought. "Look, all of you guys must've figured out by now that you're all from different years, different times. I'm from a time that I can tell you everything that's going to happen in your lives. Because where I come from, it's already happened."

The players glanced at each other knowingly. They had indeed discovered and figured out they were all from different times. That was one of the things they hadn't been able to explain or understand. Limbotown was another.

Ruth turned back to Ogilvie and, in a hushed voice, confessed, "I gotta own up—it was a real jolt seein' ol' Matty again."

The Matty Babe was referring to, of course, was Christy Mathewson. He sat one table removed from Ruth's bunch, and was quietly taking in the proceedings. The bright, college educated pitcher could see his untimely death in the faces of the other players. Like Ruth, many came from some time after 1925, the year of Matty's death. The easy-going right-hander was held in such high esteem by the other players that no one had come right out and told him. But he knew.

It had only vaguely dawned on Ogilvie that these time anomalies would naturally occur having players whose lives jointly spanned the century. He spied a grinning Lou Gehrig. He didn't know yet. Ogilvie discreetly sized up Josh Gibson and Roy Campanella, sitting with Paige and the others. They didn't have a clue either.

As if a switch went off in his head, Ruth declared to Ogilvie, "Hey, then you can tell me who I'm gonna manage for after I retire."

Ogilvie did know the answer to that one. He was opening his mouth, about to tell Ruth his future, when he finally got his first good idea since being in Limbotown. In fact, it was the first good idea he had since befriending the Alvarez family. Ogilvie had come up with a way to lure the white players into playing with the black players—and with no money involved. There was a certain risk to the plan, but it was still ingenious.

Ogilvie swallowed his answer to Ruth as if he'd gulped down his spiked coffee. Instead, he offered to all the players, "I've got a proposition for you gentlemen. I'll tell any of you anything you want to know about your future, on one condition: We're going to have a little game between you guys and the Negro League players. If you win, I have to tell you anything you want to know. You don't have to play or practice or anything after that. But if you lose, then we're all going to be playing on the same team. We're going to practice together. And we're going to play Drummond's team in a seven-game series."

Everyone at the table was speechless. Ogilvie had really given them something to think about—a chance to see their futures. No matter what Drummond had told them about not remembering anything after leaving Limbotown, this was too tempting. Even the hard-line racist, Rogers Hornsby, seemed interested.

Ogilvie could have just offered outright to tell Ruth and the others their destinies as bait to play with the Negro Leaguers. However, that alone wouldn't have been enough to seal the deal. Once they found out what they wanted from him, they would do as they pleased. In the end, it would've been patronizing. It wouldn't have lasted more than a few days. There was nothing to bind the agreement, no mortar to hold the bricks together. These hard-bitten pros needed an excuse to set aside their bigotry. A contest between the two sides could do it. Then it would be a matter of honor to live up to one's promise. He knew the word of these players meant something to them. That was the kind of cement Ogilvie was looking for. That was also the risk. If the white players won, there would be little he could do to make them play.

Ogilvie stood up and said, "You guys talk it over. I need to discuss this with the Negro players."

He left Ruth and the others to argue while he strode to the other side of the dining room where the black players were sitting. They appeared even more seditious than Ruth or Hornsby.

As he walked, Ogilvie was beginning to realize the importance of the reference books in his clubhouse office. He and Antonio had barely used them in picking their team. Now he knew the information in them would be invaluable. Without question, if the white players won, they'd be all over him for the answers he said he had. He was counting on that not happening. It would mean he'd failed to unite the team, trimming little Roberto's chance to live and, ironically, his chance to die. Of course, if the white players lost, he didn't have to say anything. No matter the outcome, the stuff in the books would help him understand his players: their lives, their reasons, their strengths, their weaknesses. Ogilvie knew that a large part of managing was being a student of human nature, something he forgot when he picked this team. He figured managing should be much easier with the advantage of a rear-view mirror. He had a lot of reading to do. He was looking forward to it.

Just as Drysdale and Clemente had said, the black players looked like they expected to be going somewhere. Their packed bags stood next to their chairs, and they had their jackets on. They had little food in front them, mostly coffee and rolls.

Their hierarchy had already been set. Satchel Paige was clearly the leader, followed by the less vocal Josh Gibson, the home run hitting machine. They sat together at the head of the table. Jackie Robinson, the first black player in modern Major League history, quietly stewed a few seats down. Next to him sat his Brooklyn Dodger teammate, catcher Roy Campanella.

Robinson and Campanella were from 1953, several years after Robinson had broken the color barrier. Since all of the other black players were from a time when baseball was still segregated, Robinson and Campanella were sort of considered freaks. The old Negro Leaguers didn't completely trust them, although they had been a valuable source of information, like confirming Drummond's claim that baseball went interracial in 1947. Robinson and Campanella even told Paige that he would finally make it to the Major Leagues himself in 1948 (at God knows what age) as a Cleveland Indian. But for Satchel Paige, it was still 1935, not 1948.

Knowing that baseball would one day be totally open just increased the frustration and anger of Paige and his teammates. Hornsby had seen to it that word was passed along to the black players that there was no way in Hell he was going to allow them to play with Ruth and the others. This insult, in the face of certain future integration, was too much for the old Negro Leaguers to take. If they weren't wanted, they didn't want to play, and they didn't want to stick around. Once Ogilvie sized up the problem, he found a way to deal with it.

117

The nobody-manager stood before Paige and the others and confidently stated, "Gentlemen, for those of you who didn't hear it yesterday, my name is Don Ogilvie. I'm going to be your skipper for the next eight weeks. All of you were handpicked to be on this team by my assistant, Antonio, and me. I'm familiar with all of your great careers. It's a pleasure to have you aboard."

The old Negro Leaguers were mildly pleased to find that this self-proclaimed white manager was treating them with some deference. But Satchel Paige, for one, was not about to be thrown off track by this little maneuver. Paige said, "Yeah, well it great you happy to have us here, but not everybody feel dat way. If the white players don't wanna play with us, we don' wanna play with dem."

Ogilvie said, "Well it's not all the white players. Mostly the ones from before 1947—and I think even some of them would like to play with you guys. They just don't want to admit it. You gotta understand they come from a time when things were different."

Paige fired back, "Yeah, well most of us come from that time too."

Seeing he wasn't making any headway, Ogilvie got right to the point. "Look, I'm arranging a little game with the white players to settle this whole thing. All you guys have to do is win, and then we all play together as one team."

Paige asked, "What makes you think we'd wanna play with 'em after beatin' 'em? You know we beat white teams like this before, a lot of times, too. And what makes you think they gonna play with us, specially if we whup their asses good?"

Ogilvie knew that the old Negro Leaguers wanted nothing more than to play with the white Major Leaguers, even if they were bigots. They wanted it more than Eliot Ness wanted Al Capone. It was their dream since the Negro Leagues were formed. And, it was true the Negro League teams more often beat the white teams in exhibition games. In fact, Ogilvie was counting on it this time. He knew Paige was speaking with battered pride when he threatened that the black players wouldn't want to play with the white players. He understood the real question in Paige's and the others mind's was whether the white players would honor such a bet. Or would they further humiliate the black players by losing, and then welsh on their promise to play together?

Ogilvie was even more confident now. "Don't worry about that," he said. "I've got some leverage if I need to use it, but I don't think I'll have to. I really get the feeling these guys will stand by their word, even if it doesn't go their way."

"Can you guarantee it?" Paige demanded.

"I can," said Don Ogilvie, getting Paige's attention. He reasoned that he could always toss the white players tidbits about their futures even if they lost, on the condition that they all played together anyhow. Of course that might not work on all of them. Still, he honestly believed the white players would keep their promise, even if they lost; and no further enticement would be necessary—only a sense of honor. Nevertheless, knowing his players' destinies would be a potent tool for manager Don Ogilvie.

"Another thing to think about," Ogilvie continued. "There's no way out of this place. I'm sure you guys already know that. Limbotown doesn't have a train station. You and your bags aren't going anywhere. Besides, I'll bet this is the nicest hotel any of you have stayed in, and the best ballpark you've ever seen." Their silence exposed them.

Ogilvie wrapped it up. "Look, you guys talk it over. I'm going to talk to Ruth and set a time for this game. I'll be right back." He walked away. A big quarrel broke out.

As the nobody-manager engaged in his shuttle diplomacy between the two sides, he knew there would be a game. He was feeling so positive about it that he ventured a look at Maggie. Catching her eye unexpectedly, he winked at her, not to be outdone by the romantic Babe Ruth. To his delight, she smiled like a schoolgirl and blushed. Whether he realized it or not, he was finally doing something to impress Maggie Briggs. She could see there was going to be a game too.

Ruth and the others were still carping as Ogilvie arrived. Dissension was rife among the ranks. As Ogilvie suspected, the support for Hornsby and Ruth was melting away faster than the polar ice caps.

At the second table sat Christy Mathewson, Dizzy Dean, and Cy Young, all pitchers. Dean, the affable, fire-balling right-hander from

Kentucky, was already a great admirer of Satchel Paige, having faced off against him in white versus black, all-star exhibition games. A native Southerner, Dean considered Satchel the best pitcher in baseball. Far from shy, he regaled his fellow pitchers with tales of Paige's blazing heat and his magic "hesitation" pitch. Mathewson and Young came from the early nineteen hundreds. Paige wasn't around yet. They were duly struck by the enthusiastic hyperbole of Dean's exaggerations. Mathewson, a thinking man, was terribly aware of his newly discovered mortality, having learned of his premature death only hours earlier. It now made little difference to him the color of the players he played with. He saw this only as an opportunity to play with the best, against the best. The modest and self-effacing Cy Young just wanted to see Satchel Paige pitch. The Ohio-born Denton True "Cyclone" Young wanted to know if the gushing Dizzy Dean was telling the truth about Paige.

At Ruth's table sat the rest: Gehrig, Carl Hubbell, Honus Wagner, Jimmie Foxx, Pie Traynor, and the mutineer, Rogers Hornsby. Hornsby had been outflanked. The only dispute Ruth and the others had was whether Ogilvie could prove his boast to tell the future. If he could, they were playing and that was that.

As Ogilvie walked up to the noisy bunch, Ruth had his same query: "Who am I gonna manage for after I retire? If you can tell me that, we'll play the Negro Leaguers. And if we win, you have to tell any of us anything we want to know."

"And if you lose," Ogilvie was fast to remind, "we all play together as one team." The talking stopped. Ogilvie demanded, "Do I have everyone's word of honor on this as a man and a ballplayer?" Then Ogilvie turned to Rogers Hornsby and asserted himself, "And that means you too, Hornsby."

The smoldering Cardinal second baseman seemed as if he really had smoke coming out of his ears. His face was red and sweaty from embarrassment, and it did appear as though steam was rising from his head like a boiling teapot. He knew he was beat. What made it all the more humbling was that he realized there was nothing he could do about it. He had no choice but to go along, or look even more foolish when the others outvoted him. They looked to Hornsby to see if he would finally give in. He was too angry to speak. He only tilted his head up and down one time. The rest of the players voiced their hearty approval. Ruth and the rest spun in their chairs to look at Ogilvie. Could this guy know their futures? They wanted to find out. The nobody-manager had their complete attention now.

"Okay, we've got a deal," said Ogilvie. He had to pause a moment and gather himself before he went on. "You're not going to like what I have to tell you, Babe. The truth is, you don't get hired to manage any Major League team."

You can imagine the tremendous pride of a Babe Ruth. After he retired from the field, managing was his only goal in life. As the best player in baseball, he expected it. That Ruth was never tapped to skipper a major league team turned out to be his biggest disappointment. Throughout his career, he was saddled with his well-deserved reputation: How could he manage a Major League team when he couldn't even manage himself? It was a rhetorical question.

Ogilvie's answer was like an arrow through Ruth's heart. Sometimes truth can be the sharpest weapon of all. A whine arose from the players, some grumbling and expressions of doubt. It was of such a small scale that it scarcely concealed their feigned disbelief. If the modern-era players knew the truth, they weren't saying—and the Babe didn't trust them anyhow.

Ruth sat in stunned silence for a second or two, then burst out, "Bullshit! You're lyin'! You don't know the future! Of course I'm gonna manage. It'll probably be the Yankees too!"

Ogilvie's new-found confidence deserted him instantly. How was he going to prove to Ruth and the rest that he was telling the truth? He hadn't thought about that. Should he have just lied to the Babe and told him he was going to manage? Most of the players wouldn't have known the difference. And Ruth would've believed him if he'd lied. He was again rudely reminded about thinking things through. He instinctively looked toward Maggie and the answer popped into his head—he hoped.

Ogilvie's reply was sympathetic, even empathetic, "Look, Babe, I know you don't believe me. I wouldn't believe me either if I were in

121

your shoes . . . but would you believe Maggie?" This question caught both Ruth and Maggie Briggs off guard.

The Babe gestured at the ravishing redhead and said the only thing he could, "If this be-u-ti-ful woman says she knows the answer then I take her word as gospel. But I don't think she knows the answer."

Ogilvie took a gamble that she knew Ruth's history, or would back him up if she didn't. He put Maggie on the spot. A hard inside slider was coming right at her. But it was what he saw in her eyes, so he went with it.

She kind of cleared her throat and began speaking. The normally poised and exquisite Maggie Briggs was a bit uneasy. "Well, Mr. Ruth, I, ah, do know the answer to your question." The one second she took to breathe before continuing seemed an eternity to both Ruth and Ogilvie. "I'm afraid Don . . . Mr. Ogilvie is telling the truth. You're not going to manage a Major League team." Maggie did not enjoy delivering bad news, nor could she lie.

Don Ogilvie's relief was nothing compared to Babe Ruth's shame. He had not only agreed to accept Maggie's word, he now had to suffer the consequences of it, even if she was wrong. Truth or not, the other players had heard the words. Ruth would not be a Major League manager. The words were true.

Ogilvie broke what was becoming an awkward pause. "Well, Babe, you can manage a Major League team. This one," he said waving to the other players at Ruth's table. "I'm going to manage the black players in the game we're playing tomorrow. Game time is one o'clock."

Ruth was still reeling from shock. Nevertheless, he somehow mustered his usual bravado. "We'll be there, Ovaltine. You just make sure your team shows up."

Having gotten the white players to agree to play the black players, Ogilvie thought the hard part was over. Now all he had to do was sew up the deal with Paige and his bunch. He wasn't worried about that. Soon he would have to worry about a bigger problem—making sure the black players won. He thought he had the edge there too. Ruth was in miserable shape, and a lot of the white team consisted of pitchers. They would have to play positions they weren't accustomed to. Plus, their pride and quest for respect would push the black players. But the outcome was far from decided. Once the two teams squared off, it would be a battle to the finish.

Ogilvie didn't have a Plan B. If his team lost, a few of the white players might join with them, assuming the black squad still wanted to play. He knew his strategy was putting little Roberto's life on the line well before the seven-game series against Drummond and Cobb. The stakes were huge. Ogilvie was not a riverboat gambler by nature. He was forced into the role by circumstance and had little choice. He knew if he didn't take a chance now, Roberto would have no chance later. He was beginning to appreciate Drummond's and Maggie's warning that "this isn't going to be easy." And if the black players won, there was still no guarantee of harmony—only a promise to play together, not a promise to get along.

Even Major League managers in the year 2000 had to deal with this kind of thing. Clubhouses and their cliques were often divided along color and cultural lines—Latin players in one group, and the blacks and whites in their own. It was long established that a successful team didn't have to get along off the field as long as they played like a team on it. Even all-white or all-black teams could have problems. The boundaries of clashing personalities and mammoth egos were not restricted by race. Playing like a team would be all Ogilvie could strive for. He hoped he would at least get the chance to try.

The brouhaha with Paige and his crowd came to an abrupt halt as Ogilvie advanced on their table. It had already been decided that they would play, as long as the white team kept their promise to play *with* the Negro Leaguers. They waited to hear what Ogilvie was going to say. He addressed the watchful group. "Gentlemen, we have a game tomorrow at one o'clock."

Paige spoke for the group. "We'll be there. But if you can't deliver on your promise about playin' together if we win, you be seeing a lot of sittin' aroun' 'til we get outta this place."

"I'll deliver. You guys just win." Then Ogilvie threw Paige a curve. "Mind if I manage you guys tomorrow?"

This was something that the Negro Leaguers hadn't thought about.

Fortunately, Paige found the novelty of it humorous. He didn't consult with his teammates before answering. "Sure, we don't mind that, if you don't manage us to lose."

Ogilvie had a ready answer for Paige. "I'm handing the ball to the best pitcher in the game—and that's what Dizzy Dean over there thinks too. That ought to make my job easier."

A broad grin creased the face of Satchel Paige. He was gratified that at least two white men recognized his abilities. Ogilvie's opinion didn't carry much weight, but the opinion of the white, Southern flamethrower did.

"We be at the clubhouse around ten to suit up an' get loose. Okay?"

"Okay," said the pleased nobody-manager.

Ogilvie walked away. He was headed back to Drummond Field to find the Alvarezes and tell them the exciting news. As he stepped past the bar, Maggie made sure he noticed her. This time she winked at him. She felt he'd earned some encouragement. He couldn't help but smile and nod at her. The little wink was more comforting than a warm mug of Ovaltine.

Chapter 9

As he left the Hotel Limbotown, Don Ogilvie noticed that his step seemed to have more bounce in it than he could recall since his Achilles tendon snapped like an old rubber band some twenty-five years earlier. Back then he was young and going to the Majors. Of course his step was going to have a little more spring in it. No, his old injury had not disappeared. Don Ogilvie just felt good—better than perhaps he should. He hadn't enjoyed any kind of vindication in decades. Now he wanted to savor his momentary triumph of arranging a contest between the black and white players, and hope it would carry over to the game tomorrow. He looked up to enjoy a beautiful sunny day in Limbotown, except for one thing. Again, there were no clouds to be seen, which was not so unusual. But he searched the sky in vain. There simply was no sun. That was unusual. He knew by the clocks at the hotel that it was almost noon. Surely if the sun shone in Limbotown it would be out and visible now. It wasn't. Whatever caused the light in this strange little burg sure didn't come from a huge mass of fiery gases. He made a mental note to ask Drummond about this.

He was still pondering the "let there be light" quandary as he arrived at the outside entrance of the visitors' clubhouse. The door was open. He made his way through the empty clubhouse, out the dugout and onto the field. There were Clemente, Drysdale, DiMaggio, Mantle, and a delirious Antonio Alvarez playing catch. Little Roberto and Maria were watching from the grass near the visitors' on-deck circle.

They'd left for Drummond Field shortly after Ogilvie arrived at the hotel.

The small group paused to consider the would-be manager. He was alone. They all assumed he had failed in his bid to retrieve his team. But the Alvarez family, at least, knew him well enough to notice the Quixotic smile on his face. Little Roberto was positive his best friend had not failed at all. He grabbed the old outfielder's glove Don had given him (which had made it to Limbotown clutched to his chest, as it was every night) and rushed toward him saying, "They're coming, aren't they!"

Don said nothing just long enough to make his answer seem uncertain. Then he knelt, picked up Roberto, and replied, "Yeah, they sure are. But first we've got to win a game tomorrow, Roberto. We're going to manage the black players in a game against Ruth and the white players. If we win, then everyone's agreed to play together against Ty Cobb's team."

Roberto was disconcerted. He asked, "Why does there have to be a black team and a white team? And why would the black team have to win?"

Don Ogilvie didn't anticipate having to spell out the intricacies of racial politics to his young friend. He searched for an answer but couldn't come up with a decent one. He tried explaining anyhow. "Things were different back then, Roberto. It's not like now, where everyone plays together. People didn't understand then that all folks are pretty much alike and nobody's better than anybody else. They didn't know that because they didn't give themselves a chance to be with each other, play with each other on the same team, like we do now. I know it's hard to understand, but you're gonna have to try. Some of these guys aren't going to like you or your mom and dad just because you're Hispanic."

Little Roberto's face filled with puzzlement. Don grimaced, thinking his remarks too pointed for a seven-year-old.

By this time, Antonio and the players had stopped throwing and walked over to join Don, Maria, and little Roberto. They heard what was being said. Roberto Clemente dropped to one knee and offered some advice to his troubled namesake. The Puerto Rican accent was thick, but the message was clear. "You gonna meet all kinda deefferent

126

people in you life, Roberto. Mose of 'em you be able to get along weez. Some people no gonna like you no matter what. Even if you never done anyting to 'em before and even if you never meet 'em before, dey steel not gonna like you. That jeest the way it is and may not be much you can do about eet. Eet really don matter cuz eet not your problem, eet theirs. All you can do ees be yourself."

Don Drysdale, the big Dodger right-hander, added, "You know, Roberto, we wouldn't be here this morning if we weren't going to play for you. We don't need a game to decide that." Clemente and the all-too-young-looking Mickey Mantle nodded their heads in agreement. DiMaggio barely tilted his head up and down once to signal his assent.

Ogilvie appreciated the support, but made a strange request. "Well, that may be so, guys, but I'm going to ask you to play with Ruth's team tomorrow. Of course, Clemente and Robinson will play with the Negro Leaguers. I don't want to give Ruth and his bunch any excuses to back out or change their minds if they lose. That means you'll all have to play to win. I know I'm taking a big chance. I just don't see it any other way." Ogilvie urged his small group of Hall of Famers: "Will you do that for Roberto and us?" They all said "sure" or "yeah," except for the taciturn Joe DiMaggio, who blinked a couple of times. Everyone took that as a "yes."

Ogilvie, realizing he hadn't been formally introduced to the great Yankee Clipper, reached out his hand and said, "Joe, I'm Don Ogilvie. It's a pleasure to have you here. Have you met the Alvarez family?" Joltin' Joe cautiously shook Ogilvie's hand and curtly said, "Yeah," at least affirming his ability to speak.

The nobody-manager recalled the DiMaggio biography that he had read the night before. It began with a photograph of the intense, enigmatic Yankee Clipper. The book unfolded by juxtaposing Ruth and DiMaggio. It was like comparing Robin Williams with the Pope: unlimited quantities of random energy and chaos versus staid ritual and powerful, dogmatic control.

If Babe Ruth was the magic of baseball, Joe DiMaggio was its mystique. Both were Hall of Fame outfielders for the Yankees. That's

127

where the similarity ended. Two personalities could have hardly been more different. And yet baseball fans universally revere them both.

Ruth was as rough and unrefined as a gravel pit. DiMaggio was as smooth as glass. Ruth was boisterous, crude, and gregarious. DiMaggio was nearly a mute. Most people could have a better conversation with the Sphinx.

The Babe very rarely made plans about anything, on or off the baseball diamond. If he did, he usually forgot them anyhow. DiMaggio's ventures into public, whether social or business, was deliberate, calculated, and measured. He was about as spontaneous as a Sunday sermon.

Ruth loved his fans and loved being around them. DiMaggio, like Garbo, wanted to be (left) alone. He cherished his privacy like a pirate treasures his loot. He also cherished his loot, hoarding it like Scrooge. Ruth got rid of money like it was carrying the plague.

The Bambino had an innate trust for life, people, and the game of baseball. Joltin' Joe was cautious, paranoid, and cloistered.

It was DiMaggio who, in 1936, "replaced" Ruth in the Yankee outfield. As different as they were, baseball fans recognized them both as something special—Ruth, for his openness, his big heart, his big bat, and even his big mouth; and DiMaggio, in spite of his detached and imperious demeanor. What they could do on a baseball field made them heroes. Their unbelievable skills and inborn ability to make the big plays—this they had in common. This in turn accounted for their appeal even if their opposite traits endowed each with a very different charisma. Their personalities wrapped their baseball gifts. The public was as eager to embrace the wrappers, opposite as they were, as much as the gifts.

And DiMaggio's baseball gifts were, to say the least, formidable. He was a superb center fielder. The Yankee Clipper, as he was dubbed, set sail in the outfield like Rommel patrolled North Africa. His silky, loping stride enabled him to chase down virtually any ball. With Yankee Stadium's seemingly endless center field, this was no small wonder. Amazing grace masked his speed. Deceptively fast, his running was so fluid it appeared effortless. It was baseball ballet. Just when you thought the ball would whiz into the gap or hit the wall, there would be the

Yankee Clipper with a mid-air pirouette to rob the batter of a hit. Once he got to a ball, he could return it to the infield with the force and accuracy of a small howitzer. He didn't have a rifle for an arm, he had a cannon. DiMaggio also employed his swift moves on the base paths, often turning singles into doubles, doubles into triples, and stealing bases in between.

His baseball mystique was born fully formed in 1941, as if spawned from the forehead of Zeus, by a record that is less likely to be broken than any other record in sports history: The insuperable fifty-six game hitting streak. It is an achievement no one has come close to since the right-handed DiMaggio did it himself. Even Ruth's home run records, once believed untouchable (both career and single season) have been breached. The DiMaggio baseball mystique? He did something no one will ever do again. Setting a record that cannot be broken passes through the door of fame and claims the mantle of greatness. There was no better year for Joe DiMaggio than 1941, the Year of the Streak. It was the season that would make him a living legend, and the decades would transform into immortality.

There are at least two other baseball records in this class: pitcher Cy Young's career win total of 514, and Rogers Hornsby's modern batting average apex of .424. Yes, these now-unattainable credentials carry perhaps the same baseball mystique as DiMaggio's hitting streak. But no, these guys didn't have the same personal charisma as Joe did. He was both stone-faced and mystic, a combination that seemed to suit DiMaggio as well as his fans.

In the pre-World War Two days of America, Joe D captured the imagination of the public and kindly distracted it from the horrible carnage and heartbreak that would soon follow. They even wrote songs about the baseball heroics of Joltin' Joe DiMaggio. Like many other ball players who joined the armed forces, Joe also lost valuable baseball time to the war.

Born to a large, Italian fishing family in the San Francisco Bay area, his father wanted him to join the family business. Joe D on a fishing boat was like Frankenstein with fire—not a good mix. Poppa's opposition to baseball miraculously vanished when the money started rolling in. All the DiMaggio boys were now encouraged to play ball. Two of his brothers, Dom and Vince, also made it to the big leagues, consigned to playing in the long shadow cast by their famous sibling. They didn't mind. Joe's luminescence reflected well on the entire DiMaggio clan.

As a kid, he was a loner. It could take years for him to develop a friendship, which he did about as often as Haley's Comet buzzed by. He was as careful as a Chernobyl clean-up worker. If a friend did anything to fail the Yankee Clipper, he was dropped from the roster faster than a bumbling rookie. Once you made it on the DiMaggio shit-list, you never made it off. It was Joe's rule. You only got one chance and one mistake. No exceptions. Trust was not a word in his vocabulary. He did, however, rely on the sanctity of the DiMaggio family, often conferring with his parents and brothers for counsel and advice.

In 1936, he was only a twenty-one-year-old rookie, and already expected by Yankee fans to be the team's next savior. His ballyhooed play for the minor league San Francisco Seals preceded him. He did not disappoint, although he almost didn't get there. In a bizarre foreshadowing of the chronic injuries that would vex DiMaggio throughout his career, he injured his knee while exiting a taxi. Most teams would've disposed of him quicker than you could say "damaged goods." A great deal of Joe's game was based on his speed. Without it, he was lost. As it turned out for the Yankees, they guessed right. The knee healed, and DiMaggio became a star his first season.

Joe, as the emerging leader of the Yanks, had many personality traits in common with the taciturn Lou Gehrig, whose fateful departure from baseball and life soon followed DiMaggio's arrival. Joe D provided continuity after the Iron Horse's farewell by having the same style as Gehrig. He wasn't trying to copy the master—it was truly his way too. DiMaggio or Gehrig would isolate and freeze out their prey. An icy stare or haughty disregard was their way to communicate umbrage. They were men of few words. For them it was a very effective technique.

DiMaggio's teammates had ultimate respect for him. Joe was never one to complain about injury or pain, and frequently played with both. It rarely affected his performance. If it did, he wouldn't play again until he thought he could get the job done up to his high standards. His fellow

Yankees were not alienated by his remoteness. They understood that stoicism on and off the baseball field was Joe's way of life. His play more than made up for any lack of fellowship. Just about every year DiMaggio played, the Yankees won the pennant and often the World Series.

He developed his trademark urbane persona after only a short time in New York. Despite his humble West Coast background, DiMaggio came to symbolize New York's sophistication, even snobbery. During the season, he lived in a New York hotel room. When he stepped out, he would often hold court with other celebrities, politicians, and fat cats of the time at his favorite New York haunt, Toots Shor's nightclub. On the outside, he exuded style, class, and power. His reserved presence only added to his elusive, intangible magnetism. He became as protective of his carefully constructed image as he was of his hoarded booty, and used his image like armor, a defensive shield to keep the masses at bay. Still, it couldn't stop the ulcers he developed.

He relaxed (if you can call it that) by drinking coffee, smoking cigarettes (both known irritants to ulcers), listening to game shows, and reading comic books. Superman was his favorite. They had a lot of similarities, especially when they changed from street clothes to their uniforms.

Remarkably, despite DiMaggio's manifest talents as a player, he wasn't elected to the Hall of Fame until his third go-around; a definite snub by the baseball writers who got to vote. Some attributed it to Joe's well-known and all-too-frequent health problems—mainly his legs and feet. Others blamed his stand-offish relationship with the press (and public in general). This minor blemish did nothing to dull the brilliance of the great Yankee Clipper on a baseball diamond. When he was in his prime, he was as polished and as hard as a real diamond.

Then there was Marilyn. The plot was right out of *A Star is Born*. Except with the real thing, the whole story was far more tragic. Joe played the part of the established star whose glow from the limelight was fading, Marilyn, the part of the young, beautiful, ambitious blonde bombshell on the verge of super-stardom. The love was there, but the timing was all wrong. When they married in 1952, Joe had just retired from baseball, wanted to settle down, enjoy his accomplishments, and let history turn him into a national icon. Marilyn wanted accomplishments and wanted to be an icon too. She would soon have both. The price, eventually, was her life.

In perhaps the ultimate stroke of irony, Marilyn, at once wrapped up in herself and oblivious to Joe's past, commented to him on her return from a hugely successful USO trip to Korea, "It was incredible, Joe. You don't know what it's like when tens of thousands of people are cheering for just you!"

The Yankee Clipper quietly and ruefully replied, "Oh yes I do."

Both Joe and Marilyn were so deeply flawed, it is doubtful their relationship could have withstood the test of time even under the best of circumstances. As it was, they divorced within a year. Joe could not bring himself to share Marilyn with her public. In those days, Marilyn could not get enough of her public. With her death in 1965 died a large chunk of Joe DiMaggio's tortured heart. He never got over Marilyn. Her demise forever etched her glossed-over memory in the stone tablet that was the Yankee Clipper's mind.

DiMaggio's first marriage didn't work out either; nor his relationship (or lack of one) with his son, Joe Jr. His only state of grace was on a baseball field. The rest of the universe was a dicey proposition for Joltin' Joe. The world was not his oyster, although he could've made it so, and so it appeared on the surface. He always believed that people, whether in baseball or not, were leech-like sycophants wanting to suck the life and fame out of him for their own personal appetites. He always believed that people wanted a piece of him that, once removed, could never be replaced—kind of like the old Native American superstition that a photograph would steal a part of their soul. It was this cynical creed that guided practically all of his thinking and decision making.

DiMaggio lived a long life, though one would be hard pressed to say a happy one. He died in 1999 at eighty-six. While his game had no detectable faults, his personal life was riddled with them.

The nobody-manager then turned his attention to Mickey Mantle, whose cherubic face would've been a natural for the Mickey Mouse

Club instead of the Yankee ball club. "Mickey, if you don't mind me asking, how old are you?" said Ogilvie trying to be diplomatic. The diplomacy was not necessary.

An eager Mantle answered, "Nineteen," in a cracking voice that could've earned him the nickname "Squeaker" too!

Ogilvie slowly nodded his head storing away this information for later use. "That's fine," The nobody-manager replied. "You don't mind playing with the Babe's team tomorrow, do you?"

"Oh no, Mr. Ogilvie, it'd be an honor," stated a respectful Mantle.

Little Roberto, on hearing his best friend being referred to as "Mister" by the youthful Mickey Mantle, was quick to correct him, "You don't need to call him 'Mister,' Mickey. His friends call him Don." Ogilvie and the Alvarezes couldn't help but chuckle, recalling how little Roberto originally befriended the downcast hitting coach.

A still-smiling Don Ogilvie said to Mantle and the others, "That's right. My friends call me Don, and I want everyone here to do the same."

A beaming Mickey Mantle responded, "You got it, Don!"

Ogilvie announced to the gathering, "I've got to go find Drummond and tell him about our game tomorrow. Game time is one o'clock, so everybody should be suited up and ready to play. You guys can do whatever you want to do until then. After tomorrow's game, I'll get a practice schedule together." Ogilvie mumbled to himself, "If there's anybody left to practice with." That cheerful possibility in mind, he walked through the home team's dugout and into their clubhouse to begin his search for Death in the Flesh—Doctor Drummond.

He didn't know where to begin looking. It seemed that Death Incarnate always materialized when needed. He figured the home team's clubhouse would be a good place to start. That's where Drummond and his team would presumably be when the Series got underway. He was glad to find the home team's surroundings no more luxurious than the visitor's, but no less so either. He was about to call out Drummond's name when he heard Death Personified's New York diphthong coming from the manager's office. "I'm in here, Ogilvie."

He made his way to the open office door and found Drummond sitting in a chair, his stubby legs planted on the desk in front of him. As usual he was wearing his black umpire outfit. He motioned Ogilvie in and asked him to sit down. He didn't wait for Don to speak before saying, "I hear you got a game tomorrow. Congratulations . . . I guess. You're taking a big gamble. If your Negro Leaguers lose . . . well, I imagine you've already thought about that. Now, what can I do for you?" As usual, Drummond knew everything that was going on and cut right to the chase.

Ogilvie was immediately put on the defensive again, and could only offer a humbling "mea culpa." "It looks like I didn't give myself much choice. You were right about the players not getting along. I didn't think that one out, so I have to work with it as best I can. I feel like a one-legged high jumper."

Drummond flashed his trademark smile that said, "I told you so."

The nobody-manager continued: "I'm gonna need the field ready, and some umpires for the game tomorrow. Hopefully, you can arrange that."

"No problem. I'll give you three umpires and the field will be ready. Hell, it's ready now. Anything else?"

"Yeah," said Ogilvie, avoiding what he really wanted to say. "Are we gonna have fans?"

Death in the Flesh gave the nobody-manager a condescending grunt. "Just the hotel people for now, a few hundred or so. When the series starts, it'll be standing-room-only, okay? I'll be providing the extra Lucky Stiffs. They're not busy anyhow."

"Build it and they will come, huh?" Ogilvie couldn't resist getting in a jibe at one of Death's few known weak spots.

"You know this *Field of Dreams* crap truly annoys me, don't you? This is not going to help you with what you really want to ask."

Drummond knew there was more on Don's mind, and there was. Ogilvie wasn't exactly sure how to approach it, so he blurted out, "Mantle's voice hasn't changed yet, and Ruth's collecting a pension."

Death Incarnate took his legs off the desk, leaned forward, fixed his gaze on Ogilvie, and said, "So?"

"Everyone else looks to be in good shape except those two. You've given me a sixth grader and a forty-year-old juvenile delinquent."

134

"Nobody specified any age or shape for your players when we made our agreement," Drummond reminded Ogilvie. "You're free to call off the deal anytime you want. But look at this way—Mantle's always had bad knees. At his age here in Limbotown, that shouldn't be a problem. As far as Ruth goes, you don't know, he may play like . . . Babe Ruth. You'll get a chance to see both of 'em in action tomorrow. Why not wait and see how they do? Last, I'll say this: All these guys were taken from a time while they were playing in the Major Leagues. As you said, all the others are in their prime. You're complaining about two players out of twenty-four. Don't be so picky."

Ogilvie didn't feel there was much he could do. He also realized that the idea of "calling off the deal anytime he wanted" was no choice at all. Roberto would die. The part about Mantle's knees was true enough, but how much big league experience he'd had was a huge question mark. Ruth, on the other hand, whatever his advanced athletic age, had too much Major League experience. He was a broken-down old warhorse ready to be put out to pasture. Or shot. As Drummond had said, though, at least he'd have a chance to see them both play very soon.

Ogilvie let the subject drop by saying, "Let's see what happens tomorrow. By the way, game time is one o'clock if you're interested."

"I wouldn't miss it for all the sunshine in Limbotown," Doctor Drummond said, again reminding Ogilvie of his ability to apparently know everything spoken or thought, whether in his presence or not.

"Since you seem to know it all, where is the sun in this place?" Ogilvie asked.

"There is no sun, only light," was the simple answer from Death Personified.

"Okay, so where does the light come from? And don't tell me it'd be like talking to a chimp." Ogilvie was determined to get an explanation—even if he didn't understand it.

"Yeah, you might actually get this one. Ever hear of ambient lighting?" Drummond didn't wait for an answer. "The light comes from around the edges of the fogbank. It's artificial, of course. It's controlled by what you'd think of as a big dimmer switch on a timer. You've noticed we don't have clouds here either. And normally we don't have a moon or stars at night. But since I want everyone to feel at home, I'm gonna have 'em. Not a sun or clouds, just a moon and stars. They won't be real, but nobody'll know the difference. It'll look like a real sunset, except without the sun. When it's dark, the moon and the stars will come out. That oughta make everybody feel a little more at ease."

"Sounds peachy, but why no clouds?" asked Ogilvie.

"You want clouds? Go to the Caesar's Palace Mall. I want the playing conditions to be ideal. No sun, no clouds, no glare and no shadows."

"How does the grass grow without real sunlight?"

"Yeah, that's a tough one for me. I've always had trouble bringing things to life," remarked a wry Death in the Flesh.

Ogilvie ignored the tongue-in-cheek reply and moved on for the big question: "Well, where are we, anyway—Outer-space?"

"Not exactly," said a cautious Drummond. "That one is a bit more complicated than the lights. Limbotown is more of a 'what' than a 'where.' It can be anything I want to make it; not just a baseball stadium and hotel. It could be as big as outer space, if I wanted . . . Let's just say Limbotown becomes whatever I need it to become. That's about all I can tell you."

The nobody-manager had to accept Drummond's sparse explanation. This one did sound like it was well beyond anything he'd ever heard of. "Wherever, whatever . . ." Ogilvie said, followed by what he thought was a kind of science-fiction sound effect. "See you at the game tomorrow."

"One more thing before you go, Ogilvie," said the Ultimate Umpire. "A word of warning about the books in your office."

"What?" Ogilvie said apprehensively; not sure if they were booby trapped, or somehow rigged by Drummond. He wasn't too far off.

"Don't let those books out of your office. They're for you and Antonio to use. Nobody else—especially not the players. They're not supposed to find out about their destinies on their own. Of course there's nothing to stop you from telling 'em what you want. In fact, you'll find them a very effective tool in managing your players. Sooner or later, and probably sooner, these guys are gonna find out about these books, and they'll try anything to get a hold of 'em. It's your job to protect 'em. If you don't, you'll lose the advantage of knowing your players' histories. You'll lose your leverage—and you're going to need all the leverage you can get. Okay?"

"Okay. Thanks for the heads-up," said a slightly baffled Ogilvie. Once again, Death in the Flesh was helping the nobody-manager. Or was he? The chunky umpire had already aided him earlier by keeping secret his arrangement to trade places with Roberto. But all of Drummond's so-called "help" came as a double-edged sword, capable of both cutting through his obstacles as well as cleaving himself. It was a "monkey's-paw" kind of help—he may get what he wanted, but not without a price or some unexpected trouble. The same was true of Maggie Briggs. He fell in love with her, and it was not at all clear whether this would help or hurt him. The books would give him insight into his players. But would they resent him if he didn't share what he found out? A gun, for instance, can either protect or harm. It depends on who's using it and why. Death Personified was giving him tools, all right, yet if he didn't use them properly, he could end up shooting himself in the foot, or somewhere worse.

A shattering thought then occurred to the nobody-manager. He asked Death Personified, with a twinge, "Hey, what's gonna stop the Lucky Stiffs from telling my players what they know about 'em?"

"Good question," replied Drummond. Seeing the worried furrow on Don's brow, he said, "No, I mean it was a good question—an intelligent question. The answer is, the Lucky Stiffs can remember just about everything—except when it comes to the players. Then, depending on what year they're from, all I let 'em recall is the players' playing days and nothing beyond that. Unless someone tells them something, or they get hold of those books . . . So take care of 'em, Okay?"

Drummond was trying to extend his too-short legs back to his desk. The attempt resulted in a miss and a pratfall. He sprang to his feet grumbling, "Next time I gotta get longer legs." Ogilvie couldn't hide his laughter as he left to retrieve Antonio to piece together their team for tomorrow's big game.

He headed back to the field and began to weigh his lineup. It wouldn't be that difficult. He barely had enough players to fill the positions anyhow. Still, he wanted Antonio's input. There was the batting order. Gibson would bat clean-up and Cool Papa Bell would lead-off, but most of the other spots were up for grabs. Another decision would be whether to move Campanella or Josh Gibson, both catchers, to first base, or leave Campanella on the bench to start.

As he emerged from the home-team's dugout, the small gathering had already broken up. DiMaggio continued his solitary workout, while Drysdale, Clemente, and Mantle resumed their game of catch. Antonio, Maria, and Roberto watched from the visitor's dugout. He asked Antonio to stay and help with tomorrow's line-up. Maria and Roberto went back to the hotel for lunch. They promised to return with some sandwiches. Little Roberto was grumpy. He wanted to stay with his father and best friend. He wondered out loud what he would do the rest of the afternoon. The fascination of Limbotown had already worn thin for the seven-year-old. Cancer, illness, and even death could be held in check in this extraordinary place, but not childhood boredom. It was a problem the players would soon begin to experience too (you know—cabin fever), until their discovery of a fleeting way out of their fog-banked container.

Maria had a ready answer for her impatient son. "Maggie said she was going to introduce you to some of the workers' children. There are some exactly your age. And Maggie said that the movie theater would be open tomorrow. Maybe we can find out what's showing." Appeased, Roberto and his mother left for the hotel.

Bench coach Antonio Alvarez and manager Don Ogilvie retreated to the visitor's clubhouse to prepare for the big game. Ogilvie found Charlie McManus and told him to ready Drummond Field. Within the hour, Maria and little Roberto returned with sandwiches and left again so Don and Antonio could finish their roster. As Ogilvie thought, it didn't take too long. They were done by 3:15 p.m. Limbotown Standard Time (LST).

With their work finished for the time being, Don convinced Antonio to rejoin his wife and son at the hotel. Don told him, "I'm going to stay here and start reading up on the histories of our players. I know we're going to win tomorrow, so I need to know about these guys if we're going to have any chance to make them into a team."

He was trying to put up a front for Antonio, even though he was not nearly as confident as he sounded. Antonio wanted to stay. Ogilvie told him he should be with his family. The ardent assistant offered to take a book with him. The absent-minded manager said, "I'm glad you brought that up." He told Antonio about Drummond's admonition that the books never leave the office, and how they were potent devices. "There'll be plenty of time for you to read these books, I just need to know some stuff now." He made Antonio agree not to tell the players anything about their past without clearing it with him first. Antonio understood and left for the hotel.

Ogilvie's real reason for getting Antonio to leave was not altogether pure. As soon as the young assistant disappeared from sight, Ogilvie went to the bottom right-hand drawer of his desk where the ever-full bottle of Scotch awaited. He'd originally intended to celebrate his earlier success in engineering tomorrow's game; now he wanted a drink because he was nervous about winning. He took two large pulls and kept the bottle on top of his desk within easy reach. He grabbed a reference book from the shelf and came upon an old photograph of a beaming Babe Ruth. The books had a surprise of their own, one that had not been revealed earlier when he and Antonio briefly used them to select their Hall of Famers. As Ogilvie studied the photo, it took on a life of its own. It transformed into a slick three-dimensional video, including narration and background music. The unconventional reference books provided by Drummond would save Ogilvie precious time, not to mention eyestrain. They would also give him all the information he needed about his players, both on and off the field. He would need to only think of a question and the intuitive books would relay all they had— in their peculiar documentary style, of course.

After getting over the amazement of the video-books, he settled into their version of "The Babe Ruth Story." He found Ruth's life was pretty much the wild orgy he'd heard about. Some of the details were shocking, revolting, and even disgusting. Naturally, Ogilvie couldn't help but see the parallel between little Roberto and the Johnny Sylvester story. If things worked out, this time there could be a real miracle.

Savoring that thought, Ogilvie delved into the special volumes, trying to absorb as much information as he could. He brushed up his recollections of Satchel Paige, Josh Gibson, and his other black players. He also learned more about the real old timers, like Honus Wagner, Christy Mathewson, Walter Johnson, and Cy Young. When these guys were born, Custer was still blissfully roaming around what would eventually become Montana, trying to figure out a way to make it into the history books. (He made it okay—just not the way he expected. Ogilvie, among many, could've given Custer a wonderful discourse on expectations gone haywire.) And if Cy Young had been begot any earlier, he might've been recruited as an Ohio regular in the Civil War—that's right, the American Civil War that ended in 1865. He was born less than two years later. Things like cars and electricity hadn't been invented yet. These ol' boys thought the 1930s-style Hotel Limbotown was a futuristic wonder.

Ogilvie hadn't noticed how many hours had passed when he heard Maggie Briggs knocking softly on his open door. He looked up at her, pleasantly surprised. She was carrying a covered tray of food. It was well past 8 p.m., and he hadn't bothered with dinner. On the other hand, he hadn't realized the time.

The magnificent redhead couldn't help but notice the open bottle of Scotch on top of Ogilvie's desk. She didn't say anything. Ogilvie knew what she was thinking, given her judgmental expression. She was cordial compared to her first tongue-lashing, when the alcoholic coach learned it was not a good idea to ask her to spike his morning coffee.

"I brought you some dinner," she announced neutrally. "It's late and the Alvarezes were worried about you. So I said I'd check on you and bring you a meal." Then it came. "Anyway, you're going to need something to soak up all that Scotch."

Ogilvie was relieved she at least got in one zinger at him. Otherwise he would've been on edge waiting for it. He didn't mind. Seeing Maggie made him yearn to confess his love for her (as if she didn't know) and bare his blistered soul. Thankfully he restrained himself from further besmirching his already-tarnished dignity. Still, he was feeling vulnerable—a combination of the booze, uneasiness about learning the destinies of his players, and his now palpable fear about losing tomorrow's game. He kept his conversation curt, wisely ignoring her dig.

"Thanks for the food, Maggie," was his simple response. As he lost himself in her eyes, he thought he saw something. She looked away quickly.

Maggie Briggs couldn't understand what was becoming, to her, an unexplained attraction to Don Ogilvie. It was more than her usual sympathy for a Challenger. Yes, she was impressed with his dexterity in arranging the game between the players. But it was more than that. She was troubled to find herself, a Chosen One, a proven Challenger, oddly drawn to this unkempt example of personal weakness, self-pity, and drunkenness. And those were his good qualities. It was starting to chafe her. She decided she would make a conscious effort to ignore these stirrings, even though she couldn't deny them. No more delivering meals, which might be rightly interpreted as showing some partiality. It might encourage the nobody-manager, who was searching for any positive sign. What was she doing, falling for a man she'd probably never see again? Even she rated his odds at none to "forget about it." What was she doing, feeling something for someone whose life was, as she put it, "a mess"? She didn't want to think about it now. The answers might turn out to be more irksome than the questions. She felt disquieted enough about the whole situation to cut short her visit. She left the would-be manager to study his unique books.

Chapter 10

O gilvie decided he'd better find out about the enemy. He knew he had plenty of time to learn about Ty Cobb. However, he wasn't thinking about Cobb or even Drummond. He was thinking about Rogers Hornsby.

Rogers Hornsby was an insufferable son of a bitch. Later in his life, he might've even admitted to it. As insufferable as he was, Hornsby was still no Ty Cobb. The Georgia Peach was in a class by himself. They'd had to invent new names for previously undiscovered mental illnesses to accommodate the creativity of Cobb's various psychoses. Hornsby was a distant second. He wasn't really deranged, like Cobb. He seemed just as mean, which was a feat in itself.

Cobb and Hornsby proved that you didn't have to be liked to be effective. Rogers Hornsby was probably the best right-handed hitter there ever was. In 1924, at age twenty-eight, he established the modern record with a .424 batting average. He entered major league baseball in 1916 at the tender age of nineteen, playing second base for the St. Louis Cardinals. After nineteen years in the big leagues, he retired with a lifetime batting average of .358.

He was nicknamed "the Rajah" or just "Raj." It was easier than saying Rogers. As contemporaries, many reasoned that if Ruth could be the Sultan of Swat in the American League, then Hornsby could at least be the Rajah of the National League. Oppressor would've been more accurate. As different as they were, Hornsby and Ruth were considered the best players in their respective leagues. One had the appeal of Santa Claus, the other the charm of Lord Voldemort. Although Raj didn't hit homers like the Babe, for a second baseman he had unprecedented power. Also like Ruth, Hornsby was both deceptively speedy between the bases and an excellent fielder.

Hornsby's other great talent, on or off a baseball diamond, was his ability to piss off anyone. He almost always said what was on his mind, whether you wanted to hear it or not. Normally it was not very nice. He didn't care who he offended.

Hornsby was crude, even by baseball standards. His language could make a Greek sailor blush, and he was known to unmercifully berate players in front of their teammates—not exactly the kind of thing that made you popular in the clubhouse. His hair-trigger temper went off early and often. He was as stubborn and unforgiving as a mule stuck in a mud-rail fence. Hornsby's idea of sensitivity training was kicking umpires in the ribs after he'd felled them by buckshot (this only a slight exaggeration). From time to time, he succeeded in pissing off his fans, managers, coaches, team owners, sportswriters, umpires, and everyone else—including the iron-fisted commissioner of baseball, Judge Kenesaw Mountain Landis.

Despite this, the Cardinals made him a player-manager until no one could stand it any longer, which turned out to be one season. Remarkably, Hornsby managed the Cards in that single year to the 1926 World Series, beating Ruth and the Yankees—yes, the same World Series in which Ruth hit his home runs for little Johnny Sylvester. Notwithstanding his unlikely World Series victory, he was traded the very next season to the New York Giants. While not nearly as controversial as Ruth's trade from Boston to New York, his exile was not cheered by loyal St. Louis fans. He may have irritated those St. Louis fans once in a while, but they considered him a god. They figured that anybody who could defeat Ruth and the Yankees in a World Series deserved that status.

Hornsby sowed his seeds of discontent everywhere he went. He distributed his mean-spirited personality indiscriminately. Not to say that he didn't discriminate. An ornery Texan, he was a staunch defender of the old color barrier, just like the Georgia-born Cobb. Had they been born some years earlier, they would've gladly joined with fellow Hall of Famer, Cap Anson, in formalizing baseball's unwritten but well-known edict against hiring blacks. It was an unwritten law that might as well have been etched in stone.

Hornsby also had other flaws and weaknesses. An avid gambler, he enjoyed a day at the track. Rumored to have bet on baseball games, the second baseman skirmished with Commissioner Landis. He was punished by Landis on occasion. There was no love lost between the two. They were both possessed of massive, unyielding egos; each believing their visage should envelop some huge outcropping such as Mt. Rushmore. (It was arguably Landis's mountain-sized megalomania that at last prevailed over Hornsby's misdemeanors, Cobb's dementia— and even Ruth's celebrity. That and he could throw a player out of baseball forever. When Landis gave you a lifetime ban, it was still enforced after your death.)

Another of Hornsby's weaknesses, if he chose to consider it that, was his genuine fondness for children. This might seem a contradiction on its face, since the adult versions of the human race were his usual victims. He liked kittens and puppies too. But when they grew up, he'd just as soon tie them in a sack weighted with rocks and leave them on the beach at high tide—that or at least kick them. Nonetheless, Rogers Hornsby was a complicated man, and to brand him a one-dimensional cretin would be unfair. That type of blanket character assassination should only be saved for Ty Cobb. Besides, Hornsby was a multi-dimensional cretin.

He was not without a conscience, however. He may have had sociopathic tendencies, but he knew enough not to cross the border into the nether reaches of that moral outback known as "Cobb-land." Still, Hornsby was just about as difficult to deal with as the maniacal Cobb.

He was a series of contradictions. He was a loner like DiMaggio, but his job required performing in front of thousands of people. A handsome guy, he could charm you with his easy smile one moment and torment you the next with a burst of obscene epithets that would make Buck

Nimble wince. Then again, he didn't smoke or drink, mainly because he was afraid those vices might hurt his game.

His swing was sleek perfection, a thing of beauty. His concentration and focus while in the batter's box was unequaled; nothing distracted him. Outside this small domain of refuge (for Hornsby and everyone else, except the opposing team), many things distracted him: his salary, other players, managers, umpires, horses, gambling, and Commissioner Landis, to name a few.

He was, to state it politely, a bigot, and was an unenlightened critic of the dismantling of the color barrier in baseball. Yet many years after he retired, he was known to help any player of any color with their hitting. It was the only thing that made him human for consecutive hours at a time. He could talk about the art of hitting endlessly. His usual dour personality would give way to spunky pep. Baseball was his only true refuge.

The Rajah was also the last of a dying breed of lobby-sitters. This was the arcane practice of literally just sitting in a hotel lobby and observing humanity pass by. People watching. Hornsby would target a plush chair in a suitable location of any given lobby and sit for hours. This must've been a relief from his normal behavior. At least his rotten demeanor would be confined to a limited area. By the 1920s, ballplayers considered this esoteric activity passé, but not old Raj. When the likes of Babe Ruth had been out carousing till dawn, Hornsby could keep pace with him without leaving his chair. Only the lure of the ponies or a poker game could make him move. He would get in plenty of lobby sitting at the Hotel Limbotown.

In the end, Hornsby was still truculent, but mellowed by age. He died in 1963 at age sixty-seven.

Ogilvie didn't recall drifting off to sleep. Again he wound up slumbering in his clubhouse office. Much to his relief, reading about Hornsby didn't produce any nightmares—none that he could remember, at any rate. But then he hadn't gotten to Cobb yet.

Antonio was standing over him, gently shaking his shoulder. He awoke, mumbled something to his assistant coach, and noticed the clock on the wall registering 9 a.m., now the morning of the big game. He immediately broke into one of his patented sweating fits, oozing moisture from practically every pore in his body, like a human osmosis filter. "Hand me that towel over there, Antonio," he said.

Having experienced Ogilvie's watery purges many times, Antonio dutifully delivered the towel. Ogilvie whipped off his shirt and proceeded to dry himself like it was his morning bath. Thinking out loud, he said, "You know, Antonio, I think I'll jump in the shower. Our lineup card is on my desk. Take a look and tell me if you think we should make any changes. I'll be right back." With that, Ogilvie dropped his drawers, wrapped the towel around where his waist used to be, and was off to the locker-room showers. Mr. Universe he was not. His pronounced gut could barely accommodate the swathe that was encircling it.

The clubhouse was just beginning to show signs of life. Charlie McManus and his crew were readying equipment and making sure everyone's belongings were in order. A couple of the black players arrived. Old Charlie directed them to their lockers.

Ogilvie exited the shower, now with a fresh towel. He re-entered his office and began putting on a San Bernardino Stampede uniform that was conveniently placed in his closet. As he dressed, he asked Antonio, "Do you think we need to make any changes to our lineup?"

Antonio's response was enthusiastic, "No. It reads like a "Who's Who" of the old Negro Leagues. Let's hope Satchel's arm holds up. He's our only pitcher."

"I'm not worried about that," said a now well-informed Ogilvie. "He pitched into his early sixties. The man has a rubber arm. But I *am* worried about winning," he at last admitted.

As Ogilvie was donning his jersey, the squat, blackball with legs, Death in the Flesh, entered the office. Behind Drummond stood a tall, thin man with a stern look on his face. He was also clad in black. Just under the stranger's nose was a pair of lips as full and red as any woman's. Upon closer inspection, they were apparently real and naturally crimson. The mounds of pulpy meat were so out of proportion to the rest of the lanky man's face that they looked like those wax vampire lips people get for Halloween. They gave the stranger a clownish expression.

146

Rather than introduce him to the man with the clown lips, Drummond got on Ogilvie straight away. Seeing sweat still pouring off the nobody-manager, Drummond remarked, "Hey Ogilvie, don't you know you're supposed to dry off from your shower before you get dressed?"

Ogilvie ignored the dig, observing that Death Personified was overly amused with his own joke.

Drummond was still chortling as he finally introduced them to the patient stranger, "Don Ogilvie, Antonio Alvarez, this is Bill Klem, your home-plate umpire for today."

The tall man with the clown lips extended his hand first to Antonio and then to Ogilvie, saying, "Doctor Drummond has told me about your game today. That's great. I understand Ruth is managing the other team." Bill Klem, respected Hall of Fame umpire of old, withdrew his hand from Ogilvie's and tried to unobtrusively wipe it on the side of his pants.

Ogilvie, used to this sort of reaction, shrugged and said, "Sorry about that, Bill. I'm a little nervous today."

Klem was understanding. "That's all right. I hear you got quite a lot to be nervous about. I hear your team is some Negro League all-stars."

"Yes," said Ogilvie, "I'm hoping you won't tolerate any name-calling or racial talk."

"Don't worry about that," stated the lippy umpire, "I run a tight ship. I never missed a call in my life. I don't plan to start now."

Ogilvie, satisfied with Klem's answer, simply said, "Welcome aboard. We look forward to a great game."

Klem, business-like as always, said: "Have your lineup card ready at least five minutes before game time. Tell Ruth to do the same." Then the tall, thin Klem and the short, dumpy Drummond—Mutt and Jeff dressed in black—left the visitor's clubhouse.

Ogilvie didn't yet know anything about Klem, except for the clown lips. Those proud protuberances, however, would actually serve to keep the white players in line. Klem, as a contemporary of Ruth and Hornsby, endured all kinds of name-calling and baiting because of those lips. His official nickname among the players was "Fish-lips." But like Ruth, he was often called "nigger-lips." As might be imagined, he wasn't fond of either label. Ordinarily, he would eject any player from a game for the insult. He was an evenhanded umpire, but also hard-nosed. His fleshy attributes would prompt Bill Klem to keep the game civil, even if his purpose were not to curb the players' bigotry, but to maintain respect for himself.

Antonio caught Don's eye. The kid was on the verge of laughing. Ogilvie cautioned him; "I know. They're hard to miss, aren't they? At least he promised to be fair."

Ogilvie couldn't help himself as he added with a grin, "I don't think he'll be taking any lip from Hornsby and his group."

Antonio, not to be outdone by his manager, added, "Let's hope what he said isn't just lip-service." They both chuckled.

"Okay, have we gotten it all out now?" asked Ogilvie. "This guy's going to be calling balls and strikes, so we've got take him seriously. Thank God he'll be wearing a mask."

"You mean on top of the one he's already wearing?" said Antonio, who hadn't gotten it all out yet.

Ogilvie tried to suppress another chuckle, but he couldn't. "All right, that's enough," he said, as much to himself as to Antonio.

By now the clubhouse had started to fill up with most of the black players and a few white players. Charlie McManus had done a fine job of tactfully assigning lockers. The arrangement mostly kept blacks and whites apart. But Charlie did put Drysdale's locker between Robinson's and Clemente's. On the other side of Robinson was Roy Campanella. This was a smart move, since the big white Dodger hurler had been a teammate of both Robinson and Campanella, and friends with Clemente. Ogilvie was pleased with this setup. He hoped the other white players would notice how well Drysdale and his black counterparts got along. They didn't.

As Ruth and the rest of his contingent arrived en masse, the combative Rogers Hornsby complained about having to dress in the same clubhouse with the black players. Provoked, the old Negro Leaguers were ready to duke it out. At least Ogilvie had some managerial experience at the high school level. He'd prevented or broken up fights before. He had been humiliated by Hornsby and saved by little Roberto only a day earlier; this time he was determined not to let history repeat itself. It was also an

148

opportune time for a new manager to exert some authority. His baseball instincts took over.

As he calmly walked between the two openly gathered groups, he loudly decreed, "Let me tell you guys the rules of conduct. Any player who touches another player in anger is outta the game. Any player that uses a racial name is outta the game. If a team has enough players ejected and you can't field nine players, that team forfeits the game. No exceptions. That also means if Ruth's team forfeits, it's the same as losing—and that means we all play together, like it or not."

A belligerent Hornsby, now standing nose-to-nose with Ogilvie, asked, "Yeah, well who made up these fucking rules?"

"I did!" said a resounding Ogilvie. "What I say goes around here, Hornsby. You better get used to it. If you wanna make a point, do it with your play, not your big yap!"

"If you weren't so old and fat, I'd kick the shit outta you right now!" was Hornsby's seemingly automatic response.

The nobody-manager could see that he wasn't going to get off light. Realizing if he didn't stand up to Hornsby that instant, his chance of managing this elite pack would fade faster than an artificial sunset in Limbotown.

"Take your best shot," he growled at Hornsby. The nobody-manager tried to swell up his chest and suck in his gut. The effort was not entirely successful. His shoulders involuntarily slumped and gravity forced his portly paunch south. He looked more like a puffer-fish than a threat.

To Ogilvie's relief, the much younger and stronger Hornsby backed off, saying, "You're just looking for an excuse to throw me off the white team. You're not worth it. Probably drown me in sweat and crush me with your belly anyway."

Ogilvie exhaled. "You're right! Why don't you tell me about it while you're getting ready." He was trying to get Hornsby and his followers to take a hint.

The hostile Hornsby had been rebuffed by the gumption (and imposing gut) of the uncommonly aggressive nobody-manager. Nonetheless, no one was as surprised as Ogilvie himself when the two sides actually broke up and returned to their lockers. A handful of the white players grudgingly understood Ogilvie's need to confront Rogers Hornsby, even though they didn't agree with the nobody-manager's rules.

Antonio stood in virtual awe of his alcoholic coach. He had never seen his friend act so sure and swift. Then again, he had never seen him manage before. Charlie McManus came over to where Ogilvie was standing in the middle of the clubhouse and presented him with his morning cup of coffee. The dark, aromatic liquid was offered more like a battle commendation than a beverage. "Here's your coffee, Mr. Ogilvie." Old Charlie winked at his manager and softly said, "Nice job not gettin' killed."

As he took the scalding mug from Charlie's grasp, both Antonio and the crusty old clubhouse caretaker couldn't help notice that Ogilvie's hands were shaking with seizure-like regularity—and it wasn't from his morning hangover. Ogilvie's adrenaline glands hadn't been exercised in years. They were going to get a helluva workout in Limbotown. He did discover one happy after-effect; adrenaline, like his love for Maggie, evidently staunched the flow of his perspiration. Unlike the day before, his "Johnstown Flood" had been dammed. He was too terrified to sweat. The thought of Hornsby, half his age, in great shape, pummeling his old, flabby, booze-soaked body evoked a horrific vision.

The nobody-manager scanned the relative tranquility of the clubhouse and noticed that one of the old-time white players was doing the same. Their eyes met and they smiled, each nodding at the other. Ogilvie would come to know this right-handed pitcher as a bright and independent thinker who would draw his own conclusions. He refused to be influenced by his turn-of-the-century peers. That man was Christy Mathewson. Ogilvie had learned enough about him to be duly impressed, and he was gratified to receive the approval of this Renaissance baseball star.

Before there was Babe Ruth, there was Christy Mathewson. Ruth may have been baseball's biggest superstar, but Mathewson was its first.

Christy Mathewson wasn't exactly born with a silver spoon in his mouth, as some thought. Such a claim would be hard to swallow, mainly because the baby Christy was conceived in a little town in Pennsylvania called Factoryville—and Christy's dad didn't own the factory. Nevertheless, young Mathewson grew up wanting for naught. His father was very well to do for the times, just not a robber baron. So Christy's spoon was only silver-plated. Nice homes, fine prep schools, and mixing with the upper crust of whatever society was available in rural Pennsylvania, was Christy's milieu.

He matriculated to Bucknell University, a prestigious ivy-league college in west Pennsylvania. He was not a P.E. major. Try chemistry. Okay, he was a major jock, and the lure of professional baseball eventually caused him to drop out before graduating. But remember—this was in the days when baseball players were considered as wild as the Wild West. Then a tall, blonde, educated, refined stranger came into town at the turn of the century and tamed its wicked ways. The fact that Christy Mathewson was boyishly handsome, almost six-foot-two, and his right arm could make pitches never before seen, didn't hurt either. He was the first respectable baseball hero. Fans rolled out the red carpet for him. Finally, here was an athlete you could take home to meet the family without fear that he would eat dinner like a hungry dog or molest your teenage daughter. This was one baseball player parents wouldn't mind their daughters marrying or their sons emulating.

Not only was he popular with the public, his teammates and opponents liked and respected him too. And with good reason. He was never petty. He was unusually forgiving, especially on the pitcher's mound. Errors didn't rattle him. His attitude was "We'll get the next one." With that kind of temperament, his teammates loved playing behind him.

Some described Mathewson as the precursor to DiMaggio: aloof, aristocratic, even regal. But Matty, as he was known, could obviously get along with anyone. The proof of that was his relationship with his notoriously cantankerous skipper, John McGraw. The old National League New York Giants manager had a vocabulary and temper that made Buck Nimble look like a first-grade Sunday school teacher. He and Mathewson got along famously. McGraw assumed the role of the gruff, crude but well-meaning manager, father; and Mathewson that of

151

the good-natured, cultured, dutiful player, son. It was a classic example of opposite attraction. That is probably why the relationship worked so well. Each perhaps admired or at least recognized qualities in the other that would be impossible to call their own.

Despite his clean-cut image, Matty was far from a goody two-shoes. He was not averse to an occasional drink while puffing on his pipe or smoking a cigarette. Curse words were known to escape his saintly lips from time to time, and informal gambling was a favorite pastime. Mathewson was an expert checkers player, and canny about cards and dice. He may not have had a typical background for the average baseball player of his era, but he surely had the common touch. He could mingle with baseball ruffians as easily as high-society matrons. He was truly the Golden Boy of early baseball.

When acquired by the old New York Giants, he wore the number six on his uniform. Sporting a fastball, curve, and his new "fade-away" pitch (which he invented and is now called a screwball), it didn't take long for New York fans to clamor with anticipation when "Big Six" took the mound. The hard-throwing right-handed strikeout artist compiled incredible records with his pinpoint control. He once had a stretch where he didn't walk a batter for sixty-eight innings. He won thirty or more games for three consecutive seasons in 1903, 1904, and 1905. He struck out an astonishing 267 batters in 1903. In the 1905 World Series against the Philadelphia Athletics, he pitched three shutout victories in six days, the last game on only one day's rest. In 1908 he won thirty-seven games! Today, twenty games is considered stellar. He won an untouchable 373 games in his career—third highest ever, behind Walter Johnson and Cy Young.

After his playing days, he joined the Army in 1918 for the final months of World War I. Too valuable to soldier, Matty's expertise in chemistry was used to study the effects of chlorine and other toxic clouds that each side had wafted over the other in that brutal struggle. As luck would have it, Big Six was accidentally exposed to the noxious gases he was asked to investigate. The results were not immediate. The contact was like lighting a slow-burning fuse. It led to Matty developing terminal tuberculosis. The life of Big Six, like a skyrocket, exploded mid-air when he was only forty-five. After having been a player-manager for the Cincinnati Reds in 1916-1917, Mathewson recovered enough to become president of the old National League Boston Braves in 1923 until his death in 1925 at the start of the World Series.

His passing was mourned not only throughout baseball, but nationwide. The first of the old-time sports heroes had died. The life of the inaugural Golden Boy of the Major Leagues burned bright to the end.

Christy Mathewson walked over to Don Ogilvie and introduced himself. They shook hands. The big pitcher was both friendly and encouraging, "Not all of us agree with this Ruth fellow and—what's the other one's name? Hornsby?" It was hard to say though if Mathewson was really speaking for anybody but himself.

Ogilvie said, "Well, it's nice to know that. Yeah, the other guy is Rogers Hornsby. That's Roger with an 's' on it. I think the 's' stands for 'shit for brains'."

Mathewson grinned. "I can see this Babe Ruth chap must've been something in his time. The other players give him a wide berth and seem to defer to his judgment."

"Yeah, Ruth was somethin', all right." Ogilvie continued. "He set the baseball world on its ear with his big bat. His big mouth wasn't too far behind."

Mathewson, coming from 1905, didn't know of Ruth or Hornsby— or any players from that era or after. Walter Johnson wouldn't come into the league until 1907. The only other players that he knew and knew him personally were Cy Young and Honus Wagner.

Mathewson observed, "It's a bit strange that these fellows recognize me, but apparently I'm not old enough yet to know of them."

"All these guys are familiar with the great Christy Mathewson," said a reverent Ogilvie.

"What's stranger is that they're surprised to see me alive," revealed a nonplussed Mathewson.

"At least you know you were around long enough to pitch yourself into the Hall of Fame. Sounds like you understand Limbotown pretty damn good," Ogilvie opined. It was all he could come up with for a twenty-five-year-old who had just learned of his own premature death. He wasn't about to tell Mathewson exactly when the big moment occurred either. He knew more than enough for now. Rationing the knowledge of the reference books, Ogilvie realized, would require judgment and restraint—in other words, wisdom. It was a faculty which, if it existed at all in Don Ogilvie, was used inadvertently and about as often as a total eclipse.

"I hope we all get the chance to play together. It would be magnificent if we could all help save the life of young Roberto," stated a sincere Christy Mathewson.

"Yes, it would," concurred an anxious Ogilvie.

The nobody-manager noticed, with some self-loathing, how well Mathewson seemingly dealt with his own mortality. Forget about being injured and losing a baseball career; this guy just realized he was checking out way before noon, and he was already thinking about someone else. Ogilvie began to feel the twinges of the embarrassment he'd been able to dull with alcohol the prior evening. Drummond's books were filled with the stories of his players, some of whose lives made Ogilvie's problems look as troublesome as a bad hair day. Out of the black players alone were the tragic tales of Roberto Clemente, Josh Gibson, and Roy Campanella. From the white team there was, of course, Mathewson—but overshadowing them all was Lou Gehrig.

Matty wished Ogilvie good luck. However, before returning to his locker, he asked him, "Do you mind if I come by just to talk sometime? I'm very curious about all the scientific advancements that have taken place—if you don't mind telling me about them."

"No, no," said a pleased Ogilvie, "Come by anytime. The office door is open to everybody." Ogilvie felt a connection with Mathewson. His request to talk would not be an idle one. Christy Mathewson would learn many things from Don Ogilvie. Don Ogilvie would learn much more from the turn-of-the-century pitcher, nee scholar and philosopher.

He hadn't gotten there yet, but the nobody-manager would come across stories of other baseball greats, their bad fortune and how they dealt with it. He would in time discover two stories that would make

154

him the most uncomfortable: Grover Cleveland Alexander and "Smokey" Joe Wood, both pitchers. He had selected neither for his team, and perhaps it was just as well. He already had his hands full and then some.

Ogilvie sought out Babe Ruth to tell him about Clown-lips Klem and the lineup cards. He could see the big man at his locker. It was much too close to Hornsby's for Ogilvie's liking. Nevertheless, he walked over to converse with the Babe. Ruth, stripped down to his shorts, was enormous. He could've been the prototype for the Spruce Goose. His size did not surprise Ogilvie.

The Bambino appeared even more hung over than the day before, the bad news of his failure to manage in the majors taking its toll in the form of a binge at the Limbotown bar. This did not surprise Ogilvie either.

But when the nobody-manager saw the Yankee great pulling on an old Boston Braves uniform, he was surprised. He was also very concerned. The uniform Ogilvie saw meant that Babe Ruth's career was virtually over; that his baseball talents were but a caricature of their vaunted past. He knew this now with the help of Drummond's special books. The Yankees traded Ruth in 1935 to the Boston Braves. He wouldn't even finish out the season. His previous two years with the Yankees saw his statistics drop like a barrel over Niagara Falls, his abilities gone almost overnight.

Sure, Ruth's condition would probably help Ogilvie and the black players prevail in today's game, but what about eight weeks from now, when they had their Series? All the training in the world could not restore Ruth's skills. Putting Humpty Dumpty back together again was not possible. Ruth was a victim of the thief from whom there is no escape—time. You can get a lot of things back in your life, but time is not one of them—except maybe in Limbotown. Still, Ogilvie could not help being expedient. If it would aid his cause today, he wouldn't worry about Ruth until tomorrow.

He engaged the huge outfielder's eyes and said, "I see you're playing for the Braves this season."

"Yeah," said Ruth while pulling on a jersey that could've been used to tent a medium-sized troop of Boy Scouts. "Probably be my last year, too," said a wistful Bambino. Then remembering what he was doing and why, his eyes tightened as he warned the nobody-manager. "Don't worry, Ovaltine! I've got plenty left for you and your band of Cuban Indians."

Ruth's boldness was heartening, except Ogilvie knew it was nothing more than bluster. The Babe Ruth of only a few seasons earlier could've backed it up, but not the 1935 model.

"I wish you the best of luck, Babe. But if your team loses, I'm counting on your word that we'll all play together," reminded Ogilvie.

Ruth ignored the reminder about what was supposed to happen if his team lost and said what he wanted. "I know I'm gonna manage in the Majors. I'm gonna prove you wrong."

"I hope I'm wrong too, Babe," Ogilvie said sympathetically. "Why don't you guys take batting practice last? You can be the home team today and use the other dugout."

"Okay with me. We won't have to play the bottom of the ninth that way," was the Babe's cutting reply.

"And, oh yeah," added Ogilvie, "we gotta give lineup cards to the ump five minutes before game time. It's some guy named Bill Klem."

"Old Fish-lips?" said Ruth. "Hell, he's from the National League. They don't know how to call strikes over there."

"Well, he's what Drummond gave us, so we're stuck with him," stated Ogilvie.

From his nearby locker, Rogers Hornsby, acting as if he was only an innocent bystander, turned and asked, "Bill Klem? Is he tall with a pair of lips that came right off a halibut?"

"That's him," said the nobody-manager.

"Damn, Jidge," said Hornsby to Ruth, as if Ogilvie was invisible. "I don't give a damn about Ovaltine's bullshit rules, but that son of a bitch Klem will throw us outta the game if we say anything about the niggers. He'll think we're talking about him!" Hornsby, who spent most of his career in the National League, knew Klem all too well.

Glad to see that Klem's reputation preceded him, Ogilvie left Ruth and Hornsby to stew and moan.

He found Antonio and told him to make sure that little Roberto was in his uniform and ready to assume his duties as batboy by game time. He also commented, "I don't think anyone will mind Maria sitting in the dugout with us. I know she'll want to keep a close eye on Roberto anyhow."

With his players in uniform, Ogilvie gathered the black all-star team to announce the lineup. With only eleven players available to play nine positions for the entire game, everyone was going to play. He decided that Roy Campanella and Clemente would start out on the bench. Everyone else would play their natural position. The Ogilvie-Alvarez lineup was a formidable Negro League All-Star team:

- Leading off and playing outfield, the speedster, James "Cool Papa" Bell.
- Batting second and playing second, the agile Jackie Robinson.
- Third and playing first, the steady Buck Leonard.
- Hitting clean-up, as always, mighty catcher Josh Gibson.
- Fifth, in the outfield, the incomparable Oscar Charleston.
- Sixth, the versatile Judy Johnson, third base.
- Seventh, and at shortstop, the acrobatic John Henry Lloyd.
- Eighth, the little dynamo outfielder, Jimmy Crutchfield.
- Ninth, the team's only pitcher, the charismatic Satchel Paige.

As Ogilvie read his list aloud to the tightly huddled group, the players began to don more of a game face for the upcoming battle with the white major leaguers. Ordinarily they would've been looser. When playing exhibition games against white all-star teams, the atmosphere was generally more carnival-like. This time was different. The honor of the Negro Leaguers had been bluntly called into question by Hornsby and Ruth—especially Hornsby. Also, they were now only moderately suspicious of their white nobody-manager, who earlier seemed ready to take a beating for them—not something seen in the days of the old Negro Leagues.

Ogilvie prepared his Negro League All-Star team for warm-ups and batting practice. When they were done, they could sit and watch Ruth's team do the same. *Maybe some flaw could be exposed and exploited,* Ogilvie waxed to himself.

Ogilvie and the team left the clubhouse and emerged into the dramatic expanse of Drummond Field. As he and Antonio followed their players through the tunnel to the dugout, a huge anxiety attack was brewing in the hollow of his abdomen. His mouth was dry, and the breath he drew had a queer metallic flavor to it. He desperately craved a drink. At the same time, he could not remember a moment when he felt more aware, more conscious, more alive. It was a different feeling from the rush of adrenaline or his love for Maggie. It was oddly empowering. His urge to imbibe was fast overcome. Ogilvie had found something far more potent than alcohol—managing dead Hall of Famers in a fight for little Roberto's life.

Regardless, his body once again became a rain forest. He grabbed two towels on his way to the field and wadded them under his armpits. He was sweaty but ready.

Chapter 11

His team took the field. It was another magnificent day in Limbotown—mild temperatures, blue skies, and the seductive green turf of Drummond Field. Ogilvie asked his players to, ". . . do whatever you usually do to warm up." Some began stretching, others ran; a few went right to the batting cage. Ruth and the white squad made their way over to the other dugout to do some pre-game scouting. With their old-style uniforms, bats, and gloves, both teams looked like a convention of baggy-pants comedians or rodeo clowns— they did to Don Ogilvie and Antonio Alvarez anyway. It was okay. The players fit right in with Clown-lips Klem and just about everything else in Limbotown.

The stands were becoming lightly sprinkled with the hotel employees and their families. The small crowd, including Maggie Briggs, was mostly bunched behind home plate. Maggie made sure everyone knew about the game. Soon they all showed up. In Limbotown you could close down a whole hotel on account of a baseball game. This is one place that had its priorities straight.

Everyone also knew of the challenge to save Roberto's life. It was one of the privileges of being a Lucky Stiff. Still, only Ogilvie himself, Drummond, Maggie, and whoever the other Chosen Ones were, knew about Ogilvie trading his life.

Death Incarnate found a seat one level up from all the others. Everybody, including Drummond, preferred it this way.

159

As the nobody-manager's crew retreated to their dugout, it would be his turn to scout Ruth's team. He didn't even know who was pitching. A couple of players were warming up in the bullpen. But it was Walter "Big Train" Johnson who climbed the Drummond Field mound when batting practice was over. This made sense to Ogilvie. Ruth knew Johnson well, having faced him many times. The fast-balling right-hander would be a tough match against Ogilvie's mostly right-handed lineup. If Johnson failed, Ruth was laden with other Hall of Fame pitchers—like Cy Young, Dizzy Dean, Christy Mathewson, Don Drysdale, and Carl Hubbell. Don Ogilvie had only Satchel Paige, but figured things were about even.

There wasn't much Ogilvie could do about the old bats and gloves. He wasn't going to try to re-train these guys five minutes before game time. Both sides would be playing old-school baseball. That would be fair. However, he did exert some managerial sway over his players.

He asked his team to, "...knock off any showboating or clowning during the game or between innings. I don't want to aggravate Ruth's team. If they turn out to be sleeping dogs, we don't want to kick 'em."

He also reminded his team that: "It might not mean much to you fellas yet, but we're playing for the life of my best friend—Antonio and Maria's son, little Roberto."

The chance of that *did* mean something to them—not nearly as much, of course, as it meant to Don Ogilvie and the Alvarezes. They had only known these people for a day or so. During that short time, they saw the nobody-manager deftly put together this contest and stand up to Hornsby's affronts to them. Their respect was also at stake. And, whether it was true or not, they could taste Ogilvie's hunger to save the life of his best friend, a little brown child.

By this time, Roberto and his mom were seated in the dugout. Roberto had on his San Bernardino Stampede uniform that said "Batboy" across the back of his shoulders.

Don Ogilvie announced to his players, "Roberto is our official batboy back home, and he'd be honored to be the team's batboy today." He added, "Maria is going to be with us in the dugout today. I'm sure you guys won't mind."

Maria was young and attractive. They didn't mind. All were quite respectful of her motherhood and marital status. Many of the players tipped their caps to her and referred to her as Ma'am or Missus. Satchel Paige apologized in advance for any foul language that was sure to be used in the heat of the game: "We might fergit and say sumpin' sound pretty bad. So we sorry already."

Maria tried to reassure them, "I've been around baseball players most of my life. Please play like I'm not even here. I can't tell you how much my husband, my son, and I appreciate what you're doing for us." Her voice faded off in a choke of emotion. There was nothing like a pretty woman's tears to bring hardened pros to their knees. They were moved. They were also ready to play serious baseball.

Little Roberto, who was now standing next to his father and under the protective arm of his best friend, stated, "You guys just let me know what bat you want and I'll go get it." His cheerfulness lightened the mood.

Paige turned to Josh Gibson and said, "It might be fun havin' a half-pint gettin' our stuff. Kind of a valet service." The old Negro Leaguers were used to handling their own belongings, from luggage to gear. The novelty of the first-class treatment they were receiving in Limbotown would not wear off during their entire stay.

At five minutes to one, head umpire Bill Klem stood on home plate. He signaled to each dugout. Don Ogilvie, butterflies the size of crows flapping in his stomach, emerged to present his lineup card to Klem. Ponderously, Ruth did the same. Klem made them shake hands.

Out of nowhere, a voice on the Drummond Field public address system requested everyone to rise for the National Anthem. Ogilvie briefly wondered if Limbotown had its own anthem. A beautiful female voice then filled the speakers with the "Star Spangled Banner." At the end of the magnificent rendition, there was healthy applause from the small audience and a few familiar chants of "Play ball!"

Water jetted from Don Ogilvie like a burst fire hydrant. Antonio, who was ready with a fresh supply of towels, affectionately wrapped one around his manager's shoulders. Ogilvie silently recognized the gesture with the tilt of his head.

His sweat glands should've erupted when he saw the white team's outfield of Ruth, DiMaggio, and Mantle trot out to their positions. Instead, his pores were clogged by the improbable sight. It was the kind of thing that baseball fans could only dream about. In New York, grown men would've wept.

Antonio remarked to Ogilvie, "How'd you think the Stampede would do with that outfield?"

Ogilvie smiled. "We wouldn't need an infield."

Added to the Babe's outfield was Gehrig at first, Hornsby at second, Honus Wagner at short, and Pie Traynor at third.

Big Train Johnson completed his warm-up tosses. Antonio made sure the players knew the batting order and readied them. Cool Papa Bell entered the batter's box as the leadoff hitter. Big Train brought his best stuff and struck him out with his first three pitches. He struck out the next two batters, too.

Ogilvie and the Negro leaguers were dazzled—not only by the sheer speed of Johnson's fastball, but the length of his arms.

Cool Papa remarked to Ogilvie, "Man, that sucker don't have an arm. That's some sort of buggy-whip attached to his right shoulder."

A consensus started to form about Walter Johnson's origins. As Buck Leonard surmised, "There musta been a brotha or a sista in the family woodpile somewhere to get arms like that."

Big Train, however, was a seventh-generation American. He was as lily white as they came. Born in Kansas and raised in California, he was not a racist—at least not by turn-of-the-century standards.

They called Walter Johnson "Big Train" for good reason. First, he was big, about six-two. Second, his fastball was indeed like a fast train that seemed to disappear into a tiny tunnel. Third, his heater moved around like the ball was lopsided. The movement was unpredictable. That's how Johnson got away with throwing only one pitch his entire career. The batter knew the fastball was coming, but couldn't hit anyhow. He could also move it up or down or side to side. It didn't look like he was throwing hard but the last pitch he threw in the inning Ogilvie estimated at a hundred miles an hour. He hadn't time yet to set up radar guns. His guess was right on target. It was no mystery how Big Train did it. He may not have been the missing link like Ruth, but he did have arms that would make most orangutans jealous. Knuckle-dragger was not the phrase that came to mind in sizing up the lanky, open-faced Johnson. Still, he could probably tie his shoes without bending over. Unbelievably, his right-arm, his pitching arm seemed even longer than his left.

Finally there was the trademark Big Train side-arm delivery. The ball would come rocketing out of Johnson's right hand by way of third base giving a right-handed batter the illusion the ball was going to hit him. It very rarely did. By the time the batter could figure out what happened, the ball would be in the catcher's mitt with the umpire singing, "Steee-rike!" He was going to be tough to get to. However, Ogilvie had learned of perhaps Johnson's only weakness. If his players didn't start hitting, he would try to take advantage of it and hope for the best. His armpits started to flow again.

Satchel Paige was not to be outdone or upstaged by anyone. Ogilvie found he wouldn't have to panic when Paige matched Johnson almost pitch for pitch and struck out Hornsby, Wagner, and Gehrig in the bottom of the first inning. The skill of Satchel Paige was only equaled by his resolve. Ogilvie wasn't sweating anymore.

Hornsby had played in these inter-league games before and faced Satchel Paige. In one game Paige struck out the stunned Rajah five times. At the time, Paige was about ten years younger than both Ruth and Hornsby. The older Babe shrewdly avoided any inter-league showdowns with the young Negro League phenom. Scuttlebutt had it he didn't want to come anywhere near the lightning-fast and devious Paige. After all, look what he had done to Hornsby.

Ruth would have to bat against Paige to start the second inning. Today, the vitiated, over-the-hill Bambino would have no choice but to face a young, strong, Satchel Paige.

Josh Gibson was often called the black Babe Ruth because of his prodigious home run power. But it was Satchel Paige, the renowned Negro League pitcher, who was able to parallel Ruth's fame.

An average Negro League game might draw 20,000 fans. When

163

Paige pitched, that total easily doubled. He was the supreme crowd pleaser, a showman, a flashy entertainer. And, oh yeah, he could throw a baseball like a magician. If Satchel Paige pulled a rabbit out of his cap, the crowd reckoned it was all part of his game. More often than not, he could make the ball seemingly disappear as it flew by the batter. He was a sorcerer on the pitcher's mound. Instead of a cape, top hat, and magic wand, Satchel employed an arsenal of pitches, a tireless arm, and his wily instincts to outwit the opposition.

Leroy Robert Paige was born in Mobile, Alabama, in the early 1900s. The official date is 1906. Many believed him to be born in 1903. Paige himself did nothing to clarify his true age. It was a matter of intrigue he enjoyed promoting. In fact, he enjoyed promoting anything about himself. He was a shameless and brazen self-promoter, who was also outspoken and brash. He was the Mohammed Ali of the first half of the twentieth century—and, like Ali, he could back up his boasts. As the popular leader of the Negro Leagues, Paige was an early and vocal opponent of baseball's color line. Whether he intended it or not, it made him a budding civil rights leader.

He was not the modest, self-effacing hero like, say, Lou Gehrig. He was more the raucous, carousing, bombastic hero—like, say, Babe Ruth. Truly, the Babe and Satchel shared many similar attributes and accolades. They were both the favorite players of their time, albeit for different American communities. They were both the biggest draws. They were both the highest-paid players in their respective leagues (although the Negro Leagues were far from as affluent as white Major League baseball). They both loved women (despite both being married), fancy cars, wild clothes, and a wild time. They both believed they were the best at what they did, and not many could argue otherwise. They both loved the limelight and the devotion of their fans. They both were outgoing, friendly, and natural born leaders. They both were born to play baseball.

Paige acquired his quirky nickname as a child while growing up in the South. He'd earned a precious few cents a day toting satchels and baggage at the local train station. The name stayed with him forever. As Paige became a Negro League star, his own baggage increased to accommodate his ever-expanding wardrobe of whimsical fashion statements. The name "Satchel" may have had modest roots, but it soon referred to the imposing collection of expensive luggage that Paige could now afford to have others tote.

Once he ascended the pitcher's mound, it was Satchel's game. He directed it, controlled it, and manipulated it—all with the toss of a little white ball. During rock fights as a kid, he developed his famous "hesitation" pitch. Making his victims duck or flinch by first faking a throw, he then quickly followed up with a missile that was fast, accurate, and seemed to come out of nowhere. He called his curve ball his "be" ball because, he claimed, "It always be where I want it to be".

Sometimes he would start a game with no fielders behind him and then dramatically strike out the side. He was often accused of showboating, but most Negro League teams had some of the Harlem Globetrotters in them. The players, the owners, and the fans appreciated the value of entertainment—the idea that a baseball game was not a life or death proposition (at least outside of Limbotown). It should be fun. He could also play hard-nosed baseball, but there was always joy in Satchel's heart when he took the field. And what a big heart he had. No one was more competitive or wanted to win more than Satchel Paige—nor did anyone have more empathy for his fellow man. Not exactly a philanthropist; he was more of a homespun philosopher. Always willing to lend a sympathetic ear, he never forgot his humble beginnings.

Paige fully expected the color barrier to fall of its own weight—which it did, in 1947. The optimistic Satchel had expected the fall would occur much earlier. He'd also anticipated that he, as ambassador and leader of the Negro Leagues, would be the first black player to cross the line. But in 1947 Paige, was already forty-something, with his best years behind him. Jackie Robinson got the call instead. This never sat well with the blunt-speaking Paige. He felt his harsh criticism of segregated baseball had denied him the honor bestowed on Robinson. More likely it was his age. He did make it to the majors the following year, and acquitted himself admirably during several stints. He pitched into his early sixties. Had the Major Leagues seen Satchel in his prime, he would've been on the same plateau as Walter Johnson, Christy Mathewson. or Dizzy Dean.

He pitched magnificently against his white alter ego, Dizzy Dean, in inter-league exhibition contests in the 1930s. Dizzy commented that if he could add Paige to his St. Louis pitching staff, the pennant could be won by late July, and he and Satchel could go fishing until the World Series in October. Dean, a Kentucky product, was Paige's biggest fan in the white Major Leagues. There were other believers who were reluctant to come forward in those pre-World War II days. Dean never had that problem. He was unabashed in his praise of Paige, and he didn't care what others thought. To Dizzy, Paige could've been green with yellow trim; it just didn't matter. What mattered to Dizzy Dean and electrified him so much was Paige's wizardry with a baseball. He could turn it into a bewitched orb captive only to his command. With Dean as the premier Major League pitcher of his time, Paige would've had to do a lot to get Dizzy's attention. Satchel Paige not only got Dean's attention, but also the white Kentuckian's public acclaim when doing so risked his own celebrity. For Dean and a growing group of supporters, greatness knew no boundaries.

Satchel Paige might play a 200-game season in summer and then go to Mexico or Cuba in the off season and play another 200. He would often pitch on little or no rest. In 1935, he reportedly pitched twenty-nine games in twenty-nine days. He must've had a bionic right arm to keep up that pace and pitch until he was old enough to collect Social Security.

Satchel wrote an autobiography, appropriately titled, *Maybe I'll Pitch Forever.* Like Dizzy Dean, he was famous for his funny aphorisms, such as, "Don't look back. Something might be gaining on you." He was the Negro League's version of Will Rogers. Dizzy Dean, on the other hand, sort of was Will Rogers. His folksy sayings amused the public first as a player and later as an announcer. If they ever put Dean and Paige together in the same room with Yogi Berra and Casey Stengel, the English language would surely be overmatched, reshuffled, and require a new dictionary.

At his 1961 Hall of Fame induction ceremony, Ted Williams, the illustrious Boston Red Sox slugger, courageously spoke of the past injustice the Major League color barrier wreaked. He pleaded for the need and right to induct into the Hall of Fame the equally talented Negro Leaguers who'd never had the opportunity to play in the Major Leagues. It wasn't until ten years later that the Hall of Fame finally added a handful of Negro League legends. Many others deserve to grace the Hall. Although part of the first bunch to be selected, if Satchel were alive today he'd still be leading the charge. Satchel Paige died in 1982 at age seventy-six.—or was it seventy-nine?

In the top of the second, Ogilvie's team could only muster a weak ground-out by Josh Gibson, followed by two more strikeouts. Big Train was throwing easy, but slinging very hard stuff. They were using the live ball. When hit firmly, it would fly out of Drummond Field like any other ballpark. Walter Johnson was blissfully ignorant of this. To him, the tightly wound white bullet with red stripes made his fastball even faster and livelier. The Negro League hitters were struggling.

To start off the bottom of the second, the much-anticipated match-up between Ruth and Paige took place. It was anticlimactic. Paige blew him away on three fast balls, with Ruth corkscrewing himself into the ground on his last swing. Most of the players in his dugout just looked away, pretending not to see the sorry remains of greatness. It was an unpleasant reminder to all of how fleeting an athlete's time. As far as Ogilvie could tell, there was little chance, as Drummond suggested, that Ruth would play like Babe Ruth—not like the Babe of old, at any rate.

In the bottom of the fourth inning with two outs, Lou Gehrig got the first hit of the game with a bouncing ball single up the middle. Paige then struck out Ruth for the second consecutive time to end the inning.

Ogilvie got his first real scare when Mickey Mantle came up in the bottom of the third. Young Mickey had looked bad striking out in his first at bat. The battle-tested Paige was too much for the undeveloped talent of Mantle. Paige immediately had Mickey down two strikes and no balls. He was winging fast balls by him. On the next pitch, Mantle literally closed his eyes and started his stroke before the ball left Paige's

167

hand. If the ball was in the dirt or over the backstop, The Mick was committed to swing at it. To everyone's amazement, the bat cracked with the sound of solid contact. The ball took off foul down the right-field line and cleared the fence. It was a hard shot but foul all the way. Mickey was almost to first base when he turned to come back to the batter's box. His return was slow, his head down. He appeared discouraged, knowing what he had done was sheer luck.

Ogilvie turned to his young assistant, Antonio Alvarez, and said, "That's what I call the longest walk. When a hitter knows he's in over his head and then almost gets lucky on one pitch. He doesn't stand a chance after that, and he knows it. That walk back to the batter's box is the longest walk there is . . . You and I have been there, huh, Antonio? Watch this. Satchel will fool him with a curve ball out of the zone for strike three."

As if pre-scripted, Mantle lunged at a curve in the dirt for a strikeout. Antonio Alvarez could tell from the look on his manager's face—Don Ogilvie didn't want this game to be his longest walk.

Meanwhile, in the other dugout, a quizzical Ruth asked the downhearted Mantle, "Is that how you hit this guy—shut your eyes and swing?" With no other ideas, Ruth was half-serious.

It was a pitcher's duel until the bottom of the fifth. Paige got a little careless waiting for the first batter of the inning, Jimmie Foxx, to swing at pitches just out of the strike zone. He didn't, and Paige walked him. Paige struck out third baseman Pie Traynor for the first out of the inning. Then DiMaggio came up. On a 1-1 fastball over the outside part of the plate, Joe D took Satchel high and deep to right center for a two run home run and a 2-0 lead. The small crowd was mostly silent out of respect for Roberto and his parents.

The white team dugout was celebrating anyhow. When DiMaggio returned to the bench to receive the congratulations of his teammates, Manager Babe Ruth told him, "Damn, son, if I knew you could hit like that, I woulda moved you up in the order. Nice swing." The always-chatty Joe D let out a hardly audible, "Thanks;" a veritable speech from the Yankee Clipper.

The nobody-manager quietly remarked to Antonio, "I know I told

DiMaggio and them to play to win. I was hopin' they wouldn't take me so seriously."

Ogilvie started to schvitz like a steam-room junkie. He had a two-run deficit to deal with, and his team had yet to get a hit or score a run in five innings. He thought this would be a good time to let his players in on Walter Johnson's one frailty.

At the top of the sixth inning, Ogilvie gathered his troops and told them, "Johnson won't throw inside. He's afraid he's really going to hurt someone. He did once. That's another story. You guys just get up on the plate and either walk or hit that outside fastball that he's been getting by you. And try not to make it look too obvious." It worked. Josh Gibson got the Ogilvie team its first hit and score on a long home run to left field. The game tightened at 2-1.

In the top of the seventh, the Negro Leaguers were on top of Johnson and home plate, scoring three more runs for a 4-2 lead. But they might not have scored at all. Joe DiMaggio nearly made the play of the game on Oscar Charleston's line drive double up the gap in right-center. Ruth was closer to the ball, but stumbled pathetically. DiMaggio took off for what could only be a defensive move to try to cut the ball off before it got to the wall. When the ball was hit, there was no way DiMaggio could get there in time to catch it. Holding Charleston to a single and a RBI had to be the strategy. Instead, the laws of physics seemed to bend for Joe D, and he left his feet, skying high in the air—only to have the ball tick the end of his undersized mitt and roll to the wall. If he had made the catch, it may well have kept his team in control. If he had been using the large, modern outfielder's glove, he would've had it. The Negro Leaguers, as well as everyone else at Drummond Field, had the same question on their minds: How did he even get that close?

Ogilvie was able to breathe a tiny sigh of relief as his team took a two run lead going into the last two innings.

The small audience, led by the cheers of Maggie Briggs, was hopeful of a win. Drummond, from his second-deck perch, was poker-faced.

Ruth replaced Big Train with Cy Young to start the top of the eighth. It was a last-minute decision by the Babe, and old Cy wasn't properly warmed-up. With a couple of walks, a sacrifice and a timely hit, the

Negro Leaguers scored two more runs for a 6-2 lead going into the bottom of the eighth.

Then Paige seemed to falter. He walked DiMaggio, the inning's lead-off batter, but it was better than giving him another homer. Then Mantle bunted DiMaggio to second for the first out. Ruth needed a pinch-hitter for Cy Young, but he was down to nothing but pitchers. The Babe must have learned something, because he picked Don Drysdale to hit for Young. For a pitcher, Drysdale was excellent with the bat. Ruth knew nothing of Drysdale, who came along decades afterward. As Ogilvie would later find out, Ruth simply asked the pitchers if any of them were decent hitters. Drysdale was the first to raise his hand. The big right-hander immediately singled to center, sending DiMaggio to third with only one out.

That's when the real play of the game occurred. Hornsby was up again, and still hadn't put the ball in play. He was hungry and mortified. Paige had dominated him. Hornsby was a frustrated racist, and also a magnificent hitter. He couldn't be held down forever. On a 2-1 fastball, the Cardinal second baseman sliced a sure-hit one-hopper past a flying, outstretched John Henry Lloyd at shortstop. As DiMaggio trotted home from third and the crowd began to groan, Pop Lloyd quickly got up and threw the ball, which should've been in left field, to Jackie Robinson at second—who turned it for an inning-ending double play. It was a close call, the ball just beating the fleet Hornsby to first base. Instead of one out, one run in and men on first and second, the inning was over for the Ruth team.

Ogilvie asked Paige about Lloyd: "Does he do this kinda stuff all the time?"

Paige was nonchalant in his reply: "Yeah—when Pop was dis young, he could float."

There was stunned but respectful snarling from the white team dugout.

Hornsby, naturally, was livid. He was jumping up and down like he was on a pogo stick, yelling obscenities at the umpires and the black team dugout. Klem warned him about his antics and threatened to throw him out of the game. This only enraged Hornsby more, and he continued his tantrum. He spewed more venom at the black team, and both benches cleared. Thank God it was a typical baseball brawl, with a lot of punches being thrown and very few landing. About half the players on each side were either looking for a fight or trying to break one up. They were rolling around on the ground, wrestling more than punching. The melee lasted less than two minutes. What Ogilvie was afraid would blossom into a full-scale race riot pleasantly fizzled almost as fast as it started. Klem ejected Hornsby from the game and banished him to the dugout on the condition he kept his mouth shut. Otherwise it was off to the showers. Order was restored to start the ninth inning. Ogilvie's squad failed to score.

It was still 6-2, the black team, going into the bottom of the ninth. Paige was cruising, and struck out Honus Wagner and Lou Gehrig to get the first two outs. With only one more out, the two teams would have to play their promised games together for Roberto's life. Only Babe Ruth, who had struck out in his previous three at-bats, stood in the way. Ruth looked like a whipped puppy (albeit, a very large whipped puppy) as he tried to ready himself in the on deck circle. Something tugged at Ogilvie's mind. Maybe it was manager's intuition. He signaled Klem for a time-out. He told Antonio, "Go to my desk. There's a bottle of Scotch in the lower right-hand drawer. Grab it and go to the other team's dugout and give the bottle to Ruth. Use the dugout tunnel." Ogilvie didn't want Bill Klem and the other umpires to see anything.

Antonio was bewildered. "What?"

The nobody-manager said, "Don't think about it, just do it. Now!"

Antonio went.

Ogilvie slowly approached Paige on the pitcher's mound. "Terrific job, Satch. I need to ask a favor. I want you to throw a couple of balls to Ruth and then groove one for him right down the middle. I need to see if he can still hit one out. I think everybody else does too."

Paige understood. He was beginning to appreciate the nobody-manager for thinking about the team's future.

Antonio retrieved the bottle of Scotch and hurried through the other clubhouse to the white team's dugout. He stood at the opening, trying not to be seen. Ruth was at the other end, selecting a new bat. Antonio

171

did that kind of loud-whisper thing. "Hey, Mr. Ruth. Pssst. Hey, Mr. Ruth!"

Gehrig, who was close to where Antonio was, watched the strange solicitation and got the Babe's attention. "Hey, Jidge. There's a kid from the other team wants to see you."

Ruth spied the furtive Antonio motioning him to come over. Ruth sighed heavily. "All right." He asked Klem to extend the timeout and walked into the tunnel where Antonio awaited.

"What is it, Kid?" he asked Antonio in a way that was not altogether polite.

Antonio removed the bottle of Scotch he had secured in his waistband and presented it to the big outfielder. "My manager, Don . . . Don Ogilvie said I should bring this to you."

Ruth's eyes lit up as he carelessly wrested the glass container from Antonio's hand. The big man glanced over his shoulder to make sure no one could see and proceeded to take three huge gulps from the bottle.

After the first one, he became more talkative. "A few years back I wouldn't even get a hangover after drinkin' all night," he told an overwhelmed Antonio.

After the second giant swig, he reminisced. "Used to be I could eat and drink as much as I want, play a game, and hit a coupla homers. No sweat. Did it all the time . . . Ain't fun gettin' old."

He wiped off the last gargantuan swallow on his jersey sleeve. "Not bad," he commented. "This oughta steady my hand and cool my head for a minute. Go tell your boss, thanks." Babe handed the bottle of booze back to a wide-eyed Antonio Alvarez and made his way to the plate.

Ruth settled into the batter's box. He glanced over at Ogilvie and nodded once. Ogilvie nodded back. Antonio made his way back to his manager's side, curious to see the effect of his offering on the Sultan of Swat.

Paige gave Ruth two outside curves that didn't draw a swing. He then let a batting practice fastball go right down the middle. The Scotch-powered Bambino, his hangover and nerves soothed by the hair of the dog, hit one of his patented high arcing shots to deep right field. The Babe of yore would've hit the ball completely out of Limbotown. This

172

version was glad to clear the fence by ten feet. Ruth was wobbly rounding the bases, but his reputation was still intact—sort of.

Jimmie Foxx, the last batter of the game, hit a harmless ground ball for the final out. The tiny throng cheered. The Alvarezes congratulated and hugged their nobody-manager. Ogilvie praised his players. The two teams even met at home plate to exchange handshakes, although it was only a formality. The nobody-manager could feel the riptide of resentment coursing just beneath the surface. Before the players left the field, Ogilvie announced another practice for the next morning at ten. There were no audible objections. This time he was pretty sure they would all show up—including the stubborn Rogers Hornsby. Upon hearing about the practice, Hornsby just kicked at the dirt in anger. He hadn't really stopped kicking since hitting into his double play to end the eighth inning.

Ruth sought out "Ovaltine" and unobtrusively thanked him for the timely boost. "Thanks for that snort, Keed." The two alcoholics understood the temporary curative effects of more liquor. Nevertheless, Ogilvie knew he would have to do something about George Herman Ruth. He tried to locate Drummond at his second level roost. Death Personified was already gone.

Instead, a smiling Maggie Briggs stood in front of him. "Congratulations," she said, extending her hand to his. This time he made sure not to hold on too long. "That was a great game. I guess now the hard part really starts."

This time he understood what she was talking about. "You're right. This isn't going to be as easy as I thought. Thanks for trying to warn me." He was more modest than apologetic. He was on a mission though, and asked her, "Do you know where I can find Drummond?"

"He really likes his clubhouse office. He can make believe he's a real big league manager in there," she informed Ogilvie with a grin. She let him go saying, "Good luck with whatever you're going to ask him."

He told the Alvarezes he would join them later at the hotel. First he needed to talk to Drummond. He wouldn't say exactly what about, only that it was: "team business."

Chapter 12

Don found Drummond in his clubhouse office.

"Well, Ogilvie, you pulled it off, so far. But you got a long way to go," counseled a confident Death in the Flesh.

"That's what I need to talk to you about. Babe Ruth didn't play like Babe Ruth, and Mantle is still an overgrown sixth grader."

"Whaddaya talkin' about!" Drummond screeched in his best Brooklyn accent. "The big ape got a homer, and the kid nearly got one!"

Ogilvie pointed out, "You know just as well as I do that Mantle shut his eyes and swung at that pitch. It was pure luck. He wasn't close to anything else the rest of the day. He was overmatched, and you know it!" Ogilvie was getting louder. "And don't even talk to me about Ruth! What the hell do you think I was telling Paige out there? My recipe for cornbread? The big blob was barely able to hit the damn ball when it was served to him on toast!" Ogilvie was giving as good as he got, but it was going to take more to get what he wanted.

"What is it, Ogilvie? What do you want this time?" asked an irritated Drummond.

"Only what's fair. I need a younger Babe Ruth and an older Mickey Mantle."

"No," Drummond said. He wasn't yelling, but he was firm.

Ogilvie was thwarted. He tried again. "Look, I've built the whole team around Ruth. If I can't have the real Babe Ruth for our Series, I might as well mail it in now. I thought you wanted some real competition.

Give me these two guys in their prime and we'll see who's the better manager—you or me." Ogilvie was trying to goad Drummond any way he could.

Death Personified laughed softly. "I told you—Death has no ego. Don't try to bait me, Ogilvie, I'm not Charlie the Tuna."

The nobody-manager was hampered and feeling desperate. He begged Death, "There must be something I can do to get this . . . some way to earn it."

Drummond was pensive for a second; then his face glowed with what he thought was a brilliant idea. "I've got some good news and some bad news for you, Ogilvie. The bad news—you're stuck with Mantle. The good news—Ruth. You just gave me an inspiration about "earning" him. Tell you what I'll do. For every week you can keep Fatty Arbuckle on the wagon, stone-cold sober, I'll knock a year off his age. That'll make him thirty-two by Series time—the same age he was when he hit sixty homers. But if he falls off, even once . . . what you see is what you get."

Ogilvie thought that this is just the kind of solution he'd come to expect from Drummond. Maggie and Drummond had both tried to warn him: "This isn't going to be easy." Yes—Death Personified would help, except it was again his monkey-paw kind of help. Keeping Ruth dry would be near impossible. Hell, he couldn't even keep himself sober. There was no other choice, though. Ogilvie was ready to settle with Drummond on the Ruth issue, but for a reason unknown to even himself, he requested one last favor. It was something that wouldn't help him.

The nobody-manager asked Death in the Flesh, "If I can keep Ruth sober, will you let him go back to 1935 in the same shape I get him into?"

Even Drummond wasn't sure why Ogilvie asked for this but replied, "Look, I can't send him back any different than I found him. I will do this—he can have one game. That's it. He'll look fat, except he'll play like whatever shape you get him into. Is that okay?"

The Ultimate Umpire didn't wait for Ogilvie to say anything. "Now get outta here before I change my mind!" Drummond wore an extra-wide grin as a conflicted Don Ogilvie left the room. Death in the Flesh already knew what was just occurring to the nobody-manager—that trying to keep Ruth sober would mean he'd have to stay sober too.

As he left the grinning Doctor Death, Ogilvie realized he'd have to make a sobriety pact with Ruth, and come up with some convincing reasons for the Babe to agree. This time he was trying to think ahead. He hadn't had a drink all day, but he was also preparing himself to drink— and in front of Maggie Briggs too. Oh well, he thought, a manager's gotta do what a manager's got do, even if it meant doing something he knew he shouldn't be doing.

He showered and changed clothes in the team's clubhouse. The place was cleared out, except for Charlie McManus and some of his men.

He walked the short distance to the hotel and joined Maria, Antonio, and Roberto for an early dinner in the dining room. The food, the service, everything, as usual, was exceptional. Don Ogilvie and the Alvarez family enjoyed a brief victory celebration, and Don and Antonio discussed what they were going to do for practices. Little Roberto was awestruck, recounting the thrills of the game—especially Babe Ruth's homerun. Despite his awful performance and contrived dinger, the Babe was still God to children. He had a magical bond with them. The only cheer from the fans for the white team had been Ruth's charity shot in the last inning, and most of that came from the kids. Ruth himself was a child. He and children everywhere—even those in Limbotown—reveled in it.

Ogilvie was drinking water all through dinner, trying to hydrate himself in advance of what was probably going to be a big night of boozing. He didn't say anything to the Alvarez family about Ruth, or about Drummond's demand of sobriety in exchange for years off of Ruth's age. He didn't want to jinx the deal before he secured the big man's handshake on it. After dinner, the Alvarezes retired for the evening. Don told them he was not too far behind. It was a white lie. He knew he had a date waiting for him in the hotel lounge, conveniently located adjacent to the dining room. It wouldn't be Maggie Briggs, however. There he would find the hulking, sulking and solitary Babe Ruth, numbing his bruised ego with hard liquor.

176

Ogilvie took a deep breath and timidly entered the faintly lit, plush lounge. Maggie watched from her usual station at the bar with some interest. She was not sure what was going on.

There were a few other players in the room, none of whom were getting near Ruth. He'd played miserably, and his teammates knew his home run was less than immaculate. If one of them had tried to approach him, they would've been harshly rejected or even ejected. Ogilvie was not sure what type of reception he would get and readied himself for the worst. He walked to the Babe's table and just stood there. Ruth looked up, bleary and teary-eyed.

Ogilvie asked, "Mind if I join you?"

To Ogilvie's relief, the soused Babe just kind of wagged a hand at him to sit down.

Ruth offered Ogilvie his gratitude again for having Antonio deliver the magic bottle of Scotch. "Hey Ovaltine, thanks for that shot. I know what you was trying to do. Everybody knows I'm all washed up. Hey— you gotta have a drink with me. You are a drinking man, aren't ya? You better be!" he said, slapping Ogilvie on the back.

"Yeah, I'm a drinking man all right, Babe. That's my problem. I'm too much of a drinking man."

"Well you better be drinkin' if you're gonna sit here, Ovaltine!" Ruth decreed.

Ogilvie had expected no less. All that remained now was for the nobody-manager to completely disillusion Maggie Briggs by ordering a drink. He decided to go all the way and asked Maggie to bring a new bottle. The patter was tart as a flabbergasted Maggie Briggs delivered a fifth that she noisily pounded on the wooden table.

"Would you like a gun and a bullet to play Russian Roulette in between gulps?" was her caustic contribution.

Ruth was too despondent to care, and Ogilvie had to swallow his pride for the time being and stick with his plan. The irony was not lost on him that he and Ruth would have to drink together in order to form a sobriety pact. They hoisted their glasses. Ruth, who was already well toasted, made a self-deprecating toast: "To a good manager, who out-managed a fat, overdone, over-the-hill dumb shit." They drank.

Ogilvie wasn't going to waste any more time. "Babe, what if I told you there was a way I could get you to be thirty-two years old again—the same age you were when you hit your sixty homers?"

Ruth stuck his finger in his ear, wiggling it around, and said, "I musta not heard you right. I thought I heard you say you could make me young again."

"That's right," affirmed Ogilvie. "Of course there's a catch. You have to stay sober. Not one drop of alcohol can pass your lips until the Series is over. Drummond's rule. For each week you stay dry, you become another year younger. If you slip up, even once, you're back to this."

"I don't believe that little bastard for one minute! He can't do that. He can't do anything."

Ruth had not taken well to Drummond's ridicule of him. He reminded Ruth too much of his feisty, Lilliputian Yankee manager, Miller Huggins, who the Babe disliked, even detested. According to Huggins, the feeling was, at the very least, mutual.

All Ogilvie could do was point out the obvious. "Look, Babe, I don't like the little bastard either. But it sure is hard to ignore this place," Ogilvie said, moving an arm around. "Limbotown is pretty convincing."

"Ah, it's all some big trick," Ruth muttered as he took another shot.

Ogilvie responded as best as he could. "Well then, he oughta be able to trick your body into being thirty-two again."

Ruth wasn't persuaded. The nobody-manager hated to do it, but he was going to have to fall back on Maggie once more. He silently snared her attention, and she understood it as a summons. When she arrived at the table, she declined both men's invitation to sit down.

Ogilvie told Maggie, "Drummond's promised to make the Babe a year younger for every week he can stay sober. Please tell Mr. Ruth Drummond can do that."

Maggie viewed the nobody-manager with an inkling of what he was trying to do. She was helpful in her reply. "Yes, Drummond can definitely do that. He could make you nineteen or even turn you into a baby if he wanted too." After a second, she added, "That would be redundant."

She continued: "If he told Don he would do that, he'll do it. And I'm sure he was very serious about the not drinking part."

She asked Ogilvie, "Does that mean you have to stop drinking too?"

"No, it doesn't," he informed a disappointed Maggie. After just the right amount of time, he added, "But I was just about to suggest to the Babe that he and I go on the wagon together. You know—a sobriety pact."

That seemed to mollify Maggie somewhat. The nobody-manager was headed in the right direction after all. Ruth broke records; Ogilvie broke bottles. Actually, Ruth broke records and bottles. Maybe they did have something in common. Sadly, it was the wrong thing to have in common—or was it? She knew what a monumental task it would be for Don Ogilvie to keep himself and Babe Ruth sober. It would be like trying to lasso a tornado. No one could refuse either of them a drink. Drummond's rules were fair but difficult. She was pleased that Ogilvie was willing to give it a try. She left them alone to carry on their negotiations.

Ruth asked, "Why would I want to quit drinkin' just to get younger? I already been thirty-two before. I like drinkin'. I like gettin' drunk."

Ogilvie tried to remember some of the arguments he'd thought of earlier: "Well, I can tell you for one thing—your teammates will never feel the same about you after today. They think you're some kind of has-been. Some of 'em are thinking you weren't that good in the first place. You need to show 'em, Babe. You need to show yourself. But that's only half of it. There are some kids here in Limbotown that are never going to believe in Babe Ruth again. You can't let 'em down. And there's a kid here by the name of Roberto who's dying. I know you don't know him yet, but all he could do at dinner tonight was talk about how Babe Ruth hit a home run. A home run in our Series against Cobb might save his life."

The "children" angle was working. Ruth started to remember the Johnny Sylvester story. "You know, I done this before. Seems to me I saved a kid's life during the '26 World Series. Hit a couple or three homers, and the lad was just fine. Can't remember his name though."

"Johnny Sylvester," said Ogilvie.

"Who?" asked Ruth.

"Johnny Sylvester. The kid's name was Johnny Sylvester."

"Nah, that wasn't it," concluded the Babe. "His name don't matter anyhow. What's important is that I done this before, and guess I can do it again."

Ogilvie wasn't about to prompt Ruth with the true facts behind the Johnny Sylvester story. The Babe was waxing nostalgic, and it was helping his cause. "Of course you can do it again, Babe. But you're gonna have to dry out to do it."

Ogilvie tried to add further incentive. "And as long as you stay sober, you can be my assistant. I need someone who knows these players. You know most of them. That could be a huge help."

"Hell, all I want to do when I retire is manage. That midget freak who thinks he's Death gives you the best baseball team in the world to manage; and what do I get? To be your assistant? No thanks."

Slightly stalled, Ogilvie lit on what he hoped to be a more clever approach. "You got to manage today. How would you like to manage up until the Series starts? I'm going to be splitting the players into two squads. I'll be rotating players from each team every few days. You can manage one squad and I'll manage the other. That's eight weeks' worth of games."

This got Ruth's interest. "Hmm. That could be all right," he brooded.

Ogilvie said, "You know, Babe, all I wanted when I was a kid and then a player was to be Babe Ruth. I got injured and that took care of that. So here I'm stuck with being a manager. You don't know how much I'd like to trade places with you."

Ruth leaped in. "Well let's do it. We'll get that Doctor Derby, or whatever that little prick calls himself, to switch us! If he can make me younger, he oughta be able to do that!"

"I'm sure he can, Babe. But the rules for this contest are that I have to be the manager. That's one I know he won't change."

With his inimitable habit of butchering names, or merely forgetting them altogether, Ruth had now taken to calling Drummond "Derby." Back in the Babe's time, the Derby was the symbol of the fool, the rube, the beguiled, the conned. Ruth was also afraid of the unknown Drummond, so he hid his fear by feigning insolence. "If I do this, there's gonna be one more thing I want besides managing a team," Ruth said in a way that sounded like an ultimatum.

"What's that?" asked a wary Ogilvie.

Ruth leaned forward and in a hushed voice said, "I want to pitch in the Series. I was always proud of my pitchin'. And one last thing," the Babe continued, "don't tell no one about it. I don't want them fellas makin' any more fun of me than they already is. If they hear I'm gonna pitch, they'll really give it to me."

Ruth was indeed a terrific pitcher. He would have to be hammered into much leaner shape to even attempt it though, but Ogilvie was willing. "You got it. I promise you'll pitch in the Series if you stay sober with me. Do we have a sobriety pact and a deal?"

Ruth held out a huge right hand and said, "Shake on it and drink on it. Starting tomorrow, no more drinking till we finish the Series."

The two men raised their glasses, drank, and returned the empty shots to the table with a bang. The pact was official. Ruth agreed to meet Ogilvie at the stadium in the morning for practice and the start of a new day.

Ogilvie didn't know at the time, but his promise to let Ruth pitch would be the single biggest ingredient in the Series' outcome. The die was cast weeks ahead, and not even Doctor Drummond knew which way it would fall.

Chapter 13

Ogilvie was awakened in his hotel room by his 8 a.m. wakeup call. Nursing what he hoped would be his last hangover in Limbotown (and maybe forever), he drank three tall glasses of water and choked down six aspirin. The sendoff with Ruth from the night before hadn't been as beastly as it could've been. All in all, he felt pretty decent.

After showering and dressing, he grabbed a quick bite in the dining room. A few of the players were scattered about, the black players having laid claim to their own area in what seemed to be an informal arrangement of de facto segregation accepted by both sides, for the time being.

Most of the old Negro League players greeted Ogilvie with a sign, a wink, some even a "good morning," the residue of victory from the day before. Their white opposites were heedless, indifferent. Ogilvie didn't care, as long as everybody showed up for practice.

A hopeful harbinger emerged as the nobody-manager got up to leave for Drummond Field. A robust, boisterous Babe Ruth and a band of white players were walking into the dining room just as Ogilvie was walking out.

"Hey Ovaltine!" Ruth said, greeting him like an old buddy. "Tell these boys what you told me last night, about me gettin' younger if I can stay off the hooch. Tell 'em that Doctor Derby squirt promised to do it." The boasting Bambino had told his compatriots about his deal with

Ogilvie and Drummond—a deal that could turn a ton of blubber back into the perfect baseball prodigy.

Ogilvie seized the moment. "That's right, you guys. I've got Drummond's word on it. But if the Big Boy slips up, even once, we'll be stuck with this version. All you fellas need to watch the Babe and keep him on the straight and narrow."

Rogers Hornsby, the now-omnipresent thorn in Ogilvie's side, spoke up. "This is a bunch of horseshit. No one can make Ruth or me or anyone younger. Whaddaya doin', fillin' his head with this crap?"

Don heaved a pent-up sigh. "I don't expect you guys to believe anything—about this place, what I'm trying to do, or anything else. But what do you have to lose? If we can keep the Babe on the wagon, how can that hurt? In two or three weeks, you might be surprised to see what happens. But there won't be any surprise unless we can keep him sober, twenty-four hours a day, seven days a week."

Just to irritate his nemesis further, the teetotaling Hornsby asked, "Does that mean beer too?"

Ruth's eyes lit up. "Yeah, beer's not booze—and it's nutritionated! Got hops and grains and all kinds of healthy stuff in it." Ruth would've made a great lawyer. He was forever finding non-existent loopholes to squirm through—not an easy task considering, his tremendous girth.

Ogilvie spread his right thumb and index finger over his forehead and shook his head saying, "Let me make this clear. Beer has alcohol in it. He can't drink beer either . . . or shoe polish or cleaning fluid or floor wax. Anything with alcohol in it! Got it?"

Hornsby scoffed, "Yeah we got it, but this is still a bunch of bullshit."

"Give me three weeks," pleaded the nobody-manager, "and if you don't see a difference, you can take him out for a big night on the town. In the meantime, I'm asking you, begging you . . . don't let him drink. Okay?"

Ruth slapped Ogilvie on the back, gave him a cheering squint (not exactly a wink), headed for the dining room, and imparted over his shoulder, "See you at the ballpark, Keed."

Ogilvie studied Ruth in awe. The depressed drunk from the night before was now a manic, backslapping optimist ready to take on the world—or at least Limbotown. The nobody-manager wondered what magic Ruth could conjure up to make this overnight transformation. Whatever the hell it was, Ogilvie wished he could bottle it and drink it. What a marvelous substitute it would've made for a fifth of Scotch.

This was typical Ruth. He did these one-eighties all the time. He could be in a horrendous slump for two weeks, and then break out of it by belting ten home runs in the next eight games. Sometimes the Babe would be injured in a game and carried out on a stretcher, only to return the next day with no sign of damage at all. These turnarounds were not confined to baseball. It was part of his makeup. It just wasn't in Ruth's nature to be down very long. Instinctively he knew life was too short for that.

Ogilvie could only imagine what it would be like to be inside Babe Ruth's head, no doubt packed with copious amounts of cotton candy, hot dogs, beer, and lots of open space. Still, there was a certain depth to him, to which he himself was not altogether deaf. On the surface, the Babe was simple. Yet there remained complexities to be dealt with—not only by others, but by the Big Man too. It wouldn't be wise to underestimate the Bambino's unconscious thoughts, buried as they might be.

As Lou Gehrig straggled behind Ruth and the rest into the dining room, Ogilvie caught him by the arm with foreboding words—"Lou, can I speak to you for a second?"—foreboding because Gehrig knew what was coming. He was the natural chaperone for the Babe. He didn't like it, but that's how things usually turned out for Gehrig when he was out with Ruth. Often times he would decline the Babe's invitations for an evening on the town because he knew it meant staying out all night, drinking and chasing women—or at least watching the Babe do it. As well as Ruth and Gehrig got along, Lou didn't approve of the Babe's nocturnal lifestyle. Gehrig was much the momma's boy and Boy Scout he was portrayed as. Still, Ogilvie got him to reluctantly agree to the task. Someone had to be there to make sure the Babe didn't drink, no matter what, and Boy Scout Gehrig was the perfect man for the job.

That death could strike down the Iron Horse of baseball was a disturbing revelation. Not only that, it cut him down in full bloom at age thirty-eight—and in plain sight, for all to see. It was a reminder that a spot in this world can only be rented. Wealth, fame, arrogance, or humility offers no protection from the setting sun. Life is death, and death means sorrow for the loved ones left behind. There is no cure, no defense.

Banish mortality and men become gods. But gods are the stuff of myth, as baseball aspires to be and sporadically achieves. Man is powerless before death, and even gods must be laid to rest at times. Lou Gehrig was no exception. He was a lustrous example.

Born Henry Louis Gehrig in 1903 to German immigrant parents, serious baseball came into his life while a science student at Columbia University. The studious Lou made a choice to pursue baseball over his education, a decision his strong-willed mother didn't agree with at first. He really must've loved the sport to risk her wrath, something he rarely did. Normally he deferred to her wishes like any good momma's boy would do. There were some departures, and baseball was one of them.

Another was his marriage to the independent-minded Margaret Twitchel. She helped Lou sever the tangled umbilical cord of his mother's domination that was not-so-slowly choking the life out of his already stifled emotional growth. They had a loving marriage. Then Lou got sick in 1939, and on Independence Day of that year—in between games of a double header on what was billed as "Lou Gehrig Appreciation Day" at Yankee Stadium—he delivered his "I'm the luckiest man on the face of the earth." That day, 61,808 fans packed the House that Ruth Built to bid farewell to their idol.

Although big, coordinated, and muscular, the young Lou did not immediately exhibit the skills that would eventually propel him to the Yankees, the Hall of Fame, and baseball immortality. A natural hitter, he had to work hard to become the smooth first baseman everyone remembers. He spent more time than he would've preferred in the minor leagues. When Wally Pipp complained of a headache one afternoon in 1925 (he'd been beaned the day before) and Gehrig started in his place, no one imagined that the Iron Horse wouldn't miss a game until he took himself out some fourteen seasons later. He was suffering the mysterious effects of amyotrophic lateral sclerosis—ALS—the incurable ailment that would become known as Lou Gehrig's disease.

He didn't have the home run numbers of his more illustrious teammate, Ruth, or the lofty .400 batting average of a Rogers Hornsby, although he hit for both power and average. What Sweet Lou did better than anyone else was knock in runs, and it was runs that won games and pennants. In 1931 he set a league record with 184 RBIs. That incredible mark was, of course, eclipsed by Ruth hitting a league leading forty-six home runs that same year, again obscuring Gehrig's star, but in full harmony with their enduring connection.

That Ruth was gregarious and bigger than life was an understatement. That Gehrig was shy, modest, and taciturn was just as true. But as a ballplayer, Gehrig was as tough as a well-done steak. He was the Clint Eastwood of the baseball diamond. His few words were always pin-point and to the nub—a lot like DiMaggio, who joined Gehrig and the Yankees shortly before Lou got sick. Together they couldn't utter a whole paragraph in a season. Still, the cold shoulder could be devastating. Being frozen out by either DiMaggio or Gehrig was worse than being cursed out by Rogers Hornsby. Like the proverbial quiet fart, Gehrig or DiMaggio could be silent but deadly.

The friendship of Ruth and Gehrig was entirely a story of the attraction of opposites. It was the extroverted veteran, Ruth, who took the demure rookie under his big wings when the Columbia man joined the Bronx Bombers during the 1925 season. Ruth embraced the reserved Gehrig on and off the field. Lou never condoned the Big Man's appetites for carousing, but they enjoyed being together, and the two occasionally conversed in their parents' native German. They genuinely liked each other.

Lou sensibly relegated himself to the Babe's presence, his majesty. To do otherwise would've been a doomed attempt to make the sun disappear by closing his eyes. Ruth was all too aware of his own exalted status, and understood that Gehrig was predestined to survive in the shadow of the huge oak tree that was the Babe. Being the baseball savant that he was, the Bambino was inherently mindful of the steady first baseman's role in his success. Having Gehrig bat just behind him in the order made pitchers honest. They couldn't walk the Big Boy with carefree abandon anymore, or Sweet Lou would come a-knockin'. As the Iron Horse protected the Babe's flank, Ruth sheltered Gehrig with his umbrella of goodwill, gratitude, and friendship.

Late in their careers, a silly quarrel broke apart the friendship when Mom Gehrig commented that the Babe's wife, Claire, was not a good mother. The Babe let the enmity fade away. Lou never did, rejecting the Bambino's rapprochement in the last days of his life in 1941. You wonder how the Iron Horse might've felt had he known that Ruth would be taken down by a horrible and enfeebling throat cancer only a few years later. How important can a grudge be?

For the Gehrig in Limbotown, the falling out had not yet occurred. For Ruth it had, and he was happy to ignore it. He was pleased that Ogilvie had assigned his buddy, Lou, the chore of being his official watchdog. Gehrig wasn't nearly as eager; giving in was more like it. However, Ogilvie did give Gehrig a powerful weapon in his quest to oversee the unwieldy Bambino. He lied and told them both that, ". . . Drummond can arrange for Mrs. Ruth to come to Limbotown if the Babe doesn't behave himself." After a while, Gehrig wished he'd gotten a nickel for every time he had to use the threat.

Ogilvie was glad to see a bustling anthill as he entered the clubhouse. Charlie McManus and his boys were busily helping the players arriving early with their gear and other belongings. He made it to his office to find Antonio Alvarez already there in practice garb, ready to receive him. As the nobody-manager changed into his baseball clothes, Antonio asked, "What are we going to do today, Skip?"

Ogilvie had a plan. "There's a terrific training room and gym just the other side of the clubhouse. Got some of the best looking weight machines I've ever seen. We're going to teach these guys about weight training. You know they didn't do that back when."

Antonio voiced his approval. The Captain and First Mate of the Titanic were heading for another iceberg.

By 10 a.m., Limbotown Standard Time, the visitor's clubhouse at Drummond Field was filled with Ogilvie's team. No one was missing.

The black players were more animated and talkative than the white squad they had beaten the day before. But there were no incidents—no fights, no race riots. The white players were standing by their word. For now.

As they continued to dress, Ogilvie climbed a bench and asked for their attention. He was a little flustered when they actually gave it to him this time. He delivered a short speech on how he envisioned the practices would go, and then launched into a blurb about the benefits of weight training, ending with, "So let's go next door and familiarize ourselves with the equipment, and then figure out a routine for everybody."

Nobody moved. Ogilvie saw expressions on black and white faces that said, "You gotta be kidding!" And then the inevitable dissent from Hornsby: "Ball players don't lift weights. Everyone knows that. Makes you a fucking muscle-bound freak! Can't straighten your arms out or anything. You gotta be flexible to play this game." Everyone, including all the black players, mumbled their assent.

The nobody-manager had just taken five minutes to explain that weightlifting, combined with stretching exercises, wouldn't do what the player's feared. Either they weren't listening or they didn't believe it. Telling them again wasn't going to help. Ogilvie then had a minor inspiration. Like his idea of only two days before, which paid off with the black versus white game, there was some risk involved, but he was getting used to taking risks.

He tried out the new tack. "Antonio, get up here," Ogilvie commanded, friendly enough. Antonio was startled, caught like a burglar in a bank vault, but made his way to the bench Ogilvie was standing on. The nobody-manager continued. "This is our assistant manager and bench coach, Antonio Alvarez, the right fielder for the San Bernardino Stampede, our ball club back home. How long you been lifting weights, Antonio?"

The young coach, savvy now to what Ogilvie was trying to do (or so he thought), quickly replied, "Three, four times a week since I was fourteen. I'm almost twenty-six now." The players gave Antonio the once over. He was average-sized for a ballplayer; six feet, 190 pounds, medium frame. To the Hall of Famers, imposing he was not.

Ogilvie then directed, "Get down on the floor and do some stretching so these guys can see how flexible you are." Antonio complied and proceeded to perform some rather convincing feats of elasticity, including the splits.

The players were struck—except for Hornsby. "Okay, so the kid's a fucking contortionist. We don't have to lift weights to learn that. Besides, we're all strong enough now."

Ogilvie then sprung the second part of his ploy by asking Hornsby, "Do you think you're stronger than Antonio?" Antonio's jaw dropped.

The solid and thick Hornsby looked over Antonio like a hangman readying a noose. "You must be crazy. I'd crush 'im like a snail."

"Well, there's only one way to find out," Ogilvie said as the rest of the blood drained out of Antonio's face. "You guys are both right-handed. How about an arm wrestling match? If Antonio beats you, then we're all going to lift weights. Okay?"

"This isn't going to turn out like yesterday's game," stated an overconfident Hornsby while flexing his hard right bicep.

Ogilvie wasn't worried, and Antonio wasn't quite as ashen now. Antonio Alvarez was the arm wrestling champ of the San Bernardino Stampede. He'd even defeated the Stampede's ox of a first baseman, Billy "Big Ass" Washington, and Big Ass was much bigger than Hornsby. The Limbotown squad wasn't wise to this fact. The young assistant just hadn't anticipated his skipper's scheme.

Antonio was about the same height as Hornsby, but the twenty-eight-year-old Hornsby was almost twice as wide, and none of it was fat. However, he wasn't nearly as scary-looking as Billy Big Ass.

Ogilvie enlisted a couple of Charlie McManus's men to position a training table and a couple of chairs in the middle of the locker room. The nobody-manager situated Hornsby and Antonio at the square battleground, laid down a few simple ground rules, and then, on his cue, let them have at it. Within five seconds, Antonio slammed the back of Hornsby's right hand to the wood like a forty-pound flounder hitting the deck. The players hooted. Hornsby's face was as red as it had been when the white players voted to play the game against the black players, as red as it had been after Hornsby struck out three times and then hit into a double play in that contest—and, as red as it had been when he was finally kicked out of that game. While Ogilvie was getting used to taking chances, Hornsby was not getting used to being humiliated.

Ogilvie scanned the room and offered, "Maybe old Raj didn't get a clean grip. How about two out of three?"

Hornsby wasn't buying. He'd gotten a good grip. He didn't intend to be further embarrassed. Grumbling obscenities, the Cardinal second baseman unceremoniously pushed away from the training table and surreptitiously retreated to his locker to rub some rank smelling balm on his right shoulder.

The players who were familiar with Rogers Hornsby knew that he was perhaps the strongest player of his day. They were convinced and awed by the medium-sized Antonio Alvarez, who had summarily dispatched the arrogant and reluctantly humbled Hornsby.

"Shall we go lift some weights, gentlemen?" Ogilvie rhetorically declared while walking towards the weight room. A string of players formed a loose line behind him.

Satchel Paige turned to the Negro League's strongest man, Josh Gibson, and asked, "Damn, Josh. You think that Antonio could beat you?"

"Not in a home run contest," was the big slugger's soft reply.

Josh Gibson was often referred to as the black Babe Ruth. As flattering as this accolade was meant to be, the Negro Leaguers and their fans always thought of Ruth as the white Josh Gibson. They had a pretty good argument too. At age twenty-four, the right-handed catcher for the old Pittsburgh Crawfords reportedly hit eighty-four homers in a 170-game season, and some 962 overall in a career that spanned seventeen seasons. Ruth hit a high of sixty home runs in a 154-game season, and 714 total over twenty years. The Babe hit a home run about every eight times he batted. Gibson hit a home run about every seven times he came to the plate.

Josh Gibson also caught for the black all-star teams that played against the white big leaguers who barnstormed the countryside in the off-season looking to make an extra buck. Big Josh hit two homers off

Dizzy Dean in one of those games. In eighteen games against white major league pitching, he hit .412.

Physically, he was what you would expect a home run-hitting catcher to look like: big, thick, and muscular. His strength and hitting power were the source of legend. Once he whacked a ball at Pittsburgh's fabled Forbes Field that supposedly didn't come down until the next day . . . in Philadelphia. He was also rumored to be the only ballplayer of any color to have hit a ball completely out of Yankee Stadium. If that was true, he'd have done something the Babe would have envied, because not even he had hit one out of "The house that Ruth built."

Gibson was blessed with a good-natured personality, a wonderful sense of humor, home run-hitting power, and absolute joy when playing the game. But that all changed in 1943 when the prodigious slugger suffered what was then called a nervous breakdown. Although he continued to play, he was never the same. It foreshadowed worse things to come. Only months before Jackie Robinson broke the color barrier in 1947, Josh Gibson died of either a stroke or a brain tumor. Perhaps it was a stroke caused by a brain tumor. It didn't matter. He was only thirty-five.

While Don Ogilvie and Antonio Alvarez demonstrated proper weightlifting technique to a still-unsure group of players, little Roberto and his mother were meeting some of the "local" Limbotown children and their parents. Maggie Briggs arranged an informal gathering in the hotel lobby. As she had promised, the striking and able innkeeper was going to make the Alvarezes' stay—and especially Roberto's—as pleasant as possible.

Maggie showed the kids where they could play. Unknown to all (except Drummond and the Chosen Ones), was a magnificent playground on the other side of the lobby, opposite the dining room. It hadn't seemed to be there before, but as Drummond had said, he could make Limbotown into anything or anyplace he wanted. A playground was not a tall order.

Drummond had told the children and their parents the same as he had the players—that they were all dead now but brought back to life for a brief time as "Lucky Stiffs." How much and what they really believed about Limbotown and Death Personified varied widely. Nonetheless, they all knew why the Alvarezes and Don Ogilvie were supposedly there: to try to save little Roberto's life. They just didn't know that Don Ogilvie's life would be sacrificed if he won the Series.

The drama surrounding Roberto made him a celebrity among the other children and their parents. He never considered himself to be or acted like he was something special. Still, he had to field questions from his new chums like, "Are you really going to die if your team loses?" And, "Are you feeling okay today?"

Although insensitive, the inquiries were only innocent curiosity. Roberto and Maria were not offended. It just didn't do much to take their minds off why they were there in the first place. The mothers and fathers who Maria and Antonio Alvarez met were mostly sympathetic, albeit uncertain. Some kept their distance, cautious of Limbotown, Drummond, the Alvarez family, and Don Ogilvie.

Part of it was the racial element again. This one wasn't confined to only the players. Drummond had stocked Limbotown with Lucky Stiffs from the last hundred years and from various races and ethnic backgrounds. They weren't all altruistic philanthropists striving for world harmony. On the contrary, they were baseball fans, subject to the same foibles and ugly prejudices as the players on Ogilvie's team. The uneasiness that pervaded the mix of black and white athletes was a meandering undercurrent for all of Limbotown. Nevertheless, the velvet-gloved, steel fist of Maggie Briggs, the beautiful and fearless manager of the Hotel Limbotown, was able to contrive a restive peace and make it work. She was a smart and clever manipulator, yet she couldn't change or control what the Lucky Stiffs believed or how they thought. It made for some interesting challenges of her own. As seemed to be the case everywhere, Limbotown included, the rainbow blend of brown, black, yellow, and white children frolicked together quite nicely—as long their parents stayed out of the way, thank you very much.

The deluxe playground was outside under the artificial sunlight and had, along with other amenities, a Little League-sized baseball diamond, which would soon be the site of daily sandlot games. Before long, Babe

Ruth and then other players would join in the fun. This was also typical Bambino. All those years at Baltimore's Industrial School for Boys left imprinted on the Babe's heart an indelible promise for every youngster. Even in the Majors, he still competed in back-lot battles and stickball contests with neighborhood kids. Such was his love for children; he couldn't help himself. The Limbotown contests would always end with Roberto and a pile of other kids crawling on top of the willing and supine Bambino like a litter of puppies overwhelming a rapturous five-year-old. The love was pure, unfettered, and soaked up by Ruth like a parched sponge. He recharged his psychic batteries this way and it took his mind off drinking—for a while, anyhow. For little Roberto and the rest, it was like playing baseball with Santa Claus, Christmas coming for an hour or so everyday.

Seeing her mix with them, it was plain to Maria Alvarez that Maggie Briggs loved children. And they loved her right back. Maria wondered if Maggie had any family of her own, if she had ever been married. She only assumed that there was no "Mister" Briggs.

As they watched Roberto and the other kids play, Maria couldn't hold back. She asked, "Did you have any children, Maggie?"

The usually vital redhead took a breath with a long exhale. "It's hard for me to talk about my life, Maria. Friendships in Limbotown can't last very long. You'll be gone in a little while, and you won't remember any of this. I will. I think you're someone I could talk to. I think we could be friends. If I shared these things with you now, it would make saying goodbye even harder. Am I making any sense? "

She was, and Maria knew it. The mother of little Roberto was in too deep to let go. "I'd still like to be your friend."

Maggie lowered her green eyes and spoke softly: "I need a friend who will be here after you've left Limbotown, Maria." A subdued Maggie Briggs couldn't conceal the loneliness in her voice.

Little Roberto's mother could bring herself to pry no more. "I hope one day you find the friend you're looking for."

"Thank you, Maria. Me too."

As open as Maggie seemed to be with all the kids, Maria knew that she would, or could, only tell her so much. Maria knew that a person like Maggie might not be allowed to divulge any more than she already had—about herself or Limbotown or Drummond, or why Don Ogilvie was really there. She felt that Maggie had something she wanted to say. Exactly what was a mystery. Eight or so weeks in Limbotown may not be enough time to find out, and then the chance would be lost forever.

Chapter 14

After the weight-training session, Don and Antonio took the players out to Drummond Field for a light workout, mainly consisting of throwing and fielding. Ogilvie shrewdly solicited the help of his players in conducting the simple drills. With only Antonio as an assistant, Ogilvie needed more coaches. He couldn't imagine better instructors than his Hall of Famers, many of whom would go on to be Major League coaches and managers themselves. By giving the players some responsibility, it aligned their interests more closely with his. It was a very small step after a shaky start.

It also gave Ogilvie the chance to hand out a couple of special assignments. The first was for Don "Big D" Drysdale, who was from 1965. The six-five right-hander was open to Ogilvie's request.

The glitch was the old timers' pitching mechanics. During their short workout, Mathewson, Johnson, and Young had all exhibited long, whirly-bird style wind-ups, with high leg kicks. Pitching from a true stretch and glide-stepping to the plate was not in their repertoire. Their pick-off moves were easy to detect and not very quick. Ty Cobb would have a field day stealing bases against these guys—which he'd had in real life anyway.

Ogilvie described the dilemma to Drysdale near the back of the bullpen and out of earshot of the other pitchers: "These guys take 'til next week to deliver a pitch, and by that time the guy who was on first is rounding third."

Big D grunted his agreement. Drysdale, who'd died prematurely from a heart attack in 1993 at age fifty-six, was a modern-era pitcher. He could help teach them the modern game. But Mathewson, Johnson, and Young knew not of Drysdale, his incredible fifty-eight-inning scoreless streak and his dauntless intimidation of batters by throwing inside—way inside. So Ogilvie began by holding a small conference in the bullpen among the "arms"—"Could you guys gather 'round for a minute?"

He told them of Drysdale's credentials in a way that made Big D accepted by all: "I think you guys have met by now. This is Don Drysdale. He plays with the Dodgers. He holds the Major League record for hit batters, but you don't land in the Hall of Fame if you're wild." Ogilvie then said, "I'm making Drysdale and Mathewson co-captains of the pitching staff. Don is going to teach you guys how to get rid of the ball so Cobb doesn't steal home while he's still in the batter's box. If that doesn't work, he'll teach you about chin music." Drysdale's smile grew.

The affable Big D was a natural-born leader, a lot like Christy Mathewson or Walter Johnson, only fifty years later. Their similar personalities would make it easy for them to work together. And Mathewson, always the progressive was anxious to learn the new techniques; Drysdale would teach them to him and it would hopefully rub off on the other relics.

The second special assignment wasn't going to be as easy. Of course, anything involving Joe DiMaggio was not easy; and asking DiMaggio to help a young Mickey Mantle was not going to agree with Joltin' Joe's temperament. The nineteen-year-old Mantle needed help in centerfield and at the plate, and the twenty-seven-year-old DiMaggio was the logical guy to give it to him—except that Joe DiMaggio was withdrawn, suspicious, and not very charitable.

The now somewhat clear-headed and forward-thinking Ogilvie had another angle. He approached Joe D, who was playing catch in centerfield. "Mind if we talk a few minutes, Joe?" he politely asked.

Without turning to look at him and while still tossing the ball, DiMaggio issued a one-word answer. "Shoot."

The nobody-manager could see the conversation was going to be mostly one-sided, maybe totally. He took a long breath and began a short soliloquy: "You know the kid, Mickey Mantle?" Joe just kept on throwing, so Ogilvie just kept on talking. "He's going to play centerfield for the Yankees after you retire. His first trip to the majors didn't go too well. He was only nineteen, like he is here in Limbotown, and they had to send him down to the minors for more seasoning. When he made it back, he went on to become a Hall of Famer. Had a great career. Probably the most powerful switch hitter the game has seen. But he almost didn't make it at all. When they first brought him up, he played right field next to a guy in center they called the Yankee Clipper. Mickey was in awe of you, Joe—intimidated too. He could barely say hello. Then one day during a game, a hitter crushed a line drive between center and right. Mickey, the young right fielder with good wheels, was going to take the ball. Out of the corner of his eye he saw the great Joe DiMaggio moving over to make the catch. He knew better than to try to show up a Yankee legend, so he put on the brakes hard, caught a spike, and ripped up his knee . . . real bad too. The center fielder didn't even know the kid about ruined his career just to show the veteran some respect. After that, Mickey had leg problems the rest of his playing days. You know what that's like, huh, Joe?" No response, only the sound of the ball smacking leather. The nobody-manager had conveniently omitted the part about Mantle's leg problems occurring long before his professional career—a childhood victim of osteomyelitis—and had worn braces. He would've had leg problems even without the DiMaggio incident. But the story Ogilvie was telling was mostly true.

He pressed on. "You saw what happened yesterday during the game. The kid was overmatched. Yeah, he had that one lucky swing, but that was it. And he doesn't really know how to play center yet. Doesn't know how to judge the ball hit straight at him or which cutoff man to hit, how to turn around and run for a ball without looking at it. Stuff like that. I was thinking . . . maybe you could help him. Give him a few pointers, some advice, show him how it's done . . ." Ogilvie paused as the Yankee Clipper turned to look at him with a blank stare that said, "You must be joking. I'm Joe DiMaggio. I don't share my professional secrets with anyone, especially a kid who's trying to take my job." What came out instead was "Huh."

It wasn't a turn-down, but it sure wasn't a yes either. Ogilvie knew he couldn't force it, so he left Joe DiMaggio to ponder his own thoughts. "Thanks for listening, Joe," he said, and walked away. This one would be a wait-and-see.

Unexpectedly, he didn't have to wait long. The next day, and every day after that, Joe DiMaggio started Mickey Mantle's apprenticeship in earnest. The story of the kid who almost lost a Hall of Fame career just to show a little reverence to an aging veteran must've gotten to Joe. Not many things did. That was Ogilvie's assumption, in any case. No one knew why DiMaggio really did anything. If Joe knew himself, he wasn't telling.

Mickey Mantle was able to come by in Limbotown what he was never able to get in real life: a kinship with Joe DiMaggio, tutelage from the master—and perhaps, all thanks to a nobody-manager.

Ogilvie was again amazed to see the power of the magic reference books in action. Drummond had said it was there. The bits and pieces he'd told DiMaggio must've struck a chord somewhere. Having the knowledge was one thing. Using it wisely was another. That his ploys, subterfuges, ruses and schemes had succeeded so far left him wondering how long he could keep it going.

After a couple of hours of practice, Ogilvie gathered his team near their dugout and told them, "I'll be splitting you guys into two rotating squads, one to be managed by me and the other by Ruth. You'll be switched around so everyone can get used to playing with each other and so we can see what combinations work best.

"Thank you, guys, for today. The Alvarezes thank you too. Now hit the showers—and don't be afraid to hit the soap."

As Babe Ruth spun to head into the clubhouse, Ogilvie said, "Not so fast, Big Boy . . . you and I have more work to do." Ruth hesitated only a second and then trotted over to Ogilvie's side. It wasn't Ruth's forte, following orders, especially from a manager, but he had made a deal, and the Babe wanted to prove he was a man of his word. He was a repentant drunk now.

It became a familiar sight in Limbotown, the legendary Bambino and the nobody-manager jogging around the Drummond Field track, taking extra batting practice—and Ruth secretly honing his pitching skills again. The regimen would in time revive both of them. The Babe predictably, Ogilvie in ways he had yet to imagine.

The intra-squad games were exciting and unbelievably played. Little Roberto and some of the other kids would serve as batboys, while most of the Lucky Stiffs, tightly seated behind the home-plate backstop, would look on. Ruth relished his role of manager, and Ogilvie let him bask in it. It turned out he was both a sharp and perceptive skipper. Despite their rotating mixture, the two squads did not produce any spontaneous racial bonds and things continued to be tense. Both in the stands and in the dugout, different colors sat on the same bench but did not mingle.

Satchel Paige was welcomed with open arms by most of the other pitchers, but that was the only exception. The reason was clear to the position players. They considered pitchers a distinct sub-species of ballplayer. "Arms" were thought to march to the beat of their own drummer, and not usually in sync. Flamethrowers Drysdale, Mathewson, and Dean made sure that Satchel Paige, the team's only black pitcher, felt comfortable in the bullpen. Whatever his pedigree, he was one of them—it just didn't spill over into the dugout or clubhouse. Satchel understood.

After a while, they all began to trade pitches and share information on batter's weaknesses. When the discussion turned to Ty Cobb one day, Cy Young offered, "He ain't got no soft spots, lessin' you throw directly at his head."

As he had promised, Christy Mathewson became a regular after-hours visitor to Don Ogilvie's clubhouse office. The well-spoken pitcher was interested in the changes in both the world and the world of baseball. Ogilvie was happy to dole out everything he could remember or muster. When Ogilvie confirmed to Mathewson that, "Where I come from, baseball's been integrated for over fifty years," Matty began his own quiet campaign among the other old-timers, preaching open-mindedness and tolerance. He didn't have to convince Dizzy Dean, already a huge fan of Satchel Paige. Dean was overjoyed to be on the same team. It was always kind of a fantasy of his, but impossible back in the 1930s.

Big Six was a very intelligent and highly perceptive young man of only twenty-five. Aware of his own early death, he was the first and only of the Lucky Stiffs to figure out that Don Ogilvie would be trading his life for Roberto's. Ogilvie sensed that he knew, and it didn't make him uneasy. The link that he felt with the turn-of-the-century pitcher was somehow soothing, and Matty seemed to exude a trust that said to Ogilvie, *Don't worry. Your secret is safe with me.* The unspoken understanding between the two men drew them closer. Mathewson was not only smart—he was also a keen student of human nature. He wasn't going to bring up the subject with Ogilvie anymore than Ogilvie was about to tell Mathewson the details of the big pitcher's death. Rather, they would both wait for the other to signal that they wanted to talk about it. Ogilvie needed this kind of confidant. He sure couldn't talk to the Alvarezes about it; and even though Maggie knew, his feelings for her made him something less than impartial when she was around. Christy Mathewson assumed the role with serene command.

For Ogilvie, the self-possessed young pitcher became a constant reminder of his own failed attempts at dealing with the unfairness of life. Now the nobody-manager wanted to be reminded. Mathewson was a lighthouse, a beacon that the wayward manager could use to guide his own tattered ship through rough waters. Ogilvie had found a friend in Christy Mathewson.

Antonio Alvarez had hoped his son would be naturally drawn to his namesake and his father's idol, Roberto Clemente. The youngster was instead attracted to Babe Ruth like he was the Pied Piper. Of course, all the kids and most of the adults in Limbotown felt the same way. It's hard to change a force of nature. More predictably, it was Antonio who was drawn to Clemente, and he tried to make his hero as much at home as he could in a place unknown to both of them.

Other than Don Drysdale, Clemente knew of but didn't really know the other players. The Pirate outfielder was from 1966. Everyone else was from before that time, and didn't know about Clemente. He was thirty years old and in the midst of his first MVP season. The old Negro League players were wary of him. Sure he was black, but he was also Latin. Although this wasn't new territory for them, they were still more suspicious of this Puerto Rican phenom than Robinson and Campanella, who were also snubbed. The old Negro Leaguers were jealous and a little resentful of their black Major League counterparts.

Ogilvie was pleased to see his young assistant befriend the isolated Clemente. They both needed friends in this strange place, and much to Antonio's delight he also got some help with his hitting.

Roberto Clemente was born into poverty in Carolina, Puerto Rico, in 1934. Equipped with the proverbial "milk-carton" glove, a beat-up ball, and a broken broom handle, he was also born to play baseball. He wasn't the first black or Hispanic player in the Major Leagues, but he was the first Latin player to make it into the Hall of Fame. This accomplishment made him an icon to all Latin ballplayers.

The Brooklyn Dodgers originally signed him to a Major League contract in 1953, but he was left "unprotected," and the then lowly Pittsburgh Pirates drafted him away the next year. In seventeen seasons with the Bucs, the right-handed outfielder led them to two World Series championships, garnering four batting titles, 3,000 hits, twelve consecutive Gold Gloves, and two Most Valuable Player awards along the way.

He glided around the outfield with the grace of a Joe DiMaggio and swung the bat with the power of a Josh Gibson, something that might be expected of someone with Clemente's staggering talents. He was the epitome of the five-point player. He could do it all, and do it all superbly. In addition to the home runs, he hit singles, doubles, and triples. He fielded like radar, ran like a cheetah, and threw like a laser-guided missile. His rifle-arm was unbelievable. Strong and accurate, he could throw out a runner at first after gloving an apparent single to right.

A 1956 automobile accident almost left him with the same fate that Roy Campanella was to suffer only two years later. The exceptional outfielder recovered, but he was shadowed by chronic back pain and a string of other injuries throughout his career. Nonetheless, when he took the field, he was ready to take whatever came, and refused to compromise his all-out style of play. The great ones always seem to find a way to overcome, and the gifted Puerto Rican was no exception.

His early dealings with the American media were often strained and misunderstood. Many were put off by his heavy Puerto Rican accent and foreign ways. Like just about anything new and different, Clemente's acceptance was slow. One problem was, he was too honest. When asked on the record about his damaged back, Clemente told reporters the truth: "It hurt." They didn't like that. Saying that it didn't affect his game sounded like an excuse to them—or even worse, whining. Either you're too hurt to play, or you don't talk about it in public. This was the standard set by the likes of Gehrig and DiMaggio, baseball stoics of epic proportion, and the media of the early 1960s encouraged it.

It was no surprise, then, that the road to the Hall was a bumpy one for Roberto Clemente. Once his teammates saw what he could do with a bat and a glove, they didn't care if he talked like Charro—or even dressed like her (he didn't)—but the press did. Although not pleased about it, he demonstrated admirable restraint and patience. Eventually the sportswriters came around. When Clemente won his second Most Valuable Player award in 1971, they finally seemed to take him into the fold—and not a second too soon.

He died the following year in a December 31st airplane crash. He wasn't on his way to some self-indulgent New Year's Eve party. Rather, the tremendously polished fielder and batsman was quietly involved in sending badly needed supplies to victims in earthquake ravaged Nicaragua. He hadn't sought or condoned publicity for his good will. Clemente was private, deep and intense. He knew that baseball (outside of Limbotown) was, after all, just a game. If he could use the game to help those in need, Roberto Clemente was humbled to serve a higher purpose.

Word of his death while going to the aid of others was devastating to the Pittsburgh Pirates, their fans, the world of baseball, and the world in general. The avant-garde MVP of the previous season was dead at age thirty-eight.

Although the Alvarez family and Don Ogilvie were all too familiar with Clemente's early fall, it never came to mind when they were in the presence of the hard-hitting, soft-handed speedster. His ebullient personality and passion for living infected those who gave in to it, and darker thoughts were gently churned under in its wake.

Apart from her earlier ambivalence, Maggie Briggs decided it would be all right if she delivered dinner to Don Ogilvie, who just about lived in his clubhouse office. She saw to it that he ate at least one healthy meal a day. He was sober now, doing well under difficult circumstances, and relentlessly hammering himself and Ruth into condition. She was going to allow herself to like Don Ogilvie. It was easier this way. This is what she honestly felt, and the changes taking place in him gave her no reason to deny her growing feelings—to herself anyhow. Whether she would ever share those thoughts with Don Ogilvie was still uncertain.

Ogilvie noticed the difference in her attitude toward him. Pleased, he believed that uninterrupted temperance would speak louder to her than being permanently marinated in Scotch. He was right.

The movie theater opened that evening. The stately art deco structure was an enticing detour for the players and the other Lucky Stiffs in this one-road town. Its façade could only hint at its spectacular interior. Once inside, the theater opened up into an august, high-ceilinged lobby dripping with extravagance. It was the kind of indulgent, gaudy movie palace built during the Great Depression, offering a delusional escape for the fiscally bludgeoned masses.

Ornate wall panels of silver and gold outlined and crisscrossed backdrops of blood-red and azure-blue terra cotta that were framed by maroon woodwork. The eclectic mix included everything from sharp-edged geometric designs to softly rounded sculpture. It was an unlikely mish-mash of Chinese, Indian, Moorish, neo-classical, and modern architecture. Somehow it all worked.

Inside the theater chamber, the lofty ceiling became a busy

intersection of gothic art encased from above by a rich blue dome. The cerulean canopy was symbolic of the faux sky that enclosed all of Limbotown. At the peak was a huge six-point opaque-glass chandelier. Its amber hue was expertly crafted with metal framing while red fabric tassels hung from its outsized, shamefully embellished chassis. The walls of the theater flowed onto a multi-colored, thickly carpeted arena that was neatly filled with rows of overstuffed red velvet chairs. As outsized and majestic as it was, the Limbotown Theater would hold no more than 1,000 people, ample for the current population of its fog-banked borough.

The movie-house manager was a kindly and pleasantly eccentric gentleman by the name of Old Jack Dumphy. His rounded torso was covered by a garish sport coat, worthy of the sleaziest used-car salesman. The too-wide tie that covered his cheap white shirt clashed with his brazen coat of many colors in a way that almost made your eyes cross. His constantly glowing, round, ruddy and heavily lined face was topped off by a toupee that redefined the concept. It wasn't real hair. It was some sort of artificial fiber that gave the appearance of fishing line. He was going for either a woman's pageboy or an old-fashioned schoolboy's Buster Brown look, except for one thing; the wig's shade of gray wasn't exactly what you would expect to see on a man of this age. It was platinum. It would turn out that, in many ways, "Old Jack" was not at all as he appeared—and he appeared like the circus had come to town and stayed too long.

He was a sociable, joking, hard-drinking, adroit selector of the fare that filled the huge silver screen of the stately Limbotown Theater. He would play mainly classics: *How Green was My Valley*, with Maureen O'Hara (who bore a striking resemblance to Maggie Briggs); *Robin Hood,* with Errol Flynn; *Captains Courageous*, with Spencer Tracy; and, much to Ogilvie's approval, *To Kill a Mockingbird*, with Gregory Peck—a film delivering its not-too-subtle message about tolerance, prejudice, and injustice.

As Maggie delivered dinner to his clubhouse office that evening, Ogilvie said to her, "I see the movie theater is opening tonight. I better make sure what Drummond's gonna show." With a hitchhiker's thumb, he blindly gestured at the volumes on the shelf behind him. "Don't want him givin' away somethin' that's in those books."

Maggie informed him, "Drummond doesn't run the theater. That's Old Jack Dumphy. You need to see him."

The puzzled coach replied, "Yeah, but Drummond's the one who really runs everything around here."

"That's true in a way. But you may have noticed that I run the hotel. Charlie McManus is in charge of the clubhouse and stadium, Burt Stansberry operates the elevator and Old Jack Dumphy manages the theater. Drummond can't do it all himself." Maggie always knew how to make her point with the overmatched hitting specialist.

"How old is this guy? You make it sound like 'Old' is part of his name."

"It is," said Maggie.

He ventured a parting question of the beautiful redhead: "Other than looking for Methuselah, how do I recognize him?"

"That's easy. Look for W. C. Fields in a really bad platinum wig." Ogilvie tilted his head, didn't say anything, and headed down the street.

The apprehensive coach approached the easy-to-spot screwball cinema boss just outside the Limbotown Theater a couple of hours before its inaugural showing. On first glance, the brashly attired film impresario seemed to have a stony scowl forever baked on a face that looked like a relief map of Argentina. It was the mug of a jowly bloodhound. But when the old guy greeted you, the glower turned into a broad grin, and his eyes twinkled with the mischief of a troll.

The nobody-manager extended his hand and said, "Hi, I'm Don Ogilvie. I hear you run this place."

Old Jack Dumphy smiled and replied, "I'm Old Jack Dumphy and, yes, I do run this place. I hear you run Babe Ruth. Congratulations, I think."

Ogilvie chuckled. "It's more like he runs me. Condolences are more like it. Talk to Lou Gehrig sometime and you'll see what I mean. I was hopin' to talk to you about what you show here . . ."

"Come with me and I'll show you my humble little sanctuary as we chat. And please call me Jack. I only use 'Old Jack' when I'm being formal."

The quirky exchange continued as the two men wandered through the empty, grandiose movie-house. After recovering from the surprise of meeting the unconventional Mr. Dumphy, Ogilvie found him to be most helpful and generous of heart. He may have looked like a buffoon, but he spoke with an educated, erudite tone: downright professorial—and at the same time, friendly.

The ruddy-cheeked theater captain reassured the nobody-manager: "I only show movies that should appeal to everyone in Limbotown, whether grownup or child. Drummond's main restriction is that I only show movies that don't give too much away about the future, and especially about the lives of the players. That's for you and your reference books. There won't be any showing of *The Babe Ruth Story*, *The Lou Gehrig Story*, or even *The Bingo Long Traveling All-Star Show*." (That film was a tribute to the old Negro Leagues, with Billy Dee Williams and James Earl Jones playing characters far too reminiscent of Satchel Paige and Josh Gibson.)

The cartoonish cinema aficionado became a tad irritated as he went on: "It's Doctor Droopy Drawer's personal directive that *Field of Dreams* be shelved, of course—not because of anything divulged in it, but because the Old Curmudgeon doesn't want his precious Drummond Field compared to that wonderful ballpark in the middle of an Iowa cornfield. You did that earlier, and it really pissed off the little bastard. I liked that. Besides, that's where he got the whole idea of a ballpark in the middle of nowhere, the farmhouse replaced by the Limbotown Hotel and Theater, and the invisible cornfield fence replaced by the 'one-of-its-kind' Limbotown fogbank."

Ogilvie thought to himself: *Movie theater manager? Not likely, and the way this guy is talking about Drummond, me, and the special books—Chosen One. Only he's too far down the road for Doctor Death.* He asked out loud: "Are you a Chosen One, Jack?"

Old Jack Dumphy stopped their slow meander and faced Limbotown's latest Challenger: "Of course, my boy, and I'll be rooting for you and the Alvarezes the whole way. I know what you're thinking.

206

I'm too old for Drummond . . . That's a conversation for another time, I promise."

Ogilvie thought, *Death Incarnate's done a pretty good job of mixing up the few Chosen Ones in between all the Lucky Stiffs, keeping me guessing*. He then had a spirited debate with Old Jack about whether to show *Bull Durham*, the classic baseball comedy that follows the zany antics of a minor league ball club throughout an equally zany season. Some of the zaniness included foul language and sexual capers that seemed to be right on target when it came to ballplayers. The clownish film buff finally got Ogilvie to let him run it uncut as a midnight show for adults only, and it quickly turned into a player favorite.

Complementing the movie theater, the hotel lounge furnished its own entertainment with a piano bar. Manned by Don Ferris, a longtime accompanist from Los Angeles, it became a Limbotown haunt. Ferris, a distinguished white-haired, pencil-mustached grandfather, knew all the standards from the beginning of time through the '60s and then some. His evening performances became instantly popular. He crooned and amazed the players and everyone else by knowing every song they asked for. He was a Lucky Stiff who Drummond had brought in from the 1980s, well after the players' times. With the exception of guys like Clemente and Drysdale, who were from the 60s, the old-timers were wowed by the snappy new tunes and racy lyrics of the future. There were many songs none of them had heard before. Who were these guys, Lennon and McCartney? And what the hell is a Beatle?

Other than baseball, the piano bar and the movie theater were just about the only games in town. They provided a small reprieve from the escape-proof fog-banked fortress of Limbotown, and stemmed what soon would become too big a problem for the nobody-manager: boredom. The players would find some solutions, none of which would help Ogilvie and the Alvarezes—not at first, anyhow.

There was another sport in Limbotown, and it became one of the players' answers to the boredom question.

Baseball players can't help but notice women, more so than most men. Doesn't always have to be attractive women either. Sometimes just willing will do. Limbotown had both attractive and willing women, although some were just attractive and others just willing. It didn't take the players long to figure out which were which. Whatever the case, the strange mating dance of the American athlete acted out its innocent to crude variations in this surreal enclave.

It all seemed harmless enough to Don Ogilvie, and helped normalize life in an otherwise strange place. Naturally, some friendships and budding romances sprouted up. Ogilvie didn't try to stop it. He knew better. It would be like trying to put out a forest fire with a bucket of kerosene. Plus, he had what he hoped would be a little romance of his own. One other benefit—it kept the Babe's mind off drinking.

His infatuation with Maggie Briggs over, the infamously horny Bambino's wandering eye had already staked out new territory and new prey. Most of the other players weren't too far behind. There was big game out there, and Ruth, the wily Lion King, was ready to feed amongst the faster, but vulnerable gazelles. Today it's called stalking, and it's against the law. In Ruth's day it was merely sport, the law of the jungle. Ruth knew not of illegal chase or of restraining orders. Anyhow, he figured if he could be hounded by his fans, he was entitled to do some hounding of his own.

After the theater opened, the players and other denizens of Limbotown established a routine of sorts. The players would practice during the day, watched by the rotating shifts of Lucky Stiffs and their families; their generous schedules allowing. They all ate dinner in the hotel dining room. Most would later catch a movie at the theater and then head back to the lounge or their rooms to close out the evening.

Don Ogilvie had his own rituals as well. After practice he remained at Drummond Field, Maggie Briggs delivering his dinner to him. Sometimes he would meet the Alvarezes at the theater for a movie; other times he'd stay in his office, brushing up on the details of his players' lives with Drummond's unique books. Near midnight he would walk over to the lounge to drink the mineral water or decaf coffee Maggie would serve him. Ogilvie enjoyed the piano stylings of Don Ferris and seeing the players mingle with the other Lucky Stiffs of Limbotown.

That first evening after the theater opened, he finished the last part of his new, nightly rounds. Ogilvie entered the hotel lounge around midnight, took a cup of decaf from Maggie behind the bar, and joined Babe Ruth and his cohorts at the piano bar. The nobody-manager offered his grip to pianist, Don Ferris: "I'm Don Ogilvie . . ."

Ferris kept playing with one hand and shook Ogilvie's outreached hand with the other: "I'm Don Ferris. We 'Dons' have to stick together. Good luck with your team."

"Thanks. How about playing some Beatles for these guys?"

Ogilvie surveyed the room. It was big enough to accommodate all the groups and cliques of Lucky Stiffs comfortably. Unlike in the clubhouse or in the stands, there seemed to be a silent understanding that the bar was kind of a neutral zone, where everyone was allowed to blow off a little steam. The atmosphere was relaxed, even free-wheeling . . . at first.

The Hotel Limbotown Lounge didn't really have a closing time. But at about 2 a.m. Ogilvie tapped a soda-drinking, womanizing Babe Ruth on the shoulder and suggested, "Jidge—I think it's time for lights out."

Ruth disengaged a moment from his sales pitch to his new lady-friend and replied, "Can't you see I got somethin' goin' on here, Ovaltine?"

"That's fine, Babe. Why don't you just take it upstairs?" Ogilvie's immediate concern was getting Ruth into shape, and that meant getting Ruth to sleep—or at least up to his room. The nobody-manager wasn't about to make any moral judgments on Ruth's philandering. Not even his best friend, the ultimate Boy Scout Lou Gehrig, could stop him.

Ruth said flatly, "Oh . . ." Then realizing that Ogilvie wasn't trying to be party-pooper after all, he said a little louder, "Oh, okay."

"But lights out, Babe, alright?" And then Ogilvie whispered, "That's the whole idea isn't it?"

A happy Bambino winked at Ovaltine, wrapped up his negotiations with his lady of the moment, and they both started for the lobby elevator. The other players had, sensibly, already turned in.

On his way out, Don Ogilvie explained to the lovely hotel manager,

"Maggie, I can help him quit drinking and I can get him into shape, but I can't stop him from chasing women."

"Without Mrs. Ruth here, no one can. And I know Drummond's not going to bring her. It's probably just as well."

He was pleased to hear she didn't expect him to conjure up too many miracles. "Goodnight, Maggie," he said, and walked the deserted, lone Limbotown lane back to his clubhouse refuge.

To their increasing frustration, the players soon discovered that none of the Lucky Stiffs, though they all professed to be fans, knew anything of their lives, other than some recollections of the players' baseball days. Even the fans from the last part of the century, who should've remembered something, couldn't. Ruth and the others smelled a rat, and his name was Doctor Derby Drummond. This left only Ogilvie, the Alvarezes, Maggie Briggs, and the players themselves as possible ways to find out about their futures. They crossed off Ogilvie, Maggie, and the Alvarez family as willing informants. They didn't know about the reference books in their manager's office . . . yet.

The players themselves, when they did remember anything, faked bad memories to dodge worrisome questions from their teammates. Who would tell Gehrig or Mathewson or Josh Gibson their destinies? And how could you prove it? No one wanted to be the bearer of bad news. That would be bad luck, and you could jinx yourself. That left only the nobody-manager with the power to dispense the knowledge— and he wasn't saying much.

Ogilvie's regular visits from Christy Mathewson and Maggie Briggs; working out with and keeping himself and Ruth sober; the habit of practice and the intra-squad contests; the sandlot games with Roberto, the local kids and the Bambino; the movie theater, the piano bar, and even the players' romantic exploits—all this became the rhythm of life in Limbotown for the first week. The novelty of it didn't last beyond that. Don Ogilvie began to worry.

Chapter 15

His fears came true in two ways. First and foremost, the ongoing racial friction. It was like trying to bind a wound with sandpaper.

Nearly as frustrating was Ogilvie and Antonio's inability to get the players to try modern gear. They clung to their old bats and gloves like life rafts. Batting helmets? Forget it. They weren't interested. Sure, guys like Drysdale and Clemente used big gloves and wore helmets because they were from that era, and they still got crap from the old timers. The players from the Dark Ages, or anytime before World War Two, thought they were having their manhood tested. After getting them to give in to weight training, Ogilvie couldn't get them to budge on the equipment. He heard things like, "I guess this glove was good enough to get me into the Hall of Fame." Or, "I brung this bat to the dance, and I think I'll take her home with me." Whatever strategy he tried failed. It would be a couple of weeks more before Ogilvie would blunder upon an idea that accidentally let him get his way.

His first attempt was met with laughter and disaster. At the beginning of the second week in Limbotown, he started a practice by having Antonio dress up in his full, form-fitting San Bernardino Stampede uniform. It included a batting helmet, a lightweight tapered bat, wristbands, batting gloves, a large outfielder's mitt, and protective guards for his exposed shin and elbow. Ogilvie tried to explain to the team the reason for each piece of gear, and that it was now legal to use.

The old-timers conjectured that present-day ballplayers must be panty-waist sissies to need all that junk.

Ruth barked to Gehrig so everyone could hear, "Jeez, Lou, the kid should be holdin' a purse and wearin' a dress and one them big floppy hats with a bird-nest in it to complete the assembly." The other players snickered—not at the Babe's malapropism (some didn't know the difference between "ensemble" and "assembly" anyway), but at the paraphernalia Antonio was modeling.

Eyeing Antonio's basket-style mitt brought forth Ruth again. "Hell, I seen a Cuban fella usin' one of them things down in Florida once. Only he was playin' Jai Alai."

Hornsby remarked, "The kid's pants is so tight, he might as well be playing in his long johns." He added, "Those things on his leg and arm are for football players, not baseball players."

With the exception of the latter-era guys, the Famers stuck to their old outfits and old ways. Even the open-minded Christy Mathewson wasn't ready to part with his favorite glove. Ogilvie wouldn't force them to change—he wanted them to do it on their own. He just needed to find a better way to persuade them. Perseverance and a brighter idea would be needed. For now he was stymied.

Ogilvie asked the disappointed clubhouse manager, Charlie McManus, to be patient: "Charlie, don't pack-up all our new gear yet. I have a feeling something is going to make these guys change their minds. I just wish I knew what." They were *both* going to have to be patient.

The fiasco also marked the introduction of "Tick" Moran, team trainer. He was furnished by Drummond, just like old Charlie McManus had been. No one knew where he came from or his history, and Tick didn't say much about himself. He was friendly enough, and looked like an average Joe of about forty or so, except for one thing. Everyone soon learned why he was called "Tick." It was a straightforward nickname. Tick had a tick all right—it just didn't want to stay in one place. The first time they met, Ogilvie noticed that Tick's tick consisted of Tick's head slightly bobbing to the right every second or so. When he saw him the next day, his head was fine but his left shoulder had a little hop in it. A couple of days after that, the tick traveled to the right corner of the jumpy trainer's mouth. It never disappeared, and no one knew where it would show up next—certainly not Tick. It became fodder for the player's penchant to gamble on anything. Soon they were laying bets on where the tiny spasm might land next and when.

Other than the nomadic twitch, Tick Moran was a well-practiced and up-to-date trainer that the players came to rely on. You may not be able to die in Limbotown (because you were already dead), but you could still suffer injury—and Tick could stitch, tape, bandage, massage and whirlpool with the best of them.

The big problem, the racial tension, got worse before it got better. As Ogilvie tried to explain to his young bench coach, "Remember this one, Antonio? To make steel you have to get two metals very hot, melt them down and then pour them together. If you survive the explosion, you have the hardest metal known to man."

Antonio's face silently asked, *What happens if we don't survive the explosion?*

Ogilvie tried to calm his anxious friend by saying, "Don't worry— we didn't come this far to lose." Neither the manager nor his green assistant had the courage of that conviction yet; nonetheless, for each other's sake, they pretended to.

Meanwhile, little explosions were taking place all over Limbotown. Groups and individuals were clashing. After keeping their distance, black players and white let their hostilities burst. The calm surface waters of Limbotown were roiling beneath, and then the tempest was no longer submerged. The Pledge of Civility, administered by Maggie Briggs and backed by Babe Ruth, was strained to its limits and finally blew up. Scuffles between players cropped up in the clubhouse, in the dining room, at the movie theater. The first real fight erupted between Jackie Robinson and Rogers Hornsby at the piano bar in the once-peaceful hotel lounge. The two combatants were also the most likely: the belligerent Hornsby, the proud Texas bigot, and the quietly smoldering Robinson: the symbol of baseball's integration. Nobody knew exactly what led up to it. The beginning of the end was Hornsby's piano bar request for "Dixie," and Robinson's refusal to "... look away, look away, look away down South ..." The fray was quickly broken up by both black and white teammates, only to leave exposed a festering sore.

The nobody-manager felt helpless. He couldn't batter, nudge, maneuver, wheedle, or proselytize his team into submission. If he thought that would've worked, he would've tried it. Something like that might have had a chance with high school kids, but not these hardened veterans. They would have to do it themselves. They couldn't be coerced, not by him. He had another idea.

Ogilvie didn't reveal his plan until he gave a clubhouse speech before practice the next morning: the old "... if you're going to hate or dislike someone, don't do it because of the color of their skin. Do it for a real reason, like they're fat and homely, or maybe too damned arrogant and good-looking for their own good." The nobody-manager was alluding to Babe Ruth and Rogers Hornsby, respectively. The players got it and couldn't have cared less.

He went on to talk about, "... lots of famous teams, where the players didn't get along off the field or in the clubhouse but somehow managed to play great ball. Like Tinkers and Chance, who wouldn't say shit to each other off the diamond, but played like a Swiss watch on it. And you guys know this happens on all-black or all-white teams too. You know your own examples. Most of you guys have been on teams like that ..."

They realized the truth of Ogilvie's words and were indifferent to them at the same time. It was about like he figured they would react.

He actually got more of a rise out of the bunch when he reminded them "... of the big picture. We're trying to save a kid's life. Maybe we can put our differences aside for now."

Having little Roberto around in the clubhouse and as batboy in the dugout exposed the players to his irresistible personality. He had already befriended the kid-loving Ruth and many of the others. The sandlot games were absolute reverie for Roberto, his chums, and the Hall of Famers too. They were starting to care about Roberto and his fate—a fate they might change, whether they believed it or not.

214

The clubhouse conference ended when Ogilvie divulged his alternative to the random rows that were escalating and becoming more frequent. The Robinson-Hornsby melee had gone too far. "I've arranged for Charlie McManus to set up a boxing ring in one of the exercise rooms. If anyone has a beef with a teammate, it'll be settled on the canvas and nowhere else. Any fights outside of our twelve-by-twelve pit means a suspension from practice and confinement to the hotel."

Almost immediately, Rogers Hornsby spewed his challenge to Jackie Robinson: "Robinson, your black ass is mine!"

Robinson accepted just as quickly. "Dream on, cracker. Get ready for a whuppin'."

"All right—we'll shorten practice today," said Ogilvie. "First match at two this afternoon. But now we play ball. Let's hit the field."

After an edgy, abridged workout, the two gladiators were allowed to punch it out. Except for the team, Ogilvie would not allow an audience. He didn't want a spectacle, or to otherwise incite the Lucky Stiffs of Limbotown into picking sides. There was enough of that already.

Ogilvie refereed the contest. Rounds were two minutes, and the principals used thickly padded gloves. Artistic it was not. A lot of flailing haymakers were launched, which even when they landed, caused more noise than damage. The players roared and whooped. The match was more like an endurance contest than a fight. After the fifth round, Hornsby and Robinson were arm-weary to the point of exhaustion. Ogilvie declared a draw and made the fighters shake hands.

Hornsby and Robinson, both second basemen, barely spoke a word to each other for the rest of their stay in Limbotown. On the other hand, the brawl seemed to deflate the antagonism between the two, and the players in general. Afterwards, there were few fights between any of the teammates in or out of the ring—but there was no unity either.

Relief came again from an unexpected source: Babe Ruth. In a way, the help was unwitting, yet help nonetheless. Ruth took seriously his managership of the rotating squad that Ogilvie had assigned him. He soon learned that skippering a mixed crew wasn't any easier for him than it was for Ogilvie. The Babe found himself compelled to be more even-handed, making decisions for the sake of a win. That might mean putting in one of the black players to pinch hit or pinch run instead of a white player. Ruth didn't like it, but he also wanted to use certain players for certain situations, and this meant going color blind—at least at Drummond Field. The players saw. One afternoon Ruth was heard pleading to Hornsby in the locker-room, "Christ, Raj, I'm not asking you to sleep with 'em, just play with 'em!"

The Bambino was having another predicament of sorts. He was beginning to take a real shine to Satchel Paige. With his contagious, captivating, fun-loving nature, no one was immune. Ruth couldn't help chuckling at Paige's jokes, sayings, and takes on life. And Paige could hardly feel any different about the mountain of a man whose bear of a laugh echoed throughout Limbotown when Satchel cracked wise. Knowledge and understanding is the enemy of fear and suspicion. Babe Ruth and Satchel Paige were finding they had some things in common: baseball, women, fun, women, a taste for adventure—and let's not forget women. The more they knew about each other, the more they found to like.

It was one thing for Ruth to pledge to be civil. It was quite another to start a chummy camaraderie with Satchel Paige, the outspoken integrationist. Paige's cohorts viewed his friendship with Ruth with similar misgiving. Happily for Ogilvie, neither listened to the warnings of their peers and soon the relationship would take an even greater turn.

A few of the practice games did produce fleeting fits of racial harmony. They were really more flashes of excitement in a tight game, when a big hit or a great play made the outcome. Sometimes the players would forget, intertwining in the heat of the moment like the black and white keys on Don Ferris's piano. Then just as suddenly they would break apart, embarrassed at their show of honest emotion.

Ogilvie took quiet note of these buds of hope. He remarked to Antonio, "Baseball has a way of breaking things down and then putting them back together in its own way. It's a long season in the pros, Antonio. Sometimes it takes the whole year to turn a bunch of ballplayers around. Sometimes it doesn't happen at all. Then, if something bad crops up, like a key injury, the players can fall apart or pull together. It's the manager's job to push 'em in the right direction. You just want to make sure you don't push 'em over a cliff."

In the beginning, Ruth wasn't showing much progress. He may have been sober, but he was still too big and too old. A discouraged Antonio reported to Ogilvie on how Ruth did in the morning wind sprints: "I asked him to haul ass, but he had to make two trips."

The nobody-manager had his most famous ballplayer try everything, from a lighter bat to a better diet. After a while he adopted both. However, the childlike Babe extracted rewards from his harried skipper along the way. The extra training sessions were like a never-ending car trip. Ruth's unrelenting nagging was like a kid asking over and over again, "Are we there yet, are we there yet?" He'd pick one thing at a time and then wouldn't quit.

Ruth's biggest coup was finagling Ogilvie to convince Maggie to give him a suite: "I need a suite, I need a suite, I need a . . . Jeez, Ovaltine, if I had me a big ol' suite I might even sleep in there sometime." The Bambino's logic was way beyond mangled, and at the same time you couldn't argue with it.

Maggie was philosophical and put it to a worn-down Ogilvie this way: "The bigger the baby, the bigger the crib."

When the other players found out about it (he'd invited everyone to a party the first night, with the Babe drinking Coca-Cola), there was some passing grumbling, nothing more. After all, a suite was the Bambino's customary abode on the road, or even at home. The others could hardly complain, given their own deluxe rooms.

In order to bribe the Big Baby into more rigorous training, the payoff was—what else? Food. Ogilvie had pared down Ruth's hoggish gluttony to something less than biblical. For Ruth, calories were no longer used as a form of measurement; instead, pounds were used—for both heft and grub. As the Babe slowly started to shed fat, Ogilvie would allow him to add another pound of chow—*but* it had to be in the form of vegetables, lean protein, or whole grains. The scrambling manager had requested the kitchen and wait staff to ignore the Bambino's orders for anything else. No junk food. No hot dogs or hamburgers, no ice cream or other desserts. They mostly complied. In due time, Ogilvie would let

Ruth have some of his favorites as an additional prize for staying on the wagon and working hard.

One evening at dinner, Ruth cashed in a food bonus and asked his waiter for a "cowling." Not sure if he was thinking about the front covering of an engine, the server returned a puzzled stare. The Babe explained, "I don't think I can eat a whole heifer tonight, so just give me one of them little ones. You know—a cowling." His table companions giggled like schoolgirls. When the waiter returned with a large, uncut prime rib roast, Ruth boasted with vindication, "I knew you had one back there!"

As he left the dining room that night, he spied Walter Johnson eating a pile of frog legs. Ruth solemnly advised, "A ballplayer from Kentucky told me be careful—if you eat too many of them things, they'll make you croak." The Sultan of Swat knew not of puns.

Despite the lighter moments, training the aptly labeled Bambino was like dealing with a spoiled, disobedient child. Keeping a close rein on The Babe was a time-consuming and exhausting duty for Don Ogilvie. Now he knew how Gehrig felt.

As the workouts continued, Ruth continued to press his beleaguered manager for more details on his life. Ovaltine was as vague as a mirage. Ruth was not satisfied, and badgered the hesitant skipper with all the charm and impetuosity of a 300-pound Saint Bernard. As he had done with Christy Mathewson, Ogilvie was fast to dole out all kinds of information about modern baseball and "the advance of civilization," things like the designated hitter and man going to the moon.

When Ruth asked about the moon landing of 1969, he earnestly asked, ". . . if anyone has discovered any of my home run balls up there."

It was during one of these conversations that manager Ogilvie made a careless slip. Ruth innocently asked him, "How do you get your 'ins and outs' on the players?"

Ogilvie absentmindedly blathered that, ". . . it mostly comes from the reference books in my office." As soon as he spoke the words he knew it was too late.

Ruth's eyes ignited like sparklers, and he clumsily changed the subject, hoping Ogilvie wouldn't recognize his goof. "Think the sun'll show up tomorrow, Ovaltine?"

Ogilvie knew. Drummond had warned him, and now he was the one who let the fox out and into the henhouse. He had only himself to blame. Vigilance would be needed in guarding the books, he reminded himself.

At the start of the second week in Limbotown, cabin fever was rampant. Sure the hotel, the movie theater, and the women were nice, but the well-traveled players were going stir crazy. Even the practical jokes, like nailing a player's shoes to the floor or cutting a hole in his jockstrap, had worn thin. By now, word had spread like the Plague about the books in Ogilvie's office. They might be the only cure for the players' cooped-up dementia. Ruth was recruiting a band of "gorillas" to commandeer the coveted tomes (lucky for him, he could pass for either a guerrilla or gorilla). A major problem was that Ogilvie almost always slept in his clubhouse office, now outfitted with a rollaway bed.

A plot was devised. Pretending to be on a mission of mercy, Babe Ruth prevailed upon Maggie Briggs to persuade Ogilvie that he should sleep in his hotel room. Ruth said she should ". . . get him out of there for the night because one of the kids lost his pet snake in there and we didn't want to tell 'im and get the kid in trouble and scare poor ol' Ovaltine half to death."

Maggie actually bought this yarn, and was touched that Ruth and his pals should be so thoughtful to the local children. When she told Ogilvie about it, he chortled and explained to her the real reason for the soft-soap story: "They know about the books, Maggie."

The normally savvy Maggie felt gullible, having been taken in by the Bambino's bamboozling. "I should've known."

Ogilvie told her, "Play along. I've got a plan too."

Talking to Charlie McManus and his boys, Ogilvie asked them not to interfere. It was customary for clubhouse staff to steer clear of player antics and pranks anyway. Still, the manager was a bit irked to learn that Ruth had already gotten the old "wink and nod" from Charlie and his crew.

After practice that afternoon, Christy Mathewson poked his head around Ogilvie's office door and tried to tip off his manager in a way that wouldn't be disloyal to his teammates: "I hear St. Patrick and Babe Ruth have driven all the snakes out of Ireland and into Limbotown."

The nobody-manager just smiled at Matty and said, "I'll be ready for 'em."

The artificial moon shone bright late that evening as four watch-capped, black-clad figures silently made their way through the only street in Limbotown. The lampposts that lined either side of the lone boulevard marked their progress. The leader, face obscured by the dark, was the size of a great silverback gorilla—unmistakably Babe Ruth. Rounding out the quartet was a fun-loving Dizzy Dean, a curious Jimmy Foxx, and a vengeful Rogers Hornsby.

While Ogilvie conveniently spent the night in his scarcely used hotel room, the tiny band confidently entered the unlit clubhouse and by flashlight fumblingly found the manager's office. When they reached the door, Ruth said in a hushed voice, "Maybe it's unlocked. I'll give it a try." Extending his big paw to the doorknob resulted in a zap of current, a jump, and a, "Yeowww!"

Ogilvie had rigged a crude, low-voltage shocker that briefly stifled the brain trust. Not only that, the Bambino's electrified scream woke old Charlie McManus, who came out of his adjacent quarters looking like a whitewashed scarecrow come to life. Spindly, hairless legs poked out from his oversized boxer shorts like pale toothpicks. His upper frame, loosely draped in a sleeveless undershirt, was a real treasure—an old, sunken chest buried between slouching shoulders. When Charlie stepped into enough light to be seen, the intruders let out a group yelp, their faces turning as white as Kabuki Theater. Thankful they hadn't frightened each other to death, they agreed it was enough excitement for one night, and the commandos abandoned their sortie for now. Next time they'd be better prepared for the nobody-manager's schoolboy tricks.

A lot of the news that Ogilvie "scooped" to Ruth or Mathewson was hastily relayed to the other players. Not all of it was believed, particularly anything Ruth came up with. Sometimes even the highly regarded

Christy Mathewson wasn't taken seriously. During regular clubhouse gatherings, Ogilvie was often asked to confirm incredible reports, with man landing on the moon coming up almost daily. Many were unconvinced and remained that way. With the exception of Mathewson and Gehrig (both college-educated scientists), the players asked a lot fewer questions about modern marvels than they did about the doom of the old reserve clause and the start of free agency. They were all happy to hear about it, only unhappy to hear it took so long.

Ruth remarked one morning in the clubhouse, "I'll bet none of them free agents is making any more than the $80,000 a year I was takin' home."

Ogilvie, biting his lip and trying not to laugh, looked at his assistant and asked, "Antonio, what's the minimum player salary for 2000?"

Pausing only a second, Antonio replied, "225,000."

"And the average salary?" said Ogilvie prompting his bench coach again.

"About two million."

Ruth and the others were dumbstruck. The Babe asked, "A year? Is that in dollars or pesos?"

Ogilvie assured them the figures were correct and added, "Don't worry, Babe. Damn, a loaf of bread costs five bucks where I come from. A tiny little house in San Francisco will set you back a million clams, easy. It's called inflation."

"Well, what the hell is inflation?" asked a noticeably irritated Ruth.

Before he could answer, Rogers Hornsby cut in. "Inflation is that thing that happened to your gut. You know, it got a lot bigger, but not a lot better." Everyone broke up.

Ogilvie thought it was a pretty apt analogy. He tried to console the Babe by saying, "If you were a free agent today, Jidge, you'd probably be the first billion-dollar player."

Ruth softly wheeled to Gehrig and asked, "How much is a billion, Lou?" The former Columbia student quietly stated, "A million, a thousand times over." Ruth grinned wide.

At the start of week three in Limbotown, the movie theater's marquis had a one-word offering for the evening's fare: *Babe*. Virtually all of Limbotown—and, of course Babe Ruth himself—thought they knew what the movie would be about. It was actually a mid-1990s film about a much-ridiculed farmer who traded in his working sheepdog for a talented little pig named Babe.

About halfway through the first showing, George Herman Ruth asked his companion, Lou Gehrig, "When am I gonna be in it, do ya think?"

Gehrig, with his droll sense of humor, deadpanned to his befuddled buddy, "You must not recognize yourself as a child."

Other players chimed in that, "The 'Babe' was so small, the movie musta been shot when he was only five weeks old." They all agreed that, "The Babe's face hasn't changed one bit. He's just a lot bigger now."

After threatening to ". . . stuff a cowling up the ass a' anyone who says another word," Babe Ruth didn't attend another performance of *Babe*.

Although very appealing to children, the parable also carried a strong and skillfully delivered message about tolerance and being different. Most didn't see that part of the story.

Some did. Roberto Clemente lamented: "I know how dat peeg feel. He nicer 'bout it dan me."

It turned out that Babe Ruth was not the only player popular with the children of Limbotown. Honus (a shortened name from the German "Johannes") Wagner, the folksy, avuncular shortstop from turn-of-the-century Pennsylvania was another choice. The "gee, shucks, gosh and golly" infielder, who had hands like shovels and legs as bowed as any bull rider's, amused and entertained the local kids with all kinds of funny stories and colorful expressions. A real favorite was Wagner's tales of his, ". . . wacky Uncle Snacky from Wes' Virginny." Seems Uncle Snacky, according to the equally wacky Wagner, ". . . had two thumbs on his left han' he used for crackin' walnuts and rollin' cigareets one-handed." Whether he was real or not was anyone's guess and the kids didn't care. They just wanted to hear stories told by Honus Wagner, as only he could, about the three-thumbed mountain man, or other peculiar characters.

Although he was only twenty-eight in Limbotown, Wagner had already aged like moldy cheese, his agreeable, craggy face and smoky voice making him seem older than he really was. Despite appearances, the "Flying Dutchman," as he was dubbed, might've been the best all-around player there ever was. Ty Cobb, naturally, had a fit every time he heard that. Nonetheless, the modest Wagner could play virtually any position on the field and make it look like he'd been born there. His bowed legs were deceiving. He had 722 career stolen bases. At the plate, his right-handed bat was like a shotgun, spraying unhittable spitballs to all fields for doubles and triples. His long arms were accentuated by the forearms of a blacksmith, and his barrel chest rivaled Buck Nimble's. All this was attached to a six-foot, two-hundred-pound frame. When he puffed on his pipe while blowing the foamy head off a beer, it was hard not to think of Popeye. Ogilvie was tempted to feed him nothing but spinach and see what happened.

When the countrified trio of Honus Wagner, Cy Young, and Dizzy Dean got together in Limbotown, it was a rainbow waterfall of slang, a cacophony of colloquialisms unheard since the last episode of *The Beverly Hillbillies.*

Chapter 16

The nobody-manager's team had been in the enigmatic Limbotown for almost three weeks. Aside from the deluxe amenities, the fraternizing, and the constantly perfect weather, all was not quiet on the western front—even if you could figure out which way was west. The infighting was less frequent, but the bad blood was sapping the strength of the players. There was no release, nowhere to go.

Babe Ruth's "Raiders" might've been thwarted in their first assault on Ogilvie's office, but more attempts were sure to come. That defeat only intensified Ruth's claustrophobia. The Bambino was like a caged beast ready to bust out of Limbotown. It wasn't much different from the feeling he would get at St. Mary's Industrial School for Boys from where Ruth would bust out from time to time. He was always either caught or returned on his own, and would face stiff punishment from Father Matthias. Ruth always felt the brief flights were worth ten times the punishment, bar one. That time Father Matthias took away Ruth's baseball privileges. He never ran away again. Now the Babe was getting that old feeling once more. As an adult, he had never been confined. It was anathema to him, a permanent Pavlovian reaction to the walled and gated St. Mary's. Ruth's patience was unraveling, and this time there was no way to escape.

That evening, as he and some of the other players rode down for dinner, he launched into a biting attack against "Burt the Squirt," as the Bambino had dubbed Burton P. Stansberry, III, the friendly and diminutive elevator operator. Their reciprocal name-calling and razzing over the first couple of weeks had escalated and culminated in Ruth's outburst.

Berating him unmercifully in the crowded booth, the Bambino was trying to overcome his cabin fever at the little man's expense. "My morning shit is bigger than you, Squirt."

Gehrig told him to, "Knock it off," but he didn't.

The tongue-lashing was vicious, and Burt's only defense was to wisely say nothing. The ferocity of Ruth's diatribe had gone well beyond witty retorts: "Go find your dick, Squirt. I'll give ya a microscope and a pair a tweezers."

Rogers Hornsby sniggered his approval.

The time had finally come for Burt the Squirt to teach Big Foot a lesson and cure his cabin fever all at once. The trim, clean-cut employee waited for everyone to get off the elevator at the lobby and then called to Ruth, "Hey, Mighty Joe Young—a word with you?"

Ruth responded curtly, "What is it, Squirt?"

Burt moved in to set the trap. "What if I told you I could get you and your buddies outta here. Take you anywhere you want to go."

For a second, the desperate Ruth was ready to nibble. Then he wised up, saying, "Yeah, right," and spun away.

Burton P. Stansberry, III, persisted. "I can prove it to you. Meet me here after you finish your dinner. Bring that swell guy, Hornsby, with you too. And don't tell anyone else."

After dinner, Ruth not only had Hornsby, but most of the other players waiting at the elevator. It was the first spontaneous mingling of black and white teammates outside of Drummond Field.

Burt explained that, "This first demonstration is only for Ruth and Hornsby. They can tell the rest of you guys if I'm telling the truth or not." He then warned, "You better keep your mouths shut if you don't want Ogilvie to find out." The disappointed group broke up as Ruth and Hornsby boarded the booth.

The doors shut and Burt asked, "Where would you like to go? The beach, the mountains, the zoo?"

Ruth said, "We ain't goin' anywhere, Squirt, 'til we get outta this box."

Burt smiled a crooked grin and said, "We'll see." He placed his hand on the elevator throttle and slammed it forward. The compartment didn't seem to move, but it made a shrill whooshing sound that slowly diminished in pitch and intensity as Burt eased off on the handle.

The compact elevator operator then announced, "The beach it is. We're here."

Ruth and Hornsby waited for the doors to open. Since they were facing front, they didn't notice that the entire rear panel of the enclosure had lifted straight up, revealing a balmy, uninhabited palm-lined beach reminiscent of the South Pacific. Burt mockingly tapped Ruth and Hornsby on their shoulders and they turned around, their mouths big as bear traps.

"Go ahead, take a look. It's all real," he goaded them. Hornsby and Ruth were too stunned to move. "Yeah, I can arrange to take you guys anywhere . . . New York, Paris, Rome, Tahiti. Wherever you want . . . now go ahead and take a look." He pushed them out of the box into the tropical paradise and said, "I'll be back in five minutes."

The panel closed and vanished, and Ruth and Hornsby were left stranded in their civvies on a deserted white sand beach. The elevator did not return in five minutes. After an hour, Ruth and Hornsby were screaming at the top of their lungs how they were going to torture Burt the Squirt, performing acts of unspeakable and physically impossible indignities upon him. Just then an invisible door slid open right in front of the hysterical pair. There stood Burt inside the elevator.

As the two approached to get in, the little man held up his hand and said, "Not until I get an apology and a promise, in front of everybody, that you're not going to insult me or call me any more names. Otherwise you can stay here forever."

"Hell, cut off my legs and call me Shorty," said a flabbergasted Ruth. "We was just funnin' ya. Besides, raggin' on ya and givin' ya a nickname is really just tryin' to tell ya we like ya."

"Well, you don't have to like me that much anymore," suggested an unyielding Burton P. Stansberry, III. "No more names, and apologize in front of everyone. If you promise to do that, you can get in." After extorting a firm pledge for public penance and no more slurs or

226

nicknames, Burt let the one-hour Robinson Crusoes back into the magic stall.

Once inside, he told them, "The other players won't be invited to go on trips until I'm sure you'll stick to your word and show me some courtesy and a little respect. They're gonna be pretty pissed off if they find out I won't let 'em use this thing 'cause of you guys." The two felt like Laurel and Hardy painting themselves into a corner, the clever little lift lieutenant having supplied the can of paint.

After their teammates heard from Ruth and Hornsby, Burton P. Stansberry, III, soon became one of Limbotown's most valued citizens. The petite, mercurial elevator cabbie was also one of the best liked.

Once the players discovered Burt's Magic Booth, the raids on Ogilvie's office took a hiatus, although they would not stop completely. The nobody-manager would find out soon enough about the Enchanted Cubicle.

Ruth needed a live hitter in his quest to regain his pitching form. No one else was supposed to know about the Bambino pitching, so Ogilvie became the hitter. In the beginning, it was tough going for both of them. As they got into shape (with Ruth shedding both pounds and years and Ogilvie just pounds), their skills sharpened. Before long, the fifty-two-year-old Ogilvie was whacking ball after ball beyond the distant fences of Drummond Field. He surprised himself. Babe Ruth was surprised too. He gained a bit more regard for his easy-going nobody-manager. He arranged for some of the players to casually drop by so they could see that Ruth wasn't just puffing about Ovaltine. Some were mildly impressed, believing that Ogilvie had probably been a pretty good power hitter in his day.

The smug Rogers Hornsby reacted with a, "Hmm. He still manages like a girl." Raj didn't approve of Ogilvie's laid-back, low-key management style. The combative second baseman preferred the "in-your-face, go-fuck-yourself" management style.

All of them wondered why Ogilvie had Ruth pitching batting practice to him.

Far more striking was the Babe. Now near the end of his third week of rehabilitation and training, Ruth was making the progress Ogilvie had predicted. It was nothing short of extraordinary, and it occurred virtually overnight. The man who had been struggling with his size, his strength, his timing, his stamina, recaptured it all in one giant gulp of Limbotown air. It was like watching a wilted rose regain its bloom, a seeming wonder like the reverse photography used in nature films. As Drummond had promised, Ruth was somehow getting younger. Whatever it was, nobody could argue with the results. Ruth was not only thumping the ball way over the fence in practice, he was now doing it in the intra-squad games against the best pitching. After his third terrific game in a row, the doubters were silenced. In that third game, Ruth not only homered twice, but also made a spectacular leaping catch of a fly ball to rob Lou Gehrig of a home run (which he good-naturedly ribbed Gehrig about the rest of the evening), and then for good measure tripled and stole home. The old Bambino's legs had returned—and with a vengeance. Ruth was the complete package again, getting better every day. It was scary.

The camaraderie between Satchel Paige and Babe Ruth officially began when they both set out for a night on the town, courtesy of Burt the Squirt's (although no one called him that anymore) amazing roaming cubicle. Neither expected to find the other there when they met Burt at the appointed time. Up to some matchmaking of his own, the bantam Burt was aware that Ruth and Paige seemed to like each other, only neither one was bold enough to do anything about it. In his own way, he was trying to help Ogilvie unify his team. The nobody-manager was oblivious to it. Sure, he'd already met the cheerful little operator, but he had no idea that Burton P. Stansberry, III, was a Chosen One with a rather unique elevator.

At exactly 10 p.m. that evening, Ruth and Paige were surprised to see each other walk toward the fifth-floor elevator landing, and even more surprised by what the other was wearing. Outlandish was a wholly inadequate description. The Babe was attired in a sort of western-style, buckskin-suede outfit and custom cowboy boots. Paige, on the other hand, must've fancied himself d'Artagnan, decked out in a foppish dark purple, velvety ensemble and a white lace shirt with puffy cuffs, placket, and collar. Stranger still, they were both donning the exact same hat, which went with neither of their getups. Ruth should've been wearing a ten-gallon Stetson or a coonskin beanie, and Satchel should've had on a plumed Musketeer's hat—or at least the one he'd had on when he first arrived in Limbotown. Instead they were both sporting large, custom-made New York Yankee caps, the design of which was forever linked to the Bambino. It startled Ruth for a second, but he quickly recovered and said, "I like your hat, Satch. But who's your tailor, Queen Victoria?"

Paige, cackling, got in a jibe of his own. "I like your hat too, Babe, but I see you swapped clothes with Davy Crockett . . . is he around here too?" They both erupted in big belly laughs and slapped each other on the back.

While they awaited Burt and his one-of-a-kind transporter, Satchel explained his Babe Ruth-style Yankee cap to the Bambino. "Burt promised me a trip to Yankee Stadium to see a Yankee game . . . where black folks sit wit' white folks and da Yanks have black players too . . . Hey, man, why don't you come wit' me?"

Ruth had been planning to go to New York as well, only the New York he wanted to see was circa 1927—high times, when the Babe was at the top of his game and at the top of the heap. Yet he couldn't resist an invitation to see the New York of the future. As the door to Burt's enchanted chamber opened, he agreed to accompany Satchel Paige to see a modern-day Yankee game: "That sounds tee-rific!" So he thought.

When Burt heard about the idea, he regretted to inform them that the elevator had some limitations that made their joint venture impossible: "Sorry guys—that's one you can't do together. Technical reasons."

What Burt didn't tell them was that the elevator could take a person into the future only as far as they had lived. You weren't supposed to show up after you were dead in real life. Burt wasn't about to tell Ruth that he died in 1948 and his mysterious transporter couldn't take the Babe beyond that year. Baseball had only started to integrate the year before, and the Yankees didn't have their first black player until 1959. Since Paige had lived until 1982, Burt had planned to take him to a Yankee game in the late 1970s where Paige might enjoy black Yankees like slugger Reggie Jackson. But Ruth couldn't go to the '70s. The Babe did a lot of magical things at the House that Ruth built, but reappearing there decades after his death wasn't going to be one of them as long as Doctor Drummond was in charge. At any rate, neither Paige nor Ruth questioned Burt's intentionally vague explanation.

Instead, the Babe invited Satchel to pal around with him at his old stomping grounds in 1920s' New York City: "C'mon with me and I'll take you to my favorite places."

Satchel was flattered, but he explained that he would have trouble getting into any of Ruth's spots—even with the Bambino's help. "Ain't no way they lettin' me open the front door, lessen I'm the doorman." Burt agreed with him.

Then Paige suggested they do it the other way around. "1927 was a good year in Harlem. I know the brothers would be happy to see ya! And when you want, we can always put you in a cab goin' uptown." Paige turned and asked, "What do you say, Burt, my man?"

The crisply uniformed, good-looking little elevator engineer was uneasy, but he okayed it. "All right," he cautioned Paige, "but don't let him out of your sight. If he goes uptown, you're going with him, so be careful. And remember—he's on the wagon. The rules count out there just as much as they do in Limbotown."

Satchel vowed watchfulness. "I got the big man's back." As Ruth got in before him, Paige observed, "And man, he got a lotta back."

Burt's elevator swooshed to its destination. The rear panel opened to 1927 Harlem, and Burt bid them good evening, saying, "At 6 a.m., wherever you are, you'll be engulfed by fog and returned to Limbotown. Until then, you're on your own. Good luck."

That was another limitation of the quirky contraption—it only worked for a maximum of twelve hours per trip. After that, you were automatically returned to Limbotown. It wasn't a permanent way out.

The pair stepped outside the panel, which closed and disappeared from sight. Paige and Ruth were on the streets of old Harlem, together, one dressed like Daniel Boone, the other like the Scarlet Pimpernel—both wearing floppy Yankee caps.

Ruth wasn't too sure how long he was ready to pal around with

230

Satchel in 1927 Harlem. He briefly thought about flagging a cab and getting uptown right away. Paige was tuned into Ruth's jitters and reassured him. "You got nothin' ta worry 'bout down here, Jidge. We all love ya, and you with me!"

Thus emboldened, Paige guided George Herman Ruth to a noisy nightclub branded by blinking red neon "Jilly's." Before they went in, he made Ruth promise not to order or drink any of the booze that would no doubt be offered or foisted upon him. "No hooch, okay?"

He reminded the Bambino of the elevator operator's warning that the rules applied here too. "Burt say Drummond be watchin' you." Satchel did not want to be blamed for stopping the miraculous recovery of the Babe's skills that everyone in Limbotown was only now seeing.

Ruth pledged not to break training: "I might have to get a sandwich or two to munch on later. If I do, I'll wash 'em down with sody-pop."

With that they entered the blaring, jam-packed rectangle of a building, only to watch a raucous party chaotically grind to a halt like a freight train that jumped the tracks.

After a lot of noise and confusion followed by whispers and stares, Satchel, who was just becoming a star himself, confirmed the crowd's buzz. "Dat's right," he spoke loudly. "I'm Satchel Paige, and dis here my frien' from the Yankees, Babe Ruth. Maybe some of you folks hearda him. He come down here wit me to tell y'all thanks for bein' fans." The crowd didn't seem sure.

At Satchel's prompting, the Babe took off his cap, waved it, and yelled, "Thanks everybody!"

There was a total hush for a moment, then wild cheering erupted. The party took off again, this time with Satchel Paige and his very special guest, the Sultan of Swat, as unofficial grand marshals. Ruth quickly loosened up, penning autographs and exchanging quips and complements from this previously untapped vein of friendly fans. He never did make it to Manhattan that night. Instead he and Paige made the full circuit of nightspots, getting pretty much the same reaction wherever in Harlem they went.

At exactly 6 a.m., and at the end of a deluxe southern-cooked feast of fried chicken and waffles, collard greens, mashed potatoes and gravy, black-eyed peas, macaroni and cheese, biscuits, cornbread, and several enormous apple pies, Babe Ruth and Satchel Paige vanished from sight. They instantly found themselves in the middle of a cloud with asphalt at their feet. They walked forward less than two steps, the fog clearing, and saw a sign: "Now entering Limbotown. Population: It depends." They knew they were "home." Ahead lay the town's single boulevard (which saw only foot traffic), the hotel, the movie theater, and Drummond Field. Ruth and Paige gave each other several more congratulatory slaps on the back, and the Babe thanked him for a great time. Cabin fever shouldn't be a problem anymore.

As they entered the hotel, two of its earlier risers witnessed an all-too-brotherly Paige and Ruth wander in the door. They didn't approve, but it wasn't because of the night on the town. The detractors had their own travel plans. They objected to the new friendship for different reasons. Rogers Hornsby was furious. He didn't say anything. He just went outside and let out a primal shriek that even Doctor Drummond heard in his clubhouse office. Josh Gibson shook his head at Paige, give him the once-over for his purple peacock suit, and advised, "Remember who you are now, Satch."

Paige looked at the back of his hands and muttered, "Yeah, like this stuff gonna wash off."

When Ruth boarded the elevator in the lobby, this time to head to his suite to shower and get twenty winks, he looked at the neatly packaged, jockey-sized Burt and said, "Amazin', just amazin'. I gotta hand it to ya, Keed. That was amazin'."

Burt smiled as his jaw jutted.

Ruth then copped a troubled expression and blurted, "Hey, you got us outta breakfast 'fore we could pony up the tab. Jeez, them nice people is gonna think I'm a real shit."

Burt was way ahead of him. "Don't worry, Big Guy, I left a C-note for you two pikers."

Notoriously huge tipper that he was, Ruth let out a throaty grunt of approval: "Yuunnhh."

The *Harlem Tattler* ran a fanciful story the next day about how Satchel Paige and Babe Ruth, ("yes, *that* Babe Ruth"), had made the rounds of several well-known Harlem locales. They claimed to be playing on the same team. The talk of a black and white exhibition team was dismissed as a hoax. When told the two were playing at a location they referred to only as "Limbotown," state unknown, one witness quoted Paige as saying, "I can tell y'all one thing 'bout where we playin'—our manager says, 'We ain't in da middla some cornfield in Iowa, that's fo' shuh.'"

Since the New York Yankees declared the real Bambino was in Philadelphia belting two home runs that same evening, the *Tattler* reasoned that the young, prank-loving Paige was surely pulling another of his outrageous stunts, this one involving an astonishing Ruth impersonator.

Paige wasn't asked to pitch that day, and he yawned all afternoon. Ruth's performance was definitely off. Half the other players were sluggish and sleepy as well. Ogilvie saw it right away. He knew something was not right. Something was up. He had to get to the bottom of it.

There'd been no recent attempts on my office, he thought. *Things are too quiet. Then Babe shows up like he hasn't slept all night, only no one in Limbotown claims to have seen him. He and Paige are seen walking into town, still in full party gear, like they haven't been to bed.* Ogilvie shook his head. It didn't add up. It was like they found a way out. Crazy. If they had, why not just stay there? Something was going on. The players were suddenly secretive. Drummond was pretending to be of little help. He, of course, knew what was going on. Passing it off, he told Ogilvie, "Look somewhere else on this one." Maggie knew too, but was even less direct.

Running out of choices, Don Ogilvie was drawn to the movie theater and the eccentric, charismatic Old Jack Dumphy. With a twinkle in his eye, the garishly garbed Dumphy said, "You're getting warmer. Why don't you try the hotel elevator?" Ogilvie was puzzled, but heeded the tip anyhow.

On the short walk over, Ogilvie had a terrible revelation about Burton P. Stansberry, III, being the purveyor of a wondrous "traveling" elevator, with the players riding it to the hilt. He rejected this preposterous notion in a flash and said out loud, "Nah."

When he reached the lobby, Burt was there to meet him, as if he expected him. "Great day to be alive, isn't it!" he said with his hallmark greeting. It was a clue for Don Ogilvie that Burton P. Stansberry, III, was no ordinary elevator engineer. He was a Chosen One; any day in Limbotown was a great day to be alive for Burt, who knew he was dead.

"Come into my office, Mr. Ogilvie," he said politely, bowing and sweeping his right arm in a welcoming gesture of entry. As Don Ogilvie got into the elevator, the whole epiphany played out in his head again. He'd been had. This damn crate could somehow transport you out of Limbotown! Burt looked sympathetically at the nobody-manager. "The Boss is always the last one to find out. Oh well. Where would you like to go?"

Ogilvie wasn't thrown off track this time. "I'd like to go to a place where you and I can have a nice little talk about the rules my players are gonna have about not using this, uh, thing. Okay?"

"Okay," said a willing Burton P. Stansberry, III.

Then it finally hit him. Ogilvie asked, "Are you a Chosen One?"

"You catch on fast, my friend," Burt chided. He added, "I'm behind you and the Alvarezes the whole way."

He wondered what Challenge the thirty-five-year-old elevator operator had to overcome. Considering his earlier exchange with Maggie Briggs, he wasn't about to ask. Then he remembered something Maggie told him. Drummond wouldn't let older people who have already lived most of their lives be Challengers. Ogilvie, at fifty-two, had just made the cut. He pondered once more why Drummond would allow Old Jack Dumphy, who must've been over seventy-five, to do whatever he had to do to become a Chosen One. Then again, he didn't know what Old Jack's Challenge was either, and things in Limbotown were not always as they appeared. Dumphy promised to tell him—he just didn't say when.

"Can't we just shut this whole thing down?" pleaded Ogilvie.

Burton P. Stansberry, III, explained to the nobody-manager that,

"Drummond wants the players to have the same distractions here that they have in the real world."

Ogilvie replied, "You'd think Limbotown was distraction enough. I guess this damn contraption can take 'em almost anywhere. That's a lot more distracting than usual."

"You'll have to take that up with Drummond," Burt said. "There are some limits that should help you. Any trip is good for a maximum of twelve hours. You can't travel beyond the year of your death, and you're not allowed to see relatives or friends, because somewhere out there is your real self, living a life blissfully ignorant of Limbotown and my Magic Touring Booth. Drummond doesn't want you running into your 'real world' self, so you aren't allowed to go to a place and time where your other self is. That's why it was okay to send Paige and Ruth to 1927 New York City on a day neither of them was really there. The real Ruth was in Philadelphia, and the real Satchel was in Birmingham."

None of this was coherently explained to the players, and they didn't seem to care much as long as they got out of Limbotown, if only for a little while. As Burt summed it up to Ogilvie, "With this thing you can actually be in two places at the same time."

The frustrated manager could only hang his head and say, "God help me."

Ogilvie came to terms with the buoyant Burt. He was reasonable, although he wouldn't turn off his traveling elevator altogether, like the chagrinned skipper had asked. That was up to Drummond.

His next stop was to see Drummond about shutting down Burt's elevator—or at least the part that took you way beyond the fifth floor.

Death in the Flesh, at his usual post in his Drummond Field clubhouse, was only jokingly compassionate to the nobody-manager's plight. "I guess I understand your concern," said Drummond with mock sincerity, adding, "They might mistake the Babe for King Kong and shoot 'im off the Empire State Building. You know, if it was closed, he would try to climb up the damn thing." The sarcastic Doctor finished by saying, "It's like Burt told you—I want Limbotown to have some distractions, just like real life. Your deal with him should make it easy!"

Ogilvie complained, "Yeah, but what if these guys go somewhere to find out about their futures?"

Drummond had a ready answer for that one too. "I've made sure they won't remember."

Turned down, Ogilvie thought of other ways to try to keep his team from flying the coop at the end of every day. One idea would require the help of the theater manager, Old Jack Dumphy.

The morning after he found out about Burt's roving elevator, Ogilvie held a clubhouse meeting to discuss the magic conveyor. The player's grumbled that he found out about it at all. It wasn't all bad news though. With a couple of restrictions thrown in, Ogilvie was going to allow the players to use Burt's elevator. If he didn't, they'd go nuts and use it anyhow, eroding what little control he had over them, "No all-night trips. Be home by 1 a.m. on practice days, 2 a.m. on off days. Ruth isn't allowed to go anywhere alone. He has to be chaperoned by at least one person of my approval—and, most important, he will not be allowed to drink any alcohol, not one drop." The rules for Ruth's return to form applied everywhere.

Ogilvie then got another one of his Limbotown inspirations. "The final rule: anyone involved in a fight outside the clubhouse boxing ring will lose elevator privileges indefinitely. Anyone using a slur will lose one trip for each slip—and that includes calling Hornsby a 'cracker-head.'" There were some chuckles, sighs, and moans, but the players accepted the rules—especially when Ogilvie said, "Burt and I have a pact on it."

It gratified Ogilvie no end that Joe DiMaggio had taken so well to the nineteen-year-old Mickey Mantle. It made Ogilvie wonder why. It must've been a combination of things. The little story Ogilvie had told him about Mantle was one. And paradoxically, Joe figured that he'd probably died young (although actually, he didn't). If that misunderstanding added to his reasons for helping the youthful Mickey, Ogilvie didn't want to do anything to straighten it out. Let the brooding DiMaggio believe what he wanted.

Perhaps because of this, or perhaps not, Joltin' Joe wasn't interested

236

in traveling on Mr. Stansberry's elevator. After dinner, Joe made a habit of hanging out in the Hotel Limbotown Lounge. It reminded him some of Toots Shor's. Almost every evening you could find DiMaggio holding court with selected visitors, an admiring Mickey Mantle usually at his side. No question his schooling of the novice Mickey would pay off come Series time.

Like Ruth, however, Mantle's progress was backward at first. During a batting practice session, DiMaggio's patience burst like a rotten watermelon dropped from a tenth floor window. He couldn't get Mantle to stop bailing out on the inside curve ball, a weapon that Dodger catcher, Roy Campanella, branded "public enemy number one."

An exasperated Joltin' Joe raced around the batting cage, yelling a veritable monologue at poor Mickey. "You got some kind of mental block. You're running scared. Who the hell you think is pitching out there? Cy Young?" The other guys broke up as DiMaggio turned around and saw it was Cy Young pitching out there.

The Yankee Clipper walked away, grumbling, "I give up."

Mantle was struggling with his confidence. Younger than the other players, he was overwhelmed in the face of his boyhood heroes. Not to say that Mickey Mantle was Mickey Mouse, but Ogilvie knew he wasn't exactly dealing with Holden Caulfield either. To turn him around, he just needed to give the budding ballplayer some assurance, not therapy. Arguably it was DiMaggio who needed the shrink.

Ogilvie came up with a way to give Joe D some help. He cued Clemente and Drysdale to tell Mantle about the great career that he was going to have, and how pitchers would shake in their cleats when he came to bat and not the other way around. Ogilvie, the select storyteller that he was becoming, did not tell Mickey that at age nineteen (his age in Limbotown) he was sent down to the minor leagues. Ogilvie was trying to build his ego, not his memoirs. It was no different than the slice of revisionist history the nobody-manager served up to DiMaggio to get him to help Mantle in the first place. Anyhow, it began to work. Mickey made real improvement and started to show flashes of the Hall of Fame player he would one day become.

Despite Burt's magic elevator, the players, as Drummond promised, were unable to remember any hard facts on their lives after baseball. So Ruth organized another foray on Ogilvie's office.

Asked to play along again, Maggie had to bite the inside of her cheeks when Ruth begged her to convince the nobody-manager to sleep in his hotel room again, because, as he put it, ". . . we was worried that poor, old Ovaltine wasn't gettin' enough rest in his itty-bitty bunk, and he's just too tired to keep up with us anymore."

Maggie had a good time recounting the story to Ogilvie, who remarked, "Well, at least they're pretending to care about me. Tell 'em I've decided to sleep at the hotel tonight. I'll have a special reception for 'em in the clubhouse."

When Ruth and his band of bunglers snuck up to Ogilvie's office that night, they were equipped with thick leather mitts, wooden slats and an old skeleton key that couldn't have opened a letter. This time they literally handled the doorknob with kid gloves. Much to their astonishment, not only was the knob unwired, the door was unlocked as well. But as the last conspirator entered the room, five large buckets of water cascaded down on them. Hearing the commotion and seeing what happened, Charlie McManus showed up to hand out towels and send everyone back to the hotel. Ruth's Raiders were not happy to be thwarted again—and this time by a prank as old as the dawn of adolescence itself.

The continuing elevator escapades and the second failed invasion of Ogilvie's office caused the defensive-minded manager to try to divert his players' attention to somewhere less meddlesome, like the movie-theater. Old Jack Dumphy's eyes flashed when Ogilvie asked him if he could show *Star Wars*.

There were only a handful of Lucky Stiffs in Limbotown from a recent-enough time to know about the futuristic space epic. When the movie's title first appeared on the Limbotown Theater marquis, not many knew what it was or what it was about. Those who did had a tough time explaining to those who didn't. There wasn't a lot of interest in the first showing, so the theater was only half full. The second showing that evening was packed. Hearing the buzz about this special-effect-laden, outer-space classic piqued the curiosity of the players and the rest of the Lucky Stiffs. They all wanted to see firsthand if the hyperbole from the first audience could be anywhere close to real. They weren't disappointed. Anecdotal, clichéd reviews like, "You won't believe your eyes," "You'll think you're on a real space ship," and, "It's better than a two-hour roller-coaster ride" still didn't prepare the old-time ballplayers and the others for what they saw—or perhaps more appropriately, for what they experienced.

As the lights came up at the end of the second showing, Ogilvie witnessed stunned silence, wide-eyed disbelief, and more hanging jaws than feeding time at the San Diego Zoo. Then, total pandemonium—crazed cheering, applause, whistling, and shouts for more. When the crowd learned there were three more episodes to come, their impatience was frenzied. The nobody-manager and wily Old Jack exchanged nods. Not even Burt's magic elevator could give you an outer-space adventure. Although the *Star Wars* series wouldn't halt the elevator trips or the marauding on Ogilvie's office, it slowed them down.

Ogilvie was forced to explain to a half-panicked Ruth and group that the film was not real. Demystifying the concept of special effects to a bunch of old dinosaurs wasn't easy. No one was relieved when Ogilvie finished up his description by saying, "Special effects are just like Limbotown. Stuff that looks real really isn't."

It was bound to happen. After a few showings of the wildly popular movies, one of the players decided that "Ruth and Jabba the Hutt are almost identical twins. They musta been separated at birth." Thus to the long list of unflattering Ruth nicknames was added, "Jabba." It didn't faze the Bambino one bit. His only questions were: "Why the hell do they call him a 'Hutt'? He looks to be a big fuckin' snail. Why don't they call him 'Jabba the Slug'?" And, "He looks to be a lot bigger than a hut. Shit, he's big as a barn. Why don't they call him Jabba the Barn?"

Since his first stumbling introduction to Maggie Briggs, Don Ogilvie really didn't say much to her. Their conversations were a lot of idle chit-chat, occasionally punctuated by one of Maggie's famous exhortations. He let her do most of the talking. It was harder to stick his foot in his

239

mouth that way. It worked most of the time. Things started to change after he quit drinking. He wasn't being lectured anymore, just counseled. On the surface, the nobody-manager was neatly dealing with a delicate racial balance, a runaway elevator, and keeping the unruly Ruth in check. Both he and the Babe were abstinent, eating healthy and working out like fiends. Admittedly, the fifty-two year old Ogilvie couldn't keep pace with the now-robust Bambino, but he did what he could, and the work showed. To Maggie it was a wonderful metaphor about his gathering composure evolving through his physical rebirth. To Ogilvie it was the release (so far) of twenty-five pounds of dead weight and the old baggage in the attic that went with it. Rejuvenated, he hadn't looked or felt better since his minor league days, decades ago. It occurred to the nobody-manager that he could've lived a lot more days like this, if only he'd chosen to.

All Maggie could see was a once-hopeless drunk quietly resurrecting the shambles of what was left of his life. As a woman, her stirrings for Don Ogilvie took a deeper root, a connection made more of love than strength—and yet more powerful than death.

He was so busy, so wrapped up in the day-to-day details of managing that he hadn't thought about drinking. Sobriety wasn't a problem right now. After all, he had gone longer stretches many times before.

Even though the Series was more than three weeks off, the pressure would soon start to mount for manager Don Ogilvie. Storm clouds were brewing on the polyester horizon. The steely clank of Ty Cobb's bloody cleats could be heard making their way into his Drummond Field dugout.

Chapter 17

The old-time players were starting to get familiar with some of the new training tools Ogilvie used. Although they still wouldn't give up their old bats and gloves, they were dazzled by some of the high-tech gadgets their modern-day manager employed. The radar gun had clocked Walter Johnson's fastball at 100 miles per hour. Video cameras were used to dissect and rebuild a player's swing.

After seeing his restored stroke on tape for the first time, the Bambino commented to Ogilvie, "Jeez, I didn't know I was so be-u-ti-ful!" The Babe was in fact making a self-deprecating aside about his bulldog mug that hovered over his still somewhat potbellied breadbasket. To Don Ogilvie, the re-flowering of Ruth was indeed "'be-u-ti-ful." His left-handed swing was power and grace, simultaneous artistry and brute strength.

The nobody-manager took the opportunity to remind his reborn superstar, "Babe, your return to younger days can vanish in the instant it takes to quaff a beer or down a shot."

It was obvious the Babe savored his regained skills and the renewed respect of his teammates. "It's the straight-and-narrow for me, Ovaltine!" he projected with conviction. Now he didn't want to risk his own downfall.

Even the weight lifting that the players had originally rejected out of hand was embraced. The results were clear. The Bambino's biceps were taking on the look of a brawny lumberjack. Some of the players liked calling him Paul Bunyan and referring to his bat as the "axe." Ruth especially enjoyed the comparison, since Drummond had earlier christened him "Babe the Blue Ox" under less-flattering circumstances. Ruth noted that, "Yeah, that Paul Bunyan was a helluva woodsman . . . but didn't they name that foot condition after him?"

His arms now sculpted like Michelangelo's David, Ruth couldn't resist taking a page from "The Beast"—Jimmy Foxx, the old Philadelphia Athletics' infielder. "Double X," as he was also known, already had the arms of a blacksmith. His trademark was his sleeveless jersey. The tailored garment allowed a convincing display of his thickly muscled guns. It wasn't all show either. Foxx was renowned for his home run power, hitting 58 in 1932 and then winning the Triple Crown and the MVP award the next season.

Ruth came into the clubhouse one afternoon donning a newly designed jersey that mimicked the Double-X style. His teammates immediately jumped the big showoff with catcalls and jeers.

Little Roberto, clubhouse mascot and batboy, took seriously the mostly affable attack and came to his hero's rescue. "It's his constitutional right!" insisted the civic-minded seven-year-old. "The right to bare arms!"

"Yeah, the kid knows his stuff," bellowed the Bambino. "It's the law!"

Only little Roberto and the Babe actually thought the Second Amendment referred to limbs. In Roberto's case, at least, the mistake was understandable. The players laughed and told the fired-up batboy not to worry. They weren't going to violate anything so elusive as the Bambino's rights. They had something more "material" in mind. The next morning, all of Ruth's jerseys had been neatly carved like so many slices of roast beef. When he went to fetch one off a hanger the thin strips fluttered carelessly to the floor.

As Jimmy Foxx passed Ruth's locker, he said, "I hear they got a terrible moth problem here."

"Not after I squish the shit outta the fat fox that did this," threatened a miffed Babe. After the third shredded shirt he retrieved unraveled into threads, even Ruth's big hand couldn't muffle his belly laugh.

They had been in Limbotown a month, with the Series another month away. Race riots and boredom contained, the obstacle this time was complacency. None of Ogilvie's twenty-four players believed they would have any difficulty defeating a team of just Ty Cobb and some rube pitcher. The nobody-manager wasn't so sure. Limbotown and Drummond had their devices.

Ogilvie's mind kept drifting back to two things Drummond had said: "This isn't going to be as easy as you think," and "My team has only two players, but we're going to cover every position." After four weeks in Limbotown, location unknown, he had fallen in love, struggled with fractious players, negotiated a sobriety pact with a soused, over-the-hill Babe Ruth, and corralled a fugitive elevator. He thought he already knew what Drummond meant by, "This isn't going to be easy." Now he wanted to stew on the conundrum Drummond had presented: "My team has only two players, but we're going to cover every position."

He sought Maggie's advice that evening when she brought him dinner in his clubhouse cubbyhole. "So how are two players gonna cover all the positions, Maggie?"

Again, she wasn't clear. She wasn't allowed to be. However, she did encourage the perplexed manager. "Find out as much as you can about the other team. You've done okay so far." Then she cautioned, "But nothing around here is as it seems. The 'this-isn't-going-to-be-easy' part isn't over with. That's the most I can say."

By now he knew enough not to let that warning pass. "I kinda figured. Thanks."

Maggie lingered in Ogilvie's doorway for a moment, with her hands on her hips in a way that made his mind start to drift. She noticed and turned to leave, saying, "You better keep your mind on baseball." As always, she was right.

The nobody-manager quickly shook his head to clear the fog and then cruised down a stadium corridor and found Drummond in his office. He asked, "How about an exhibition game between my team and Cobb and that Hillbilly guy?"

The foxy little umpire wouldn't do it and tried to change the subject just a bit too fast. "Not today, Ogilvie. That's what the Series is all about.

Hey, Buddha's almost starting to get down to wooly-mammoth size, huh?"

The discerning manager sensed he was onto something. For the next few days, he hounded Death in the Flesh unceasingly, like Ruth had hounded him on just about everything.

He finally cornered Drummond in his clubhouse office for the umpteenth time and demanded, "We need an exhibition game! We need an exhibition game!" It wasn't easy outlasting Death, but Ogilvie had plenty of practice with the Babe.

Drummond finally relented. "Jeez, Ogilvie, leave me alone—you're killin' me here, which is impossible and annoying. All right already, I'll let youse guys come to a practice! Fugetabouta game. That's all you're gettin'. Tomorrow at one. Now get outta here!"

Unlike Ruth, who seemed to eventually get everything he asked for, Ogilvie only succeeded in getting Drummond to let the Hall of Famers watch Cobb and Higgins work out. He would have much preferred a game, but this was as far as he could get with the unpredictable Death Personified. As it was, a practice was all Ogilvie would need to have all of his questions answered—even if he couldn't believe the answers.

He hurried to tell his team the news. They weren't excited. Watching Cobb and another hayseed work out wasn't exactly their idea of kicks. When they came anyhow, they weren't prepared for what they saw. It was like the first showing of *Star Wars* all over again, except this time as a horror movie.

The task had been sitting there like a rotting chunk of Babe Ruth's leftover "cowling." Don Ogilvie slipped into his office easy chair, holding a special baseball book. In it was the biography of Ty Cobb. He knew roughly what it would say. That's why he wasn't looking forward to the chore, but it needed to be done. He wanted to refresh his memory and hunt for any clues that Cobb might've hidden between the lines.

If Kenesaw Mountain Landis was the Evil Emperor of Baseball, then Ty Cobb was its Darth Vader. If Joe DiMaggio was the Mystique of Baseball and Babe Ruth its Magic, then Ty Cobb was its Dark Side. He was the Bad Seed, the Anti-Ruth, the Prince of Darkness. No, he was never on a mission to destroy Major League Baseball, he just represented all that could be treacherous and wrong about one of its stars.

Cobb wasn't just the meanest baseball player of his time, he was the meanest of all time—the King of Mean. Whoever came in second place would be light years behind. The chip on Cobb's shoulder didn't go away when the game was over, unless he heaved it at you. He mortified teammates, managers, other players, umpires, and fans—as much off the field as on. During his playing days for the Detroit Tigers, he bragged of pistol-whipping to death a helpless victim over a dispute about a petty amount of cash. Although never officially linked to that crime, there is no reason to dispute Cobb's admission to it. He had numerous run-ins with the law during his baseball days, mostly assaults and batteries. Afraid his enemies might jump him, he always carried a gun. An all-too-accomplished clubhouse and street brawler, Cobb supposedly never lost a fight. He had plenty of opportunity too. In one famous brawl with a burly umpire, Cobb was quoted at the outset as saying, "No rules. I fight to kill." He then proceeded to pummel his prey into submission by mercilessly banging his head against the ground until pulled from the now-defenseless ump by horrified onlookers. Cobb was frothing at the mouth like a mad dog ready to finish the job.

Much has been written about why Ty Cobb was the way he was. Some attributed his notoriously bad attitude to an overbearing father who objected to his son's plans to become a professional ballplayer. Cobb's father was a successful businessman and wanted his bright boy to be a banker or a lawyer. The father died before the son gained fame as a hitter. One theory had it that young Ty never got over his father's disapproval, and this, in turn, accounted for his overly aggressive play and antisocial behavior.

Another view insinuated that it was how his father died that explained Cobb's infamous enmity. The senior Cobb was shot to death by his wife, Ty's mother. The shooting is still surrounded by controversy. There were several different versions, ranging from terrible accident to cold-blooded, premeditated murder. One fact is undisputed: Ty's mother shot her husband upon his unexpected, early return from a business trip. The rumor mill ascribed the killing to a scandalous love triangle, Ty's father the odd man out. A sensational trial followed, and young Ty's mother was acquitted, apparently much to his relief. His own doubts aside, Cobb remained outwardly loyal to his mother, even after her death.

Neither the senior Cobb's disapproval of his son's career nor the way his father was killed can explain Ty Cobb's madness. By the time these events took place, he was already in his late teens, and just about to make it to the Detroit Tigers. He had already been cruel and incorrigible for years. The only explanation was that Tyrus Raymond Cobb was born that way. It came as a part of that thing that makes us all what we are— be it good, bad, or something in between. Ty Cobb was never one to be in between. He always went all the way—damn the umpires and infielders, and full cleats ahead. He liked being bad.

Today, if properly diagnosed, Cobb's violence and hatred might've been dulled by a baseball-sized Prozac. Heavily medicated, he might've turned into the Mr. Rogers of baseball. On the other hand, there was no doubt that Cobb's seemingly endless supply of psychotic energy defined his ferocious play on the field and his raw actions off it. A drugged Cobb probably wouldn't have made it to the Hall of Fame, or even to the Major Leagues. Maybe Beethoven wouldn't have been Beethoven were he not the offspring of a syphilitic mother, which eventually made him deaf. Would Modigliani have painted masterpieces if he'd had glasses? Sometimes the disabilities make the genius. Cobb was the most savage player the game has ever seen. With that came the deranged personality. One could have hardly existed without the other. But Ty Cobb was no Dr. Jekyll-Mr. Hyde. He was all Mr. Hyde, all the time.

The venom and epithets that regularly spewed from Cobb's thin lips would've rivaled a mutinous band of Ghurkas. His bench jockeying was laced with humorless insults, threats, and-not-so-polite invitations to "dance." He had no friends on his own team, the Detroit Tigers, or anywhere else in or out of baseball. It must've been lonely being Ty Cobb, yet at the same time he didn't want pals. And he wasn't what you would call a fun guy to be around anyway. Cobb liked the "me against the world" arrangement. It fit in well with his blossoming paranoia.

The Peach was an infamous bigot and proud of it. Being born in rural Georgia in 1886 didn't help. Were it possible, Cobb would've raised the Confederacy from its ruins and fought the Civil War anew. As it was, he fanned the flames of his own personal battles of intolerance and hatred. He once vowed never to set foot on a baseball diamond if the opponents had any black players, and he confidently predicted that Major League Baseball would never be integrated. Summing up his unapologetic beliefs, he declared, "The darkies' place is in the stands or as clubhouse help." He was never one to mince words.

Then he admittedly broke his own rule when he agreed, along with some other Tiger teammates, to an exhibition series in Cuba. Seems that for the right amount of money, this Prince of Darkness could be persuaded to do just about anything. His love of the almighty buck knew no bounds. Even his staunch distaste for the color black could be made to bend by sufficient piles of the color green. The series played in Havana showcased Cobb's talents, except the legendary Negro league shortstop, Henry "Pop" Lloyd, upstaged him. Cobb was out-hit by Lloyd, and despite high-flying razor-edged cleats, the fearless infielder tagged out Cobb more than a few times. Ty refused to shake Pop's hand or otherwise concede the Major League-caliber play of any minority. What a wonderful sense of sportsmanship he possessed. While he couldn't stand the idea that any white player might be his equal, that a black player might be so compared was too much for the racist Georgia Peach to bear. Money aside, he never again played in a mixed game.

Although he would not admit it, Ty Cobb resented Babe Ruth. The rancor was more on a professional than a personal level, although Cobb managed to make it personal. This was hard to do, considering the Babe's expansive nature and gregarious ways. Cobb felt that Ruth's homerun hitting would eventually destroy the game, making meaningless the minutiae of baseball strategy. He was wrong, of course. What really tormented the Peach was the Bambino's popularity and the belief that Ruth was the better player. That did it for Ty. Publicly Cobb would claim indifference to the Babe, stating that the other major leaguers knew who was the best, and that was all he cared about. Privately he seethed. Cobb figured himself the better all-around player, and he was right. But Ruth drew the fans and the fans' adulation—not only because of his unprecedented home run power, but because of his contagious appeal as well. Ruth was so easy to like, and Cobb was so easy to hate.

The dam broke in the 1924 off-season. The Bambino was invited to an event at a hoity-toity Georgia lodge of which Cobb, the avid hunter, had long been a member. When he found out that the Babe had been picked as his bunkmate, the Peach was heard saying, "I'm not living with any nigger!" He often referred to Ruth alternatively as, "The Big Ape," "Polecat," "Niggerlips," "Nigger-boy," or just "the Nigger." As founder of "The Ty Cobb School of Southern Pride and Prejudice" and its only instructor, student, and alumnus, "Massa" Cobb was at the head of the class. His idea of winning friends and influencing people usually meant an opening insult followed by a quick kick to the groin. Even the happy-hearted Bambino rapidly grew to dislike the villainous "Georgia Prick," as he rightfully re-dubbed him.

Strangely enough (although perhaps not), Cobb also held fellow racist Rogers Hornsby in low esteem. In spite of their similarities, Cobb bashed the great right-handed hitter for his weak defensive skills, accusing the second baseman of being unable to catch pop-ups. The bitterness came from Hornsby's undisputed prowess at bat. That was Cobb's self-declared realm, and even a right-handed hitter from the other league wasn't allowed to poach. Brother bigot or not, Cobb wouldn't cozy up to anyone who dared to stack up against him.

The same could be said for Cobb's predictably stormy relations with baseball czar Kenesaw Mountain Landis. Although both were resolute segregationists, near the end of Cobb's career the stern-faced commissioner unloosed a bombshell scandal on the Georgia Peach. He and venerable Cleveland Indian outfielder-manager, Tris Speaker, were accused of fixing and betting on games. Both were eventually cleared but left besmirched, though the charges seemed to have substance. Pete Rose would've been mildly impressed. By then, Cobb had friends in high places, and Landis had to consider whether tossing out two of the game's greatest players for indiscretions of years earlier would only reopen the ugly wounds of the-all-too-recent Black Sox disgrace. After all, the chicanery that Cobb and Speaker were accused of was an unofficial "spoils" system that most players tacitly went along with.

Landis decided not to ruin any lives this time. Following their interim suspensions, neither played for their old teams again. Cobb played his final season for Connie Mack's Philadelphia Athletics and retired after the 1928 season.

One of the few players the Georgia Peach could stomach was Christy Mathewson. If Mathewson chose to tolerate Cobb, it was either magnanimity or madness. As a National League pitcher, Big Six was not a direct threat to Cobb's status as the best hitter. It wasn't Matty's job to bat, and Cobb, an American Leaguer, didn't have to face him. Mathewson was a poised, educated ballplayer who even Cobb admired. Fatefully, both Cobb and Mathewson were in the same Army unit in WWI when the big hurler was accidentally exposed to poison gas. Ty, The Prince of Darkness, escaped injury, and Christy, The Golden Boy, slowly died from the damage done by the gas. When one considers Cobb's long, unhappy life and Mathewson's early demise, one might be tempted to believe that only the good die young.

As you might've guessed, the Georgia Peach's personal life was anything but peachy. First wed to Charlotte "Charlie" Lombard, Cobb sired three children, all of whom he finally left hurt and disaffected. To his family he was cold, demanding, and not around much—and those were the halcyon days. His inevitable divorce from the small and delicate Charlie was an ugly, brutal struggle. To the surprise of no one, Charlie filed on grounds of extreme mental cruelty. For years after, Cobb did everything to secrete the true extent of his enormous wealth. That he would defraud the mother of his children and his offspring too was justified with Cobb's bitter, gnarled logic. Besides, he really didn't care. His second marriage was also barbaric—but thankfully for this wife, brief.

Contrary to what most people believe, Cobb didn't amass his fortune after he had comfortably retired from making an unparalleled amount of money playing ball. He had been investing right along—smart investments, too. By the time the Georgia Peach became a multi-millionaire in the early 1920s, he was already the Plantation Master of his own financial fiefdom. Buying into a small, unknown beverage company with the quirky name of Coca-Cola only turned out to be the gold cap on a silver bottle. In 1922, at age thirty-five, Ty Cobb was hitting .401 and making more money than any player or owner in baseball—and that, just from the money he made outside the game.

At the same time, the crazy-eyed Tyrus was an early advocate of players' rights. Even though he was the highest-paid athlete of his era, Cobb easily saw the need for a players' union, minimum salaries, disability benefits—and that most dreaded taboo of all, free agency. Cobb knew that baseball was a shameful monopoly protected by no less than the federal government. When asked if he thought baseball was a business, the Peach replied, "If it isn't, General Motors is the biggest sport there is." Naturally, those who were its target largely debunked his progressive opinions. And as would be expected, the many players who shared his views didn't really want his support. To them, Cobb was a lot like Kaiser Wilhelm pleading for peace as his troops dug in for the winter at Versailles.

No one can deny that Ty Cobb's baseball achievements remain unfathomable. He was the best all-around hitter the game has ever seen. It must be remembered that the bulk of his twenty-four major league seasons were played in the old dead-ball era, when hits and runs were that much tougher to come by. This makes his career numbers even more stupefying. For decades Cobb held the record for lifetime steals, hits, and batting average. He won the hitting title twelve times. Nobody else has come close. There were many who clubbed more home runs. A few hit for higher average. But none had the tools, the command, or the presence that Ty Cobb had in the batter's box or on the base paths. He was scientific as well, and he set the standard for the modern game to come. He studied pitchers' moves, catchers' throws, and ran like a raving banshee with flashing spikes hungry for flesh and bone. Cobb knew the power of the psychological game. He had a million ways to get to you. He wanted you to believe he was a lunatic who might kill you and had no trouble convincing most people of that. It happened to be true. If they had a category for most demented player, Cobb would hold an unbreakable record.

The one possible frailty in the Georgia Peach's game was defense. In the outfield his fleet feet could get him to most any ball. Still, corralling the pesky pill and making a strong, accurate throw to the infield sometimes eluded his usual flawless play. Although he batted left, he threw right-handed. Perchance this ambidextrous combination accounted for his occasional defensive lapses. On the other hand, he just wasn't blessed with a great arm, either right or left; but it was only a minor defect.

A more glaring blemish was the fact that Cobb appeared in three World Series and won none. Only adding to his simmering anger was his poor performance in those championships. Cobb would bristle with rage when confronted on the subject. He often claimed that the Tigers would've never made it to any World Series without him (he was probably right), but he unflinchingly blamed his post-season meltdowns on others' miscues and mistakes. This was typical Cobb that did so much to endear him to his team, the press, and fans everywhere.

After he left the game, one apparently generous thing Cobb did for many years was give retired players like Mickey Cochrane, the Hall of Fame catcher (and Mantle's namesake) a few bucks now and then. These guys had fallen on hard times, player pensions were still decades away, and Ty would discreetly make payments to them. Cochrane never turned down Cobb's donations, but even the grateful, bean-balled former catcher disliked him. The idea that Ty Cobb would make such an overtly charitable gesture belied his true self. He was never moved by a spirit of giving, only out of guilt, superiority, or greed. In short, even when it looked like Ty Cobb was trying to do something good, it was invariably tainted by some impure or sinister motive—harsh words, perhaps, with which an honest Cobb would have to agree. He always prided himself in being able to outfight or outsmart anyone, and it didn't matter to him how he did it or how it looked.

Cobb himself looked as if the acorn bounced off the bark. Beady eyes were close-set and piercing. His ears flew from the side of his head, while his nose, crooked and long, led to his crabbed and gaunt mouth. Hair did not like growing atop his pate, and the Peach's legs curved like they'd been formed around a forty-gallon barrel. But at six-one and 200 pounds, well heeled, and the premier ballplayer of his time, Cobb had his share of female companions. He even had a brief stint with the future

Mrs. Babe Ruth, the lovely Claire Hodgson, although there is no reason to believe that this resulted in the animosity between Cobb and Ruth. Cobb had already decided to dislike Ruth long before the Sultan of Swat married this charming socialite.

After two-and-half decades of reckless abandon on and off the base paths, the constant mauling of Cobb's body finally took its toll. The decline continued after his retirement from the game. As the cantankerous Peach grew older, his tantrums, histrionics, paranoia, obsessions, self-abuse, and overall insanity became yet more chronic. He didn't mellow with age. Instead, the old left-handed hacker acquired a serious drinking problem that he had, ironically, tongue-lashed Ruth about years earlier. Failing eyesight and complications from diabetes were just the beginning of the end for Tyrus Raymond Cobb. In 1961 he died at age seventy-four, decimated from cancer, the ravages of his own excesses, and his tireless inner demons.

The big day of the Ty Cobb workout couldn't have arrived soon enough for Don Ogilvie. Although making progress with his group, the nobody-manager needed more help. They were all lifting weights and practicing hard, but many still wouldn't part with their old gear. Meanwhile, the optimistic Ogilvie prayed that the Georgia Peach at least wore a batting helmet and used a big outfielder's glove. If he didn't, there would be no chance of convincing his crew to convert. But that was a minor problem compared to the rife indifference of the clubhouse. The twenty-four Hall of Famers were not menaced by the thought of taking on Ty Cobb and some hillbilly pitcher. Ogilvie was hoping the exhibition would provide a reason for his band to stay focused and learn today's game. So he was also hoping that Cobb and Hillbilly Higgins would put on a good show, something that would snap his players to attention. But who was going to be intimidated by a two-man team? And how were Cobb and Higgins going to cover every position? The answers would be mind-boggling.

There was no practice game for Ogilvie's players that afternoon. Instead, they would sit in the dugout and watch the "Cobb Squad" train. Loyal bench coach Antonio and an anxious nobody-manager were alone in their dugout, wolfing down a couple of sandwiches about twenty minutes before the workout was to start. A minute or two later they heard some stirrings on the other bench and saw what appeared to be Ty Cobb in sweats, with a large, rusty file honing his steel spikes to a fine edge. It was a ritual Cobb usually saved for games, to terrify the other team—or in this case, its coaching staff. After a short while, he retreated to his clubhouse only to reemerge a few seconds later, this time in full playing gear.

Ogilvie husked an enthusiastic, "Yes!" when the Ty Cobb he saw was wearing every piece of modern gear known to baseball. Maybe now his old-timers would take notice. The uniformed Peach once again backtracked to the locker room, and then something preposterous unfolded. A second or so more, and there were two uniformed players in the home team's dugout at the same time. It was hard to make out details, and at first Ogilvie and Antonio assumed the second guy was Hillbilly Higgins. However, on closer inspection he looked to be a dead ringer for Cobb. A look-alike relative in the dugout, perhaps? That theory didn't hold up for an instant as two more uniformed figures joined the group. Both players turned their backs and Antonio and Ogilvie could see the name "Cobb" stamped in large block letters across their jerseys. Antonio gaped at Ogilvie and vice versa. What was going on here? Moments later about ten more "Cobbs" walked into the dugout, followed by a beaming Doctor Drummond. The constant warnings about, "This isn't going to be as easy as you think" and "My two players are going to cover every position," raced through Ogilvie's mind again—and this time he knew why. The sometimes helpful, sometimes deceptive Drummond had duplicated Cobb sixteen times! The sneaky Little Bastard had cloned the game's best hitter like so many sheep—or, in this case, piranha.

As the exasperated Ogilvie was commenting to the unbelieving Antonio, "We're in deep shit," Death in the Flesh strutted over to gloat.

"Told you my team was gonna cover every position."

"You lyin' son of a bitch!" yelled an angry nobody-manager. "You said you only had two players, and I count about sixteen or seventeen Cobbs over there. That's a whole damn team!"

"I didn't lie," said a still cheerful Drummond. "I do have only two players: Cobb and Higgins. You won't see anybody else. Just like I promised. You made the assumption that two players meant two bodies. Bad assumption. I tried to warn you by saying we're gonna play every spot. Now you know how."

Ogilvie was furious, mainly with himself. Everything Drummond said was true. He had tried to tip him, and he still didn't see it coming. He should've known better. He let off some steam at Death Personified by saying, "Cloning Cobb is a crime against nature. This is like letting the 'Boys from Brazil' grow up."

Drummond was laughing and talking as he walked away to rejoin the Cobb Squad. "I told you this wasn't going to be easy."

Soon Ogilvie's Hall of Famers began filtering into their Drummond Field dugout. Ruth immediately asked, "Hey Ovaltine—who the hell are all the stiffs over there?"

"They're all Ty Cobb. Drummond has duplicated him sixteen times. It's called 'cloning.' That's how they're gonna play every position. The sneaky little bastard is pulling a fast one, and there's not a damn thing we can do about it."

"Clowning?" repeated an uncertain Bambino. "Hell, why can't the little Derby Bastard clown me about twelve times?"

"Not necessary," Ogilvie deadpanned. "One of you is worth a whole circus."

The Babe paced down the bench muttering, "I knew it. We're playing a buncha clowns."

"Lord have mercy!" moaned Satchel Paige. "Sixteen Ty Cobbs plus the original! Shit, wit dat many Cobbs in one place, I know where we be now—hell!"

The rest of the team was alternately confused, irritated, incredulous, frenzied, or all of the above. They had been tricked. Again. Drummond the Bastard was to blame. Again. Ogilvie struggled to calm his players as the Cobb Squad began stretching and warming up. While they simmered, what turned out to be the original Ty Cobb slowly walked over to the visitors' dugout and took a good look. Ogilvie's team did the same. There stood the Georgia Peach in all his glory, the epitome of the present-day ballplayer. It was evident that Cobb had taken to weight

254

training too as his six-one frame rippled with strength. His tight-fitting suit emphasized his carved physique. He leaned on a tapered bat as he held his large, basket-style glove. A batting helmet, batting gloves, protective guards for his right elbow and shin, and lots of colorful sweatbands, further trimmed Cobb's outfit.

Ruth, a natural antagonist to the Peach, couldn't hold back. "Look, boys! Remember this asshole? I just can't seem to remember his name . . . Oh yeah, I remember now. I seen it on a flyer in the Post Office. Ty Cobb! Says you're wanted for fuckin' some guy's horse to death!" Ruth waited for his teammates' chuckles and added: "Hey Ty, whaddaya doin' wearin' all that crap? Ya big fuckin' sissy!"

Cobb, who rarely smiled, did, and retorted, "You big fuckin' gorilla idiot, I'm wearin' all this crap so me and my sixteen copies can pound you and your gang of assholes into the ground for good!" Then Cobb started in on Ruth and the others in earnest. "I see yer with the niggers now, Babe. Right where you always belonged, you big fuckin' overgrown ape!"

With that, the black players and Babe Ruth were ready to charge Killer Cobb, but Ogilvie held them back saying, "That's just what he wants you to do. He's trying to get you guys riled up so you'll play mad and stupid in the Series. Don't fall for it." The agitated players held up.

The Prince of Darkness then took a different angle. The slit-eyed Peach spied Maggie Briggs sitting in the stands behind home plate with Maria Alvarez and most of the Limbotown workers. Cobb shouted to her. "Hey Maggie, your boyfriend's a pussy. Why don't you come to my room tonight and I'll show you what a real man can do!" This time it was Ruth and the others holding Ogilvie back.

Maggie, ignoring Cobb's crude proposition, commented to Maria, "I feel like the Bride of Frankenstein. Frankly, I'd rather Norman Bates had a crush on me."

The Georgia Peach walked away smirking, his bench jockeying having hit its marks. He retreated to his pack of Cobbs for batting practice. That's when Ogilvie noticed that some of the Cobbs were different. Some hit for power, others line drives. When they took the field, some seemed a few years younger and not as buffed, like the middle infielders that needed to be quick. Drummond had developed his Cobbs to play according to their positions—"Cobbs for All Seasons." Ogilvie had to give Death in the Flesh credit. The team of Cobbs was anything but one-dimensional. Each Cobb was specially trained and coached.

The towering figure that took the mound was a sight so striking, even grizzled old Charlie McManus had to shake his head. At six-foot–seven, the pitcher with the name "Higgins" stitched on his jersey was rail thin, with nothing but legs, knees, arms, and elbows. He had more angles than an octagon. He looked like a benign Icabod Crane, but his fastball was anything but benign. After a few warm-up tosses, the right-hander began to throw hard, real hard—Icabod Crane with a hundred-mph fastball. His over-the top style was different than Big Train Johnson's, but the velocity was the same, maybe better. Ogilvie had Antonio put the radar gun on him just to check. Sure enough—one hundred, then he got one up to 103! So this was the vaunted Clarence "Hillbilly" Higgins. Nothing but hundred-mile-per-hour fastballs so far, and he wasn't even pressing—a nice, smooth delivery, lots of movement on the ball. Ogilvie peered down the bench to see what the other players were doing. There wasn't much talking or joking, just some quiet comments about shortening swings or starting them sooner.

Satchel Paige was heard to say, "Damn, he throw that ball like he mad at it, and the only way he gonna get even . . . be throwin' it harder the next time."

Then, out of nowhere, Higgins unleashed one that seemed to dissolve in midair. In a millisecond, the ball made a terrific pop, hitting the catcher's mitt so hard it almost knocked over the Cobb-replica playing there. Antonio couldn't believe his eyes or the radar gun—113 mph! The Hall of Famers were reeling. Higgins couldn't throw this hard all the time—but one ball in ten like this would be enough to keep a hitter guessing . . . or praying. The 113-mph fastball would make Higgin's hundred-mph fastball look like an off-speed pitch, almost like a change-up. A hundred-mph change-up! On the next pitch, Higgins dropped down to his average of just over a hundred miles per hour, and he stayed there the reminder of the outing, dealing nothing but the hard stuff.

Just when Ogilvie and his boys thought they had seen the worst of it, the first Cobb in line climbed into the batter's box and went down in a heap as Hillbilly Higgins whizzed a fastball a little too far inside, about head high. This happened a few more times with the other Cobbs, leading Ogilvie's players to think that Higgins had a wild streak. It was the kind of thing a batter would keep in the back of his mind. It gave a flame thrower an edge by keeping the hitter off balance—or just plain scared to death. A batter takes his career, even his life in hand every time he steps into the box. It takes grit to face down a hundred-mph fast ball that comes from just sixty feet away. At that speed, the deadly little rocket could easily maim or kill you—a part of the game players never discussed. It was so well understood by them, it didn't have to be.

It was hard to say if Higgins was so clever that he was wild on purpose, or he was really wild. Either way, it gave him the advantage—not to mention that the blurry white projectile came at you like a fireball from hell.

Ogilvie didn't see the twenty-year-old Higgins throw one curve ball, slider, or anything else but that hellacious, wild fastball. Changing speeds with it would make the orbed missile very hard to time and hit. *At least*, Ogilvie thought to himself, *all we have to worry about is a one-pitch pitcher, who could only weaken over a best of seven series.* Then again, Walter Johnson had made it to the Hall of Fame on just the fastball. Still, no pitcher in the world had ever thrown every game of a seven-game World Series. But this was not the world, this was Limbotown—and what Ogilvie didn't know was that Hillbilly Higgins had a few more flights of fancy up his wings that he wasn't going to show until game time.

When a Cobb would duck an errant Higgin's heater, Ogilvie would remind his team, "You can see why that dumb shit 'Corn on the Cobb' wears that batting helmet. Without it, one slip-up and you're creamed corn." The players grunted.

Ogilvie could hear his crew asking each other if anyone had heard of Higgins before. None had. "Drummond says Higgins was still in the backwaters of Tennessee when he was just about to be discovered," the nobody-manager told them. "Then a train flattened him. He was twenty. That's why you've never heard of him. Nobody has—until now, I guess." The players grunted again.

During outfield drills, other Cobbs were making spectacular catches using the big basket glove: over the shoulder, over the wall, shoestring style, and fully extended midair. The Cobbs were cutting down a lot of hard-hit balls scattered to the rambling hinterlands of Drummond Field. It was quite a show.

Ogilvie turned to Ruth, DiMaggio, and the other old-timers and observed, "Yeah, with a glove like that, this place would play a lot more like little old Shibe Park than Yellowstone Park." The players grunted again.

As the practice was breaking up, the real Ty Cobb once more strode by the visitors' dugout to spit his parting poison. This time he looked straight at little Roberto, who was dutifully sitting between his father and Don Ogilvie, and sneered, "Get ready to die, you little brown bastard." A horrified Roberto burst into tears.

Ogilvie and the rest held back a livid Antonio as his hardened manager advised, "Stay here. I'm gonna take care of this asshole right now."

Babe Ruth and Don Drysdale tried to stop Ogilvie from getting killed—or at least seriously mutilated—until Christy Mathewson stepped in. "Let him go. He knows what he's doing."

Ogilvie appreciated the vote of confidence from Matty, only he didn't know what he was doing. He came up with a plan of sorts. If it didn't work, he'd be flat on his ass, knocked out, and looking really stupid—pretty much the way he was when he got good and drunk.

The taut manager stood nose-to-nose with the bitter and cruel Cobb. Ogilvie was a good twenty-five years older than the Georgia Peach, who goaded, "Who are you, old fella—the clubhouse janitor?"

"No!" Ogilvie hollered, surprising even himself, "I'm the manager of this team that's gonna kick your ass in a coupla weeks, and I'm the guy whose gonna kick your ass right now for scaring a poor, defenseless kid who never did anything to you."

Cobb snickered, "You're too old to bother with."

Ogilvie heaved a sigh of relief. He knew he couldn't hold up in a real fight with Cobb. He had something else in mind. "Well how about a little contest?" The nobody-manager's team having heard these words before, knew Ogilvie had a fix cooking.

"One free shot. Stand there and take it, and we'll see who gets up. You can go first." Now the team wasn't so sure. Neither was Ogilvie, but it was too late to back out now.

Don Ogilvie was calling upon his long-buried boxing skills. He had done some sparring in college and wasn't half bad. For him, learning to hit a baseball was easier than learning to hit a head. The boxing skills had come in handy occasionally, but not for, as Obi Wan Kenobi would say, ". . . a long, long time." Now was going to be one of those times.

Unbelievably, the violent, wily Cobb wouldn't be provoked. "All I'd be doin' is make these idiots feel sorry fer ya. Get lost."

Reading the Cobb biography a day earlier was about to pay off. Ogilvie pulled out the big guns. "I hear your momma met your poppa at a family reunion, Ty. Or was that where she killed him?"

"God, now he's done it," Ruth groaned to the bench. The players thought Ogilvie had finally lost it. Ruth and Antonio wanted to help, but Christy Mathewson held them back again.

A double insult to both of his parents was more than an insane Cobb could stand. His pale countenance was aflame, and his eyes darkened into black voids. Barely under control, Cobb confirmed, "I go first?" Then he coughed up a noisy load of mucous and ejected it at the nobody-manager's feet, saying, "You got a deal."

Mad Dog Cobb cranked up on what would be a tremendous left hook to Ogilvie's right cheek. The nobody-manager tracked it all the way in and rolled back on his heels just before Cobb's fist reached him. He was already falling backward, trying to lessen the blow. It rocked him off his feet and onto his butt, but at least he was conscious. Cobb turned away to gather his gear and walk off the field. As he did, Ogilvie slowly came to his feet, moving and rubbing his jaw to make sure it wasn't broken. He tapped Cobb on the back.

When the unwary Georgia Prick spun around, Ogilvie stated, "My turn," and swiftly connected with a wicked straight right hand to the very point of Cobb's weasely jaw. The Peach's knees folded like a deck chair on the Titanic. He went sideways faster than a Greek sailor on leave. A stunned visitors' dugout along with the spate of fans, cheered and whooped for the equally stunned victor.

"Get this piece of shit outta here, he's litterin' the field," Ogilvie shouted to the other Cobbs.

As the Cobb clones mopped up their original gene pool, they vowed revenge. "Watch your back Ogilvie. We'll remember this for the Series."

Ruth, Antonio, and little Roberto led the team onto the field to hug, backslap, and congratulate Don Ogilvie. He was shaky but dry. He wasn't a nobody-manager anymore.

Chapter 18

After the crazed events of that day, Maggie Briggs found Don Ogilvie in his clubhouse office and asked him, "Would you mind eating at the hotel with me this evening?"

Fearing another raid on his precious reference books, he asked, "What did Ruth tell you this time, Maggie? That he lost his Medal of Honor in here? I gotta keep these guys out."

She convinced him that, "Nothing like that is going to happen tonight, I promise. I just wanted to know if you would join me for dinner. Just you and me." She didn't have to ask twice.

When Don Ogilvie entered the dining room, he was taken aback by what happened. Babe Ruth actually stopped eating for a second (okay—he still had a huge turkey leg in his right hand), stood up and announced, "There he is, the man of the hour—our manager. The guy with the best right cross in baseball!"

Then everyone got up and gave him a rowdy standing ovation. The hotel staff too. Ogilvie was uncomfortable with fanfare. Ruth loved this kind of stuff. Ogilvie wasn't used to it, and found all the attention unnerving. He gave an embarrassed wave to acknowledge the acclaim. He liked being the anonymous, nobody-manager. Those days were over. Maggie grabbed his now-famous right arm and led him to a small booth where they would eat.

The meal was pleasant, but constantly interrupted by well-wishers, players, and other Lucky Stiffs who dropped by the table to offer words of encouragement, such as, "You really showed that bastard Cobb!" and "We'll kick his ass again come Series time!"

While they were enjoying dessert, Maggie let him know that she couldn't help being impressed, although she didn't approve of how he did it. "He could've killed you!" she said, in a way that made Don Ogilvie's heart melt.

His reply was meant to be flippant. "I didn't know you cared."

Expecting one of her snappy jabs, instead she got up from the table and, as her eyes moistened slightly, told the unsuspecting manager, "Well maybe I do." Maggie Briggs left a speechless Don Ogilvie to ponder his coffee.

The next morning, Ogilvie couldn't believe the scene as he entered the clubhouse. A very busy Antonio Alvarez was helping trainer Tick Moran and old Charlie McManus fit all the players for batting helmets, elbow and shin guards, and even big gloves. No, it wasn't anything Ogilvie had done. Not even his punch-out of Cobb would've made his players go modern. The credit had to go to a wild-armed Hillbilly Higgins, who threw a 113-mph fastball that could just as easily end up in your ear as the catcher's mitt. Of course, once they saw Cobb using all his rigging, they weren't about to let him have the upper hand.

From the moment of the Cobb knockout, Ogilvie finally tasted respect from his team. Getting the black and white players to play together didn't do it. Going on the wagon and training with Ruth didn't do it. Whacking some balls out of Drummond Field didn't do it. It was whacking Ty Cobb around that did it. Of course, the other stuff didn't hurt. But the moment Don Ogilvie stood up to a much younger and stronger Ty Cobb, he got everyone's attention. A few of them—Mathewson, Paige, and Ruth—had already come around. Now he had the whole bunch. Even Hornsby was quiet, possibly counting himself lucky that he hadn't tasted Ogilvie's knuckles during their earlier showdown. They didn't all get along, but from then on, they all answered to one man—Don Ogilvie.

One of the things Ogilvie was now able to do was convince Walter Johnson to pitch inside. Born with a gentle heart, Big Train had once injured a hitter by throwing too far inside. That he was reluctant to throw near a batter was perhaps his only weakness. It allowed a player to crowd the plate. Cobb always capitalized on this and hit Johnson hard throughout his career. But now Johnson had seen Cobb stand in against a guy who threw harder than him, who threw inside and sometimes threw wildly to the backstop. He also saw Cobb using a batting helmet and other gear for protection. The time had come for Big Train to learn how to brush back Cobb, the butcher.

The following day, while Johnson and Don Drysdale were tossing in the bullpen, Ogilvie came by and casually asked the lanky Dodger right-hander, "Hey Big D, what will you do if Cobb crowds the plate on you?"

"He'll have a hole where his right elbow used to be," answered Drysdale while still flinging it. The six-five Drysdale was known for firing at batters when it served a purpose, which in his judgment seemed to be most of the time. Ogilvie stepped over to Walter Johnson and asked him, "Would you like to learn about the pitcher's 'best friend'?" Big Walter said he was finally ready. Ogilvie and Drysdale exchanged grins as their skipper counseled, "Big Train, just listen to Big D, and don't be afraid to let go."

"Don't worry, Walter," promised the Dodger ace, "this is gonna be fun."

As Johnson and Drysdale huddled, the old maestro himself, Cy Young, wandered into the bullpen. Ogilvie surprised the first Major League pitcher to serve-up a no-hitter by saying, "I know how Cobb's been reading your pickoff move."

Young was puzzled. "How?" he asked, referring both to how Ogilvie knew that Cobb knew and how Ogilvie knew in the first place.

Don Ogilvie smoothly obliged the turn-of-the-century pitcher with a nod and a smile. "The stupid old bastard used to brag about it all the time after you retired, Cy. Only he didn't figure on somebody coming along later and using it against him. But that's just what we're gonna do."

"That son of a bitch used to swear to me up and down it was just dumb luck. Well I'll be a . . . What the hell was I doin' anyhow?" Ogilvie relished telling Denton True "Cyclone" Young about the tiny elbow movement that tipped off the fleet Peach. Young slowly wagged his head and said, "Well now, a feller oughta be able to fool 'em good knowing that." As Manager Don Ogilvie walked away, the Ohio-born pitcher with the most wins ever, declared, "Good scoutin' on that vermin. Thanks."

Right-handed little Roberto had been trying to learn to bat left-handed from Babe Ruth for weeks. He wasn't doing too well. Finally it dawned on the Bambino that little Roberto threw right, not left.

Confirming that he was a natural righty, Ruth advised the youngster, "Jeez kid, I know you want to bat left, but you're really a righty. Talk to Raj—you know, old Hornsby. He's the best right-handed hitter there is."

Even Roberto could see that hitting lefty wasn't working, so he didn't feel too rejected when the Sultan of Swat sent him to the Rajah. It didn't matter to Roberto that Rogers Hornsby was a bigot and hadn't said two words to him. He could teach him how to hit.

The Cobb exhibition caused Hornsby to do some looking in the mirror. Yes he was a racist, but he also liked children. Yes Cobb enjoyed children too—he ate two or three for breakfast every morning. Although he kept his distance from the seven-year-old Roberto, Hornsby secretly admired his courage and his knack for being so comfortable around bombastic ballplayers—himself included. Then there was Cobb. Was he, Hornsby, as bad as the Vile One? The scare the Georgia Prick put into little Roberto, by telling him to prepare to die, was something not even the hard-hearted Hornsby could take. Attacking an adult was one thing. Picking on a sick kid was quite another.

All Roberto did was go to the second baseman's locker after practice that day and say, "Hey Mr. Hornsby, Babe Ruth says you're the best right-handed hitter there is. I'm right-handed too. Can you teach me to hit?" The innocent question was so explosive under the circumstances that it was as if the seven-year-old had yelled, "Fire in the hole!"

The usual clubhouse drone choked off like a turbine with a two by four thrown in its blades. Hornsby, tired, was already half undressed and headed for the showers, and the little batboy had given the surly second baseman every opening to rip into him and turn him down. After a sigh, a short dramatic pause, and everyone in the clubhouse holding their breath, his reply was disarmingly casual and very un-Hornsby-like: "Why not? Grab your bat, kid, and we'll get started." Hornsby's reaction to the whole idea caught everyone off guard.

Little Roberto wasn't taken aback when the Raj decided to help him. He smiled and nodded at the players as they left the clubhouse for his first lesson. Everyone else did a double-take. The hookup of this improbable duo did more to mend a torn clubhouse than the hookup of Don Ogilvie's fist with Ty Cobb's chin.

After his momentous Cobb clocking, Ogilvie spent more time at the Hotel Limbotown. That's where Maggie was, and Maggie was being awfully friendly of late.

Ogilvie almost always remembered to secure his office against Ruth's Raiders, even though there hadn't been an attempt in weeks. But about ten days before the start of the Series, he forgot one night. Sure enough, Ruth's Rascals got lucky. Finding an unlocked, un-booby-trapped clubhouse office, they gingerly drew near the all-knowing reference books. Ruth deftly hoisted a volume from its shelf and began to rapidly thumb through the pages. He couldn't believe his eyes. All the pages were blank! A quick check of the other books revealed nothing but white paper.

"We've been had," concluded a disappointed Bambino.

"You sure have," said the raspy New York-accented voice coming out of the dark. Only it wasn't old Charlie McManus this time—it was Death Personified. The perpetrators were dismayed by his presence as he stepped into Don Ogilvie's office. Whoever or whatever the little oddball really was seemed beyond their ken, and they weren't sure of his true intentions or if he even had any.

Ruth was instinctively afraid of Derby Drummond. He would never let his pals know, so he hid his fear behind his usual bluster: "We been caught by Yoda!"

"And you're being led astray by Jabba the Hutt," Drummond said to the others. "You guys aren't supposed to be here, and you know it. I'm only lettin' Ogilvie tell you what he wants to tell you about your futures.

These books will always be blank for George H. 'Hindenburg' Ruth and the rest of youse. So get outta here and go back to the hotel. You're gonna need all the rest you can get before my team of Cobbs humiliates ya."

"Ah, ya fat little fireplug—we're gonna trounce that Georgia Prick 'til he screams for mercy," shot back a boastful Babe.

"You're a big loser, Ruth! You'll see come Series time. The resta youse guys better get him outta here before I decide to turn him into a pumpkin."

At that, the other players held back a Babe Ruth pretending to go after the sarcastic Death in the Flesh, who walked away chuckling.

"Come on, Jidge," said a resigned Jimmy Foxx. "There ain't nothin' for us here."

While little Roberto sprouted as a right-handed hitter under the guidance of Rogers Hornsby, his father, Antonio, couldn't say the same of his schooling by the great Roberto Clemente. The Hall of Fame right fielder learned what Don Ogilvie already knew. Antonio Alvarez wasn't going to make it to the Major Leagues—at least, not as a player. Clemente thought he had a good shot to make it as a coach or one day as a manager, but the thoughtful Hall of Famer could no sooner undo Antonio's dream than could Don Ogilvie. Clemente came to Ogilvie's office and told him of his dilemma. "Antonio a strong guy, but no strong player."

He added that, "'Ee a good teacher, patient, everybody like 'eem, listen to 'eem. Know a lot of baseball. Smart guy but no smart-aleck. Antonio be a good manager in a few years."

Ogilvie exhaled. "If only I could get him to see that."

The Puerto Rican speedster was relieved to find his manager had known for some time. "Don't worry. 'Ee grow up to be terreefic manager like you. You see," beamed a buoyant Clemente.

It warmed Ogilvie to his cleats to devour a few desperately needed crumbs of praise. At the same time, he wondered if he really was the terrific manager Clemente thought he was. What had he done with his life compared to the players on his own team, whose lives were cut short or forever changed before their careers had even ended? There was

Clemente dying while on a mission of mercy, Roy Campanella rendered a quadriplegic in a tragic auto wreck, Josh Gibson's brain tumor, Christy Mathewson's poison gas—and, of course, Lou Gehrig and his namesake disease. Ogilvie's old injury paled. What had Don Ogilvie done to face his fate? Hide in a bottle? What had he done with his life to deserve the respect of these men? He didn't belong in the same room with most of them. Who was he fooling? Not himself anymore.

Then there were the others he'd read about, who made him feel even more self-loathing—in particular, Grover Cleveland Alexander and "Smokey" Joe Wood.

Old Grover was the prototypical crafty veteran pitcher in every way. He didn't have overpowering stuff, so he just kept you guessing . . . and missing. Alexander was a twenty-six-year-old rookie when he came up with the Philadelphia Athletics in 1911. While in his early thirties in 1917, he was drafted, went to war, and came back forever shell-shocked, epileptic, and with a nasty drinking problem. Things really went bad after that. He made it to the Hall only to die sick, penniless, and alone. Ogilvie mournfully figured that if he'd ever made it to The Show, he would have busted apart somewhere along the line, just like old Grover did—not a joyous thought for the former nobody-manager.

More annoying was the story of Smokey Joe Wood. The lightning-fast right-hander was a peer and equal of Walter Johnson. Their duels were legendary. At age twenty-one, Smokey Joe suffered an arm injury that would mark the end of his far-too-short pitching career. What did he do? Hit the bottle and give into his demons, like old Grover and Don Ogilvie? No. He worked on his hitting and became a respectable outfielder. He wasn't a great player anymore, never made it to the Hall of Fame, as he surely would have if his arm hadn't blown out. Joe just loved the game way too much to give it up. When he couldn't cut it on the field anymore, he became manager of the Yale baseball team for twenty years. That's what Smoky Joe Wood did with his bad break. What had Don Ogilvie done with his? It shamed him to think about the answer. He was a loser.

And Maggie? She would soon see what a loser he was too. He didn't deserve her approval either.

For the first time in weeks, he looked to the lower right-hand corner of his desk. The bare thought caused the drawer to slide seductively ajar. There beckoned the honey-colored Scotch of salvation. It was strange how his recent victories worked to set off his self-destructive ways. Telling himself he didn't deserve success made simpler the idea of rejecting it altogether. It was easy to be a failure. It was harder to be on top.

Things were abruptly jolted back into focus when a bounding Roberto entered the clubhouse office saying, "Hurry up. Maggie's waiting to have dinner with all of us."

This wasn't about poor, old Don Ogilvie. This was about the life of a young boy and his parents, the real reasons to live or die. Maybe Don Ogilvie's life wasn't worth much. Maybe Don Ogilvie didn't deserve to live . . . but little Roberto did. He slammed the desk drawer shut and left for dinner, the beast held at bay for now.

After eating, and alone in the clubhouse again, the nagging feeling returned. Fighting it, Ogilvie wound his way through the stadium to Drummond's clubhouse office. He was sweating for the first time in weeks.

"I thought I'd find you here," he said as the stubby umpire peered at him from behind his desk. "Some of my boys been askin' about a place of worship—you know, a church. I could use one myself," the unsteady manager threw in as an aside.

"I figured your Stiffs for mental cripples, Ogilvie, but not you," shot back an acid-tongued Death Incarnate. "You won't find any church here. That's for sissies or idiots. In Limbotown you gotta do it yourself, by yourself. The answers are all in here," Drummond said as his palm thumped his chest. "You just gotta believe that. I thought you were doin' a pretty good job so far. Don't fuck it up, Ogilvie. I want you straight for the Series." Drummond paused. "I've helped you too much already. Now get outta here," he commanded.

Ogilvie was not calmed by Death, as he hoped he would be. Instead he found himself strangely drawn to the movie theater and the eccentric Jack Dumphy. He asked the man with the light of life in his eyes how he was able to become a Chosen One at such an advanced age.

"What makes you think I'm as old as I look?" Happy Jack playfully replied.

"Hell, you're at least seventy-something, and you know it."

"Seventy-seven, but I don't look a day over eighty-six, do I?" Jack said in a voice as loud as his sport coat. "I'll let you in on a little secret. When I became a Chosen One, I was only seventeen. Drummond almost didn't allow it because of my age. When I made it, he let me become whatever age I choose. For now I like old. Besides, if you count all the years I've been dead, I'm well over 200! Now that should make me old enough to help you with whatever is on your mind," declared the perceptive Dumphy.

Ogilvie told him.

"It's nerves, my boy . . ." concluded the youngest Chosen One of them all. "Trust who you are. Don't look to others. I'm sure Drummond already told you that. Don't look to the bottle either. You know better. It may be okay for me, but not for you. Don't be afraid to fail . . . and don't be afraid to succeed. That's what's really bothering you. It's a fight to get to the top. Staying there is even harder. Success is a burdensome thing. You not only have to be strong enough to carry the burden, you have to want to carry it."

The depth of Jack Dumphy's eyes spoke a truth that Don Ogilvie was forced to see. Then the old, young man added, "I think you're ready."

The former nobody-manager thought to himself, *That's one opinion.*

In the beginning, the practice games relaxed him. They didn't count. Plus, it was rare grist to mill a batch of Hall of Famers. After the Cobb exhibition, all that changed. Ogilvie wasn't a nobody-manager anymore, and it wasn't going to be a battle against only two. The Cobb Squad was its own fully cast all-star team. Training took on a new urgency. Everyone felt it, and none more than Manager Don Ogilvie. Then, in an avalanche of seconds and minutes, the Day of Reckoning arrived.

Chapter 19

The night before the first game, Don Ogilvie sat alone in his clubhouse easy chair. He was anxious but prepared. He was fit, having lost some forty pounds now. He had overcome his sweating hex, his need for a drink, and his search for help from above. In Limbotown he was the master of his destiny—at least according to Drummond and the Chosen Ones. Sure, just like in the real world, many things were beyond his control. Here he was learning to stop worrying about what he could not do and start concentrating on what he could, like not putting his mouth around a bottle. That was the only defense for the unexpected. When life throws you a curve, you have to learn to roll with the punches. Mixed metaphor or not, this was one of the lessons of Limbotown. It was a variant of the Alcoholics Anonymous credo of admitting to and then giving into a "higher power"—whatever that may be. Here, you were the higher power. Here, you had to give in to yourself. Although it was not a comforting thought, it was strangely uplifting. He was ready to give his best and accept what would come. Then again, he figured he had no other choice.

As always, there wasn't a cloud in the synthetic sky on opening day for the Limbotown World Series. It was noon, and the Drummond Field stands were beginning to fill up for the first game's one-o'clock start. This time the spectators weren't only Limbotown workers. From the reaches of the mysterious burg's fogbank filtered fans from the last hundred years and from every walk of life. Apparently materializing out of nowhere, in all there were almost 40,000. As Ogilvie had earlier learned from Drummond, these Lucky Stiffs were "Loose bodies, 'dead' baseball fans from every era. They weren't busy anyhow."

Even more surreal were Drummond's announcers. Stationed behind and above home plate sat an unlikely pairing: the eloquent and gentlemanly Hall of Fame broadcaster from the old Brooklyn Dodgers, Red Barber; and a later Hall of Fame Lucky Stiff from the Chicago Cubs, the irrepressible Harry Caray. The pre-game chatter was different than usual.

"Hi, I'm Harry Caray, and my partner for this Series is the incomparable Red Barber. Says here, Red," recited Caray while thumbing through a stack of papers, "that this is the year 2000 and we're all dead—except for the manager of the Hall of Fame All Stars, a Don Ogilvie, and his assistant, Antonio Alvarez, his wife Maria, and their seven-year-old son, Roberto." His white hair tousled, the old, black-goggled and rumpled Harry Caray asked his partner, "How do I look for a dead man, Red?"

The well-groomed, diplomatic Barber sized up the dreadful-looking Caray and said, "Just fine, Harry. You know, we've been told this Series is all about little Roberto Alvarez's life. According to our host, Doctor Drummond, Roberto has a rare form of cancer, a type of leukemia. There is no cure. Now Doctor Drummond says he will spare the boy's life if Roberto's best friend, Manager Don Ogilvie, can lead his Hall of Fame squad to victory in this seven-game set. Little Roberto will be in his team's dugout as batboy for the duration of the Series. Okay, I'll admit it's a bit hard to swallow that Doctor Drummond is, as he claims, Death—or, Death Personified—but there's a lot of things that can't be explained here in . . . where are we, Harry . . . Limbotown? Is that in the lower forty-eight?" asked the dulcet-toned Barber in his signature soothing and subtle southern accent.

"Yeah, good question, Red," agreed the befuddled Caray, who made up an answer anyhow. "Limbotown: Go straight until you hit the fourth dimension, make a left at Purgatory, and it's three light years up on your right. Here's another one for you, Red: Where the hell do you think we're broadcasting to?" In fact, they could only be heard within the confines of Drummond Field, which Death in the Flesh had outfitted with built-in radios and headsets. Some of the early fans not around for the start of broadcast baseball had to be told about it by those who were.

"And, it gets weirder, Red," continued a skeptical Harry Caray. "The opposition and home team is made up of only Ty Cobb and a young pitcher named Clarence 'Hillbilly' Higgins. And here's the twist: These two are supposed to play every position! Boy are they going to be busy!"

"Well, Harry," said Red Barber, scratching his head while reading more, "it also says here that there are actually seventeen Ty Cobbs. Drummond claims to have duplicated the original sixteen times. This I've got to see. Yes, suh."

"It's almost as crazy for the Hall of Fame team, Red," commented a wide-eyed Harry Caray. "We're supposed to have Honus Wagner and Christy Mathewson on the same team as Roberto Clemente and Don Drysdale. These guys were born decades apart, but it says here they're all about the same age. Now that's a neat trick if you can do it. If it's true, this could be a World Series for the Ages."

"Let me try to set the scene here at Drummond Field, Harry," continued a helpful Red Barber. "The seats in this magnificent ballpark are quickly filling up with fans that look like they've come from many places and times. The feeling is festive, like the Fourth of July. To go with our perfect weather, there's a slight breeze coming from . . . what direction is that, Harry?"

"That a-way."

"Well folks, we can't tell you East, West, North, or South, but the breeze is blowing from left field to right," continued Barber.

"Doesn't look like sun and shadows will be a problem either, Red. Apparently there is no sun here in Limbotown. According to our information, we have what's called ambient lighting . . ."

As was his tradition, during the seventh-inning stretch of every game played, Harry Caray would lead the crowd in singing *Take me out to the ball game*. The part about "I don't care if we ever get back" took on a new meaning in Limbotown.

Field Level, Aisle 5, Row 4, on the third-base side behind home plate, was typical of the crowd. Some were dressed in old-fashioned high collars and bowties with bowler hats. Some were in suits with baggy pleated pants and jackets with wide lapels and colorful, wide ties. Others wore far more casual attire, ranging from shorts or jeans and tee shirts to polyester leisure suits and velour jogging outfits. It wasn't hard to tell what era people were from—at least for the first couple of games.

In the beginning, the trousers-and-tie set viewed the jeans–and–sneaker club with suspicion and even downright scorn. Who are these half-naked, ill-clad heathens, they wondered? The post-WWII crowd was amused rather than outraged by their bygone alter-egos and tried to befriend them. It was rough going. Everyone had to deal with the whole Limbotown thing—that it was really the year 2000 and they were all dead now (having been told so). Not to mention the absurd idea that some creepy little umpire, who claimed he was Death Personified, set up an "other"-Worldly Series with a down-and-out minor league coach, managing a team of dead Hall of Famers against a bunch of Ty Cobbs in order to save a dying boy's life. Whew!

Then there were the cultural differences from generation to generation. The turn-of-the-century folks were shocked and appalled at the language, clothing, and overall undisciplined freedom of their latter-day incarnations. What were Negroes (some used other words) doing in the stands with white people? Again, the post-1940s group would have to explain that integration had finally become a reality just short of a hundred years after the Civil War. However, Drummond had nimbly put the fans together in a way that avoided a riot. He also made sure the many Drummond Field ushers were well trained and up-to-date, expertly defusing any would-be "time"-bombs with cheerful explanations, always ending with, "Enjoy the games!" They would.

Soon their mistrust would dissolve and their curious children would mix, drawing in their parents too. Baseball can do things like that.

In Aisle 5, Row 4, ten-year-old Simon Stuffington sat in his best knickers next to his high-collar, World War One-era father, Charles, a Boston banker. While a bowler hat topped his poppa's tweed suit, an authentic Boston Red Sox cap whose style was more Russian Revolution than American ballplayer topped off Simon's outfit. It captivated eleven-year-old Barry Goldstein, who sat with his dad, Mel, just on the other side of Simon and Charles. Barry and his dad were from Cold War Chicago, 1964, and Barry held on his lap his precious, full-sized Mickey Mantle outfielder's glove. Simon had never seen such a huge, elaborate mitt before. The enormous cowhide caught his eye. As their fathers eyed one another guardedly, the youngsters briskly worked out the terms of a straight across trade: Simon's Red Sox cap for the big glove. The boys wrapped up their deal, but not their conversation. Simon was breathless to hear about 1964. When Barry told him about astronauts being shot into space by giant rockets, Mr. Stuffington spun directly toward Mel Goldstein with a glare and said, "Kindly have your child cease from filling my boy's head with folderol."

Mel Goldstein broke the uneasy silence by uttering, "But it's true. You wouldn't believe what science has done. Some of it's good, too. I'm Mel Goldstein, and this is my boy, Barry. Looks like our two kids already hit it off." Mel Goldstein reached out a big hairy, friendly hand from his amply filled polo shirt.

An apprehensive Charles Stuffington decided to be adventurous as they shook hands. "Charles Stuffington here. Would you mind if I ask you a few questions?"

The gregarious Mel grinned and said, "You got it, Charlie," and the two were off to the races.

"Do you mean to tell me that they not only allow Negro fans to sit right alongside white fans but they also let Negroes play on the same team as whites?" asked a doubtful Charles Stuffington.

Mel Goldstein resounded, "You bet! See, Jackie Robinson was the first Negro player in the Bigs. He came up with the old Brooklyn Dodgers in '47, right after the War."

"Good, Lord! How long does the Great War last?" complained Charles Stuffington.

"No. I'm talking World War Two," informed Goldstein.

"There's going to be another World War!?" Charles Stuffington was upset.

"Don't worry," comforted Big Mel, "we win."

After a short pause, Mr. Stuffington asked, "Why do they keep saying Ruth is a Yankee? Everyone knows he plays for the Boston Red Sox."

"You're not going to like the answer to this one, Charlie."

Their pre-game workout over, Don Ogilvie was holding a clubhouse meeting. He marked the progress of his players and how they'd become a team. He didn't have to remind them of how he won their support. And he probably didn't have to remind them about Roberto either, but he did. All the players, including Rogers Hornsby, had grown to like the Alvarez family. They liked Antonio because he was friendly and helpful and knew when to stay out of their way. Then, too, he was the father of Roberto. They liked Maria because she was pretty and smart, and the courageous mother of a dying child. They liked Roberto because, well, he was Roberto. Precocious, disarming, unbowed by Hall of Fame ballplayers and even Death, the little batboy had won their hearts, and it was with their big hearts they would play for him.

Ogilvie's words drew them around. "I know things didn't start off too well. I think it's important we remember that. We may not start this Series off too well either. If we don't, we need to keep our heads because anything can happen in a seven-game series. We need to remember that even if things go well today. We can't let up, win or lose. Roberto's taught all of us that. There may be a lot of things that are more important than baseball, but not today, not here. Today we get to do what we love and have it mean something more than we could ever imagine. The Alvarez family and I thank you for this.

"We know nothing worthwhile comes easy. You guys know it too. Baseball usually isn't life or death. And you can't play that way. You can't play scared or too careful. You gotta play hard and loose. There's a team full of Cobbs in the next clubhouse that think they can beat us. I say they can't . . . let's go prove it."

The low-key rally broke up with a lot of pent-up energy in the room. It was noisy and tense, and as expectant as the maternity ward at County General. The players pulled on their uniforms and tended their gear.

That's when old Charlie McManus handed Ogilvie, Antonio, and

275

little Roberto their new jerseys. "Here, you better wear these so you look like the rest of the team." The new shirts had stitched across the front, "Ogilvie's All Stars".

"Whose idea was this?" asked the former nobody-manager.

Charley smiled, "Everybody's." It was the players' way of saying that it was Don Ogilvie's team now. Antonio and Roberto knew about the tribute and proudly donned their new armor.

Ogilvie let the players go to the dugout first, holding Antonio, Maria, and Roberto behind. He told them, "Whatever happens, remember one thing: I'm ready for this. If we don't make it, we can leave here knowing we did our best. I've learned that's all anyone can do."

They hugged and held back tears. With Antonio and Roberto in tow, Ogilvie left for the bench while Maria went to sit behind home plate with Maggie. Drummond brought his gang of psychotic Cobbs into their dugout, and head umpire, old Fish-lips Klem, asked each side for lineup cards. The crowd was restless, confused, and thrilled, much like Red Barber and Harry Caray.

"Well, Red, I don't believe it. Looks like there are a lot of Ty Cobbs on the home team's bench. They all look like Cobb anyhow."

"Let's see if they all play like the real Ty Cobb," wondered a distrustful Barber.

"Look, Red!" pointed out an excited Harry Caray. "Isn't that the Babe himself in the visitor's dugout? Says here when he got to Limbotown he was forty years old, but his manager, Don Ogilvie, made a deal with Dr. Drummond to make him thirty-two again. He does look terrific. Also says that part of the agreement was keeping him off the bottle."

Caray covered his mike with his hand and said to Barber, sotto voce, "If Drummond hadda made me that same deal, I woulda had to turn him down. Gotta have my Budweiser by the fifth inning or my throat freezes up."

Barber nodded while Harry gave a confirming pat to the large plastic chest at his feet that housed many ice-cold Buds. As Caray checked inventory, Barber picked up for him.

"Well, Harry, there are the rest of 'em: Gehrig, Foxx, Satchel Paige,

Josh Gibson, Honus Wagner, DiMaggio. This is quite a team. We have players from the old Negro Leagues playing right alongside the old Major Leaguers. This is something I've never seen or could've imagined, folks. And playing against a team of Ty Cobbs? Well, this could be some Series. Yes suh!"

The crowd quieted as they were asked to rise for the American national anthem. Although Limbotown was not known to be in the United States (or anywhere else for that matter), Drummond allowed the custom, which helped normalize a setting that was anything but normal.

Many at Drummond Field were cynical, even contemptuous of the notion that Drummond was Death Personified and could spare a life. After the fans began talking to each other, theories were flung about—some logical, others bizarre. The bizarre ones were usually closer to the truth. Nevertheless, it made for split loyalties. The Drummond-managed "Cobb's Crusaders," as their uniforms proclaimed, had their fans. Not all in the crowd were swayed by the story of little Roberto. Many didn't believe it. Those who did didn't press those who didn't, because they knew they couldn't prove it. But just before game two, Red Barber interviewed a gutsy and ingratiating Maria Alvarez, and there wasn't a mother at Drummond Field who didn't root for her—even if some still didn't believe her.

Drummond let the visiting All-Stars have last ups for the opener. After that, the "home team" would alternate every game. The first three games would be played on consecutive days, followed by a day off, then two more games in a row with another day of rest. If the Series still wasn't decided, the last two games would be played on successive days. If there was a seventh game, Ogilvie's All-Stars would have the last at-bat.

Christy Mathewson started the opener for the All-Stars and retired the first three Cobbs he faced. Ogilvie's team would finally take their first cuts of the Series. The stadium was buzzing as Clarence "Hillbilly" Higgins climbed the mound for his warm-up tosses. He was a riddle to the fans because no one had ever seen or heard of him before. Once you saw him, the rangy right-hander with the screaming fastball was not the type you were likely to forget. The Hall of Famers could attest to that.

Harry Caray was blown away. "This daddy longlegs of a pitcher is throwing flame out there, and he's just warming-up. This can't be right. Our radar gun has him hurling at 107 miles per hour! Wow!"

An astonished Red Barber found himself saying, "I don't think I've ever seen anyone throw this hard . . . warming up or in a game."

After Higgins threw his practice darts, the real Ty Cobb, who was playing catcher, to better needle and unnerve his opponents, walked toward the visitor's dugout and vilified Ogilvie. "You'll pay for that sucker-punch, you spineless son of a bitch. You'll pay with your best friend's life! This game is the first nail in his coffin." Sneering, he spit and walked away. In each succeeding game, Cobb would select a new object of his hatred and dedicate the Crusader's anticipated victory to the chosen victim.

Ogilvie and Antonio put their arms around Roberto, who shouted at Cobb, "We're not afraid of you. You got nothin'!"

Fish-lips Klem bellowed, "Play ball!" and Higgins started mowing down batters with high heat. He never let-up, striking out the side in the first inning without so much as a foul ball. The radar gun had him up to 112. Ogilvie tried not to look worried for his team's sake. He knew he would have to be patient. He expected to drop this game. The idea was to let Higgins tire himself out. As the Cobb Squad's only pitcher, there was no way he could keep throwing this hard before he got a day off. It was a sound strategy, thought Manager Don Ogilvie.

And while a valiant Christy Mathewson would only allow one run, it might as well have been ten. The contest wasn't as close as the 1-0 score suggested. Higgins made the solitary run hold up by pitching not only a no-hitter, but also a perfect game. In fact, not one ball thrown by Higgins hit fair territory. Overall, there were three foul balls. One was caught for an out. Everyone else struck out. That was the extent of the Hall of Famers offense in Game One. Even in Limbotown, it must've been some kind of record.

Cobb's Crusaders, meanwhile, scored their only run in typical Ty Cobb fashion. Cobb One, the original, bunted for a single with one out in the fourth inning on a bang-bang play at first. He stole second easily, and then on a razor's edge, nabbed third. "Campy" (Roy Campanella) shot a bullet to Pie Traynor, but the ever-elusive Cobb slid to the left field side of the bag and got a toe on it before the diving infielder could slap the tag on him. The next at bat, Cobb trotted home on the second out, a squibber to first base. The rest was Hillbilly Higgins unloosing thunderbolts.

After the game, Ogilvie told his team not to be discouraged—Higgin's arm would be tired and sore tomorrow. Still, there were a lot of shell-shocked ballplayers wandering around the locker room—and who could blame them? The stadium was awed by Higgins mastery, his supremacy. This was not a guy nibbling at the corners. Every hitter was challenged, and he skunked them every time. They had as much luck against him as Isadora Duncan had with long scarves. This guy could demoralize a team.

Red Barber predicted, "It could be a short Series for the All-Stars if Higgins can keep this up for another three games. But I don't see how he can."

For the start of Game Two, Higgins ascended the hill again. Ogilvie's strategic gem about the big country hurler wearing out his arm collapsed as fast as you could say "ambidextrous." Higgins was taking his warm-up throws, except now he was dealing from the left side! Icabod Crane could bring it with either arm! The good news was that he wasn't as fast left-handed as he was right-handed. The bad news was he was now mixing in curves, screwballs, and sliders. After enduring seventeen Cobbs, Ogilvie thought he had seen it all. Now this. What else could Drummond heave at him?

"Well, Harry," offered a dazzled Red Barber, "now we know why the Cobb team only needs one pitcher. He's really two. He can give that right arm a well-deserved rest today. This is sure not something you see every day. No suh!" Barber was handed a note. "I've just been informed that Manager Don Ogilvie and his Hall of Famers are only finding out now, like us, ladies and gentlemen, that Higgins can deliver as a righty or a lefty. As a manager, not the kind of thing Don Ogilvie can be happy to hear about. His team won't be able to count on this youngster wearing down quickly . . . they're going to have to win some games, make him work, and hope fatigue sets in."

"Higgins is only twenty years old, Red," Harry Caray interjected. "Hell, when I was twenty I didn't get fatigued until I was thirty-eight. Ogilvie better make another deal with Drummond to age this freak about five years a day, or this thing could be over before he breaks a sweat."

Sauntering by the stunned visitors' dugout after Higgins completed his left-handed exhibition, the original Ty Cobb dedicated the second game to Jackie Robinson. "Which one of you niggers is Jackie Robinson?" he growled just low enough that the umpires couldn't hear him. Robinson began to step out of the dugout and was held back by Paige and Gibson. "You're the special coon that started it all, huh? Too bad you play second base. My spikes are hungry today . . . for dark meat."

Ogilvie protested to Klem, who shooed Cobb away. "He said 'nigger,' Bill. You're supposed to throw him out for that!"

"If I catch any of 'em, I will. But I gotta hear it first." Klem returned to home plate.

The crowd had heard about Cobb's first dedication to Ogilvie, and while they cared little about him, they didn't like that little Roberto was Cobb's cudgel. As word spread about the Jackie Robinson affront, the crowd divided and the Cobb fans were stalwart again. The rest could only hope to be vindicated by the Hall of Famers. Maybe today they would bust out. Maybe Jackie Robinson would explode.

It was a miracle that Jackie Robinson didn't explode—at least in public. In private, he fumed and boiled over many times. Jack Roosevelt Robinson held in a lot of things: not just racial taunts from ignorant fans and players, but things far deeper, like deference and dignity and equality.

In his only parallel with Babe Ruth, he desperately wanted to manage a Major League team when his playing days were over. He wanted to be the first black skipper in the Bigs. It was not to be, yet another frustration for the first black ballplayer to be inducted into the Hall of Fame.

280

It wasn't easy being Jackie Robinson. For one thing, there was his pledge of stoicism in the face of naked racism. It was a reluctant promise extracted by Dodger General Manager Branch Rickey, the man credited with engineering Robinson's rise to the Majors and sometimes referred to as the Abraham Lincoln of American baseball. It's a workable comparison—especially since Rickey's reasons for breaking the color line were no more pure than Lincoln's. They were both moved, at first, by economics rather than idealism.

Rickey, much like old-time New York Giant Manager, John McGraw, saw an opportunity to improve his team and increase gate receipts. When the rough-and-tumble McGraw tried to sneak in two black players in the early 1900s and pass them off as "Cuban" Indians, the result was not nearly as favorable as Rickey's straightforward attempt with Robinson decades later.

The Dodger general manager and part-owner was a visionary who saw the time was right. Cloaked in the vestments of righteousness, Rickey was truly more interested in tapping into the staggering pool of talent in the Negro Leagues. That he could do so under the guise of justice and morality only aided his crusade. Rickey's goals may have been expedient, but the outcome was hard to argue with.

In the Second World War, black servicemen distinguished themselves and honored their country—a country that had a segregated Army and a largely segregated populace. Many of these soldiers, whose heritage went back to the Buffalo soldiers of the Civil War, gave their lives to protect the freedoms they themselves never enjoyed. The hypocrisy became so obvious that the United States Supreme Court finally dismantled, abandoned, and discarded the absurd idea that the races could remain "separate but equal." But that didn't happen until 1954, almost ten years after WWII, and almost ninety years after the Civil War. (Sometimes justice is a little like geology—you know that glacier is moving, you just can't see it.)

In 1941, Jackie Robinson left UCLA (the first athlete there to letter in all major sports) and his southern California home to enlist. He graduated Officers Candidate School as a lieutenant, only to be ordered to the back of a military bus, which he refused. Robinson was actually court-martialed, but then acquitted. Sacrifices like this— not the least of which, giving one's life for country—eventually embarrassed the Armed Services into integrating, although full parity has yet to be achieved.

After an honorable discharge, Jackie landed a spot with the Negro League's Kansas City Monarchs in 1945, and two years later he was starting his first Major League game as a Brooklyn Dodger.

Jackie Robinson was a man of fierce pride and intense emotions. He was also a man of his word. So when he first came up, he kept his promise to Rickey to hold his tongue and his fists as he endured everything from the jeers of his own teammates to death threats from anonymous cowards. It took its toll.

There was some help along the way. When Robinson became a Dodger in 1947, some of his teammates threatened mutiny. They didn't get very far. Charles "Pee Wee" Reese, the Kentucky-born Hall of Fame shortstop and Dodger captain, put a quick stop to it. Reese's support of Jack wasn't just confined to the clubhouse either. During Robinson's first season, he took the field for a game that might've been played in any major league stadium of the time. The catcalls and ridicule were so barbaric that it spurred Reese to walk across the diamond and put a sheltering arm around a black man who was only trying to do his job— which was to play baseball. That silent gesture spoke with deafening voice. Jackie Robinson may have been alone, been the first, but at least he had a friend—and a white friend at that. Pee Wee Reese was, in fact, what Branch Rickey claimed to be: someone who realized that underneath the color-coated façade we all wear, there was a person with feelings and aspirations and fears, like we all have. The courage shown by Pee Wee Reese may not have been as profound as the courage it took to be Jackie Robinson, but his compassion was unrivaled, and Robinson never forgot it.

The Dodger's black second baseman played the game like there was no tomorrow. And in Robinson's case, he could not be sure there would be. Who knew how serious the death threats were? Considering the bitter and scathing resistance by players, managers, sportswriters, and fans, the terrorizing couldn't be taken lightly. Most men wouldn't have been able to stand up to it. Robinson did. He took his rage and fright and frustration and turned it into baseball excellence. He was Rookie of the Year in 1947 and helped lead the Dodgers to the National League pennant. He made them a better team, filled the stands, led them into post-season play, and replenished the team's coffers, something Branch Rickey was happier about then than his budding stature as baseball's emancipator.

Robinson left baseball in 1956 with a .311 batting average and 19 steals of home. His reckless antics on the base paths were something unseen since Ty Cobb.

After retiring, Robinson held various civilian positions from which he tried to champion the principles of civil rights, in and out of baseball. He not only wanted to see black managers, he wanted to see blacks in the front office—and one day, black owners in the Major Leagues. He lived to see none.

When he died in 1972, he was old before his time. The burdens, the battles, the struggles, finally sucked the life out of him. He died knowing there was much work left to be done. By his example, he blazed a path for others and called on them to pick-up the trail and carry on the journey. Many did.

"A life is not important except in the impact it has on other lives." This self-written epitaph was sheer understatement. At a mere fifty-three years, the life of Jackie Robinson measured by his own yardstick, was very long indeed.

Chapter 20

In Aisle 5, Row 4, Mel Goldstein and son Barry again labored to explain about Jackie Robinson and the intricacies of racial desegregation to Charles and young Simon Stuffington. This time the Goldsteins couldn't help but notice their WWI-era companion's more relaxed dress. No ties or stiff collars today. Charles was wearing a jaunty cap, and Simon had on a new-style Boston Red Sox cap he got for free from one of the many Drummond Field vendors.

Big Mel was winding up his conversation with Mr. Stuffington: "So ya see, Charlie, baseball is different in the early '60s. It's normal for teams to have Negro and white players and for fans of all colors to sit together. Gosh, it's just baseball. Nobody's gettin' married or anything."

Charles Stuffington and son Simon were being dragged forward decades in only days, whether they wanted to or not. Simon found it exciting, exhilarating. The handlebar-mustachioed Charles wasn't so sure.

Red Barber's prophecy held up for game two. The now left-throwing Higgins mystified the All-Stars with a convincing assortment of hard sliders and tricky curves mixed in with a hundred-mph fastball. Compared to the day before, when the players were trying to catch up to break-neck pellets, today they were lunging at the off-speed stuff and swinging late at the heater. They did better, managing eight foul balls this time. But they were no-hit again, in another perfect game.

The only highlight for the All-Stars was Campanella and Robinson hooking up to throw out various Cobbs on every attempt to steal second base. Although Robinson didn't show it, you could feel his satisfaction as he tagged out the Cobbs sliding spikes-high. On a Cobb's last attempted steal of the game, he finally managed to slice up Robinson's glove hand. The wound required some stitches that the unruffled infielder later displayed like the Red Badge of Courage.

Tomorrow Higgins would be back with his right-arm javelin for game three, with a day off after that. Ogilvie had two games left to solve the puzzle, find the hole, and discover the weak link in Higgin's game, if there was one. He was beginning to think there wasn't. Higgins wasn't tiring, and he wasn't wild like he wanted Ogilvie's All-Stars to believe. He threw like an old hand that had pitched against Hall of Famers before. Yet he'd never been in the big leagues, and he was only twenty when he died. How did he get the poise, the composure, the mental toughness to do what he was doing to these grizzled veterans? When Ogilvie asked Drummond about it after the game, he didn't like what he heard. As it turned out, Drummond had let Higgins practice against all sorts of dead Hall of Famers, not just Cobb. He had faced Ruth, Gehrig, Foxx, and the rest of them many times before. Not only that, there had been many World Series' in Limbotown with the Hall of Famers being skippered by Hall of Fame managers! Drummond told him that none of the Hall of Famers, in whatever combination, and whoever their manager was, had ever won so much as one game against Hillbilly Higgins. This was another piece of cheerful information Ogilvie wouldn't pass on to his All-Stars.

This time, Death Personified didn't have to remind him that "This isn't going to be easy." He expected to hear Drummond say, "This is hopeless, you fucking idiot! I've got the best pitcher there ever was. He's beaten every dead Hall of Fame player and manager. Why do you, a drunken, over-the-hill minor-league batting coach think you can do anything but lose?"

The Lucky Stiff Hall of Famers weren't allowed to remember their at-bats against Higgins, but Higgins was allowed to remember. He may've been twenty, but he had the experience of a well-seasoned Major League pitcher. The Big Hillbilly was neither awed nor fearful of

Ogilvie's All-Stars. To the contrary, he was confident and knew all their weak spots. Drummond tried to justify his scheme: "I couldn't let him pitch against just Cobb. That wouldn't be right. He needed to see some other hitters too."

"What would've been right was to let my players remember their at-bats against Higgins," Ogilvie responded.

"Oh, come on," moaned Death Personified. "For the last eight weeks your guys have seen the best pitching around, not to mention all the guys they faced before that." Ogilvie was stymied by Death again.

Cobb dedicated the third game to Babe Ruth. In a horrific pre-game exchange, the two unleashed profane bombardments of mythic dimension. Clown lips Klem threatened to expel them both if they didn't break it up. The fans, polarized in game two by Cobb's blasphemy of Jackie Robinson, came together after they heard about the attack on Ruth. Cobb went too far this time (and pretty much all the time). Desecrating the Bambino was un-American, sacrilegious. The fans wouldn't stand for it. Those who had backed Cobb's Crusaders were turned around. The team of Ogilvie, Ruth, Paige, Gehrig, and little Roberto was the darling of the entire crowd now. The onlookers loved an underdog, and they also despised Cobb for his unrelenting death march against an innocent seven-year-old boy. Even if it wasn't true, Cobb believed it. The spectators wouldn't abide this unthinkable cruelty.

Game Three saw Hillbilly Higgins return to his right-handed lightning with predictable results. The All-Stars managed a couple of high pop-ups in fair territory, but they were no-hit once again. At least it wasn't a perfect game. Higgins walked two batters. The only flicker of life for the Hall of Famers was provided by Ruth, and it turned out to be a false alarm. In the fifth inning, the Babe guessed right on location and speed and clobbered a towering fly ball down the right-field line. It peeled foul long before it cleared the fence. A collective groan welled up from the crowd as the Babe slowly paced back to the batter's box, head down. It was the longest walk. The same long walk Don Ogilvie and Antonio Alvarez had seen Mickey Mantle suffer when he was overmatched by Satchel Paige in the black and white game. It was much easier to take, seeing the inexperienced nineteen-year-old Mantle do it against the cunning Paige. It was almost unbearable watching Ruth, in his prime, broken by a twenty-year-old pitcher that nobody had heard of. As the ball carried foul, it carried with it the hopes of Don Ogilvie, the Alvarez family, the All-Stars, and their Drummond Field followers. The Bambino was dreadfully outclassed, and on his return to the plate, he struck out swinging on the next pitch.

Cobb's Crusaders scored three runs against a host of Ogilvie's pitchers and fielders. The former nobody-manager substituted freely. He was searching for offense, desperate for it. It never happened. There was a day off now, and that could only help Higgins. They were down three games to none, and no team in the history of Major League baseball had ever come back to win a World Series with that record. Not a one. And no one had ever beaten Higgins and the Cobbs.

The fans were glum that afternoon, eerily hushed as they filed out of Drummond Field and disappeared into the enveloping fogbank that only they could somehow penetrate. As always, they would be back for the next game.

The day off after game three was the longest, most agonizing day in Don Ogilvie's life—longer than the day he realized his career as a player was over, longer than the day his wife left him, and even longer than the day he found out about Roberto. He felt truly helpless, impotent. He was Ishmael the pariah, the sole survivor of the Pequod, left only to narrate the portentous tale of the tormented Captain Ahab and his crazed obsession with the Great White Whale. Or was he Ahab too? All he knew now was that he was desolate, hollow, an echo.

He threw himself into watching videotapes of Higgins. Maybe there was something there. He had to give his hitters some help. Good Christ, he was supposed to be a hitting coach, if not a manager. Bleary-eyed and sleepless, he came up as drained and empty as a whiskey bottle at an Irish wake. He had a nagging feeling though, as if he had seen something but couldn't bring it into focus. What good was a feeling if he couldn't use it?

The mood at the Hotel Limbotown was somber after the Hall of Famers went down three games to none. Instead of gab and laughter, the habitually noisy dining room was reduced to the sound of silverware

287

clanking against plates. What with Higgins' domination of the best baseball had to offer, hope was just another four-letter word. It would take a miracle to begin a most implausible comeback, and Hillbilly Higgins had seen to it that he was the only miracle at Drummond Field.

Before the start of the fourth and perhaps final game of the Series, Babe Ruth gave Roberto his lucky rabbit's foot to hold for him. "I think you better keep this today," he told the youngster. "Maybe if I give it to you, it'll start workin' for me." A hushed Roberto slipped the hair-and-bone talisman into his pocket—and not a moment too soon.

The Prince of Darkness strode over to the All-Stars' bench and delivered his final dedication straight to little Roberto. "I don't like pickin' on children. There's nothin' personal about it. But you goin' down today, Kid. That's the way it has to be." Even though offered as a partial apology, when the fans found out, their furor filled the air.

Rested, Higgins came back in game four as a left-hander—the side that had all the curves and sliders, and fast balls too. He was on his way to an unheard-of fourth consecutive no-hitter, and the end of the Series.

An indomitable Satchel Paige held the Cobb Squad to one run. But now it was the top of the ninth, the All-Stars last at bat, Roberto's last chance, Don Ogilvie's last shot. Not one Hall of Famer had collected even one hit against the immutable Higgins. As the All-Stars Cool Papa Bell took the batter's box in the top of the ninth, Roberto unobtrusively slipped Babe Ruth's lucky rabbit's foot into Don Ogilvie's back pocket. The former nobody-manager was transfixed on the game and he didn't notice Roberto's sleight of hand. Bell struck out swinging.

Then it hit him. It came into focus. He had seen something. Higgins had a "tell." The six–and-a-half-foot Hillbilly was tipping his pitches! His right foot was the giveaway. He kept it parallel to the mound for the fastball. It drifted toward the plate for the slider, and even more for the curve. It was subtle, but Icabod Crane's right foot was like reading a barometer. The more the foot pointed home, the slower the pitch; the closer to the rubber, the harder it came. Ogilvie tested his theory as Rogers Hornsby took his cuts. This one should be a curve. Higgins threw a curve. This one a fastball. Higgins dealt the heater. And this one a slider. Slider it was. But Hornsby fanned and now there were two outs.

Ogilvie signaled a time-out and motioned Joe DiMaggio back from the on-deck circle.

He huddled his team. "You guys think you might be able to hit this robot if you knew what was coming?" He hastily dispatched the secret.

Red Barber was prescient as he told the stadium, "Well, maybe Don Ogilvie has some special words for his players. Down to their last out, he, the Alvarezes, and the All-Stars, are all going to need something special. Yes, suh. It's one thing to be shut out four games in a row, and something else to be no-hit four straight."

DiMaggio entered the batter's box with Roberto's life dangling by a wisp. Then there was a crashing crack of the bat so clear and crisp, it blew through the stadium like a sonic boom. The Cobbs in left and center scrambled in vain to catch up to the low liner that split the fielders and bounded off the wall on the fly. DiMaggio smoothly slid into second and hopped up, standing tall. The crowd wildly cheered the first hit of the Series for the All-Stars, coming with two outs in the ninth inning of game four. The Yankee Clipper barely nodded to Don Ogilvie to signal that the tell was real.

A buoyant-looking Babe Ruth then stepped into the box. This was what the crowd had been waiting for, praying for. The game was on the line and the Sultan of Swat was up. You couldn't ask for more than that. A home run could win it. This was the kind of situation the Bambino feasted on—food for his famished ego. Ruth let the first pitch go by for a strike. He gyrated toward Ogilvie with a motion that said, "Don't worry—I'm on him." The stadium held its breath. The next pitch was a fastball. Ruth turned loose a left-handed tomahawk that launched the ball high into the air, completely out of the stadium and over the Limbotown fogbank. Drummond Field erupted. The players celebrated crazily. Ruth was mobbed at home plate, and the ushers had to keep the fans from trying to join the on-field romp. Hornsby and Robinson found themselves embracing by accident, then pulling apart and embracing again, this time on purpose.

Drummond contritely commented to the Cobb standing next to him in the dugout, "Man, that thing got outta here fast."

After another base hit, Higgins managed the third out on a hard-hit line drive to third. He left the field shaking his head, wondering how the All-Stars seemed to know just what was coming.

It was 2-1 All-Stars, with Cobb's Crusaders coming up in the bottom of the ninth. Only now the Cobb Squad's aura of invincibility had been burst apart like an over-inflated sex doll. The sly, screw-balling left-hander, Carl Hubbell, set the Crusader's down in order. The victory was vacuum-sealed. It was one of those games that was, as Red Barber told the departing fans, ". . . magic, absolute magic." Everyone there knew they had been a part of something that beckoned from another place.

There was a new feeling in the stands as the peripatetic throng poured out. There was a new feeling in the All-Stars' dugout and clubhouse. There was a new feeling in Limbotown. There would be a contest after all.

That night at dinner, Ogilvie asked Antonio and Roberto, "Do you guys know where this thing came from? Doesn't the Babe carry one like it?" He was holding Ruth's rabbit's foot.

Roberto smiled and replied, "Yeah, it was the Babe's, but I'm pretty sure it's yours now." Don didn't ask for an explanation. He didn't need one.

Hillbilly Higgins didn't tip his pitches when he threw right-handed, and the tell was gone when he threw left again. Drummond wouldn't let the All-Stars steal anymore wins. Death in the Flesh had known about Higgin's tell all along, but Ogilvie was the first to figure it out. All the Hall of Fame players and managers before him hadn't picked it up, but the old minor-league booze hound from San Bernardino had. Drummond was impressed, and that was hard to do. Sure Ogilvie had done a good job with his team (and himself) under trying conditions, but that meant nothing if they couldn't win. Ogilvie and his All-Stars were the first to do that too. And even though he was anything but human, Death Personified felt a peculiar, uncommon sensation—which he nonetheless recognized right away as reluctant admiration. He grimaced, laughed, and felt chagrined all at once.

In game five it finally started to happen. Higgins right-arm torpedo

290

lost a few knots, and the All-Stars began to hit. He was human after all. Evidently Drummond hadn't concocted him like Frankenstein's monster.

The next two games produced some of the best baseball ever seen anywhere, anyplace, anytime, in the history of the Universe—Limbotown included. Pale words when compared to the action on the field. It was unreal. The battles became gritty, hard-fought, gutsy affairs, with each team coming back time and again. It was like two heavyweights trading their best blows in the center of the ring. With both teams knocking the ball, plays were being made. But that's not a fair way to describe it. More like Hall of Fame plays were being made routinely, stuff that had the crowd shaking its collective head in disbelief. Magnificent but nerve-wracking if you were a manager, heaven if you were a fan—except for one thing: Roberto. By now everyone was so wrapped-up with the Alvarez family that they were ready to go after the Cobb Squad with pitchforks and clubs. None were allowed in the stands, thankfully.

Cobb's Crusaders were becoming frustrated. The Game Four triumph had given the All-Stars a shot of badly needed "kick-ass" juice. And the secret Drummond let slip to Ogilvie (this one turning out to be in favor of the All-Stars)—Higgins had never pitched the fifth game of a seven-game series because he'd never had to. This was new territory for him and, despite his nickname, and origins, he didn't like the hilly terrain.

Equally vexing for the Cobbs was Ogilvie's exploitation of every flaw they had, and some they didn't even know they had.

In the fifth game, Cy Young used his "new" pick-off move to nail a Cobb leaning off first base. The vile clone flew into a rage, yelling so hard its normally wan face looked like Rudolph's nose. Old Cy had to take his cap off and cover his mouth to hide his grin.

It was really testament to Ogilvie's superior managing. Drummond claimed to be running the psychotic Cobbs, and he was probably doing as well as anyone or anything (including Death) could do. Still, the Cobbs had a mind of their own and did what they wanted to. Sometimes they followed Drummond's signals, if they met with their approval. Yet Ogilvie was out-thinking and out-maneuvering Death and his sinister

Cobb henchmen. He anticipated their attempted steals and called for pitchouts or fastballs to help his defense pick off, cut down, and uproot the evil clones. It also didn't hurt to have the familiar Dodger duo of Campanella and Robinson defending.

The Hall of Famers broke up a 2-2 tie in the bottom of the eighth. Robinson socked a double in the left-centerfield gap and took third on a Jimmy Foxx ground ball out to first. DiMaggio popped up to shallow left, not really deep enough to score Robinson. The left-field Cobb caught the ball and, without warning, Robinson broke for home. The throw arrived well ahead of him. The All-Star bench groaned. As the slippery second baseman came barreling down the line, he juked to his right and slid back to his left, faking catcher Cobb out of his jockstrap. Robinson's right foot swiped the bag clean. The All-Star bench and the fans went bonkers. Robinson had outfoxed the butcher of the base paths at his own game. Ty Cobb was beside himself. Then again, he couldn't help it. There were seventeen of him.

The Hall of Famers held on to win game five, with the left-handed Carl Hubbell again closing-out the left-handed Cobbs in the top of the ninth. Cobb's Crusaders were mesmerized by the old New York Giant's southpaw screwball, and the last Cobb to strike out for their second straight loss angrily broke his bat over his pumped-up thigh.

In the first inning of game six, Walter Johnson hit the real Ty Cobb in the ribs; and then did it two more times when he came up after that. Klem threw Johnson out of the game. Cobb was upset by Johnson's new aggressiveness. No more crowding the plate on him. Drysdale showed his approval by plunking two more Cobbs himself when he took over for Johnson with two outs in the seventh inning. Even though Klem ejected Big D, that did it for the Cobb Squad. With the score tied 3-3, the clipped Cobbs and the rest of their bench charged Drysdale on the mound. The All-Star dugout instantly cleared their bench, and a five-minute brawl ensued. Order, or at least a simmering semblance of it, held as uneasily as a pressure cooker on fire. The umpires tossed out a couple of more players from each team. Despite the ejections, the bench-jockeying and trash-talking on both sides escalated into vicious diatribes.

Fish lips Klem had to threaten more vetting to dull the dagger-sharp barbs.

The Cobbs Drysdale nicked came with an expensive price tag, however. Dizzy Dean took over with two outs and Cobbs on first and second. The next clone sliced a double down the left field line just inside a diving Judy Johnson. The low liner drove in the first Cobb from second base. As the next one puffed from first around third, Roberto Clemente (in left field so Ruth could be in right) played a tricky carom in the corner and made a throw so hard it almost knocked over Josh Gibson before the homeward-bound Cobb-replica had a chance to do it. Gibson arose from the collision holding the ball in the air, and Klem emphatically rung up the furious Cobb Clone for the last out of the inning. But it was 4-3, Cobbs.

Luckily, the All-Stars were hitting the left-handed Higgins, even with the tell now gone. And they weren't too worried about Higgins throwing at them either. Ogilvie reminded his hitters that the Big Hillbilly wasn't as strong now, and Klem vowed to boot him out of the game if he retaliated. As the Cobb Squad's only pitcher, Drummond couldn't afford to have Higgins ejected.

With one out in the top of the ninth and the All-Stars still down 4-3, Roberto Clemente singled sharply to center, bringing up Ruth. Lightening would not flash again as the Bambino corkscrewed himself into the ground for strike three on a wicked Higgin's slider, and two gone. The crowd moaned.

That brought up the right-handed Josh Gibson against the left-handed Hillbilly. The All-Star bench and the fans were tense. Gibson had yet to get a hit. Down to the last out again for little Roberto. The big catcher must've liked the first pitch he saw because he slammed it clean out of Limbotown and over the fogbank, just as Ruth had done two days before—except to left field instead of right. No matter, same result. One of the first to greet Gibson as he crossed home plate was the Babe, who shouted, "Show-off." Gibson's laughter caromed around Drummond Field as he basked in the backhanded compliment from the biggest show-off of them all.

Again the screw-balling Hubbell got the final outs, but this time he had to struggle mightily for them. As the lone left-handed pitcher on Ogilvie's roster, he was very effective against the all left-handed lineup of the Cobb Squad, except he was getting tired too. Yes, he had struck out Ruth, Gehrig, and Foxx in order in the 1934 All-Star game, but he was a starter like the other Hall of Fame pitchers, not a reliever. "King" Carl wasn't used to being in a game every day. Ogilvie wished he had another left-hander to use in relief. And he did. Would he have the grit to use him in game seven if he had to? He had already made the promise he would.

Somehow the All-Stars took games five and six and forced game seven, with Higgins appearing like he might be ready to fold up for good. At the end of game six, it looked like the Big Hillbilly had just flown in from the Afterlife—and boy were his wings tired.

That night, the dining room at the Hotel Limbotown was hot with the fever that nothing could stop the All-Stars now. Even Don Ogilvie allowed himself to imagine it when he saw the beams of hope bursting out of little Roberto and both of his parents. But he should have known better. Maggie Briggs, for one, wasn't celebrating yet. Having seen too many Challenges go awry, she subscribed to Yogi Berra's philosophy: "It ain't over 'til it's over." Nonetheless, Don Ogilvie thought to himself, *Nothing can stop tomorrow's game. Nothing can stop us from winning.*

Chapter 21

The morning of game seven found the former nobody-manager once more waking in his clubhouse office. He rose to a familiar sound that somehow seemed out of place. He had heard this sound so many times before, so why couldn't he name it? As he quickly dressed and grabbed a cup of coffee, he headed for the dugout tunnel where the noise seemed to be coming from. The familiar thrumming got louder. Then just as he reached the dugout, his head sank with sudden recognition. It was raining, and raining hard. The blue skies of Limbotown were nothing but liquid gray. Drummond Field was awash with swept-away visions of victory. This was the final straw, the last Drummond deception, one he could no longer take.

He knew right where to find the little charlatan. The Fat Fraud would be at his clubhouse desk, pretending to be a big league manager—his favorite diversion.

Ogilvie charged in unannounced. Drummond was expecting him. Ogilvie was not the type to blow his top, but now he couldn't help himself. For whatever reason, he had taken the team radar gun with him. Maybe he was hoping to shoot Drummond full of neutrons. Instead, he threw the useless weapon at Death's head, causing him to duck. Then Ogilvie let loose a barrage of cursing rant. Somewhere in the hail of accusations was his main complaint: "You know we've got Higgins on the ropes. He's ready to fall apart. This rain-crap is just a way to get him some rest, you weasely, slimy bastard!"

When he was finally exhausted from his own tirade, Drummond asked him, "Feeling better now? Both of us know that weather is unpredictable. Hell, rainouts in any World Series can happen and do. It's no different here . . . I promise you that tomorrow we'll play for all the marbles. Now quit your bellyachin'."

He was never sure quite how he did it. How Drummond always seemed to be able to make his most outrageous ploys somehow acceptable: Limbotown, Seventeen Cobbs, Hillbilly Higgins, The Magic Elevator, now a rain delay. Maybe he accepted it, Ogilvie reasoned, because there was nothing he could do about it. Limbotown may not have been real, but it sure felt like the ragged road of life with all of its switchbacks, sinkholes, and washed-out bridges along the way. It just seemed to Don Ogilvie that he found every hazard, every peril—or perhaps they found him.

Maggie Briggs decided she'd taken a big enough chance already. She and Don Ogilvie were running out of time. After the All-Stars' third loss, she knew that the Series might be over the next game. She would never see the reformed manager again. And she didn't want to say goodbye. When the All-Stars started winning, she didn't have to. If the Hall of Famers won the last game, Don Ogilvie would be a Chosen One, and there would be many future Challenges they could both witness. If the All-Stars didn't win, she wouldn't have time to tell him what was in her heart, and she would be burdened by it for eternity—which was a lot longer than waiting at the doctor's office. The rain was her last reprieve.

She acted swiftly. She hinted for the Alvarez family to retire early from dinner that evening, leaving her alone with Don Ogilvie. Maria Alvarez, not having been told a thing, knew exactly what was happening, and her effervescence spilled over the table like uncorked champagne as she quickly gathered up her husband and son.

Never one to waste time or words, Maggie said to the unsuspecting manager, "I want you to stay the night with me. I think you'll like my room." Her intent was unmistakable.

The simple words caused the former nobody-manager to freeze up in a way he hadn't since they first met. He didn't know she had a room, figuring he would never see it even if she did. It made sense, though. He couldn't picture her sleeping hanging upside down like a bat in a broom closet.

She led him through a locked door at the far end of the bar that everyone assumed housed supplies. It did. *Maybe she does sleep in a broom closet*, he thought. Beyond the supplies was another locked door leading to a short hallway and another door—the entrance to Maggie's room. He hesitated to cross the threshold, and she had to take him by the hand. As she closed the door behind them, she turned until she was eye-to-eye with him. Without a word, she slowly raised her cupped hands to caress and cradle his face. She drew him even closer and gently pressed her lips against his. At first, he was surprisingly reluctant to let go, too unbelieving to finally receive what his soul ached for. But her mouth was the taste of warm butter and wine, and soon all of his thoughts spun endlessly away. He never wanted to leave this new-found Nirvana. After a time he couldn't measure, the kiss broke off as tenderly as it started.

Maggie opened her eyes and told him, "It's been a long time since you've been kissed by someone who loves you as much as you love them." It was just the sort of way she would tell him, "I love you."

"I'm betting it's been a long time for you too, Maggie."

Then they chorused together, "I'll always love you . . . no matter what happens tomorrow." They laughed at their corny pledge and kissed again.

It was a night he would never forget, nor did he ever want to. During the evening, Maggie shared everything with him, including the astonishing details of her life and her Challenge. Don Ogilvie was humbled again. Now they both knew the terrible and the wonderful of each other's lives. Now they were closer than lovers.

Buoyed by a real love rather than a one-sided romance, Don Ogilvie, after falling asleep in Maggie's arms, curiously awoke in his familiar clubhouse office. He wasn't concerned, curious being pretty much the norm for Limbotown. With that thought in mind, he hurried out the dugout tunnel to check the skies. Back to Limbotown blue. His pulse pounded: game seven today.

Red and Harry set the scene. "It's a funny thing about that rain delay, don't you think, Red?"

"Well Harry, this whole place is on the 'funny' side. Yes, suh. But one thing's certain—today there will be a game seven for the climax of what has turned out to be a most improbable Series, a most extraordinary story of a dying child, his parents and a minor league coach, a strange venue called Limbotown, and the assembly of the most talented assortment of Hall of Fame ballplayers to ever grace a diamond. And what a magnificent stadium it is, ladies and gentlemen. We have witnessed history . . . no—we are witnessing history. The best ballplayers from the first half of the twentieth century, all in their prime, black and white, playing with each other and against a common foe—Death and his team of Ty Cobbs.

"Then the startling revelation of one Clarence 'Hillbilly' Higgins and his wings of wonder. When he showed he could dominate with either arm, Ogilvie's All-Stars looked to be finished. They hadn't gotten a single hit.

"Down an impossible three games to none, they came back to win the dramatic fourth game in the ninth inning on a double by DiMaggio and a home run by Ruth, the first hits for the All-Stars! You were there, ladies and gentlemen. You saw what Harry and I saw.

"That was a game for all time. A magic game, if I may say again. Yes, suh.

"Next we oversaw two brutal, punishing contests, with each team handing out and taking terrific blows, the All-Stars managing to eke out wins each time. In game six, the drama of Ruth in the ninth inning again. But it was not to be. Desperation time for Ogilvie and the Alvarez family as the hitless Josh Gibson stepped to the plate. Bam! And the All-Stars are on top! A tired and courageous Carl Hubbell, massaging the last, hard-fought outs for an amazing comeback: True drama. Nothing as dramatic—and perhaps a young life is at stake. Whatever the outcome, today's game will finish this amazing story . . . one way or the other."

The air in All-Stars' locker room was heavy with the business at hand, so Ogilvie tried to lighten the mood and relax his Hall of Famers. "Hey, listen-up everybody. Jidge says anybody that hits a home run today gets to sleep in his suite. That means you won't have to see him all night."

Thinking of Higgins, Ogilvie whirled to Antonio and said, "Go get our radar gun. I left it in Drummond's office."

The young bench coach wasn't exactly thrilled with the idea of retrieving the misplaced gun in enemy territory, but he went anyhow.

Making his way through the Cobb-only clubhouse to Drummond's office felt to Antonio like swimming through shark-infested waters with a bloody seal tied around his neck. Before he could knock on the office door, something stopped him cold. Maggie Briggs was in there talking to Drummond, and that same something told him not to go in. He stepped to the side and could overhear what Drummond was saying to her: "I don't care how you feel about this guy or the kid. You know how it is with me—nothing personal. If the All-Stars win today, I take Ogilvie's life and the kid lives. If not, the kid dies. Whatever happens, happens. Why do you think I'd try to rig anything? I never have before."

"Yes, but you don't think he's ready yet . . . ready to be a . . ."

As Antonio raced through the doorway, he shouted, "Ready to be a what? A dead man? Call it off! I call it off! This isn't right. I won't trade Don's life for my son's."

The unflappable Drummond replied, "It's not your call, Pal. This deal is between Ogilvie and me. Only he can call it off, and I doubt very much he's going to do that."

Antonio turned his shock and anger toward Maggie, "You knew all along. You knew if you told us we wouldn't have any part of it." Maggie blanched at the pain in Antonio's voice.

"Forget it, Antonio," Death advised. "She wasn't allowed to tell. That's part of the arrangement too—and you're not supposed to know anyhow."

Maggie pleaded with Antonio, "I wanted to say something so many times, but I couldn't. I've had to carry it with me. I had to give Don his chance, and Roberto too. Let Don try to do this . . . like I did once."

Antonio suddenly saw everything now. And that sight brought with it the acceptance that this was right after all. An inexplicable peace overtook him and told him it was so.

Maggie saw the new calm in his eyes and said, "Let me tell Maria."

When Antonio returned to the All-Star clubhouse quiet and empty-handed, Don Ogilvie took a good look at him. Antonio had that glazed-over stare, like Moses after his first trip to Mt. Sinai.

Guiding him into his office and closing the door, he put his arm around his young bench coach and asked, "How did you find out?"

"I overheard Maggie talking to Drummond." Don tightened his lips. Antonio continued: "I see all of it now. Maggie's going to tell Maria . . ." His voice choked and the two men embraced.

Don Ogilvie whispered, "This is something I have to do . . . please let me explain it to Roberto."

Maggie made her way to the stands to sit with Maria as always. This time would be different. Maria's reaction was almost identical to her husband's. After a brief flare-up, the flames vanished and were replaced by the feeling that things were somehow as they should be.

"I knew something like this was part of it. And I knew you couldn't tell us," Maria softly said.

"I was always afraid you would guess anyhow," Maggie confided. "I'm glad you know everything now."

His young assistant asked Ogilvie if he could tell the players. "I'm not sure that's such a good idea, Antonio. It might be distracting."

Antonio returned a crooked smile and said, "Let me be the Manager this time."

Don Ogilvie couldn't refuse what he had been trying to make Antonio into all this time. He was ready to be a manager. Ogilvie gave him a pat on the back and said, "You better get Roberto out here first."

The energetic batboy came running into the corridor outside the clubhouse. "Dad says we need to talk."

They found a nearby bench. Ogilvie awkwardly launched into a spiel. "You know, Roberto, if we win this game today, you're not going to be sick anymore. And there's nothing in the world, or even in Limbotown, that I want more for you. You need to grow up . . . and be alive. You're so lucky to have such wonderful parents, wonderful people. They'll let you grow up the way you should." He was struggling for more words and finally gave up on the roundabout approach. "Sometimes

... look, you're my best friend, so I'm gonna have to tell you flat-out: if we win today, I'm not going back to San Bernardino with you and your folks. This is hard to say . . ."

"You mean you're going to die," Roberto said sadly.

"Yes," he said in relief.

"Because of me."

"No. Because of me. I'm the one who made this choice, Roberto, not you. You didn't choose to get sick. Now I'm choosing to try to help you; and I've been given a way to do that. This was an easy thing for me. You made it easy for me. Let me do this for you. Okay?"

"But who will be you? No one can be you . . . I'll miss you too much." He wasn't bawling, but water ran from his eyes.

Ogilvie had a big lump in his throat. "No one can be me. I don't want anyone else to be me. You can always remember me, Roberto. And when you do, then it'll be like I'm with you."

The kid added, "Yeah, but you're the only one who ever told me what some of those swear words meant . . ."

Ogilvie busted up. His laughing made Roberto laugh, and they hugged. "No more of this. We have a game to win," declared Ogilvie. The two had reached an understanding.

Antonio came into his own as he gathered the Hall of Famers and told them about Ogilvie's deal with Death.

"I'm about the same age as a lotta you guys—and maybe that's all we've had in common here in Limbotown, 'cause I'm sure not gonna be a ballplayer like you guys are, not a Major Leaguer. I know that now. But some of you are fathers like me. Some of you will become fathers. Some of you just like kids—like my kid, Roberto. That we've got in common, and all of us thank you.

"How can we know if this is real or not? I don't know. But I just found out from Drummond that if we win and Roberto lives, he's gonna take Don Ogilvie instead. That was part of the deal they struck in the beginning; something Don knew and didn't say anything about. If it is true . . . well, Maria and I never would have agreed to it in the first place. Drummond said he didn't need our consent to do this, only Don's—and only Don can call it off. He's not going to. This is the way things have played out."

That's when the former nobody-manager and little Roberto walked back in. "It's true. But don't feel sorry for me," Ogilvie stated. "I don't. Not anymore.

"You guys deserve the truth, and this is only part of it. I know all about you. It's time for you to hear the truth about me. I didn't do too well after I injured my foot. That's how I became a drunk. I didn't get back into baseball until just a few years ago. Before that, I worked in a grocery store. And before that, well, I was just living inside of a bottle. Then, I got another chance."

As the tormented tale of Don Ogilvie was laid bare, Christy Mathewson smiled. Don Ogilvie had made the longest walk, and this time he wouldn't come back to strike out. Not with this team . . . his team. The way his players saw it, they were playing this last game for two lives now. Peculiar that, by winning, they could only save one. But that's the way their Manager wanted it, and they would follow him into Cobb's Hell to do it.

As the stands filled for the last time, Red Barber told the entering herd, "We've just been handed some new information, ladies and gentlemen. Seems there's yet another twist to this already convoluted story. We know—or at least have been told—that if Ogilvie's All-Stars win this Series, this game seven, little Roberto's life will be saved. Now we have just been told that part of the bargain is Manager Don Ogilvie's life in exchange. That is, if the All-Stars are victorious today, young Roberto lives, but his best friend gives up his life in return. If it's true, that's going to take some of the glory out of winning for the All-Stars. Yes, suh."

"If it's true, I'll eat my ice chest," scoffed Harry Caray, who candidly added, "Well, maybe I'll just drink it."

For this last game, the real Ty Cobb abandoned his spot behind the plate and ominously assumed his usual position in centerfield.

Despite his players' respect and admiration, and their supreme effort for him on the field, the rested Hillbilly Higgins and the Cobb Squad were unstoppable. It was as if they were riding a fire-eating dragon, and it spewed, spit, and vomited flame on command. Ogilvie went through pitchers like Madonna through a frat house. Even though his hitters were finding Higgins, when the All-Stars would score a precious run, Cobb's Crusaders would score two. It was 4-2 Cobbs in the bottom of the sixth. The Hall of Famers scored another run on a scrambling triple by Honus Wagner, followed by a Buck Leonard sacrifice fly that just missed being a homer.

"That came close to tying it up, folks. The All-Stars are only one back now," reported Red Barber. The fans sighed as the lead sat at 4-3 at the end of the inning.

The Crusaders threatened again in the seventh, putting runners on first and second with one out. Ogilvie made a pitching change. The next Cobb clubbed a spiraling missile to center and DiMaggio saved two runs from scoring when he made a blind, gravity defying, over-the-shoulder stab for the second out. But it hobbled him with a twisted knee.

The taciturn Clipper got Ogilvie's ear as he limped in and said, "Put in the kid. I got a feelin'." The rest of the bench wondered as Ogilvie replaced the incomparable DiMaggio with the green Mickey Mantle.

With the All-Stars down 4-3, the next Cobb clone hit another wicked shot to center that made Mantle look like he was tap-dancing on an icy stairway. DiMaggio winced and the rest of the players moaned as the two runs DiMaggio had just saved came in to score. It was 6-3 Cobbs, and Ogilvie was forced to swap pitchers again. With two out and a Cobb on second, the next clone hit another mean drive to center, and half of the All-Stars covered their eyes. This time Mantle made a fabulous circus catch. But the damage was done. As he came slowly trotting into the dugout, Ogilvie gave Mantle an encouraging slap on the rump and DiMaggio told him to ". . . shake it off."

Cobbs roamed the bases again in the top of the ninth, and Ogilvie needed one more reliever, a left-handed reliever to face the left-handed Cobbs. His right-handers were being hammered. The southpaw, their 'meal-ticket' Carl Hubbell, was out of the question. He had given everything he had over the last several games, and one day off wouldn't do for him as apparently it did for the remarkable Higgins. Everyone knew Hubbell was the only lefty the All-Stars had. That's when Ogilvie did it. He called in a gamboling Babe Ruth from right field and met him on the mound. Mantle was moved from center to right, and Ogilvie brought in the speedy Jimmy Crutchfield to play center. Ruth, the Lefty from Boston, to the surprise of everyone, the shock of some, and the delight of others, was going to pitch. Drummond and the Cobbs licked their chops, but not for long. The trim, side-wheeling Bambino made the Cobb Squad look foolish as he fanned three in a row, stranding two runners, and savoring the contest with his nemesis like extra onions on a hotdog. Nonetheless, it was still 6-3, Cobb Squad, heading into the bottom of the ninth.

The first two All-Stars made easy outs, and that brought up the Babe for one last hack. The crowd was anxious and disappointed. A home run here wouldn't even tie the game, but it would keep it alive (and Roberto too), and narrow the deficit to two runs.

As the Babe started for the batter's box, Drummond came tearing up the dugout steps as fast as his stubby legs would take him, yelling at Klem. "He's out of order, he's batting out of order."

Ogilvie had him batting in the pitcher's spot. Klem and the other umpires huddled and decided that the little bastard was right. When Ruth was moved to pitcher, he still kept his place in the batting order and Crutchfield, the new player, took over the pitcher's spot. The cagey manager hardly protested. His hope was to extend the inning long enough to have Ruth at bat when it counted most. But there were two outs and the Babe wouldn't be due up for four more at-bats!

A wily Red Barber told the Drummond Field audience, "Strangely, this can only help the Hall of Famers, ladies and gentlemen. If Drummond had let Ruth bat out of order, that would've been the last out, and the end of the Series. The umpires wouldn't have a choice—those are the rules. Now the All-Stars have a chance with one out left."

A moment later, the fast-flying Jimmy Crutchfield barely beat the throw on his bunt down the third-base line.

Mantle was now up with two outs and one on in the ninth inning of game seven—too much pressure for a rookie. Ogilvie would have to pull him for a pinch hitter. But he didn't as DiMaggio's "feelin'" made him stop. Instead he grabbed Mantle by both arms, stared firmly into the scared kid's eyes, and said, "Mick. Look at me. You're home in your basement with your dad. Hit it just like he taught you. He's watching you."

"It looks like Ogilvie is going to let the young Mickey Mantle stay in there," Barber told the crowd. "With all that talent on the bench, he must be playing a hunch."

Mantle swung wildly at the first pitch, and then Higgins had him down two strikes. Mantle looked at Ogilvie, who only stared back. The young center fielder dug in hard and swung with all his might at an inside fastball. He fisted it on the fly past a leaping Cobb at shortstop. The ball fluttered into shallow left field for a single as a happy and relieved Mantle rounded first base. Joe DiMaggio exhaled.

Gehrig was up next. A homerun would tie the game. Instead, a heart-stopping base hit was squeezed-out—a looping, "seeing-eye" pop-up to right field. It was an anemic, fluky rally, with the fans going nuts.

Implausibly, Ruth, in his proper batting spot, came to the plate with the bases loaded and victory in reach. A grand slam could do it.

"Well folks," said an excited Red Barber, "this is baseball at its best, its most dramatic—Babe Ruth coming to the plate with two out in the bottom of the ninth and the Series on the line. A grand slam could win it. A grand slam might save a life."

Drummond was livid. His strategy had boomeranged on him. If he'd let Ruth bat out of order, that would've been declared the third out by the umpires, and the All-Stars would've lost the Series. But the Ultimate Umpire wanted to show what a smart manager he was. Now he'd outsmarted himself. Calling for time, he went to Higgins on the mound and asked him if he wanted to walk Ruth, let a meaningless run score, and face whoever Ogilvie might put up next.

Harry Caray commented, "If they walk the Babe here, I think it's going to be a very unpopular decision with the crowd."

The fans were mutinous. Josh Gibson saw Higgins looking into the dugout, and waved at him to remind him of his winning home run in game six, and that he was available to pinch hit. No, Higgins would pitch to Ruth. That's the way he wanted it. Fire against fire. "Okay," said Drummond. "He's a big loser anyhow. Go get him."

The big hillbilly came right after the Bambino and had him down two strikes swinging. You could almost feel the wind off of Ruth's bat as he whiffed at the angular pitcher's frenetic fastball. Higgins then turned careful and threw three balls to see if Ruth would bite at a bad one. Ruth barely held up each time, the fans twisting in their seats like human corkscrews. Ogilvie signaled for time and met the Babe halfway. "Where do you think he'll put this last one, Jidge?"

"As hard as he can on the outside corner."

"Me too . . . look for it up. Take him deep."

As Ogilvie returned to the dugout, his shoulders twitched and he said, "I have a strange feeling that I've done this before, Antonio."

"I've had a strange feeling ever since we got to Limbotown," confided the young assistant.

The pitch came outside with everything on it that Hillbilly Higgins had left. Ruth's bat boomed with a thunderclap. Drummond contorted in the dugout, muttering, "Shit, I don't believe it!"

Ty Cobb raced back to straightaway center field, tracking the stratospheric ball all the way. It seemed to be suspended in mid-air. Then with a towering leap, he reached far over the fence and snatched Ruth's home run. And with it he snatched Roberto's life . . . and with it he snatched Roberto's life.

The All-Stars' dugout was motionless. The crowd sat silent. Paralyzed. After a minute or two, they began to shuffle out. Only the murmur of dejected mothers and fathers could be heard trying to comfort their heartsick children (and each other, too).

"Boy, you hate to see this happen, but it happens sometimes," was all a dazed Mel Goldstein could muster for his shaken twelve-year-old son, Barry.

Charles Stuffington, in his own turn-of-the-century way, counseled his boy as well. "No tears in public, Simon. You have to be brave. Many a courageous young man is dying right now in the Great War. We don't know for certain that young Roberto will die. Life is only fair by accident—although, I must admit, it's not an easy thing to get used to."

Red Barber tried to explain it to the departing fans this way: "We know that no living thing can conquer death, ladies and gentlemen.

Perhaps all we can do is try to slow it down a bit. And that's what the Alvarez family, Don Ogilvie, and little Roberto hoped to do—slow it down so Roberto could grow up. Sometimes things don't turn out as they should—in baseball or life."

As Ogilvie, Antonio, little Roberto, and the rest of the players dragged into the clubhouse, not much was said. Maria and Maggie came in. The Alvarezes exchanged hugs and quietly made the rounds to thank everyone. Even in defeat, in disaster, they thought about others. It tore at the players to be praised for their effort, their desire, not for their victory, their conquest.

Unexpectedly, Drummond entered the room. He had the chutzpah of a Nazi at a Bar Mitzvah. "I just wanted to say what a terrific job you guys did," he said, raising his voice so everyone could hear. "That was really somethin'. Best Series ever. I guess I just wanted to say no hard feelin's."

As the players watched in stony amazement, Death Personified turned around and said to George Herman Ruth, "Well, Mr. Ruth, maybe you're not the loser I thought you were. Only a great catch saved it."

"You're lucky I didn't hit that ball to Kingdom Come, Derby! Sure felt like I got all of it," the hunched-over Bambino wailed from his bench. Then, much softer, he added, "Musta got under it hair and hit it too damn high."

"One more thing, "Drummond announced. "Tonight's your last night in Limbotown. At midnight, you'll all be taken back to where you came from, like nothin' happened—and you won't remember a thing. Even though you won't remember, I hope you enjoyed your time here. I know I did . . . and good luck to youse guys. And thanks."

At the end of his queer little appearance, Death retreated. No one was sure what to make of it, except Maggie, and as usual she wasn't saying anything.

After the clubhouse emptied, Drummond came back and actually tried to console Ogilvie. He was apologetic, respectful to the heartbroken manager. "You really surprised me, Pal. It takes a lot to do that. You came as close as anybody could. It took a great catch to do it. Another inch . . . well, I'm not trying to make you feel worse. I think you did an unbelievable job, an impossible job. Can I congratulate you?" As Drummond put out five chubby fingers, Ogilvie wasn't exactly sure what he was being congratulated for. There could be dignity in defeat, valor in defeat, and even acclaim in defeat, but not congratulations. He shook hands anyhow.

A bit later, Ogilvie cornered Babe Ruth on his way to the dining room. "Jidge, could you do me a favor?" the modest manager asked.

"For you, friend, anything," said Ruth, meaning it. Still, he was a bit puzzled at the triviality of the request.

"Could you autograph this ball for Roberto?"

The Bambino raised an eyebrow as he said, "Sure. But ya know I already John Hancocked a few balls for him. He ain't lost 'em, has he?"

"No, no, nothing like that, Babe. Drummond is serious about not letting anyone remember anything about this—Limbotown, the Series, and everything in between. Except for me. I'm the lucky one who gets to remember it. That was part of the deal: I gotta live with it. Drummond won't let the balls and stuff you gave Roberto go back home with him. Anyway, I was thinkin' that if I can get this one back, maybe I can use it to cheer him up when things get rough."

Ruth grabbed the ball, mulled for a second, and then rapidly scribbled his scrawl. "Here you go, Boss. That's tough luck for the kid. I still think I hit all of that last one. Hey, another thing. I hope you get to remember this too: I didn't get along with most of my skippers, but I had a couple of good ones in there. Outside of Father Mathias, you was the best, Ovaltine." Then Ruth whispered, "If you don't think God is listenin', you was better than the ol' Father too."

Coming from a guy who only wanted to manage and knew he never would, Ogilvie was humbled once more. He wondered if anyone could ever believe that Babe Ruth would say such a thing to the likes of him. But his thoughts swung to Roberto, and the sting overpowered Ruth's words.

As Doctor Drummond had promised Ogilvie, he returned Babe Ruth to 1935 as a forty-one-year-old Boston Brave who only looked fat and overdone. While he had complained about it his first day in Limbotown,

Ruth did not miss his game against the Pittsburgh Pirates that late May afternoon. He felt remarkably spunky, even though he had been out until the wee hours the night before, mourning the retirement of the old Bucs' shortstop, Rabbit Maranville. Outward appearances aside, Ruth was still in the terrific condition Ogilvie had pounded him into in Limbotown. The former nobody-manager had bargained for one game for Ruth, and Drummond, as usual, was good to his word. Jidge hit three home runs that day, the last one estimated at six hundred feet, clearing the roof over the right field stands in spacious Forbes Field. It was the only ball ever hit out of the enormous park. It was also the Babe's last home run. Many urged him to retire after that game. It was his last gasp of greatness. Now stripped of the skills he'd regained in Limbotown, Ruth didn't finish the season. The Braves inauspiciously gave him his unconditional release. A career that began with the loudest bang baseball had ever heard ended in a whimper. Yet the stamp he left on the game would never fade.

Everyone gathered in the hotel dining room for The Last Supper, Limbotown style. The players sat at their usual spots, and Ogilvie, Maggie, and the Alvarez family at theirs. Throughout the evening, they were visited by the loyal Limbotown staff and the team: individually, in pairs, and in small bunches. Burton P. Stansberry, III, Jack Dumphy; they all came to pay their respects and say goodbye. What started out as disbelief and disdain by the players was ending with their homage to Ogilvie, Antonio, and Maria—and, of course, little Roberto. Bittersweet was the main course of the evening.

More bittersweet was Maggie telling the former nobody-manager that they couldn't spend the entire night together. It wasn't allowed on the last night before his return. He was still alive and she was still dead. Besides, at midnight, Limbotown Standard Time, no matter where you were or what you were doing, you were sent home. That's how it worked.

Maria and Antonio let Roberto stay up way past his bedtime. Around 11 p.m., they said their final goodbyes to Maggie and went off to their room. Maggie told Roberto, "I don't need to tell you to be brave, because you already are. Just remember: your mom and dad and your best friend are going to need your help when you get home." Roberto knew exactly what she meant. She hugged him for a full minute.

Don Ogilvie tried to pass his last moments in Limbotown with Maggie Briggs. She was unusually sanguine. She made Ogilvie promise to "... be strong, don't fall off the wagon or let the Alvarezes down. You have to be there for Roberto. It won't be easy."

Ogilvie laughed out loud when she said that. "'This isn't going to be easy' is the motto of this place. Don't worry, I'm expecting it this time. Even the stuff I haven't thought of yet, if that's possible." Maggie found his mouth and he flew off again in love's grip.

The kiss was a goodbye kiss, and he left her at the hotel. He took the short walk to the stadium for the last time. He entered a deserted clubhouse and went out the dugout tunnel to take a final look at majestic Drummond Field and dream of what might've been. What actually happened was incredible enough. It may have been too much to save Roberto's life too.

Drummond appeared out of nowhere again. Now that he was leaving, Ogilvie was finally getting used to it. "Who knows, Don, maybe I'll bring you back here as a Lucky Stiff to manage some games. You were the only one to ever figure out Higgins. Of course you'll remember everything when you get back, but you won't remember any of this after you die. Sorry I can't do anything about that. You gotta be a Chosen One for that to happen. So if I bring you back, you won't remember Maggie or anything. But maybe I could introduce you to her again. She'll remember you. Whatta ya think?"

"It'd be like me showing up with amnesia. Then I'd fall in love all over again and have to leave without remembering anything. Sounds like a ball. I'm sure it'd be just about as fun for Maggie. Don't do us any favors."

"Well, let's see how long you feel that way," Death speculated as he withdrew into the dark.

Don Ogilvie retired to his clubhouse easy chair and sleep overtook him as the clock circled midnight. Twisted flashes of Limbotown crammed his head like warped reflections on a chrome bumper. Every dream ended the same way.

Ty Cobb raced back to straightaway center field, tracking the stratospheric ball all the way. It seemed to be suspended in mid-air. Then with a towering leap he reached far over the fence and snatched Ruth's home run. And with it he snatched Roberto's life . . . And with it he snatched Roberto's life.

Chapter 22

When Don Ogilvie awoke, there was no doubt he was back in his studio apartment in San Bernardino. It was as if he'd never left. And maybe he never did. Still, what other way was there to explain his new physique? Death Personified returned him in shape and forty pounds lighter. Drummond wanted him to believe it was real and left him some reminders. That was one of them. His memory of Maggie Briggs and their night together was as vivid as the noonday sun that never shined in Limbotown. That was another. He checked his small duffel bag that returned with him. Ruth's rabbit's foot and the autographed ball were still there. More reminders.

He didn't have time to wonder any more. It was supposedly the same morning in San Bernardino—still July 17, 2000. It was 10 a.m., and time to get to work: as batting coach of the Class A Stampede.

When Don Ogilvie entered the Stampede clubhouse, Buck Nimble did a double-take that almost snapped his head off at the neck. "Jesus fucking Christ, Ogilvie! What did you do to yourself? You look great! Damn, you look like you lost fifty pounds overnight. Hell, after the news about Roberto, I didn't figure to see you today. Figured you were out gettin' shitfaced . . . wouldn't't've blamed you, either."

"As a matter of fact, I did get drunk . . . for the last time in my life."

"Well fuck me in the ass sideways 'til my gums bleed! If that's what your last bender will do for ya, I'm grabbin' Squeaker, the Ripper, and

Mrs. Buck for a big ol' fuckin' party. What kinda magic poison was you downin'?"

"Humble pie."

"Huh? Never mind. Look, if you wanna be with Roberto today . . ."

"No. I think I should keep doing my job. I'll see Roberto later this afternoon."

As Don Ogilvie left the cool clubhouse to prepare for batting practice in the midday heat of the California desert, the jaws of Buck Nimble, Squeaker, and the Ripper were as slack as a small school of large-mouthed bass.

Roberto rushed to the door when the bell rang. As he had hoped, it was Don Ogilvie, with a hard-creased smile on his face. The seven-year-old batboy leapt into his best friend's arms as he entered the small apartment.

A slightly mystified Antonio and Maria weren't sure they recognized the hitting coach for the San Bernardino Stampede as he returned Roberto to ground. "Wow, you must've dropped forty pounds in your sleep. How'd you do that?" asked a narrow-eyed Antonio.

"It looks like you've been to one of those fat farms for about six weeks," observed Maria.

"I had this dream last night that you and Babe Ruth were running around a real nice baseball field and you both lost a bunch of weight," Roberto chimed in. "Then there was this big game we played against some real mean guys and we lost. A lot of other stuff happened too, but I can't remember it now."

"Well, that's exactly what happened Roberto," Don said winking at his parents. "I must've had the same dream, because I can't explain this either," Ogilvie said, putting a hand where his paunch used to be.

After the tight-knit group sat down for dinner, Don asked about Roberto's upcoming treatments and volunteered to take Roberto when he could, or "just go along for the ride."

"I know with Don helping me I'll get better," pronounced the sure youngster. The unsolicited vote of confidence gave Ogilvie a sinking feeling in the pit of his now-reduced gut, but he made sure to squeeze out a grin anyhow.

Maria and Antonio were happy to hear Don's offer to help. It could only cheer Roberto's spirits. But they knew from past experience that the unreliable hitting coach, although well meaning, probably wouldn't be able to hold up for long.

After Don left and Roberto was tucked into bed, they wondered who the familiar stranger was that showed up at their apartment that evening. Maria conjectured, "It's like he's gone away somewhere and come back a new man . . . not different really, just better. We'll have to see . . . something happened besides Roberto getting sick." Her intuition was almost as good as her son's.

Now Don Ogilvie was the first to get to the ballpark and the last to leave. He was even better with his "students" than he was before. He had some new tools. Somewhere he had acquired patience and wisdom . . . and strength. Buck Nimble had expected his spotty hitting instructor to crumble under the weight of Roberto's tragedy. Instead, it seemed to transform him.

But dealing with Roberto's illness was getting harder every day. The constant Limbotown admonition of "This isn't going to be easy" kept rolling around his head like a loose marble. The sorrow he felt and the grief he saw in the eyes of Maria and Antonio was almost too much to take. Keeping up a light-hearted front for Roberto was terribly difficult. Ogilvie had to muster all his newfound strength, and still it wasn't enough. He believed he had left his bitterness behind. Limbotown did that. Or did it? It rankled him because he still harbored a small yet intense fury over Roberto's approaching death. It burned in him like a tiny, super-heated ember of discontent. Given more air, it could ignite and consume him, just as his bad foot had. He needed an ending to this feeling, or it would end him. As Drummond had warned him, "If you lose, it may be harder to come back and watch Roberto die. You may want to stop living yourself." Don Ogilvie was not suicidal, but he pondered drinking for the first time since his return to San Bernardino—and for him, drinking was just about the same as suicide. The thought

314

made him loathe himself, which made him want to drink all the more. He had to break this deadly cycle before it broke him. But how? How had he done it in Limbotown? Yes, he'd trusted himself and the Alvarezes, but it was something more than that. Finally he remembered, and the warm answer came rushing into him like a bubbling hot springs. From some unknown corner of his heart, he felt the perfect love of Maggie Briggs, and he was as strong as a Babe Ruth home run.

Something else Drummond had told him was also true: After Limbotown, ". . . you might value your own life a little more." So one way he could honor Roberto was to value his own life a little more. He wasn't going to quit on himself now. He had failed in Limbotown, but maybe this was another chance. The sad irony of it struck him as he thought, *I set out to save Roberto's life and he lands up saving mine.* He wasn't embarrassed about it. Humility had become a way of life for the nobody-manager.

Nonetheless, he decided to test himself. On the way home from the game that afternoon, he stopped by The Spigot, the sleazy little joint he got roasted in the night he'd heard about Roberto's leukemia. Owner-bartender Oly Nevin went bug-eyed as a trim, fit version of Don Ogilvie sat down.

Ordering a boiler maker, the batting instructor put a grip around each glass and quickly turned them over without spilling a drop. "With hands like that, I don't think I should take up drinking again. What do you think, Oly?" If old Oly was thinking anything, he didn't say. He paused, stunned as Don left a ten-dollar bill on the counter and walked out.

Ogilvie may have passed his test. He may have exorcized his bitterness, but it didn't lessen the pain. That evening at the Alvarez apartment was still just as grueling.

He had trouble falling asleep that night, and when he finally did, he had a vivid hallucination of Maggie Briggs smiling and telling him to "Hang on—you're almost home." He really didn't understand what she was saying, but he decided to follow her advice anyhow. She'd never led him astray before. He hoped that her appearance was more than a mirage in some windblown oasis of his mind.

As the Stampede's season drew to a close, so did little Roberto's life. He slipped faster than expected. Ogilvie believed this was really Drummond's way of being merciful: don't drag out the inevitable—save Roberto and his parents (and Don Ogilvie too) from a woeful, lingering death.

Buck got the flu during the last week of the season. He shocked everyone when he asked Ogilvie to take over managing for him. The championship was on the line.

In the first game, the Stampede were holding onto a one-run lead going into the bottom of the ninth, the opposition up. With one out, a man on third, and a two-and-one count on the batter, Ogilvie called for a pitchout. He guessed right on a surprise suicide squeeze. The batter lunged, missed the ball, and the Stampede catcher easily tagged out the runner coming home. The game ended on the next pitch, the hitter swinging at a curve in the dirt—the pitch called for by Ogilvie.

The next day, against a different team, the interim manager knew he had to do something to break up the powerful combination of their numbers three and four hitters—Chuck "Bronco" Cheney and Juan "Loco" Lopez. Loco, the right-handed clean-up man, was a dead-pull slugger who tried to take everything deep to left field. The three-hole batter, Bronco Cheney, could hit just about anything, but he ran more like a Clydesdale—he just wasn't very fast. So even with a man on first, Ogilvie ordered the dangerous but slow Bronco walked. Then he had the Stampede pitcher throw nothing but stuff on the lower outside part of the plate to Lopez. The scheme paid off when Loco pulled into three ground ball double-plays in his three at-bats—and another San Bernardino victory.

For the last win to clinch the championship, Ogilvie used seven pitchers to perfection to preserve a one-run lead over the last four innings.

Ogilvie didn't disappoint. He wrung out three victories to earn the title.

The championship, however, was not joyful for him. Roberto was too sick to be at the games—and Antonio and Maria were, of course, with their ailing son.

What Ogilvie didn't know was that the scouts in the stands became more interested in him than the talent they were sent to look at. He had baseball smarts, keen strategies, and an eerie feel for the game. He didn't rattle either. The tighter the game, the better he managed—and managed to keep his team relaxed. The players obviously believed in him, and his belief in them gave them confidence. Either a manager has this kind of trust or not. Usually it's something you're born with. If this guy wasn't born with it, he'd sure picked it up somewhere along the way. Where had Buck Nimble been hiding this guy? Where did he come from? The old scouts wondered where he learned to manage like that.

Despite winning the Pacific Coast League Championship for the second year in a row, Buck announced that there would be no San Bernardino Stampede next season. The minor league franchise had just been sold to the Seattle Mariners. The new owners of the Dodgers were reshuffling their minor league clubs, and all the players and coaches were being transferred or let go. Old Buck was going to manage a Dodger Single-A team in Florida.

After the playoffs, Buck asked Ogilvie into his office. The redoubtable coach figured he was going to be cut loose. But Nimble surprised him instead. "Fuckin'-A, Ogilvie. Those last three games you pulled outta your ass musta impressed the hell outta someone, 'cause the Cedar Rapids Kernels want you as their new skipper." Ogilvie stuck a finger in his ear and wiggled it around. It sounded like he was going to be playing baseball in the middle of an Iowa cornfield after all.

"Don't try to be so fuckin' cute about it! You heard me right." Buck let it sink in for a second and then dropped the other cleat on him. "I got some bad news too . . . well, maybe not so bad in a way . . . Antonio's gonna be released. I know, I know . . . it's a lot to dump on him right now, except I figure you'll be needin' some of your own coaches, and Antonio's gonna be a natural, once he gets over the shock of not playin'. You're gonna have to help him with that . . . I wanted to tell you first so you could break it to him in your own way. You're a lot fuckin' better about that stuff than I am." Buck, of course, was about as diplomatic as a small nuclear device.

The Big Skipper was right as far as Ogilvie was concerned—it wasn't all bad news. Antonio could be his assistant, his bench coach just like in Limbotown. He would have to help him get over losing both his career and his only child. If they worked together, he prayed they wouldn't be constant reminders to one another about Roberto's death. He hoped they would be able to help each other. Ogilvie decided to wait a day before telling Antonio about being cut and asking him: how would he like to be a coach? He told Buck, "Yeah, I'll take him with me."

Little Roberto was at the hospital every day now. He was becoming too weak to take his treatments, so they were stopped. He finally lost what was left of his appetite, and then he seemed to lose his will to live. That was the toughest thing to see. The kid who believed he could conquer Death had his spirit broken. Ogilvie knew what that was like. He figured little Roberto had a week left, or maybe just a couple of days. It was almost over now.

That evening, as he said goodbye to the bedridden and barely conscious Roberto, Ogilvie slipped Babe Ruth's rabbit's foot into his fragile grasp.

His phone urgently ringing awoke Ogilvie the next morning. It was Antonio at the hospital. He was so excited he had trouble talking. He burst into laughter! "It's a miracle. It's a miracle, Don!" He was hysterical. "It's gone. They can't find it. It's gone. First, Roberto said he felt great this morning. He was hungry. And then when they gave him his blood tests, the nurse kept getting a strange look on her face and saying, 'That can't be right.' Maria and I didn't know what to think. Then the doctor comes in and he says the same thing! And here we are four hours and a hundred tests later and they're telling us it's gone. They can't find it! Roberto's cancer is gone. No more Leukemia . . . You better get down here right away."

On the ride to the hospital, Don Ogilvie put it all together. If Roberto was truly healthy, it was Drummond's doing, and that meant Drummond would be looking for him. That was fine. If Roberto was cured, Ogilvie wanted Death Personified to find him. He knew he would whenever he wanted to. He had a feeling it would be sooner rather than later. *But what made Drummond change his mind?* he wondered.

The scene at the hospital was bedlam. The doctors, the nurses—and especially the Alvarezes—all believed they had been part of a miracle. And they had. Maria and Antonio thought it was God's answer to their prayers. Little Roberto thought it was Don Ogilvie's love and loyalty, and the doctors thought they just got lucky. Such a last-minute cure was rare. Maybe it was the treatment, or somehow the body healed itself. It was one of those things they put in the *Enquirer*, right next to the article about a sixteen-year-old "virgin" from Swampgully, Alabama, giving birth to triplet space-aliens. None of them suspected that it was Death who'd spared little Roberto's life. But Don Ogilvie knew, and he knew the price he would have to pay. He also knew he wouldn't be getting back any change.

Nevertheless, the doomed hitting coach had no problem joining in on the celebration. Hell, he took the lead. Downing 7UP like champagne, they took Roberto home from the hospital as a healthy boy. Yes, he was still weak and underweight, but with the return of his appetite, his energy and body would soon be rebuilt.

Ogilvie left the Alvarez family with the promise that he would be back in less than an hour. His first stop was to see Buck. When Ogilvie told the skipper about Roberto, he wanted to throw a party right there in the clubhouse, only that's when the foul-mouthed manager remembered to tell him, "Fuck, Ogilvie, I almost forgot." He pulled a scrap of paper from his pocket. "I took this message from your new employer; says you gotta have a physical today . . . Yeah, it's only a formality . . . for health insurance, I think," shrugged the hulking skipper. "Hell, you're in the best fuckin' shape of your life! This 'finger up yer ass' thing oughta be a piece of fuckin' cake for ya!"

Buck, spurning badly needed reading glasses, took the note he was holding, squinted, and moved it back and forth like a slide trombone, trying to decipher his own writing, "Yeah, at five this afternoon. It says you gotta go to 418 East 4th Street. See a Doctor Dur. . . no, Drummond. That's it, Drummond!"

Well, at least now he knew how much time he had left. About three hours. He swung by his place next, and then headed back to the Alvarez apartment to say goodbye.

Roberto was still too frail to be moved around much, so the burly Buck rounded up as many of the Stampede as he could find, and they all went to the Alvarezes' place to celebrate. They danced around like drunken priests, with Roberto's normally pious parents supplying all the holy water they could handle.

Don Ogilvie knew that he would not be around to see the next morning. He had a lot of work to do. During the revelry, the newly hired minor-league manager cornered Buck and convinced the "King of the f-word" to replace him as a coach with Antonio. Ogilvie concocted a tale that he had just returned a call from a message on his answering machine and had found out that he was "inheriting" a staff with the Kernels and there was no opening for Antonio. "I know you'll get to take some of your own coaches, Buck. He may not be able to hit much, and he may be young, but he sure can teach other players how to hit. I've taught him everything he'll need to know. Besides, you can't find a better person than Antonio." Buck finally agreed, and the reformed hitting coach made him shake on it.

Ogilvie pulled Antonio and Maria into another room. "Buck says I gotta go for a physical in a couple of hours, and then I'm taking off for Iowa for a couple of days," he lied. "You know, sign contracts, meet the owners." He paused, then said, "Antonio, Buck wanted me to tell you . . . you're being released." Maybe he wasn't any more diplomatic than Buck, but Antonio took it better, coming from him. And compared to having Roberto's life back . . .well, there was no comparison. Still, it was Antonio's personal dream being snuffed out, and Ogilvie knew how that felt, so before shock set in, he added, "Buck's gonna be managing in Florida next season. Nice place for families. He needs a hitting coach to replace me and wants you to be the guy. You know I'd take you with me if I could, but they tell me I don't get to pick my own coaches—not yet anyhow. Promise me you're gonna go with Buck. I have to know that before I leave town."

It was all too much for Antonio in one day. His son cured, being let go, then being offered a new career as a coach, and not being able to take his family to Iowa with Don Ogilvie and the Single-A Kernels.

Maria spoke for him, "Don't worry, Don. I'll make sure he does the right thing." She always did.

"I need to talk to Roberto for a minute . . . alone, if that's okay."

Ogilvie shooed a few people out and shut the door to his best friend's room. They smiled at each other, then Don pulled a ball from the small bag he'd retrieved at his apartment. "I've got something very special for you, Roberto," he said. He tossed the orb softly to his friend, who was propped up in bed. The boy examined the new baseball, and then his eyes went wide. "Is this really Babe Ruth's autograph?"

"I guarantee you it is."

"How did he know to put my name on there?"

"That's a long story. All I can do is promise you that it's real."

Then the little batboy grabbed the furry paw lying in front of him and asked, "Do you know where this cool rabbit's foot came from? Mom and Dad don't know, but they said I could keep it if I want. They found it in my hand at the hospital this morning."

The smiling nobody-manager replied, "I'm pretty sure it was Babe Ruth's, but I know it belongs to you now."

After a few seconds, little Roberto asked, "You're not coming back ever, are you?"

"No, I don't think I can, Roberto. That's partly why I gave you this ball. Promise me you won't say anything about it to your Mom or Dad until tomorrow, okay? It's no big deal. I just want to make sure they let you keep it. After I leave tomorrow, I know they will." The two friends hugged and Don Ogilvie said, "You know, not since I was a kid did I ever feel like I had a home . . . until I met you and your folks. As a ballplayer, you're always on the road or gettin' traded. I think I've found another home now. I'm going home, Roberto, and it's always good to go home. It's just that we won't be together in the same way. Remember, though—I'll be with you every time you think of me."

"I'll think about you a lot, Don." They hugged again. "Will you think about me?" the youngster asked, voice unsteady and eyes watery.

"All the time, Roberto. That way, whenever you think about me, you know I'll be thinking about you too."

On his way out, he embraced Antonio and Maria in what they

thought was a congratulatory hug for all of them: for Roberto's miracle, and for Don and Antonio's new jobs. For Don Ogilvie, it was, of course, a last embrace. Only little Roberto realized they would never see him again. Antonio and Maria believed he was simply leaving to manage another team.

Don Ogilvie was ten minutes ahead of schedule as he pulled into the parking lot of the modest medical center that housed Doctor Drummond's office. He found the right door, took a deep breath, and entered. His fears instantly melted away like butter on a baked potato.

"You're the only person I know who would show up early for an appointment like this," a familiar, soothing voice teased him. He fell into the open arms of the beautiful, white-clad nurse.

"What made him change his mind?" Ogilvie asked Maggie Briggs as they came up for air.

"He'd better tell you himself," she replied as she led him to another room with a large desk in it. Or maybe the desk only looked large because a stubby, white-smocked Doctor Drummond sat behind it.

As usual, the roly-poly Embodiment of Death didn't waste any time. "Okay Ogilvie, there's nothing in here you can throw at me, so I'm gonna tell ya straight: you won. That's right—you won the Series. The big fat boy did hit that last one out . . . hit it right outta Limbotown . . . but I kept it within reach and let Cobb make the catch. Sorry about that, Ogilvie, but I needed to see how you was gonna hold up if you lost. Now don't get mad. I was gonna keep my promise and let the kid live anyhow, even if you didn't hold up. I just needed to see what you was gonna be good for as a Chosen One. Now I know."

Stupefied, all Ogilvie could think of saying was, "How could you let the Alvarezes go through that? Roberto was just a few days away from dying. You let them suffer for no good reason, you miserable son of a bitch!"

"Yeah, well, life is full of sufferin'. You oughta know that. You're bein' the miserable son of a bitch, not me. I spared the kid's life. I gave you this shot in the first place. If it wasn't for me, all of youse woulda suffered, and the kid woulda died anyhow. Would you'a liked that better?"

Drummond hadn't lost his knack for silencing Ogilvie.

"This was part of your Challenge too," added Drummond, "a part you didn't know about."

Death in the Flesh told the batting coach, "Now close your eyes. We're going back to Limbotown and pick it up with Ruth's last at bat." Don did as he was told, and he could hear the crowd at Drummond Field. When he opened his eyes, he was lost in the moment.

The big hillbilly came right after the Bambino and had him down two strikes swinging. You could almost feel the wind off of Ruth's bat as he whiffed at the angular pitcher's frenetic fastball. Higgins then turned careful and threw three balls to see if Ruth would bite at a bad one. Ruth barely held up each time, the fans twisting in their seats like human corkscrews. Ogilvie signaled for time and met the Babe halfway. "Where do you think he'll put this last one, Jidge?"

"As hard as he can on the outside corner."

"Me too . . . look for it up. Take him deep."

As Ogilvie returned to the dugout, his shoulders twitched and he said, "I have a strange feeling that I've done this before, Antonio."

"I've had a strange feeling ever since we got to Limbotown," confided the young assistant.

The pitch came outside with everything on it that Hillbilly Higgins had left. Ruth's bat boomed with a thunderclap. Drummond contorted in the dugout, muttering, "Shit, I don't believe it!"

Ty Cobb raced back to straightaway center field tracking the stratospheric ball all the way. It seemed to be suspended in mid-air. Then the spinning globe appeared to catch a second wind, and it skyrocketed over the Limbotown fogbank, disappearing into Grand-slam land. Four runs scored to win the Series. The fans, the players, and all the rest, exhilarated and spent, spilled onto the field. The party was on.

Don Ogilvie looked skyward, and he was able to see the sun—true light! But he was the only one. It was huge, and it swallowed him up.

Maggie escorted him through the Limbotown fogbank to show him what was on the other side. This time he was able to get through.

The Alvarez family was instantly returned home, with Roberto's miracle cure intact. They had no memory of their time in the elusive Limbotown.

The morning after, in San Bernardino, just as Drummond had promised, Don Ogilvie was found in his apartment easy chair, dead from a heart attack. The building handyman had let himself in to fix a leaky faucet, and then called 911. When the paramedics arrived, they called the coroner.

The scattered Ogilvie clan arranged a simple funeral at a small San Bernardino mortuary a few days later. They seemed a little surprised that anyone else came. Buck gathered up whatever remnants of the Stampede were left, and Antonio and Maria brought a healthy, but still recovering, Roberto with them.

After the brief service, Buck held sort of a wake back at the deserted Stampede ballpark. The small group dwindled to only Antonio, Maria, little Roberto, and Buck Nimble. They sat in the dugout.

Maria tearfully said, "I can't help but feel that Roberto's cure and Don's death are somehow connected." She always was a smart cookie.

They were all saddened by the minor league coach's death, except, strangely, for the little batboy himself. He reassured the rest that Don Ogilvie was finally at peace: "I know he's okay. He's home." As proof, the seven-year-old Roberto reached into a pocket and produced an autographed baseball given to him by his best friend the day they'd said goodbye.

"This is fucking weird," Buck surmised while inspecting the ball. "It's got stamped on it 'Limbotown World Series. Ogilvie's All-Stars versus Cobb's Crusaders. D. Drummond, Commissioner.' Now ain't that funny. That's the name of the sawbones I sent old Ogilvie to for his physical. And him bein' in the best shape of his life . . . go figure. I guess you never know when it's comin' sometimes."

"Isn't there a Limbotown somewhere in Ohio with a Double A-team?" Antonio wondered.

324

The ball had handwritten words on it, which Buck also read out loud: "Somethin' else on it: 'To Roberto, from your biggest fan, Babe Ruth . . .' Damn if that ain't the Bambino's hand . . . I seen it a lot." On the other side of the ball was Ogilvie's handwriting. Buck coughed and kept on going: "And one last one: 'Keep this ball to remember me by, Roberto. I've made the longest walk. I'm home now. Your best friend always, Don'."

Breinigsville, PA USA
14 March 2011
257590BV00002B/1/P